WHO IS ANNA STENBERG?

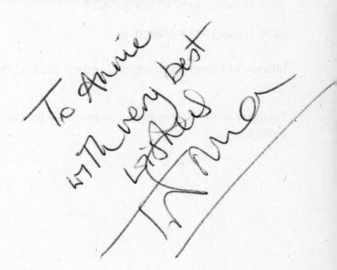

Liminal Books

Liminal Books is an imprint of Between the Lines Publishing. Liminal Books name and logo are trademarks of Between the Lines Publishing.

Between the Lines Publishing
1769 Lexington Ave N, Ste 286
Roseville MN 55113
btwnthelines.com

First Published: October 2023

ISBN: (Paperback) 978-1-958901-62-5

ISBN: (Ebook) 978-1-958901-63-2

Library of Congress Control Number: 2023942383

WHO IS ANNA STENBERG?

Tracey Norman

To M, who listened, commented, listened some more, and who reacted in the right way at every stage of this journey. And to A, who...did not. Both of you made this book what it is. Thank you.

Chapter One

Lying in the dark, my sleep-muddled brain struggled to work out where the noise was coming from. Footsteps pounded along the hall below and I leaped out of bed, grabbing my robe. My heart beat faster as I heard raised voices and a flurry of activity.

Throwing my robe on and clutching it around me, I went out onto the landing in time to hear my uncle shouting instructions.

I ran down the stairs as the hall clock chimed out midnight. My blood froze in my veins as I saw my uncle in the hallway, his face ashen. When he spotted me, he dropped his doctor's bag and hurried to me. Catching my hands in both of his, he pulled me into a tight hug. To my amazement, when he drew back, I saw his eyes were glistening with tears.

John, my father's valet, was lighting the lamps. That done, he hurried to the end of the hall and disappeared through the green baize door which led to the servants' quarters. From beyond, I could hear him shouting for Mrs. Armitage, the housekeeper. None of our servants ever shouted. My heart began to thump. The sound of running footsteps echoed along the servants' corridor.

I stared at my uncle. He was breathing heavily, his expression strained. 'Uncle Geoffrey? What is it?' My voice cracked. Deep down, I knew.

'It's your father, my dear.' The words tumbled over themselves as they rushed towards me. 'I'm afraid he's escaped. We have to get you somewhere safe. I fear he will come back here and...' He tailed off, his face greyer than before. 'His mania has not improved while he has been in our care. If anything,

1

he has become more fixated on his strange beliefs than when he first came to us.'

A wave of light-headedness swept over me, making me stagger. My uncle slipped his arm around my waist, half-supporting, half-carrying me into the parlour. He settled me into a chair and then hurried to the window, checking the fastenings of the shutters and giving them an experimental rattle while I watched him wide-eyed. He glanced over at me and paused, and I could tell he was viewing me through professional eyes. He strode across to the decanter on the sideboard by the door, poured a strong measure, then came over and knelt in front of me, holding out the glass. Like an obedient sleepwalker, I took it and sipped, coughing as the sharp flavour hit my throat. He made me drink half the contents before he took the glass and put it by the chair leg.

'How?' I whispered. 'How did he get out? I thought the asylum was secure.'

My uncle let out a frustrated sigh. 'It is, my dear, it is,' he said. 'Your father is a clever and resourceful man. More so than any of us realised. I'm not certain how he managed it, but it seems likely that he joined a group of professors who were being shown around the facility this evening and followed them out at the end of the tour.'

I stared at him, my jaw dropping. 'What?' I gasped. 'How on earth could he just walk out?'

My uncle held up his hand. 'I wish I had answers. The orderlies are being questioned. I suspect he convinced one of them to assist him.'

'What shall I do?' I asked, feeling numb. 'If he does come here and is determined to get into the house, how can we prevent him? Only John would stand a chance against my father, if it got that far. Poor Parsons is far too old to be able to take on someone with military training.'

'I have already sent one of the orderlies to the police station.' Shifting to practicalities, Uncle Geoffrey's voice became more business-like. 'I have asked for someone to be stationed here permanently until your father is found. As an extra precaution, however, I feel it would be best if you move to my lodgings at the asylum until then.'

'What!' I exclaimed. 'The asylum?'

'He has just escaped from there, and I doubt he will be keen to return. It is the one place where I believe you will be completely safe.' He got to his feet and helped me up. 'Now, let us go and pack a bag for you. My carriage is waiting outside. We need to make haste.'

I nodded like an automaton and followed him as he hurried for the stairs. Once in my room, we found my maid Eliza packing a case for me, tears streaming down her face. When we entered, she wheeled around with a sharp cry, only relaxing when she saw who it was. Fresh tears began to fall as she stared at me in fear and bewilderment. I ran over and hugged her before turning my attention to the items I would need to pack.

My uncle let out a soft 'Aha!' at one point and left the room, returning a couple of minutes later with one of my father's suits. He held it out to me. 'Just as a precaution,' he said, 'may I suggest you wear this? I know what you're thinking, but please consider: he won't be looking for a young man.'

The fact that Eliza did not throw up her hands in horror at this unorthodox suggestion drove home the seriousness of my predicament. My stomach lurched and a wave of nausea washed over me.

Eliza finished packing the case and we went behind my screen so I could put the suit on. The starched shirt collar was uncomfortable and the jacket far too big – I shared my father's height, not his build – but the trousers were a revelation, and I was amazed at the freedom of movement I suddenly had when I was not encumbered by skirts, petticoats and corset. Eliza drew my hair back into a ponytail at the nape of my neck, tucking it inside the jacket so it was out of sight. My uncle handed me one of my father's hats and when I put it on, I was taken aback at how like him I looked. In the dark, with my collar turned up, I was certain I would pass as a boy.

Eliza took my bag and hurried downstairs with it as I crossed to my jewellery box and took out three or four items, most of which had belonged to my mother. I stuffed them in my pocket and followed my uncle out of the room. As he collected his bag and gave John and Parsons some final instructions, a thought struck me, and I went into my father's study. He kept money in one of the desk drawers. There was a tiny, nagging voice at the back of my mind suggesting it might be advisable to take some.

There was nothing useful in the first drawer. In the second, I found a letter opener, which I slid into my sleeve. The third drawer was full of notebooks. I took a few out and dumped them on the floor so I could see what else was in there, finding a roll of banknotes tucked away in a back corner. I pocketed it and started putting the notebooks away, but my hands were trembling so badly that I dropped one. It bounced, flipped and landed on its back, pages falling open. Muttering a quiet curse, I leaned down to pick it up, then stopped, staring.

There were drawings, notes, maps, strange symbols, words I had never seen before. Reaching out slowly, I picked it up and leafed through. Page after page was covered in untidy writing that I didn't immediately realise was my father's because it was so different from his usual neat script. This was obviously something to do with his illness. On impulse, I stuffed some of the books into another pocket, marvelling at the ease with which men could carry items.

Dashing back into the hall, I met John and Eliza, coming to find me. John helped me into one of my father's heavy and cumbersome overcoats. He stood back, looking me up and down, then gave a small, satisfied nod and bowed.

'You look very good, Miss,' he said in a reassuring voice. I tried to smile, my eyes filling with tears. Uncle Geoffrey, who had opened the front door slightly and was peering into the dark street outside, glanced back and blinked at me for a moment, as if he had seen a ghost.

Are you ready?' he asked.

I took a deep breath. 'Yes. I think so.'

My uncle signalled to John, who began to extinguish the lamps in the hall. When he was satisfied that we were not going to be illuminating the entire street, he opened the front door and headed along the path towards his carriage. I paused to give Eliza a hug, then went to the door.

As I did, I saw the driver topple from his seat at the front of the carriage. My uncle yelled, a terrible, animal sound which was cut off by a dull thud. John sprang over to the door, pushing me behind him. Outside, we could hear the unmistakeable sound of men fighting and John ran down the path towards the carriage, disappearing behind it. Eliza and I stared at each other in horror as

4

Parsons appeared at the end of the hall. 'This way, Miss, quickly!' he called. 'Eliza, close the door!'

'What about John?' Eliza quavered.

'John knows he will need to go to the back. Do I as I say, girl!' the butler snapped, and Eliza slammed the door. I heard her bolting it and turning the key in the lock as Parsons led me into the servants' quarters.

The baize door swung closed behind us and Parsons ushered me towards the kitchen. 'The police will be here soon, Miss,' he said. 'Find somewhere nearby where you can hide safely. Perhaps the church near the park. That's not too far away. As soon as the master has been taken into custody, this will all be over.' He gave me a quick, avuncular smile, opening the door into the kitchen yard and looking around. The sounds of fighting could still be heard. I had a chance to get away, but I feared for John and my uncle, and for the poor driver.

'It's all clear, Miss,' said Parsons. 'Get yourself somewhere safe. Quickly!'

There was a sudden crash from the front of the house and we both froze. The horse squealed and I could hear the clatter of hooves. Parsons caught his breath and ushered me out into the kitchen yard. 'Please, Miss, hurry,' he begged. 'If anything should happen to you…'

He tailed off, and I stared at him, unable to form any coherent thought. There was another crash, this time from the front door, and I heard Eliza scream. Parsons groaned. 'Miss, please, you have to get to safety. Please.'

I nodded and he ushered me to a gate. I realised it led to an area behind our summer house and felt a sudden shame that I had never seen this part of my garden before.

'There is another gate to your right, Miss, just over there,' Parsons whispered, pointing. 'It's unlocked, so John can get back in. It opens onto the street. Head away from the house and then take the next road on the right – you can get back onto the main road from there and make for the church.'

'Thank you, Parsons,' I managed to choke out, fear gripping my throat and wrenching my stomach so much that I feared I would be sick. Gripping my bag, I ran to the gate, opened it and peered out. The street beyond was dark and empty, a few tendrils of fog swirling around. I stared in terror along the side of my house towards the corner, expecting my father to appear at any second. The horse was quiet now, but there were still a few scuffles and yells. Someone ran across the road at the corner, hefting a cudgel. It was Soames, valet to our neighbours the Fortescues. He was a tall, heavily built man who, like my father, had been in the army and knew how to handle himself.

It was now or never. I took a deep breath and stepped out into the street, pulling the gate closed behind me. Biting my lip, I glanced back over my shoulder at the house, then turned and ran into the dark.

Chapter Two

I pounded along the street, lugging the bag, which kept bumping into my knee, making me stagger. I had only gone a short distance before becoming breathless, wincing with each painful spasm in my chest as I hurried along, keeping to the shadows whenever I could. There was no sound now except my boots on the cobbles. A police whistle screeched at one point, but it was impossible to tell from which direction the sound had come.

Head down, I slowed to a half-jog, my muscles screaming in protest. I had always thought myself active, but this short burst of speed had proved that the stamina required to run any distance was very different to that required to last the evening at a ball. I cursed myself for not thinking ahead, for not preparing, whilst a more reasonable voice countered each criticism. No one could have foreseen my father escaping from a secure institution like St Bernadette's. It was a private facility with excellent staff, including my uncle, who had been kind and compassionate, helping me at every stage when it became evident that my father could no longer remain at home. I suspected that my uncle was partly motivated by a desire to find out whatever he could about the disappearance of his sister, my mother, when we had been travelling in Germany three years earlier. My father's mania had sprung from this trauma, along with his visions of strange demon-like creatures and the obsessive building of bizarre-looking weapons. I had insisted that he remain at home for as long as possible, but after he had tried to attack me with one of his weapons, my uncle had stepped in, and my father had been removed to St Bernadette's.

I vividly remembered the devastating day he had been escorted from the house by four burly orderlies, spitting fury and insisting I was some inhuman creature which needed to die. After he had gone and the house had fallen silent once more, I shut myself in my room and sobbed for hours.

He had been in St Bernadette's for about eight months, I realised. I wondered how long he had been plotting his escape.

The streets were dark, and most were deserted. I was so lost in thought that it took a while to realise I must have taken a wrong turn. I should have arrived at the church by now, but I had not even reached the park. Where was I? Trying not to panic, I stopped at the next corner. I squinted up at the building, looking for a street sign, but fog was drifting in from the sea and it was impossible to tell if there even was a sign, let alone read anything. The buildings around me were unfamiliar, and there was a pervasive, sour stench of cabbage and ordure. I had strayed into a poorer district; the houses here were tiny and crammed close together, and one or two had people sleeping in the doorway. I gave them a wide berth, crossing to the opposite side. Two men were staggering around on the corner as I approached and, wary, I slowed, terrified that they would hear my heart thumping in my chest. I could smell drink on them, even from a distance. I was expecting some unpleasant comment or confrontation, but they ignored me. It was only when I had passed them that I realised just how liberating my new outfit was. They had not seen a tall young woman. They had seen a tall young man.

I turned another corner, hoping to see something I recognised, but found myself looking down the length of a dark alley. Panic rose in my throat again as I turned to retrace my steps and I started feeling angry. I was a young woman of means who had been sheltered all my life and accompanied everywhere I went, which was usually only to friends' houses, church, one or two appropriate shops and the occasional walk along the seafront or in the park, to which I was driven in the carriage and collected afterwards. I was even driven to the ruins of Dover Castle, not far from my house, to walk. Why on earth had Parsons thought it safer to send me out into the streets alone at night? Why had I not run upstairs and hidden in the attic? I shifted the bag to the other hand and huffed in frustration. Parsons had done what he thought was best.

Getting lost was entirely my own fault. The disguise, at least, had been an excellent idea.

I wandered along for a while, recognising nothing. The town looked very different in the foggy night and there was almost no moonlight. Houses loomed at me out of the shadows, dogs ran across my path, some stopping for a sniff, and the further I walked, the more I saw people sleeping in doorways, sometimes two or three of them huddled together for warmth.

I reached another corner. To my left, I could hear the unmistakeable sound of the sea, and the scent of herring wafted towards me on the breeze from the area on the foreshore where they were hung to dry. *How on earth had I managed to get all the way down here?* I wondered in amazement. Mrs Armitage would have a fit when she found out. One thing was certain. As soon as I was home once more, I was going to make a few alterations to my daily routine, one of which would involve getting to know Dover better. I felt incredibly stupid and useless and, I had to admit, embarrassed at my lack of knowledge.

Turning to my left, I walked in the direction of the sea, racking my brain for some landmark I would recognise. Suddenly, I remembered that for Elizabeth's last birthday, her parents had taken us both for afternoon tea at the Lord Warden Hotel. There would be someone there who could help me contact my uncle, and I had sufficient money to obtain a room for the night. From where I was, I would need to turn to my right and follow the shoreline. That gave me confidence and I started walking again, quickening my pace in order to get there as soon as possible. The fog was thinner here than it had been in town, so I thought I should be able to see the hotel's lights in a few minutes.

I was cold in spite of my father's coat and pulled it closer around my neck with my free hand. Every time I changed the bag from left to right, I moved the letter opener to the opposite pocket, fingers wrapped around it, just in case. I had no idea what I would do if anyone challenged me and was thankful that I had managed to avoid trouble. My footsteps sounded unnaturally loud on the cobblestones, and I slowed, trying to walk more quietly. I did not want to attract any attention.

Too late. The hairs suddenly prickled on the back of my neck, and I became aware of someone behind me. My heart started thumping. What should I do? Should I run, and hope the hotel was just ahead? There was still nothing which would indicate a grand building, no lights, no faint sound of music. Around me, there was a jumble of warehouses, eerily silent and sinister in the fog, which I did not recall from my trip with Elizabeth. I decided to speed up. Perhaps there was a fisherman or a ferry agent somewhere who might help me. Perhaps it was a fisherman or a ferry agent who was behind me. I turned to glance over my shoulder, and, as I did so, a hand grabbed my arm and spun me around. I gasped and staggered, staring at a young man of about my own age. He was stockier and slightly shorter, squinting up at me from beneath the brim of his cap.

'Haven't seen you around these parts before, friend,' he said, a sneer in his voice indicating that he considered me anything but a friend. 'Lost, are you?'

I shrugged, trying to appear casual, my fingers gripping the letter opener. It was in my left pocket. There was no way I could swap it to my dominant right hand without him noticing.

'Which way to the church?' I asked, making my voice as deep as I could without, I hoped, sounding ridiculous.

He snorted. 'Church? What are you, a priest?' He peered at me again. ''Bit young for a priest, aren't you?'

'I am studying,' I replied shortly.

'I like your coat,' he said suddenly, his voice hard. 'I could do with a coat like that.'

I caught my breath. *Please*, I thought, *please leave me alone.*

He took a step forward and I instinctively stepped backwards. He gave a cackle of laughter and dived forward, but I managed to sidestep him, staggering clumsily to my left and catching him in the thigh with the bag. He swore as he regained his balance and advanced on me. 'Not very friendly, matey,' he spat. 'Now give me that coat.'

'No,' I faltered, forgetting to change my voice. He stopped, stared hard at me, then crowed with laughter.

'Well, now I've seen everything!' he exclaimed, advancing again and forcing me to retreat towards one of the buildings. 'You one of them actors I've heard tell about?'

I said nothing, just kept backing away. Too late, I realised he was herding me towards what looked like a narrow alleyway between two warehouses. 'That's it, my dear,' he hissed. 'Just keep walking. I think we need somewhere a little more private for our…discussion.' He chuckled and in the weak light, I saw a faint glint of metal. He had a blade.

The blood was roaring in my ears as I stumbled backwards towards the alley. His voice and my footsteps sounded far away, and I struggled to stay conscious as the few shapes I could pick out in the darkness swam at the edges of my vision. I thought I saw something flit behind him, but I was so terrified that all I could do was focus on his leering face.

When he had backed me into the alley, and I was standing against the wall in something which squelched beneath my boots and stank of fish and the privy, he held the knife up and said, 'Throw me the bag.'

'What?'

He swore again. 'Are you stupid? I said throw me the bag.'

'No,' I said, surprised at the sudden strength in my voice. There was no way I was letting go of the bag. My mother's jewellery was in it and that was all I had left of her.

He stopped, clearly taken aback. 'I think you need to be taught a lesson,' he said, advancing on me. As soon as he got close, I swung at him with the letter opener, catching him on the cheek. He yelled in pain and anger, and I saw the blade flash dully as I kicked him in the leg as hard as I could. He staggered, already off-balance, and fell heavily, sprawling in the muck on the ground. Seizing the opportunity, I dodged his flailing arms and started for the mouth of the alley, but he hooked my right foot with one of his as he scrambled to his feet. This time it was I who fell, landing heavily and losing my hat. I dropped the letter opener, and it bounced out of sight, so as he launched himself at me, I grabbed the bag in both hands and swung it upwards. It caught him under the chin and launched him backwards, his mouth slamming shut with a loud snap. I tried to scrabble to my feet, but my legs were like jelly.

He got to his hands and knees and advanced on me again. I brandished the bag as best I could, sickened by his mocking laugh. It looked as if his mouth was bleeding. All I could focus on was the knife, which he was holding about a foot from my face. 'Give me the bag or I will cut you to ribbons,' he hissed. 'You hear me? Cut. You. To. Ribbons.' With each word, he jabbed the knife towards me, ending with it just beneath my chin.

A terrible cold sensation washed over my entire body, leaving me feeling numb. There was such a rushing, pounding noise in my ears that it was hard to make out his words and there was a strange fog at the edges of my vision. I stared at him, frozen with fear. Time seemed to stop.

The fog was not at the edges of my vision. It was all around us, thick and cloying, a strange musky tang filling my nose and throat, making me choke. It took my attacker longer to notice because he was so fixated on my face, but as it wafted between us, he glanced quickly around. 'What the…?' he muttered, then turned back to me and grabbed the bag, trying to yank it from my grasp. I clung on in desperation, waiting to feel the sting of the blade as it sliced into me.

Suddenly, the odd, musky smell grew stronger, and something launched itself at my attacker from the depths of the fog. Between the fog and the darkness, I could not make out any details, just grunts, a leathery sound and something hard grating across the cobbles. My attacker screamed and suddenly shot backwards at an unbelievable speed, disappearing into the dense, swirling cloud. The scream was cut off by a terrible wet gurgle and then there was silence.

I lay there in the filth, gripping the bag, hardly daring to breathe and too terrified to move, my dull brain unable to comprehend what was happening. The fog started to thin as I watched it, almost hypnotised by its gentle dance. The musky smell faded away and the stench of fish and human excrement assaulted my nostrils, jerking me back to reality. I coughed and spluttered, my stomach heaving.

'What's going on? You all right?'

I yelped at the sound of the voice and jerked around to see a figure at the end of the alleyway, peering into the gloom, trying to see where I was. It was a female voice, young. 'Hello?' she called. 'Are you there?'

I started to scrabble to my feet and as soon as she heard the noise, the girl hurried towards me. She gasped as she bent down to me. 'What happened? Are you hurt?' she demanded, holding out a hand to help me up.

When I didn't move or respond, she snapped her fingers in front of my nose and I recoiled with a cry, banging my head against the wall behind me. She squinted at me in the same way as my attacker, her eyes widening in surprise and what looked like concern.

'I won't hurt you,' she said, her voice gentle. 'I have somewhere safe you can hide for the night if you want. I'm guessing you aren't used to being out on your own at this hour?'

I shook my head. She gave a little nod and held out her hand again. After a moment's pause, I reached out and took it, my own hand shaking. She pulled me to my feet, and I saw her looking up at me, clearly not expecting me to be so tall. Taking in my clothes, her face creased into a twisted smile, then, as if remembering something, she turned and stared down the alley, frowning. 'Where did he go?' she asked. 'What happened?'

My voice crept back. 'I-I don't know where he is. Something pulled him away from me and he disappeared into the fog.'

She whipped round and looked hard at me. 'What fog?'

'It was...it appeared suddenly and then just vanished,' I said weakly.

The girl looked towards the mouth of the alley, then back the other way, but it was too dark to make out much detail beyond one or two crates a few feet away. She seemed to be listening to something, but I could only hear the sound of the waves. A moment or two passed, then she seemed to reach a decision. Gripping my arm, she hustled me down the alley and back onto the street.

'I have a hiding place nearby,' she said. 'It will only take us a few minutes to get there. Did he hurt you?'

'No,' I said, trying to force my legs to work properly. They still felt like jelly, and I couldn't decide whether they were doing the right thing or not. 'He was about to, but –' I broke off, choking back a sob.

'I'm curious about your clothes,' she said candidly as she led me through a gap in a fence around an old, disused warehouse. 'But that can wait until you feel better. What's your name?'

Something made me pluck a name from my imagination rather than use my real one. She gave me a sideways glance, as if something in my voice betrayed the lie. I saw her shoulders move in a little half-shrug and she pushed open a battered door at the back of the warehouse, pulling me in after her and barricading the entrance with some crates and a barrel. 'Welcome to my humble abode,' she said with a smile. 'I'm Anna. Anna Stenberg.'

Chapter Three

I had never been in a warehouse before, let alone a crumbling, abandoned one. It felt like a cathedral, the ceiling high above my head and the far corner shrouded in darkness. The previous occupants had left behind all sorts of things – scruffy office furniture, empty crates, broken pieces of wood, a yard broom with half a handle, and a pile of mouldy old sacks which seemed to fill the entire building with their stench. I wrinkled my nose as I looked around. This was not how I had planned to spend the night.

Anna caught sight of my expression, her own becoming scornful in response. 'It's not exactly a palace,' she said pointedly, 'but it's safe. I sleep upstairs. Come on.'

She picked her way across the litter-strewn floor, her skirt swishing over the planks and dead leaves. There were only one or two windows high up in the walls, half the panes broken or missing. The hollow echo of our footsteps worried me. What if some nightwatchman caught us? I shivered, trying to stop myself from imagining new horrors. After the night I had had thus far, I just wanted to sink into the oblivion of sleep.

I began to make out the shape of a staircase in the dark corner and, looking up, saw there was a floor above us, extending over about a third of the building's length. We headed up, Anna pointing out rotting and missing steps. I put out one hand to steady myself against the wall. The bricks felt slimy, and damp and I dropped my hand with a shudder, wiping it on my coat. *At least it is just for tonight*, I told myself. *Or what remains of tonight, anyway.*

15

We reached the top of the stairs and I saw it was divided into rooms; offices, perhaps. Some seemed intact, but others were missing doors and some of the walls had either fallen or been knocked down. The whole place oozed decay and neglect and I wondered how Anna could stand it.

She opened a door and jerked her head towards the room beyond. 'In here,' she said. 'Hurry up. The cold gets in quickly.'

Obediently, I moved past her and found myself in what had once been an office. There was a heavy-looking writing desk next to the door, and a chair with no back stood beneath a blocked-up window. One wall was shelved and there was a pile of old documents and various other bits of rubbish in one corner. Inconsequential details sprang out at me as I looked around the room. I saw a pen with no nib, a broken clay pipe, an empty inkwell coated with dust. A couple of thin mattresses, a moth-eaten carpet bag and some ratty blankets lay against one wall. A pile of candles and a damp-looking tinder box sat on one of the shelves. Next to the mattresses, there was a small wicker basket containing an apple and something about the size of a book, wrapped in cloth. Anna lit a candle and stuck it into a large lump of wax on the edge of the desk, then shoved the desk along the floor so it blocked the doorway. I felt my shoulders relax a little. This would do.

Anna glanced into the basket and huffed. 'I don't have much in the way of food,' she said. 'Are you hungry?'

I shook my head. 'No,' I said. 'I'm just tired.'

She nodded and started arranging the mattresses and dividing up the blankets. 'There you go,' she said.

Exhausted, I sank down onto the mattress, which was so thin it was almost useless. It stank of damp and mould and fish. All at once, something snapped within me, and I burst into tears.

Anna hovered while I sobbed, waiting until the flood had become a trickle. I fumbled in my various pockets for a handkerchief, but finding none, was forced to use my sleeve. The coat was filthy anyway, I thought, remembering my fall in the alley, and struggled to take it off. Anna helped me, then took the coat and laid it over the desk, giving it a quick inspection.

'Just mud and dirt,' she said. 'Most of it will probably scrape off once it's dry.'

I nodded, drawing my knees up to my chest and wrapping my arms around them, trying to make myself as small as possible. I had never felt so wretched in my life and all I wanted was to go home. In the morning, I would pay Anna to guide me, I decided. If she lived on the streets, she must know the town very well.

'What happened?' she asked suddenly, kneeling in front of me. Her oval face was earnest, her eyes intelligent. There was something about her voice, too; it reminded me of my own. Hers was a little rougher around the edges, but beneath the coarse veneer, I sensed refinement. Was she a runaway, perhaps?

She said a name and I frowned at her, puzzled, until I saw the triumph in her eyes. 'Ha!' she exclaimed. 'I thought that was a lie.' She shrugged. 'No matter. Perhaps you should think of a better one. Something you can actually remember.' She reached out and touched the cuff of the suit jacket. 'Does he have a name?'

'My father?' I asked, confused, then realised what she meant. 'Oh…no. This was just to get me to safety. The suit belongs to my father. We're the same height.'

'Useful,' she observed. 'So, what should I call you?'

I had no idea why I was so reluctant to give her my real name, but there was a nagging feeling in the pit of my stomach. Shame had much to do with it, I supposed; we had kept my father's illness as quiet as possible to help him maintain his dignity and pride, and to avoid embarrassing the family. Despite everything, I felt I still owed him that same loyalty. Not even my best friend Elizabeth knew all the details, so I certainly was not about to reveal anything to this stranger, even if she had saved me.

Remembering her question, I dragged my flitting mind back to our conversation and racked my brain for a name for my disguise. 'Viktor,' I suggested.

'Viktor.' She tasted the name on her tongue. 'All right. What happened?'

'Why do you want to know?'

She sat back in frustration. 'Look,' she said, 'I understand. You have no idea who I am. But if helping you has put me in danger, I need to know. For your sake as much as mine,' she added.

I felt guilty. It had not occurred to me that, if someone was determined to rob me, Anna might be in danger too. It was clear I was a target – I was alone and wearing expensive clothes. Anna could have simply robbed me herself, or worse, when she found me lying in the alley, yet she had offered me shelter. Embarrassed and uncomfortable, I nodded.

'You're right. I apologise,' I said. 'I have had a horrible experience tonight and am finding it hard to make sense of it all.'

'Start at the beginning,' she suggested.

I took a deep breath, trying to unravel my tangled thoughts. 'Something happened tonight which meant I had to leave my home in a hurry,' I said. 'My life was being threatened. That is why I am wearing this suit. They were looking for a girl, not a man. I was trying to get to the church by the park but got lost in the dark and ended up here.'

'And met the charming gent I heard you talking to in that alley,' she finished.

A shudder coursed through me as the memories swirled round in my head. His leering stare and ugly laugh, the stink of him. 'When I saw I was at the seafront, I knew I had taken the wrong road, so I stopped for a moment to get my bearings. I thought the best thing would be to make for the hotel. Suddenly, he was right there.'

She frowned, little creases appearing between her eyebrows. She was about my age, I thought, perhaps a little older. Her frown reminded me of my mother, and I felt my heart lurch as a fresh wave of pain and grief struck it, all the more powerful for being unexpected.

'You were lucky. He could have hit you over the head or stuck a knife in your back.'

I went cold, remembering the glint of light on the blade. 'He had a knife,' I whispered, shocked, then let out a long, juddering sigh that ended in a sob. Anna reached out and stroked my shoulder.

'It's all right,' she said. 'You're safe now.'

I looked at her serious, earnest face and nodded. 'I know,' I said. 'Thank you.'

She smiled, then moved to the other mattress and lay down, curling up in the thin blankets. 'Tell me about the fog,' she said.

Biting my lip, I thought back to the moment when the fog had filled the alley. 'My thoughts are jumbled,' I said. 'I am not sure what happened. One minute there was no fog, then the next, I could hardly see anything more than about a foot away. Then he seemed to shoot backwards away from me, as though something was pulling him.'

'Did you see what it was?' she asked, raising herself on to one elbow, intense and fascinated. I shook my head.

'No. There was a strange smell, though, and I heard a noise like a parasol being shaken. Something scratched along the ground, too, I think, but that is all I remember. I thought I was going to die. I have never been so terrified.'

Anna nodded; her face thoughtful. A strand of dark hair fell down over one eye and she tucked it behind her ear before meeting my gaze. Her eyes were either blue or green, or perhaps grey. The candlelight made it difficult to distinguish the colour, but it did not hide the tilt of her jaw or her clear skin. What really lay under the layers of dirt and the patched, ragged clothes?

As I thought this, my stomach lurched again, either in confirmation or as a warning; I wasn't sure which. Before I could decide, she started asking questions again. 'What are you going to do tomorrow? Are you going to go to the church?'

I considered. 'I need to find out what has happened at home,' I said. 'The problem is that if I just march up to the front door, I might be putting myself and others in danger.'

She raised an eyebrow. 'You think the person threatening you will be watching your house?'

'He was, tonight,' I said.

She caught her breath at that and stared at me. She was probably wondering what I could have done to make someone threaten me. I had to admit I was wondering that myself.

'Could you take them a message, perhaps?' I asked suddenly, half an idea forming in my mind. 'I will tell them to pay you, of course.'

'Let us see what the morning brings,' she said evasively, settling down again and shifting the carpet bag beneath her head. 'In my opinion, you might be better off if you stay here for a day or two.'

I started to protest, but she held up a grimy hand and I fell silent. 'Consider,' she said. 'For someone like you, living a sheltered life, there are obvious boltholes you'd run to. Relatives, friends, church... they are the first places someone would look for you. Would they think to look for you here?' She waved her hand at the squalid surroundings, and I saw the logic in her suggestion. Unless he had seen me entering the building with his own eyes, my father would never believe for an instant that I would choose to seek refuge in such a place. 'You have to do the unexpected now. If your life is at stake, you can't risk being predictable.' She paused and something on my face seemed to strike a chord with her, for her own expression softened. 'Stay here with me tomorrow. I'll go out early and get some food. I think you need time to unravel your feelings.'

'Yes, I do,' I murmured. I pulled the blankets around my shoulders and lay down on my side. I threw one leg over my bag, wrapping my fingers around the handle. Anna's suggestion was sensible. I did need some time to work through the traumas of the last few hours. This horrible, abandoned building had provided me with an unexpected haven. Besides, if the worst had happened and my father was still out there somewhere, it would make sense to keep my distance until I made contact with my uncle, or perhaps the police.

Anna closed her eyes and soon I could hear the gentle, even rhythm of her breath. Tired as I was, sleep evaded me with grim determination, so I watched the flame dancing above the stubby candle on the desk. My eyes grew heavy, but the events of the night were wheeling around in my mind, faster and faster, until I felt as though I was being physically shaken as my attacker's face repeatedly loomed out of the chaos.

I wasn't being shaken, I realised, I was on a horse. What I felt was the gentle rolling rhythm of a horse's sedate walk. It was soothing, until I realised the reins were being pulled from my grasp and I was falling. I gasped and opened my eyes to find myself staring straight at Anna.

She was kneeling next to me, her face only inches from mine, gently easing my bag out from under me. As I gasped, she froze, and for a few long seconds, we just stared at each other. She looked sheepish, and as the silence stretched into a minute, she moved back, letting go of the bag and holding up her hands. Her face twisted into a rueful smile, and she shrugged. Stunned, I shot out a hand and grabbed her wrist, sitting up as I did so. She caught her breath as my fingernail scratched her, and tried to wrench her arm free, but I held her firmly.

'Is this why you want me to stay here?' I demanded. 'So you can rob and murder me yourself? Is it?'

Her jaw dropped. 'I would never hurt you!'

I laughed, surprised at how bitter it sounded. 'Really?' I scoffed. 'I have no doubt that when you saw me, you thought it was your lucky day.'

'Not everyone who lives this way is a criminal,' she retorted. 'Listening to you, I realised I wanted to help you. I could have left you where I found you.' She met my disbelieving expression with one of openness, which surprised me. 'All I wanted was to see if you had anything in there with your real name. Calling you Viktor feels strange.'

She seemed genuine, but I found I could not believe a word of it. With a snort of disgust, I shoved her hand away from me with such force that she fell backwards onto her mattress. Her eyes met mine and I saw pain there, but after everything I had been through, I had no energy left with which to care. I pulled the blankets around me again and lay down, curling around my precious bag. At that moment, the candle guttered.

'I won't touch it again,' Anna said quietly into the darkness. 'You have my word.'

Chapter Four

I was awakened by a hand on my shoulder, shaking me gently. 'Good morning,' Anna said. 'I need to go out and find us something to eat, but I didn't want to go before you were awake.'

I blinked at her, uncertain for a moment where I was. She gave a quick smile, then got up and shoved the desk away from the door. The loud, grating sound startled me and made me cringe. I watched her deft, firm, decisive movements and thought again about her attempt to take my bag. Had she been telling the truth? Was she simply trying to find out my name?

'Close the door after me and push the desk against it,' she instructed. 'When I come back, I'll knock six times, three sets of two, like this.' She demonstrated. 'Then you'll know it's me.'

'All right,' I said.

There was a slight pause, as if she had been expecting me to say something else. When I stayed silent, she opened the door and went out.

Anna had lit another candle and I realised the room would be pitch black otherwise. I sat up, groaning as my spine creaked in protest. I had no idea what time it was or how long I had been asleep. As I stretched and flexed my arms and legs, my joints complained, and I decided it might help to walk about for a few minutes. I was cold, so I pulled on the filthy overcoat, and buttoned it. As soon as I had warmed up, I would see if I could clean off any of the muck.

I went to the door and peered around the frame, listening for footsteps or voices. Outside, I could hear shouting and the clanking of winches as the docks burst into life, but the warehouse was quiet. Nonetheless, I decided to take my bag with me. Just in case.

There was a pile of sacks up here, too, tucked into a corner in one of the other rooms, as though someone had been using them as a bed. I moved cautiously from one room to the next, looking through the rubbish on the shelves and kicking at items on the floor to see if there was anything I could use as a weapon. *The letter opener had been worse than useless*, I thought. Mind you, so had I.

As I wandered, my mind returned once again to the strange fog and the memory of my attacker's face as he shot backwards into its midst. My steps slowed as I sank into the reverie, only snapping out of it when I reached the last room. I had found nothing useful; deep down, I had not really expected to.

My joints felt a little looser, but I was still cold, so I went back into Anna's room and wrapped the blankets around my shoulders, then perched on the backless chair. After a few minutes, I began to feel restless. I needed something to occupy my mind, so I opened my bag and pulled out one of my father's notebooks. It was too dark to read by the candle's feeble glow, so I went into one of the other rooms, which had a small square window, coated with dust and grime. The glass was broken in one corner, so I held the book next to it and leaned against the wall, bag at my feet, trying to understand my father's scribblings.

The first few pages were relatively neat and read rather like a diary, but I was three pages in before I realised he was talking about his trip to Germany with my mother. My uncle had told him to try medicinal bathing, I learned, and had recommended a place called Bad Elster in northern Germany. It had only been operating as a resort for a couple of years but was gaining a good reputation.

For a moment, anger flared within me. Neither my parents nor my uncle had shared any of this information with me. My mother's favourite phrase had been 'when you are older'. It was ridiculous how I was considered old enough to be turning my thoughts towards making a good marriage, but too young to be told about the treatment my father was having.

I shoved the book into my pocket, letting my anger burn inside me. Suddenly, I was angry at everything and everyone. At my father for going to war and leaving us behind, terrified that we might never see him again. At my mother, for vanishing without a trace in Germany. At my uncle for his part in the deception about my father's treatment. At Parsons for sending me out alone in the middle of the night. At Anna for trying to steal my bag. Angry at myself. Especially at myself.

With horrible clarity, I realised how weak I was. Everyone saw me as either a target or a chattel, unsuited to any form of responsibility and useful only for what I could provide for others, be it in the form of a dutiful wife or the contents of a bag I was too pathetic to defend. Something had to change, I decided. Starting right now.

I would need to learn how to defend myself. Perhaps Anna could help me. If this was how she lived, she must have a few tricks up her sleeve. When she returned, I would ask her.

Something struck me as I stood leaning against the wall in that ruined building. Even in the depths of his mania, my father had a purpose. No matter how ridiculous its nature might seem to those of us who could think rationally, he still had a purpose. My uncle had a career which gave him a purpose. Tending to my father had given my mother a purpose.

What was my purpose?

The question rolled around in my mind, even as my subconscious pointed out, quite reasonably, that I was only seventeen and had plenty of time to map out the rest of my life. Ignoring my subconscious, I started running through my skills, categorising them according to their usefulness. Embroidery and watercolour painting went straight into the useless pile, as did piano playing. Languages, however, gave me plenty to consider. I spoke French, German and a little Italian. Perhaps I could do something involving languages. But what?

I huffed out a long breath, frustrated by the lack of immediate answers, as well as the knowledge that my gender would limit me if I tried to carve out any sort of career. That made my anger flare up again, until I thought about the fact that I was dressed as a man. The kernel of an idea, a tiny seed, formed in the back of my mind and I stared out through the broken glass, toying with it.

I had been there for a while when I saw him. The window was at the side of the warehouse and looked out onto the roof of the building next door. It gave a view of a slice of the street; the front of what looked like a chandler's store and part of the building next to it, as well as the mouth of an alley between the two. There, leaning against the wall, stood my father.

I let out a noise that was somewhere between a scream and a hoarse, ragged cry, ducking out of sight, my breath coming faster and faster as panic gripped me. How? How was he here? Even I had no idea exactly where I was. How had he found me?

Taking a deep breath, I risked a quick peek out of the window. He was still there, looking around. He was bare headed, his hat in one hand.

I slumped to the floor, unable to think. Should I run? I did not want to barricade myself in Anna's room, as she had instructed. There was only the one door. If he found his way into the warehouse, I would be trapped.

It suddenly occurred to me that I should be watching my father to see where he went. Hastily, I scrambled to my feet again and peered out. He was still there, looking up and down the street, watching the activity around him. The street was full of carts and sailors, boys with lobster pots and women with baskets on their hips all bustling to and fro. At any other time, I would have found the scene fascinating, for it was so different from everything to which I was accustomed. Now, everything moved in slow motion, with my father at the epicentre.

He looked much older than when I had last seen him eight months earlier. His dark hair had a peppering of grey now, and he was thinner, more haggard. His beard was sparse and his moustache short and neat, not the luxuriant growth of which he had been so proud. The clothes he was wearing did not fit well; the trousers were too short, and the jacket was too big, hanging from his shoulders and emphasising how gaunt he had become. If he had not been trying to kill me, I would have pitied him.

The sound of quiet footsteps on the staircase jerked me into high alert and I held my breath, listening. I realised I had neglected to close the door to Anna's room. The footsteps reached the top of the stairs, went on for a few feet and stopped.

I heard Anna swear under her breath.

'Anna!' I gasped, hurrying from the room. She swung round, raising a wooden plank like a club, relaxing when she saw it was me.

'What are you doing?' she started, but I interrupted.

'My father is outside!'

'What?'

'My father is here!' I repeated, knowing I was making no sense and my wild eyes and panicked breathing had alarmed her. 'Please, I have to leave! He must not find me! Please help me, Anna, please!'

She stared at me. 'The person threatening you is your father?' she said quietly. All I could do was nod.

'Where is he?' she asked.

I pointed to the room I had just left, struggling to summon the words. 'Look out of the window. He's standing by the alley next to the chandler's.'

She disappeared into the room, returning a moment later. 'Thin man, holding a hat?' she asked. I nodded again. She set her lips in a thin line. 'Help me pack,' she said. 'We can't leave any evidence behind.'

She showed me how to roll the mattresses and tie them with twine, then gathered her meagre belongings. 'We'll hide the mattresses outside,' she told me. 'They are too bulky to carry with us.'

We were ready to leave in less than five minutes. Anna looked out of the window again while I hovered at the top of the stairs in agitation, shifting from foot to foot and petrified that my father would burst through the door at any moment. Anna reappeared and we hurried down the stairs and ran for the door.

'He's still there,' she said as we emerged from the dim building into a dull, chilly morning. She led me to a pile of barrels, some broken and rotting, and shoved the mattresses into a gap, out of sight. That done, we went to peer around the side of the building. She glanced at me, reached up to adjust my hair and collar, and gave me a reassuring smile.

'It will be all right,' she said. 'Come on. I know you're scared, but you need to try your hardest to look like you're just out for a stroll. And walk like a man.

I'll link my arm through yours.' She did, looking up at me earnestly. 'Be brave, Viktor. You can do this.'

All I could manage was a smile so weak it hardly even qualified as one. We turned away from the road and walked through the yard behind the next warehouse, then the next. The third building backed directly onto the waterfront, so we had no alternative but to head back to the road and go around the front. Anna went ahead of me. I watched as she wandered to the corner of the building, looking up and down the road. She put her basket down and leaned against the wall, then made a show of rubbing the small of her back as if she was in pain, which was my signal to join her. I stayed in the shadow of the building, ready to bolt.

'I can just make out the top of his head,' she muttered. 'Come, let's hurry. There's a cart approaching. We can slip out in front of it, and it will give us some cover if he looks in this direction.'

As the cart rumbled nearer, we emerged from the alleyway and walked briskly along. I let Anna set the pace, which was much faster than my usual stroll. I was reminded again that my life had no purpose. I did not even need to walk anywhere in a hurry, for heaven's sake.

Every now and then, Anna would glance over her shoulder. We made our way past the harbourmaster's office and turned right, away from the docks. From there, Anna led me down road after road, saying very little and turning occasionally to check that we were not being followed. Several people – mostly women – gave me odd looks as we went past and I realised that, in their eyes, I was a man out in public in a filthy coat and without a hat. I turned my collar up and tried to huddle down inside the coat as far as I could, unable to stop myself from staring into the eyes of everyone who passed us, expecting each one to be my father.

After about half an hour or so, Anna relaxed and smiled at me. 'There,' she said. 'You made it. I said you would.'

'I made it because of you. Again.' I forced another weak smile. 'Thank you. Again. And I am sorry.'

'Sorry for what'' she asked.

'For being so pathetic and incapable,' I started, but she hushed me.

'Look,' she said, 'you might think I know all there is to know about living in this way, but believe me, I don't. I make mistakes all the time. I've lost everything I own a dozen times. I've gone days without food, and days without conversation.' Her expression was serious as she looked up at me. 'I'm not going to pretend I understand exactly what you've been through in the last couple of days, but I think you're dealing with it admirably.'

I scoffed, but she went on. 'I mean it. For someone who has probably never been out on their own before, you're coping very well. In spite of everything, I haven't heard a single word of complaint from you.'

'Why would I complain?' I asked. 'You have helped me so much. I hope I will be able to repay your kindness one day.'

'You will,' she said with a smile. 'Now, enough of this. We need to go somewhere safe for a while, so we can decide what to do next. Luckily for you, I know just the place!'

Chapter Five

The sky was darkening as we walked along, heavy clouds gathering and the threat of rain cloying in the air. I glanced up and scowled, hoping we would find somewhere to shelter before we had to add 'soaked to the skin' to our list of misfortunes.

We made our way past a string of shops, of which I knew only the milliner and the chemist a little further on. People bustled past on the pavement and the road was full of carts, carriages and horses. I had never stopped to look properly before. There was a grubby urchin selling newspapers, shouting out the headline in a strident voice. I was relieved that there was no mention of my father. Hopefully, that meant my uncle, and everyone at home, was safe.

As we walked, I became aware of the extraordinary freedom I now possessed. Several people who jostled me called me 'sir' and although I did get a few sideways glances, no one challenged me. As I no longer needed a governess, Mrs Armitage usually accompanied me to town. She was sweet and kind, but I was always aware that she was taking time away from her duties in the house. Errands were completed as efficiently as possible, and she did not encourage window-shopping or dawdling. Today, though, with Anna by my side, I could look at everything for as long as I wanted to. It was strange. Everything looked and smelled the same yet was somehow different.

I spotted a telegraph office up a side street as we crossed the main road and pointed it out to Anna. 'I need to send word to my uncle that I am safe,' I said.

'I'll keep watch out here,' she said. 'Be as quick as you can.'

I hurried inside. There was a fire blazing in a small grate, and I stepped up to it, holding out my hands to its cheery warmth. The thin, pale man behind the counter gave me a disdainful sneer as I approached, and my polite smile melted as I realised how I must look, caked with dirt and without a hat. However, something in his gaze irked me. I was not used to being regarded in such a manner.

'Good morning,' I said pleasantly, remembering to keep my voice low. 'Please forgive my appearance. I was attacked…'

I got no further. On hearing my voice, the clerk's eyes widened, his demeanour changed, and a genuine look of alarm settled onto his angular face. 'My dear young sir!' he exclaimed. 'May I be of any assistance?'

'That is very kind of you, but I am, luckily, unhurt. Only my pride has suffered. And my hat,' I added. 'I lost most of my money, of course, and will be unable to purchase a new one until I can contact my family.'

'You are from out of town?' he asked, reaching for a telegram form and pushing it towards me.

'It was not the welcome I was expecting,' I said, trying to keep the conversation as vague as possible. I scribbled a message to my uncle, signing it with my initials. Keeping the bundle of notes in my pocket out of the clerk's sight, I worked one loose and produced it as payment. He handed over my change, and as I was pocketing it, he suddenly stood up, making me start. He didn't notice, however, for his attention was fixed on a small chest of drawers behind him. He squatted down and I heard a drawer opening and the sound of objects being moved. He stood up again, holding a rather battered cap in his hand.

'I thought it was still here,' he said with a greasy smile. 'It ended up in our doorway a couple of weeks ago when we had a dreadful gale. No one has claimed it, so perhaps you can make use of it.'

I eyed the cap for a moment before thanking him and accepting it. I handed him a couple of coins, half-expecting him to refuse them in the circumstances, but I was not surprised when he nodded and slipped them into his pocket.

'I shall return later,' I told him. 'There will be a reply.'

'Of course, sir,' he said with a small bow. 'I'll send this for you now.' I nodded and thanked him again, then left the office. As the door closed behind me, I heard him calling, 'Tom! Got a telegram for you to deliver, lad. Look lively!'

Anna was leaning against the wall, eyes darting from face to face, her purple shawl drawn close around her neck against the cold. 'Done?' she asked as I appeared. When I nodded, she said, 'Come on, then. Not far to go now.'

'I need to come back in a couple of hours,' I told her. 'I sent a telegram to my uncle, so there will be a reply before too long.'

'All right,' she said. 'For now, let's just get off the street and try to warm up a bit.'

We started walking down the road again, Anna setting a brisk pace. 'We can take a short cut through the market,' she said over her shoulder as I hurried to keep up. I put the cap on, pulling the peak down over my forehead. Catching sight of Anna's curious stare, I explained how I had acquired it. She laughed. 'That was a stroke of luck!' she said.

I was about to ask where we were going when I was almost knocked off my feet by a small boy in the blue postal service uniform. We both staggered off balance and Anna dropped her basket as she grabbed my arm. The lad quickly straightened himself. I saw he had a telegram clutched in his fist.

'Beg pardon, sir!' he gasped, his face flushed red with embarrassment. 'Didn't mean no 'arm, sir.'

'You need to watch where you're going,' Anna chided as he turned and fled, vanishing into the crowd. I leaned down to pick up her basket and the cloth-wrapped item, but she got there first, almost snatching it from the ground where it had fallen. I said nothing, although I did give her a sharp look. It seemed she was permitted to search through my belongings, but I could not even touch hers. Yet again, I found myself speculating about her background. She had been living on the streets long enough to learn to survive, yet not long enough to completely shed those little habits which hinted at another, gentler life.

Anna's stomach growled loudly, and she gave a little chuckle. 'In all the excitement, I forgot our food,' she said, shifting the carpet bag into the same hand as the basket and lifting the edge of her shawl to reveal a lumpy bundle wrapped in cloth and tied round her waist with twine. She glanced around, then led me towards an alley. I hung back, a gnawing feeling working its way through my stomach. Anna paused when she realised I was not following, turning puzzled eyes towards me. 'What's wrong? You must be hungry, surely.'

'Why are we going into an alley?' I had not intended it to come out as a whine, but even as I said it, I knew I had never sounded so petulant in my life. My anger at myself flared again. If I was going to deal with this situation at all, I had to become stronger. Whining did nothing except emphasise how unsuited I was to life outside my privileged sphere.

To give Anna credit, she showed no impatience. She raised one eyebrow and said, 'We are not the only hungry people around here, you know. If we sit out in the open to eat, all we are doing is making ourselves targets. I had to work hard for our breakfast, and I intend to enjoy it!'

Once again, she was introducing me to things which had never occurred to me. As I followed her, I considered the gaping crevasse which separated my lifestyle from hers. When I was able to return home, I thought, I would do something to help the poor in the city. That would give my life purpose. In the meantime, I would try to view this horrible situation as a learning opportunity, to see for myself what help was needed, where and by whom. The thought was comforting.

We leaned against the wall about half-way down the alley and Anna fished a couple of bread rolls from the bundle around her waist. I accepted one gratefully, deciding that Anna would consider it rude if I asked exactly what she had done to obtain it. I suspected it was stolen, which did not sit well with me, but I said nothing, wolfing it down in a few bites, grateful for its weight in my empty belly.

'Where are we going?' I asked, watching as she finished the last of her bread. She shook crumbs from her shawl, pulled it more tightly around her shoulders and considered for a moment before answering. When she spoke, I had the impression that she was choosing her words carefully.

'A man I know at one of the posh schools sometimes helps me. We can go to him.'

'A teacher?' I asked. She shook her head.

'No. You'll see.'

I leaned down to pick up my bag, which was lying at my feet. As I did so, a shrill scream numbed our ears, followed by men yelling and women shouting to each other. Anna and I exchanged glances and hurried to the end of the alley to see what was going on. As we did so, however, something odd happened.

By the time we reached the end of the alley, which was only a few feet away, we were surrounded by fog so thick that we could no longer see the street beyond. Anna gave a low cry, and I froze, wide-eyed, as the all-too-familiar stench from the previous night crawled into my nostrils and clogged my throat. I choked, panic rising. I caught Anna's arm.

'We need to go,' I gasped. 'This is exactly what happened last night!'

She stared at me, her mouth agape, but before she could say anything, we both heard a soft, low growl from somewhere in the fog in front of us. It was unlike anything I had ever heard before. Not a dog, I could tell...but if not a dog, then what was it?

Anna caught her breath, staring at the swirls of fog as though transfixed. She took a couple of steps towards it, heading deeper into its swirling mass. I grabbed her arm.

'What are you doing?' I hissed. 'Please, we have to go!'

She blinked at me, as though she had forgotten who I was. A flicker of something which looked like irritation passed across her face, disappearing almost at once. 'Yes...yes,' she said in a distracted voice. 'Come on.' She turned and pulled me along, away from the fog, hurrying towards the far end of the alley.

Not looking back for fear of what I might see emerging from the fog, I followed her along the alley. After dog-legging a couple of times, it opened onto the next street and as we emerged, we were almost bowled over by a petrified-looking woman who was running away from the road we'd just left.

Anna caught hold of her arm and started asking what was happening, but the woman shook her off. A man and two other women followed, then a girl of about our age. We started running alongside her and Anna caught hold of her arm and asked what was happening.

'Some madman stuck a knife in one of the post office workers!' she gasped. 'Let go of me! I have to get away!'

Anna released her arm, and we watched as she darted away. The two of us stared at each other as we realised that the post office worker had to be the man in the telegraph office.

'Quickly! Come on,' Anna said, her voice grim and her lips set.

We looked behind us in time to see the dense cloud of fog begin to dissipate. People were emerging from within it, and their terrified faces galvanised us into action. We started running as fast as we could, Anna leading me on a dizzying series of left and right turns that soon had me utterly lost, my lungs burning and tears stinging my eyes. Rounding a corner, the school stood before us, an ornate building of shining grey stone. I remembered it vaguely, having been there once or twice with my father when I was younger – one of his army friends had been a porter. The thought of being able to take shelter behind a door which locked made me run faster than I ever thought possible.

Anna pointed to one of the archways, beyond which I could just make out more buildings and a well-kept lawn. As we ran beneath the arch, I saw that this part of the school was arranged in a square, around a central lawn. Anna slowed to a walk, for a group of boys were crossing the lawn, one or two of them eyeing us with suspicion. Trying to appear nonchalant, we made our way to a door in the far corner of the building. Glancing over her shoulder to make sure no one was watching, Anna opened it and we slipped inside, closing the door behind us.

We were in a whitewashed corridor which stretched out to our right and turned a corner to our left. Anna turned right and headed along the corridor, which branched off to the left half-way along. At the end of that corridor, there was a stout wooden door on the right marked 'Porter'. Anna hurried over and knocked briskly. A moment later, the door swung open to reveal a tall, well-built man of around forty. His handsome face was rugged, and his blue eyes were sharp. He raked both of us with a piercing gaze, then stepped forward and glanced along the corridor. Satisfied, he gestured to us.

'Well, come in, then,' he said. 'If you've come here to hide from someone, hanging around in the corridor isn't going to be much help, now, is it?'

Chapter Six

For a moment, I stood staring at the man. He was wearing smart black trousers and waistcoat and his immaculate white shirt was open at the collar, sleeves rolled up to his elbows, revealing a pair of muscular forearms. He looked extremely capable, and I darted past him into the room, joining Anna by the small fireplace in the far corner. He closed the door and locked it, then took Anna's shawl and hung it carefully from a hook behind the door.

'Please, sit down,' he invited, and Anna perched on the edge of one of two green armchairs by the fire, holding her hands out towards the warmth. The man turned to me and held out his hand. 'I am Arthur Phillips, sir. Porter at this fine establishment. May I take your...'

He tailed off as I removed the cap, staring at my face. His eyes widened but he controlled himself with an effort. 'May I take your coat?' he asked in a strained voice.

I shrugged the overcoat off and handed it to him, feeling self-conscious and awkward. Noticing the dirt, he laid it over a small square wooden table, fetched a clothes brush from a dresser next to the fireplace and began working on the coat with firm, practised movements.

'Arthur, this is...Viktor,' Anna said by way of introduction. 'I see you have already noticed that Viktor is not all he seems.' I glanced at Arthur, feeling awkward. He smiled at me briefly, then looked at Anna.

'Well, I thought I'd seen everything,' he said mildly. 'I suppose you've run into a spot of trouble and need somewhere to hide until the hue and cry dies down.'

Anna bit her lip, and we exchanged glances. She seemed reluctant to say anything, and I suddenly realised she was waiting for me to speak. It was my problems which had brought us here, after all. I took a deep breath and gave as concise a description of events as I could. Half-way through, Arthur put down the clothes brush and listened with the greatest attention until I had finished.

'That's quite a story, miss,' he said. 'Now, then, how about I put the kettle on and make us all a nice cup of tea while we work out what you should do next.'

Without waiting for an answer, he busied himself at the fireplace, then took crockery from the dresser and, after moving my coat and wiping down the table, he set out cups and saucers and produced a fruitcake, which he cut into slices.

'The first thing to do,' he mused, 'is, I think, to send another note to your uncle and get the messenger to wait for a response. There's a boy here who can take it. He works in the kitchens, but he often does odd jobs for me.' He looked at me, as if awaiting my approval, so I nodded. He went to the dresser again and this time produced a pen and a few sheets of writing paper, which he laid on the table beside me. I picked up the pen and stared at the blank pages.

'I have no idea what to write,' I said.

'Keep it brief and vague,' Anna suggested. 'The telegram boy was long gone by the time the man at the office was attacked, so I'm willing to wager he got to your uncle safely. But now it is unsafe for you to try to collect the response.'

'We have no proof that it was...that my father...' I stopped, my voice cracking. Anna looked at me, sympathy in her eyes.

'I know,' she said gently, 'but you still need to be able to communicate with your uncle. He may be able to send his carriage for you.'

I considered. The attack at the telegraph office was, in all probability, an unfortunate coincidence, I thought. It was unlikely that my father had followed us from the docks; we had been some distance from him when we had been forced back onto the street and the cart had given us decent cover. If he had followed us, that meant he had seen us at the docks and had managed to keep us in sight all the way back into town whilst remaining hidden himself. I shuddered, thinking of all the doorways and alleys we had passed. The thought that he had simply flitted from one to another behind us made me feel sick. Yet Anna had kept an eye on who was behind us. Was it possible that he had managed to outwit her? Was he somewhere nearby even now, plotting and waiting?

Arthur took the kettle off the fire as it boiled and filled a large teapot, which he set on the table. Seeing my expression, he laid a hand on my shoulder. 'Keep it simple, miss,' he said.

'Wait a moment,' I said, as something occurred to me. 'My uncle is the only relative I have. Obviously, I would seek him out. All my father needs to do is watch anyone carrying messages to the asylum. One of them is bound to lead him to me eventually.'

Arthur's eyes narrowed. 'I fear you may be right, miss,' he said, rubbing his chin. 'Perhaps the safest thing for you to do would be to go to the police station and request that they escort you to your uncle's quarters at the asylum.'

I shook my head. 'My father escaped from that asylum,' I said. 'Whatever he is suffering from, Mr Phillips, I can assure you he is not stupid. He was there for eight months, plotting and observing, I have no doubt, hence the ease with which he was able to make his escape. If he knows how to get out of a place like that, I can guarantee he will also know how to get in. I would not feel safe there.'

Arthur nodded and picked up the teapot to fill my cup. I watched him, trying to reconcile the man with the domesticity. My father was a similar age and had been a similar build before he went into St Bernadette's, but I had never once seen him pour tea, much less slice cake and lay out plates. Somehow, Arthur's precise, careful movements gave everything he did a subtle strength. My father, by contrast, would have looked awkward and uncomfortable.

'Would he really try to get to you in the place he just escaped from?' Anna mused.

'If he is being driven by the idea that I have to...to die, then would it matter where I was?' I asked, my throat tightening. Anna frowned at me as she considered this. Her face darkened.

'If that's the case,' she said, 'then surely the safest thing for you would be to leave town altogether. Arthur, what do you think?'

Arthur paused for a moment. 'Well,' he said, putting the teapot down and picking up the milk jug. 'Far be it from me to throw in my tuppence worth, miss, but it seems your options are rather limited. Staying with your uncle seems to be out of the question. I am inclined to agree with your assessment of that particular situation.' He pursed his lips. 'I also think your father would keep an eye on your friends' houses. It's what I would do.'

I stared at him. He had given me the tiniest glimpse behind the curtain. Yes, he was a porter to rich young students, performing menial tasks in a deferential manner, but he carried himself like a warrior from centuries past. He had an air of danger about him, in spite of the manners, and I suspected he had led what might be termed 'an interesting life'. For the first time since leaving my house, I felt safe.

'Do you have any connection at all with the school, miss?' Arthur asked. 'Any brothers who have studied here?' I shook my head.

'No, none. I came here once or twice with my father years ago, when I was a child. One of his friends...' I broke off, as something occurred to me. My voice was quavering when I spoke again. 'One of my father's old army friends used to be a porter here. I think his name was Fielding.'

Arthur nodded. 'I've heard the name. He isn't here now, though. Retired, if I remember correctly, a few years back. Your father's only connection was Fielding?'

'To the best of my knowledge,' I said. 'My father did not discuss personal matters with me.'

'In that case,' Arthur continued, 'this may well be the safest place for you at the moment. A hotel would be no good; there's no real security in a hotel.

Here, though, there are plenty of locked doors. Why don't you two take that room for the night, and I'll sleep in one of these chairs?'

He indicated a door in the corner of the room which I hadn't noticed. 'My bedroom,' he explained. 'It's small and very basic, but it has a number of advantages. One tiny window quite high up in the wall. No one will see you and no one can get in. One door. To get to it, someone would have to pass through this room. Which means they would also have to get past me.'

He spoke simply. There was nothing boastful about Arthur at all, I realised. He had complete confidence in his own ability, and it was infectious. I had complete confidence in his ability, too.

'The doors to this building are all locked at night,' Arthur went on. 'That's part of my responsibility, so I'll have to go out for a while.'

I finished my tea and Arthur refilled my cup with a smile. 'I know that look,' he said. 'When I was in the army, there was no such thing as a decent cup of tea. Whenever I was on leave, the first cup of tea was like tasting a little piece of Paradise.'

He offered me a slice of cake, which I accepted gratefully and bit into with relish. I'd demolished half of it before I realised what I was doing and froze, the cake half-way to my lips. Anna grinned at me, and Arthur's mouth was twitching at the corners. 'No need to stand on ceremony here, miss,' he said. 'Empty stomachs need filling, don't they?'

As Anna and I devoured the cake and Arthur plied us with tea, I found myself relaxing. From the light-hearted banter between Anna and Arthur, I guessed that they had known each other for some time, so I ventured to ask how they met. Arthur gave a little chuckle.

'Caught her trying to pinch my watch,' he said. 'Thought it was some cocky little urchin like it usually is, but when I looked down, there she was, all big eyes and sweet smile.' Anna flashed her sweetest smile at him, and we laughed. 'I thought it was my duty as a concerned citizen to try to set her on a better path. Of course, I failed dreadfully.'

Anna pretended to be affronted. 'You old reprobate,' she chided. 'You deserve to have your watch pinched.' It was said with deep affection, however, and he reached across the table to hug her, dropping a kiss on the top of her head. My heart lurched as I recalled my father doing the same thing when I was a child. I watched as he held her at arms' length for a moment, his keen eyes taking in every detail of her face.

'You're all right, though,' he said. It was more confirmation than a question, but Anna nodded, patting his arm.

'I am,' she reassured him. 'A little adventure makes the days less dreary.' She turned and winked at me. Unsure how to react, I simply smiled at her.

Once the cake was finished, Arthur had some work to do and suggested that we both have a bath. There was a cupboard in his bedroom which when opened, turned out to be a recess in the wall into which a small bath had been fitted, along with a sink and privy. I felt filthy after all the running and a night in the warehouse on Anna's dirty mattresses, so I accepted gratefully. Anna was keen to bathe too, so while Arthur busied himself at the table, cleaning boots and sewing buttons onto a jacket, the two of us went into his bedroom and started running a bath. I saw Arthur had shifted the table so it was directly opposite the door, and he had stacked three of the wooden chairs, planting the fourth so he was facing the door, ready to deal with whoever might come in. He received only three callers, however, one teacher and two boys, and none of them stayed long.

I looked at the books on Arthur's shelf and found, to my surprise, that he had a penchant for Byron, my favourite poet. Anna bathed quickly while I sat awkwardly on the bed, my back turned to give her some privacy, then she did the same while I took my turn. The warm water was soothing, and I scrubbed my skin energetically, trying to exorcise the horrors of the past twenty-four hours by washing them down the drain.

By then, it was lunchtime and Arthur had to undertake some duties elsewhere in the school. I had offered to help him with some of his work, so I was distracting myself with the buttons he had asked me to sew onto a coat, while Anna had pulled one of the armchairs as close to the fire as she could, as though trying to absorb its warmth and store it for later. She had snorted softly when I'd offered my help, but when I glanced at her, I saw the hint of a smile.

Arthur was only gone for around an hour, but I was on edge the whole time. Although she exuded an air of nonchalance, Anna, too, was alert. At one point, she came and sat at the table with me, watching as I sewed, then suggested a technique which would make the fastening sturdier. I sewed the next button using her technique and she watched, then nodded approval when I'd finished. 'The thread won't wear quite as quickly now,' she explained, then went back to the fire, curling up in the armchair, her watchful eyes on the door.

When the door opened, Anna grabbed the poker and leaped across the room, overturning one of the wooden chairs. She skidded to a halt when she saw it was Arthur returning from his rounds. He carried two or three coats over one arm and a covered basket in the other and didn't even flinch as she launched herself at him. He nodded at Anna as though he was just passing her in the street, then hung the coats neatly over one of the chairs and placed the basket on the table. Anna lowered the poker and went to put it back, murmuring an apology. Arthur smiled, his eyes twinkling.

'No need to apologise, now, is there?' he said. 'Unless, of course, the apology was for your terrible footwork. What have I told you about fighting in cramped spaces?'

Anna blushed and Arthur chuckled. 'Come and have some luncheon,' he said, taking the cloth from the top of the basket to reveal some bread, a small selection of cold cuts, some fruit and some cake. 'Made a quick visit to the kitchen,' he explained. 'Called in a favour or two. I believe dinner tonight is roast chicken, so make sure you leave enough room for it.'

Anna and I bustled about, clearing away the mending and laying the table. I wondered how long we would be able to hide in Arthur's little sanctuary. Danger seemed to be following me around and I was worried about drawing Anna and Arthur into my troubles, even though they both appeared happy to help me and were more than capable of taking care of themselves. As we tucked into our luncheon, I found myself thinking once more of the creature in the fog. What on earth was it, and why had it started appearing? Did it, too, think I was an abomination that needed to die?

'Are you all right?'

Anna's words snapped me out of my reverie, and I stared at her for a moment without understanding who she was. She gave a sympathetic smile and reached out to squeeze my hand. 'Try not to think about it too much,' she said. 'I doubt it will help.'

I nodded and forced myself to eat. Although the food was delicious, and in spite of my hunger, not even the fragrant aroma of warm bread could excite my appetite. Anna kept glancing at me, so I made more effort. It was either enough to satisfy her, or she became bored, for she stopped. After a while, we heard the clock outside chiming and Anna got up.

'I need to go out for a while,' she said, wrapping her shawl around her. 'I shan't be more than an hour.'

Arthur nodded. 'Be safe,' he told her.

She smiled at him, then went to the door. As she opened it, she caught sight of my expression. 'Don't worry,' she said. 'I'm coming back.' She shot me a quick smile, then disappeared into the corridor, closing the door behind her.

Arthur chuckled fondly and shook his head, then looked at me with a warm smile. 'Now then, miss,' he said, 'how about we clear these dishes away, and afterwards, I show you one or two little tricks I know about fighting dirty?'

My laugh was bitter and brittle. 'I don't even know about fighting clean.'

Arthur regarded me for a moment, one eyebrow raised. 'Well,' he said, 'we'd best see what we can do to address that, hadn't we?'

'Yes,' I said. 'Yes, we had.'

Chapter Seven

Arthur taught me several techniques to use if attacked; how to stand, weight placement, the correct way to throw a punch, and different methods of using an attacker's weight against them, as well as one or two dirty tricks. He was a patient teacher, and I was surprised at how much I enjoyed the feeling of power some of the moves gave me. After I had successfully thrown him twice, he got to his feet with a satisfied smile and nodded at me.

'You're an excellent pupil, miss,' he said. 'You're a quick study. Remember what I've taught you, and you'll do well. Practice with Anna. She'll be able to help you develop the skills.'

I nodded, glancing at the clock on the mantel above the tiny fireplace. Anna had been gone for well over an hour. Arthur caught me looking and gave me a reassuring smile.

'Don't worry about young Anna,' he said. 'If you're going to spend any time with her, you'll find she has particular habits. This is one of them. She says she'll be gone for an hour, but, just between you and me, that girl has no idea about the passage of time.' He chuckled. 'You wait and see, miss. In a little while, she'll swan in here without a care in the world.'

It was difficult to return his smile, but I tried as hard as I could. I sat down in one of the chairs by the fire, biting my lip, and Arthur came over and put a hand gently on my shoulder. I looked up at him. A tiny smile was playing at the corners of his mouth and his eyes were kind. 'I know things must seem very strange for you at the moment,' he said quietly. 'Life has dealt you a poor hand,

44

but I get the feeling you're strong, miss, inside and out. I think you and Anna might be good for each other.'

'In what way?' I asked, feeling the sting of tears in my eyes at his kindness. 'Anna seems very capable to me. I am not sure she needs anyone.'

'Ah, now, that's where you're wrong,' he said, straightening up and casting a quick glance towards the door. 'We all need others, just in different ways. Even young Anna, though she might not admit it.'

I sighed. 'I feel so inadequate, Arthur,' I said. 'I wasn't brought up to deal with something like this, and I don't want Anna to feel like she has to act as my guardian.'

'Practice those techniques I showed you, miss, and I can guarantee you will never need a guardian again,' Arthur said, with such quiet confidence that, for a brief moment, I truly believed I could do anything.

Unsure how to answer, I murmured that I would certainly do my best. Arthur seemed satisfied and excused himself to undertake some of his chores. I offered to assist, and when Anna finally arrived, pink-cheeked and cold, she found us both drinking tea and sewing. As she closed the door, she gave a merry laugh.

'Look at you two gentlemen, sewing away!' she exclaimed. I looked at Arthur, then at myself, and we all burst out laughing. It was a much-needed antidote to the tension which had been mounting within me since Anna's 'hour' had passed.

'You've been gone for a while,' I said, keeping my voice light. 'Where did you go?'

Something flickered over her face – annoyance, perhaps, then it vanished, and she smiled and joined us at the table, reaching for some sewing and accepting the cup of tea Arthur pushed across to her. Her hands looked cold, the knuckles dry and red. She caught me looking and flushed a little, setting the cup down and moving the sewing to her lap so her hands were hidden. I fixed my gaze onto my own work and said nothing.

The silence continued for a while, then Arthur, glancing at the clock, announced that he had some tasks to carry out elsewhere in the school and we should keep the door locked while he was gone. He put on his black coat, smoothing down the lapels and ensuring his shirt cuffs were even, then folded the mended clothes neatly, took a box of shoe polish and brushes from the dresser and went out. As the door closed quietly behind him, Anna reached for the black thread, cut a length and rethreaded her needle, then looked over at me.

'Had any more thoughts about what you should do?' she asked. She looked watchful.

'I think you are right,' I said. 'It might be best if I leave Dover for a few days.'

She nodded thoughtfully and turned her attention to her sewing. A minute or two passed, then she said, 'It just so happens that, when I was out, I happened across a pair of tickets to Calais. Interested? We could go on to Paris, perhaps.'

I gaped at her. 'How on earth…?' I began.

'Are you interested or not?' she demanded. 'How I got them isn't important. You'll have to understand that, if we're to travel together. I know this is all new to you, but if you ever want to stand a chance of fitting in, you're going to have to learn to be a lot more accepting. Otherwise, you'll stand out like a sore thumb.' I stared at her, the embarrassed blush warming my face. Anna's gaze softened a little. 'I'm sorry,' she said, in a more reasonable tone. 'I didn't mean to snap. I seem to have become a little sensitive over the years. Forgive me?'

She smiled and held out a hand. After a moment, I reached out and took it. Her fingers squeezed mine and her smile grew broader. 'Paris will be fun,' she said. 'I haven't been there for a while.'

'Paris is beautiful,' I said quietly when she lapsed into silence, lost in her memories. 'I would enjoy seeing it with you.'

Anna flashed me a quick smile, got up and went to the dresser. She opened the cupboard and looked inside. 'Hungry?'

'No, thank you,' I said.

Anna found an apple and took a bite, closing her eyes as she savoured the taste. It occurred to me that it was probably some time since she'd last had easy access to food. I said nothing. Every time I opened my mouth, I either revealed my naivety or asked some gauche and insensitive question. Anna's way of interacting with the world was completely alien to me. Still, all I had to do was get through the next few days without being robbed, attacked, or discovered by my father. If I kept my head down, maintained my male disguise, and tried not to annoy Anna too much, I might be all right.

Anna snapped her fingers right in front of my nose and I gasped, startled out of my reverie. She was smiling at me. 'I don't know what on earth you were just thinking about,' she said, 'but stop it. It was making you frown far too much.'

I managed a little chuckle as my heart rate slowed back to normal. 'I was thinking that I would need to be sure not to annoy you too much over the next few days until I can go home again,' I said. She stared at me for a moment, then threw her head back and laughed merrily. Her laugh was infectious and very soon, the two of us were giggling away like schoolgirls.

All at once, she shushed me, covering her mouth with her hand and glancing guiltily towards the door. 'We'd best be quiet, otherwise we might get Arthur into terrible trouble,' she said. 'He's been very good to me. I'd hate to replay that by losing him his position here.' I nodded, trying to quell my laughter, but failed miserably and ended up making the most awful snorting sound. It would have given poor Mrs Armitage a fit. The snort set Anna off again, and for the next few minutes, we struggled valiantly to control ourselves, with varying degrees of success. Anna had to put down her sewing at one point and wipe her eyes, which set me off again.

'I like you, *Viktor*,' she said, stressing the name. 'Don't worry, I don't want to know your real name. I understand why you don't want to tell me. To be honest, I would do the same if I were in your position.' She picked up the sewing again, finished off the buttonhole she was mending and folded the garment neatly over the back of one of the armchairs. 'I am rather looking forward to travelling with you. I'm guessing you will travel in those clothes, yes?' She pointed to the shirt and trousers, and I nodded.

'I have no choice.'

'It would make sense to pose as brother and sister,' she said, taking the tickets from what looked like a hidden pocket attached to the inside of her waistband. 'The boat leaves from the docks at eleven tomorrow morning, tide permitting. We'd better make the most of the luxury we have here.'

I was about to remark that Arthur's small, spartan room was hardly luxury, but caught myself just in time and said instead, 'Once we reach Calais, what will we do?'

Anna shrugged. 'What I always do,' she said. 'See what happens. Improvise.' Something in my expression gave her pause and she smiled. 'Don't look so worried,' she said. 'I know it's not what you're used to, but think about it for a moment. You'll be able to go anywhere you like, whenever you want to. There won't be anyone telling you what to do or making sure you're being modest and behaving like a proper young lady. You might actually enjoy yourself.'

I considered. She was right. It might be the only opportunity I would ever have to experience that sort of freedom. As soon as I was back at home, everything would go back to normal, including my shopping trips with Mrs Armitage, and being driven somewhere in the carriage so I could go for a walk. Now I thought about it, my life seemed rather ridiculous. Perhaps if I tried to view this entire dreadful situation as an opportunity, it would help me to deal with it a little better.

Something occurred to me in the midst of my musings. 'What about travel papers? Mine are at home.'

'Don't worry about that,' Anna said. 'It'll be taken care of. I know someone.' Her eyes flashed at me, daring me to retort. I gave a little sigh. In the circumstances, forged papers were the least of my worries. I searched around for a way to redirect the conversation.

'Do you have any favourite places in Paris?' I asked. 'One of mine is Notre Dame.'

We started discussing our experiences of Paris and the various places we would like to see if we made it that far. After the first few minutes, the conversation started to flow and, before long, it felt like I was chatting with my best friend Elizabeth. Anna was fun, knowledgeable and, it seemed, completely unflappable, taking everything in her stride.

Including me.

Arthur came back towards dinner time with more mending and another basket, this time containing a large pot full of roast chicken, potatoes and vegetables, along with bread, cheese and more fruit. He had also, somehow, managed to get hold of a bottle of wine, so we hastily cleared the table and set out plates and cutlery. The three of us ate heartily, toasting each other. It was with a comfortably full belly and a much lighter heart that I bade Anna and Arthur goodnight before heading into Arthur's room to prepare myself for bed. I was exhausted. I was not used to so much walking in one day and my muscles were complaining, especially after my training session with Arthur, but I did not want to look weak in front of either of them, so refrained from commenting. I guttered the candle as I slipped beneath the blankets, but sleep refused to come. I lay there listening to the murmur of Anna and Arthur's voices as they talked quietly. Curious, and hoping to learn more about Anna, I pushed back the blankets and tiptoed over to the door, pressing my ear against it.

'Where this time?' Arthur said. 'I'm guessing Paris, seeing you were both talking about it earlier.'

'Yes,' Anna replied shortly.

'It could be a good cover for your activities,' he remarked.

'Maybe,' she said thoughtfully. 'We shall see.'

Frowning, I pressed my ear more firmly against the door, my heart pounding and a terrible feeling of nausea rising in my gut. So, I was to be used as cover for some street thief's illegal activities. I had clearly been mistaken about Anna. I had thought we were beginning to find an understanding, but I had misread the signs. She was using me. Well, I thought, as I got back into the bed, two could play at that game.

Chapter Eight

Sleep evaded me that night. I was not surprised. What did surprise me was how devastated I felt by Anna's betrayal. It was with difficulty that I kept reminding myself that she owed me nothing, that I was encroaching on her life, and she was already being kind enough by taking me under her wing. I was not entitled to her friendship as well. As the two of us lay top to toe in Arthur's bed, I stared at the wall, listening to Anna breathing. I had pretended to be asleep when she finally said goodnight to Arthur and tiptoed into the bedroom.

It was a struggle to process my thoughts, but I realised I needed Anna. Part of me had been happy to attach myself to her for the safety and security her company and knowledge offered. I, who had never been allowed independence, suddenly had all the independence I could ever hope for, but had no idea what to do with it, or even how it worked. My current situation would not last for long, I knew, yet I didn't know how to survive in the meantime. I had felt so much more confident earlier, before I'd overheard Anna. Now, I was just a naïve girl with a bit of money, who knew nothing about how the real world worked. Part of me kept pointing out that I had never been given the opportunity to find out, but I knew if I used that as a defence, it would soon wear on Anna. No, I decided, I would need to bury my fears, if I could, and watch everything going on around me: how people interacted, the things they said, how they dealt with different situations. Overwhelmed, I buried my face in the pillow, soaking away the hot tears which burned my eyes.

The next morning, I awoke with a terrible headache, which did nothing to improve my mood. I was barely able to bid Anna good morning, as I was having serious doubts about the whole concept of going to France. Yes, it would give me unlimited freedom, the likes of which I had never experienced in my life, and never would again. However, I would be travelling in the company of someone who was only tolerating my presence because it served her ends.

Even as I thought that, my conscience poked me in the back and pointed out a few hard truths. I had more than enough money to travel to France on my own, to secure a room at a good hotel; I could even engage a companion if I wanted to. I could spend a week or two travelling around Calais and its environs in perfect comfort. I did not have to sneak around with a thief, living on my wits. No, the truth of the matter was that I had immediately latched onto Anna as the adult, the one with experience and authority, subconsciously seeing in her a temporary replacement for Mrs Armitage. I sat on the end of the bed, fiddling with the stupid shirt cuffs, missing Eliza dreadfully. Anna glanced over and saw me slumped there, tears threatening as my fingers clumsily tried to fasten the unfamiliar cuffs. Her expression softened and she came over to kneel in front of me.

'Here, let me,' she said, reaching for the cufflinks, but I snatched my arm away.

'I can manage,' I said, my voice more sullen than I had intended.

She sighed. 'No, you can't,' she said. 'Let me help.'

After a pause, I stretched my arm towards her. She dealt with the cufflinks, and she fastened the cuff buttons, then looked up at me, her eyes taking in every detail of my expression. 'What is wrong?' she asked.

'Nothing,' I said. 'Thank you.'

Anna narrowed her eyes. I saw they were grey, and she had a sprinkling of pale freckles across the bridge of her nose. For a moment, she looked as if she was going to speak, then she gave a little shrug and got up, moving over to her bag, and checking the contents. I saw her tuck the cloth-wrapped object into the bag. It was roughly the right size and shape to be a book.

There was a knock on the bedroom door, and we heard Arthur's voice. 'Ladies, breakfast is served,' he said. 'How are you this morning? All right?'

Anna went to open the door. 'Morning, Arthur,' she said with a smile. 'We'll be with you in a moment. What are we having?'

'I thought some good strong tea wouldn't go amiss,' replied Arthur. I could hear him bustling about in the other room, the clink of china and rattle of cutlery. I could smell toast. Suddenly ravenous again, I quickly fastened my boot laces, shrugged into my father's jacket and followed Anna out of the bedroom.

Arthur greeted me with a smile, which faded into a look of concern when he saw my expression. 'Come and sit down, miss,' he said, his voice soothing and gentle. 'I'll set a few things in motion for you today, if you'll permit me. Nothing much, just to put your mind at ease so you can enjoy your time in France.'

'That's very kind of you, Mr Phillips, but you really don't need to trouble yourself," I started, but he held up a hand, his blue eyes twinkling.

'You're right, miss, I don't need to, but I want to, don't I? You're in a bit of trouble you can't handle alone, so I think I should send a telegram to your uncle once you've left the country, to tell him where you've been. He can reply to me and I can send word to you in France. An intermediary if you will. How does that sound?'

My eyes filled with tears. 'I think you are very kind, Arthur,' I said, 'and I am more grateful to you than you can imagine. Thank you. I think that would be a very good solution, but what if my father finds out somehow?'

Arthur shrugged and for a moment, his eyes flashed like steel. 'Don't concern yourself about that, miss. I am more than capable of taking care of myself and I'm not going into this blind, now, am I? Come and sit down by the fire and I'll cut you some bread to toast. The toasting fork is hanging there on the hook.'

For the next hour, the three of us ate, drank coffee and chatted about everything and nothing. Anna let slip that she had an older brother and a younger sister, but changed the subject immediately afterwards, giving me no opportunity to ask about them. I wondered where they were.

Breakfast done, Arthur produced a couple of cloth-wrapped bundles which smelled of bread. 'You'll be hungry by the time you get there,' he said. 'Put these in your bags to keep you going, then give me a hand with these dishes.'

Anna kept glancing at the clock. At half past nine, once we had stowed the food bundles in our bags and cleared away the breakfast things, she started to get fidgety and collected her few belongings from the bedroom. At quarter to ten, she suddenly announced, 'I have to go out for a while. I'll see you at the ferry.'

I stared at her, but she had turned away and was gathering her bag. 'All right.' My voice shook. 'Where shall we meet, and at what time?'

'I won't be long,' she said, a hint of impatience creeping into her voice. 'I have an errand to run.'

'Don't you worry, miss,' said Arthur, giving Anna a look which made her curl her lip a little. 'With your permission, I will escort you to the ferry and wait with you.'

'Would you?' I exclaimed in gratitude. 'That is so very kind of you.'

'Well, now that's settled,' Anna said, 'I'll be on my way, and see you at the ferry.' She looked over at the clock on the mantel, tutted briefly and then was gone.

Arthur followed her gaze. 'Best get yourself ready, miss,' he said. 'Time's getting on. I'd like the two of you to be safely on board as soon as possible. Perhaps you could write down your uncle's name, and give me your initials. When I send my reply, how about if I use your initials and give Stenberg as your last name? That should throw people off the scent, eh?'

I agreed and jotted down the information on a piece of paper he handed me. As I passed it back, he caught my hand and squeezed it.

'You'll be just fine, miss,' he said.

I nodded, a lump rising in my throat. Arthur gave me a reassuring smile, then turned and went over to the dresser. He rooted around in one of the cupboards and emerged with a small bottle of Rowland's Macassar oil. It was the three-and-six size bottle, half full. He held it out to me.

'The more you can do with your appearance, miss, the easier you'll find it to blend in,' he said. 'This should last you for a few days. I would hope that, by the time it runs out, you will be back at home again.'

I reached out and took the little glass bottle, tears stinging my eyes at his thoughtfulness. I opened it and shook a few drops onto my palm, inhaling the familiar scent of coconut and ylang ylang and trying not to remember smelling it on my father's hair when he kissed me goodnight. 'You have been so very kind to me,' I said. 'I don't know how to express my gratitude, but when I return from France, you can be assured that I will have thought of something suitable.'

Arthur smiled. 'There's no need for that, miss,' he said, reaching for his coat and starting to put it on. 'Knowing you are safe will be reward enough for me.' He went to the grate, raked the coals, then cast a quick eye around the neat little room. 'Now, are you ready?'

I took a deep breath and closed my eyes for a moment. This was it. Decision time.

I knew I should go to my uncle and trust him to locate my father and keep me from harm and, in truth, that was what I longed to do more than anything. Yet something stopped me and as I stood there, frozen, my eyes squeezed tightly shut, I realised I was excited. The turmoil in my stomach was a mixture of concern for my uncle and fear for myself but, woven in between them was an almost delirious excitement. The thought of the freedoms I would enjoy was overwhelming. Easter was only a fortnight away, then the social season would begin. There had been talk about my coming out during this season, and a fine gown was being made. I had been dreading it. I was taller than many of the young men I had been introduced to at social gatherings and I did not have Elizabeth's grace, or, for that matter, her ability to simper at the ridiculous posturing of these young dandies. Despite Mrs Armitage's assurances to the contrary, I doubted I would find a man who would want to marry me. I fully expected to be confined to spinsterhood. If that was the case, I reasoned, then why not make my spinsterhood worthwhile and actually have some fun?

I opened my eyes and looked at Arthur, who was regarding me with great concern. 'Yes, Arthur,' I said, my voice sounding stronger than I had expected. 'I am ready.'

A wave of relief passed across his face, and he nodded, giving me a big, beaming smile. 'I'm very glad to hear it, miss,' he said. 'That's the spirit. Now, then, shall we?'

I put on the cap and my father's coat, which, I saw to my relief, was now clean. Arthur must have been working on it. Impulsively, I seized his hand and squeezed it. 'Thank you, Arthur,' I said. 'For everything.'

'You're most welcome, miss,' he said, glancing over at the clock. 'Now, we'd better make our way to the ferry.'

We walked out into another grey, dull day and almost immediately saw a paperboy coming towards us with his wares. I fished in my pocket for a coin and bought a copy, then paused for a moment to flip through the first few pages for anything about my father, but I could see nothing. I would read it properly on the ferry, I thought, folding it up and tucking it into my bag.

Arthur set a brisk pace and I had to hurry to keep up, until he suggested lengthening my stride. 'We should have practiced some of this sort of thing last night,' he mused, watching as I struggled to change my gait. 'That's better miss. Now, swing your arm a little more and try to relax your shoulders. Chin up – you're a good-looking young man, miss, be proud of it.'

I glanced at him and saw that he was grinning. We both burst out laughing and as we made our way along the seafront towards Admiralty Pier, Arthur gave me little tips about how to sit, stand, order drinks and hail cabs. I drank it all in, cataloguing each snippet. As we walked, I kept looking around, fearing I would see my father lurking somewhere nearby, but I recalled Uncle Geoffrey's words from two nights previously: he would not be looking for a young man.

As we neared the pier and passed a paper mill, I realised the Lord Warden Hotel was much further along the sea front than I had thought. It was hardly surprising that I had been so disoriented that night. It loomed ahead of us, grand and elegant, surrounded by carriages, with harassed-looking porters bustling between them, steering luggage trollies around impatient horses. Had

I reached the hotel the other night, would I already be back at home, or would I be hiding, terrified, in a room in the Lord Warden?

As I mused, I spotted two figures walking around the side of the hotel. One was a stout young man in a brown frock coat, a green paisley waistcoat, and trousers in a large plaid pattern of greys and purple. His Ascot was a deep, rich purple and he sported enormous dark whiskers. He was escorting a slender young woman in a pretty tweed walking dress with pink, green and purple checks. She wore a small, plain black felt hat with a matching tweed band, and she was carrying Anna's battered old carpet bag.

I stopped dead and stared, forcing Arthur to stop too. He followed my gaze, and I heard him clear his throat softly.

The young man and Anna were deep in conversation and when they reached the corner of the building, they paused. The young man took an envelope from his coat and handed it to Anna. She gave the contents a quick glance and then tucked it into her bag. She said something, he replied, then she began walking away from him. He stood where he was for a moment, then pulled a pipe from his pocket and clamped it in his teeth before sauntering off in the direction of town.

'We'd best get to the ferry, miss,' Arthur said.

'But...Arthur, it was Anna! Did you not see her?' I exclaimed, so taken aback that I forgot my manners and used his given name.

'I can't say as I did, miss,' said Arthur smoothly, then began to ask me questions about the fighting techniques he had shown me, testing my memory. I answered vaguely, distracted by what I had seen, but it was only after I had collided with a short matron in a gaudy, bright red travelling suit that I stopped craning my neck behind me to try to spot her again. As I staggered, Arthur deftly caught the woman's elbow, stopped her from falling and apologised on behalf of his clumsy nephew. The woman huffed and tutted, giving Arthur a rather stiff nod. He bowed as she swept off, a harassed-looking manservant trailing in her wake with two large suitcases.

People were boarding as we approached the ferry. We waited near the boarding ramp as a crowd of people surged around us, gentlemen waving hats to those already on board, one or two ladies waving handkerchiefs. I felt a sudden surge of panic as the crowd pressed in on us. We were hemmed in on all sides, with the steamer at our backs and no escape route. I tried to shrink back behind Arthur, but he caught my arm and gave it a firm squeeze.

'All right there, my lad?' he asked, looking pointedly at me, and I swallowed. For a moment, I had forgotten my disguise. I nodded and took a deep breath as the people nearest us jostled past, then, suddenly, Anna appeared, looking terse. I stared at her. There was a tilt of her head that I hadn't seen before and she looked every inch the confident, affluent young woman. Under my gaze, she reddened a little and turned her eyes towards Arthur.

He leaned down and kissed her cheek with affection. He said something into her ear that I couldn't hear over the clamour from the crowd and the cries of the sailors as they prepared the steamer. Anna stepped back, smiling, then pushed me forward to take her place. Arthur shook my hand formally, then leaned over and said into my ear, 'Remember everything I told you, miss, and you will be fine. You make a very good young man. Be safe, now, and happy travels.'

'Thank you, Arthur,' I said, feeling tears threaten. I blinked furiously for a moment as I stared down at my feet, then, with a deep breath, I turned to Anna. 'Shall we?' I said, offering her my arm.

Chapter 9

As we stood in the midst of the throng of travellers waiting to board, Anna kept her eyes turned back towards Dover, her expression inscrutable. She said nothing about her attire, and I was afraid to ask, so we inched our way towards the boarding ramp in silence. We climbed up the slatted ramp carefully, Anna lifting her skirts, and smiling at the sailor holding out his hand to assist her. She took it and stepped onto the deck, then produced the tickets and what I presumed was the forged travel documents and handed them over. The sailor gave them the briefest of glances.

'Welcome aboard, sir, madam,' he said, then turned to the passengers waiting behind us. Anna and I moved towards the stern so we could wave to Arthur. As we squeezed into a tiny gap next to the rail, trying to spot him, Anna glanced up at the smoke belching from the funnels and frowned.

'We should move to the other end once we are under way,' she said, 'or we'll be showered with sparks from the funnel.' I glanced up and nodded, then turned my attention back to the mass of shouting, cheering, waving people on the quayside. I caught sight of Arthur, standing a little way away from the crush of bodies, and waved my cap. A moment later, he saw me and lifted his arm in response. Anna produced a handkerchief to wave. Glancing down at her, I saw her eyes were excited, but she looked tired and pensive.

Soon enough the steamer was ready to sail, and the funnel spewed out a vile cloud of thick black smoke which showered us with sparks and grit. The gentleman next to me started coughing and one or two people pressed handkerchiefs to their mouths and noses. As the helmsman started steering the boat away from shore, I gazed back at Dover, the elegant houses lining the seafront, the castle standing in silent watchfulness on the hill near my home. I gripped the rail with one hand, the other clutching my bag, and hoped it would not be long before I was back.

Someone bumped into me and jolted me back into reality. I retreated through the crowd of passengers, aiming for a space beneath the ship's wheel, which was on a raised platform above the deck. The helmsman was focused on his work from within his white lead-painted canvas shelter and slowly, the steamer moved away from the shore, leaving behind everything I knew.

I stood there, listening to the captain giving orders above me. 'Make your head East by North, please,' he boomed, and the helmsman repeated the order. I heard the noise of the wheel as he turned it, and the captain thanked him. Another thick cloud of smoke belched from the funnel and made me cough.

Anna appeared, pushing her way through the passengers towards me, smiling and nodding as she did so. She reached me and squeezed my arm. 'Come, let us go around to the bow and get out of this awful smoke.' We started making our way along the deck. The clouds overhead were heavy with the promise of rain and I wished I had thought to stop off on the way to the ferry to buy an umbrella. Still, we could always go below deck if it rained.

After a little manoeuvring, we managed to get to the rail near the bow and stood looking out to sea, the endless grey of the water merging with the endless grey of the sky. I took a deep breath, feeling a little of my tension ease. For a while, neither of us spoke, then Anna said, 'Now you are completely safe and in no danger whatsoever, so will you promise me that you will try to have at least a little fun?'

I looked down at her face and saw she was genuinely earnest, so I forced a weak smile and nodded. 'I will try. I promise.'

We had not been at sea for long before the wind picked up and we decided to retreat below deck, where it was still cold, but less likely to result in the loss of another hat. Clutching my cap in one hand, I led the way down the stairs, the handrail coated in greasy residue from the smoke. We found seats and I took out my newspaper. I had read a couple of pages when something occurred to me.

'I wish I had thought to buy a newspaper yesterday,' I said. 'If anything had happened to my uncle, it may have been reported. The disturbance was sufficient for our neighbour's valet to become involved.'

'I have a copy of yesterday's newspaper, but I saw nothing such as you are describing,' Anna said unexpectedly, and reached into her bag. She drew out a crumpled Times and handed it to me. 'I sometimes pick one up if it's been left lying around,' she shrugged when she caught my curious look.

I thanked her and folded my paper so I could glance through hers, which was a dog-eared mess. I started smoothing the pages so I could turn them without tearing them, when I spotted something in the personals on the front page.

'A.S. Saturday L.W. 10 a.m. G.'

My heart leaped. If 'A.S.' was Anna – and it had to be, surely - then 'G' must be the young man with the pipe and 'L.W.' was the Lord Warden Hotel. I stared at the words for a few moments before forcing my eyes to look over the rest of the page. Worried though I was about my uncle, I found all I was thinking about was Anna.

When I started reading, she got up and went to look out of one of the windows opposite, one hand tapping the glass in an incessant tattoo. I watched her, fascinated and more confused than ever. Who was 'G'? Was he the brother she had mentioned? How did a pickpocket living on the streets gain entrance to somewhere like the Lord Warden, and emerge like a butterfly from a chrysalis in a beautiful outfit that I would be delighted to wear myself? Not that I was a fashion icon, far from it; being tall made me tend towards plainer garments to make myself less conspicuous. Anna's walking dress was not new, but I had had one very similar myself two or three years ago, in a pretty forget-me-not blue. Perhaps 'G' had stolen some poor rich lady's clothes so Anna could travel in style for a change. After all, our tickets were stolen. Why not her clothes as well?

For someone who turned her nose up at so much of what I said and who seemed proud of her ability to travel around Europe without paying for passage, Anna was clearly not averse to experiencing the good life when the opportunity arose. As I thought about this, I suspected I was being unfair. I knew nothing about her – nothing I could trust, anyway – but the evidence was right in front of me. Anna Stenberg was not what she seemed, any more than I was myself.

I amused myself for a minute or two imagining Anna as a rebellious princess escaping a life which restricted her adventurous nature. As I watched how she moved, all those tiny little unconscious gestures one makes, I could see the tell-tale signs of an upbringing not unlike my own. Perhaps our current circumstances were more similar than I had imagined.

Wondering if I should broach the subject once we were safely in Calais, I turned back to the newspaper and started reading in earnest. I was hoping for some little snippet of information, yet at the same time dreading the thought of seeing my uncle's name in print for such a terrible reason. Page after page yielded nothing and, relieved, I put the newspaper into my bag. The sea was rough, rocking us violently from one side to the other. Anna came back to sit with me, looking pale.

'Are you all right?' I asked. 'Do you want to get some air? It has become rather stuffy down here.'

She nodded and picked up her bag. I followed suit and we made our way to the deck. The wind had become a fierce gale. Spray hit us as soon as we emerged, and I grabbed my cap before the wind claimed it. Anna almost fell as the boat rolled sharply to one side but caught hold of the rail and managed to right herself. She muttered a curse which made my jaw drop, but I had no time to react as we lurched to the opposite side and this time, it was my turn to lose my footing. As the two of us scrambled around, the captain bellowed from somewhere just above us.

'Come up to a point, if you please!' The wind snatched his words when they were hardly out of his mouth. The helmsman shouted something back that I could not make out and, as Anna and I inched our way along the deck, trying to find something to hang on to, the steamer began, almost imperceptibly, to turn more into the wind. Two sailors ran past us towards the bow. There were a number of hardy souls on deck, but many of them were doing their best to get below, staggering towards the steps. One poor lady slipped and fell, and it took three men to help her to her feet and down to the lower deck. Anna and I exchanged glances and followed them. So much for fresh air.

The rest of the journey was spent on our feet, swaying and staggering in discomfort as the steamer ploughed its way through the turbulent sea. I had never endured such an unpleasant sea crossing before and thanked my lucky stars I did not get seasick. That would have been the last straw.

'If you could get a job,' I asked suddenly, as a distraction as much as genuine curiosity, 'any job at all, what would you choose?'

Anna considered. 'I'd be an explorer,' she said. 'Perhaps an archaeologist. You?'

'At the moment, I would settle for anything which does not involve travelling!'

Anna laughed. 'What really excites you?' she asked. 'Pretend men don't exist and that you could do anything in the world. What would you do?'

'I would be some sort of researcher,' I said. 'I love history and solving puzzles. I would have someone to bring me a fresh pot of tea every hour and sharpen my pencils.'

We were both laughing now. 'I'd have someone to write up my notes as I dictated them,' Anna said in a dreamy voice. 'A private secretary. After we write up our discoveries, we'll get back on our camels and find somewhere else to explore.'

'You would travel by camel?'

She smiled. 'But of course. That's what one does when one works in Egypt, you know. I'd like to be the next James Burton and work in the Valley of the Kings."

'Maybe we could go to Egypt after Paris,' I suggested, caught up in her excitement.

Her face fell slightly, and her smile dimmed. The moment had passed. She shrugged and was about to say something when the steamer lurched again and a man standing nearby collided with her, sending them both staggering into two other people. There was much chaos as they helped each other to their feet and one man, who was looking rather green, suddenly turned and fled up the steps to the deck. I heard the faint sounds of retching and hoped he had made it to the rail.

We swayed and dipped and rolled our way to Calais and I have never been more relieved to see land than when I finally spotted France on the horizon. The sea had calmed somewhat, so Anna and I risked the deck, finding it a great deal more agreeable. The captain, a stocky man with salt and pepper whiskers and dark eyes, looked relieved, and the exhausted helmsman clung to the wheel with grim determination. The crew started bustling about in earnest, the captain shouting orders. The funnel belched out more clouds of soot and grit and the valiant steamer edged its way towards the harbour past a dozen little sailboats, which bobbed about in our wake.

'That was the longest sea voyage I have ever experienced,' a man near us said in a loud voice which dripped relief. His companion, a tall, thin man with a hook nose and lanky blond hair, gave an ugly braying laugh, prompting several people to glance over in disapproval.

'We'll be a while yet,' he chortled. 'These damn steamers are the devil to steer. I'm just relieved that we can dock. Last time, I had to get one of these local fishing fellows to row me ashore and the bounder charged me more than my passage to Paris!'

'Opportunistic swine,' exclaimed his friend, and they started pushing their way towards the boarding ramp, discussing the greedy and ungrateful poor on both sides of the Channel. There were a few unimpressed mutters once they had gone. As their voices faded away, Anna rolled her eyes at me.

A few minutes later, we realised that the irritating man had been right, and it was indeed going to take a while to dock. Anna and I went to the bow to look at the view. Most of the passengers were on deck now, and the sailors kept having to shoo them away from the area around the boarding ramp. I turned my back and stared out at Calais, looking at the long pier to our right as it stretched out into the ocean. There were fishermen on the shore mending nets, and beyond them, some racks for drying fish like those on the beach in Dover. The houses in front of us fascinated me, for they were so narrow, I found it hard to picture how one would fit any furniture into the tiny rooms.

At long last, we docked and finally were able set foot on solid ground. We were waved through the customs check with scarcely a second glance by the bored-looking official. He stopped the people behind us, though. Glancing back, I was amused to see the obnoxious blond man and his friend with outraged expressions on their faces as he squinted at their papers. It took us both a few minutes to find our land legs and we walked slowly along the harbour from the steamer, Anna's hand tucked in the crook of my arm. We were both looking around, but after a few minutes, I realised that Anna was not studying our surroundings as I was. She was trying to spot something. I attempted to follow her gaze, but everything around us was normal, everyday life – sailors and fishermen, messengers, people on bicycles, a trio of women selling fish, half a dozen ragged children with bulging bellies and hollow eyes, carts, horses, shouting, and everywhere the stench of coal, fish and the sea.

'Wait here,' Anna said suddenly. She hurried away, leaving me, as always, it seemed, unaware of what was happening. I shook my head and sighed, then looked around. The railway station was right next to the harbour, yet, despite that, I seemed suddenly to be in an oasis of calm amidst all the chaos around me. I took in the smoke from the paddle steamers in the harbour and more distant plumes rising from the train at an unseen platform beyond the station building. The wind was zinging through the rigging on the sailboats with a crisp whistle, and gulls wheeled and dived in the grey sky, their harsh shrieks piercing the cacophony of voices around me. As I watched them, I was brushed aside by a well-dressed couple, whom I recognised from the steamer. They were directing three porters, who were struggling with two enormous trunks. I moved away just as one of the porters tripped on the uneven cobbles and fell. The trunk crashed to the ground and the corner on which it had landed cracked. The couple started an almighty fuss as the poor man scrambled to his feet, apologising. It was clear they spoke little French, and the man spoke little English. Not wanting to become involved, even though I spoke fluent French, I sidled off and went to lean against a wooden building nearby. I felt a little guilty and I knew that had Mrs Armitage been there, she would have sent me over to act as intermediary. As I stood there, considering this tiny rebellion,

Anna reappeared around the corner of one of the warehouses opposite, beckoning to me. Picking up my bag, I went to her.

'I've managed to secure some transport,' she said with a beaming smile.

'Transport?' I asked, puzzled.

'To Paris,' she said with exaggerated patience.

I blinked. 'We are not staying in Calais?' I asked.

'The man I was talking to lives in Amiens and is happy to take us that far, as long as he chooses where and when we stop,' she said.

I was in a whirl. I had rather thought we would spend the night in Calais and then move on tomorrow, but this was Anna's world now and I had to start trying to see things as she did. I had already realised how leisurely my life was. Anna's went at a different pace. I took a deep breath.

'Excellent,' I said, hoping my voice wouldn't betray my nervousness by cracking or wobbling. 'But before we go, I do need to send word to Arthur.'

'We can stop off on the way,' she said. 'It's a bit of a walk from here. Come on.' She started walking away, her skirts swishing over the cobbles. I had to run to catch up.

'Anna,' I said, as I reached her. 'I am not going to pry into your life, but I am curious about your garments. Will you tell me –'

She interrupted. 'Did anyone bother us on the boat? No. Why would they? We looked like them. No one challenged us when we got off the boat, either. We have small bags, and now the French have done away with passports, they had no reason to suspect us of smuggling. Unless it was something very tiny indeed,' she added with a laugh.

'I would like to know what is going on,' I said, sounding far braver than I felt.

She stopped and wheeled round. 'Nothing is going on,' she said. 'What are you talking about? Come, let's go and send word to Arthur. And stop being so paranoid. Try to enjoy this. You're safe now.'

She slipped her hand into the crook of my arm once again and marched me to a smart carriage parked up not far away. A couple of urchins were stroking the horses but as we approached, they turned and fled. I looked up at the driver. He was around thirty, I guessed, tall, lanky and tanned, wearing a good overcoat and a warm felt hat. He jumped down, gave a little bow and extended his hand. I shook it.

'Bonjour, Monsieur,' he said. 'I am Henri Martin. You are M. Stenberg, the brother of Mademoiselle Anna, yes?' He had a deep, rich voice and a pleasant, warm smile. He looked trustworthy, I thought, as I returned the smile and confirmed I was Mademoiselle Anna's brother. He opened the carriage door and helped Anna in, then waited until I had followed her.

'We will stop for the night in Vieil-Moutier,' he said. 'I have friends along this route who are happy to give me food and shelter for a night. I am certain they will also welcome you.'

'Merci, Henri,' Anna said, then proceeded to ask him, in perfect French, how far it was and what time we should expect to arrive. I asked a couple of questions too, but did not really focus much on his replies. I was too busy wondering what other surprises Anna had up her sleeve and how many of them might reveal themselves before we reached Paris.

Chapter 10

The journey to Vieil-Moutier was to take us well into the evening and I was very glad that Arthur had given us food. Before setting out, we made one very brief stop in Calais so I could send him a message. Unnoticed by Anna and Henri, I took the opportunity to slip into a nearby bank, emerging with three-quarters of my money exchanged for francs. Disappointed that there was to be no sight-seeing, I pressed my face to the window, eager to see what I could before the carriage reached open countryside. Buildings loomed, then were gone as we made our way through throngs of people, past carriages and carts; the uneven streets making my teeth rattle. Calais disappeared behind us in what seemed like a blink of the eye. Once we left the outskirts, Henri whipped up the horses and we set off at a brisk pace. The countryside was pretty and looked much like home, although it was flat, with a few gentle hills in the far distance. After a while, I got bored of looking at trees and fields and the occasional ramshackle farmhouse and rummaged around for one of my father's journals and the bundle of food.

'Where did you learn French?' I asked Anna, who was sitting opposite me, her eyes fixed on the landscape. She gave her habitual little shrug.

'I told you I travel,' she said.

I took a deep breath. 'Look, Anna,' I said, 'I am not asking for your life history, but if we are to travel together for a while, I would rather not spend the entire time feeling like I have offended you in some way. We both have aspects of our lives we would rather keep to ourselves. I cannot respect your boundaries if I have no idea what they are.'

She looked at me then, as if seeing me for the first time, and when she smiled, it was genuine and made her eyes shine. 'You are right,' she said. 'I am sure you have a hundred questions. I apologise. I am always rather fraught when I travel.'

As she spoke, I noticed the change in her voice. It was softer, far more refined. 'I am guessing you travel a lot,' I said, being careful to keep my voice even. 'Your French is superb.'

'Thank you. Yours is, too,' she said. 'Governess?'

I smiled and nodded. 'Mademoiselle Vannier. You?'

To my surprise, she reddened, sighing. It was a while before she answered. I let the silence hang between us.

'Let's just say I travel around for most of the year. Sometimes I work and sometimes not.'

I stared. 'The pickpocket is a disguise?'

'I wear the pickpocket as you wear Viktor,' she said.

I smiled. 'I thought as much,' I said. 'I noticed things which made me suspect our backgrounds were more similar than you would admit.'

'You did?' she asked with a slight bristle.

'You move like a lady,' I said. 'You sew like one, too.'

That made her laugh, and to my relief, it served to clear the air somewhat. 'You're observant,' she said. 'A useful skill.'

'What work do you do?' I asked. 'I'm guessing you are not an archaeologist.'

'Sadly not,' she said. 'My work is…specialised and requires a significant amount of discretion. Forgive me that I cannot say more.'

I looked at her, thinking back to the conversation I had overheard. 'At least tell me whether or not it is illegal,' I said.

She frowned at me, looking genuinely confused. 'Why would it be illegal?' she asked.

I decided to come clean. 'When I met you, I thought you were a thief. And last night, Arthur said something about your activities.'

Understanding flickered across her face. 'You overheard us talking?'

'I was unable to sleep,' I replied.

'Unsurprising,' she said, regarding me through narrowed eyes. 'Was that why you were in such an awful mood this morning?'

It was my turn to blush, and I looked down at the journal in my hands. 'It sounded as though I was nothing more than useful cover for something unlawful.'

'I am not doing anything unlawful. I promise,' she said, so seriously that I realised she was telling the truth. She reached out and took my hand, squeezing my fingers. 'I have been travelling like this for about three years now and I have become used to being alone. It will be fun to have a companion, but it may take me a little while to become accustomed to the idea. Will you be patient with me?'

'Of course,' I said. 'If you will be patient with me.'

She released my hand, sat back, and nodded. 'I will.'

Pleased, I sat back too, the padded seat hard and uncomfortable. 'What is it like to have work?' I asked. 'I always found it ironic that all I was destined to do with my life was become a wife and mother, when the rhyme says Saturday's Child works hard for a living.'

Anna looked at me, her gaze intent. 'You were born on a Saturday? So was I.' She thought for a moment, then said, 'It's interesting. You meet a variety of people, and it opens the door to all kinds of experiences you might not otherwise have. As you might expect, you also encounter people who believe a woman's place is in the home.' She rolled her eyes.

The carriage gave a violent jolt, and I saw Henri had turned the horses onto the verge. We stopped and I heard him jump down from the box. Anna opened the carriage door. 'Is everything all right, Henri?' she asked in her perfect French.

'A short pause to water the horses, Mademoiselle,' Henri replied with a little bow. 'Are you both comfortable?'

We assured him that all was well and clambered out of the coach as he started to unhitch one of the horses. I stayed near the carriage, watching for thieves, as Anna took a flask from her bag and followed Henri to the stream.

As the horse bent its elegant neck to drink, Henri took the flask and leaned down to fill it so Anna could keep her skirts dry. Watching them chatting easily, I mulled over what I had learned and felt a little more tension ease. An old man in an equally aged haycart rumbled past and shouted what I took to be 'Good afternoon' in an accent so thick I could scarcely decipher it. I raised my hand and returned the greeting, watching as the horse jogged along, the clopping of its hooves familiar and hypnotic. A cloud of hay stalks and dust rose in its wake, and I coughed as they clogged my throat and stung my eyes. The cart continued along the road for a while before turning off into a field.

All around was peace and serenity. Behind me, I heard Anna laugh and the soothing ripple of the stream. I wandered to the front of the carriage and stroked the horse. Another cart was approaching from Calais, and I moved around the carriage, so it was between myself and the road. A tiny part of me still expected my father to appear at any moment.

Henri brought the first horse back from the stream, hitched it up and then took the other for a drink. Anna came back and offered me the flask, but I suggested she kept it for the journey. Instead, I wandered upstream of the horses and knelt at the edge of the bank to drink. The water was cold but refreshing and I felt a little better as I returned to the carriage, smiling at Henri as I passed and trying to remember what Arthur had told me about lengthening my stride. I hoped I didn't look like I had problems staying upright.

We were underway again before too long. As we set off, I unwrapped the food which had lain on the seat beside me, forgotten during my conversation with Anna. There was bread, cheese and an apple, and a smaller package of cold chicken. I ate hungrily, setting aside a chunk of bread and some of the cheese for later. Henri seemed to be convinced his friends would take us in, but I wanted to be prepared if they did not.

When we had stopped, I had slipped my father's journal into my coat pocket. I took it out again and opened it. The spiky writing on the first page, while recognisable as my father's, was blotched and untidy. Some of the words ran into each other and even on the first page, where he was writing about Dover's weather, he had pressed so aggressively on the page that the nib had torn the paper.

I frowned at the pages, turning them slowly. For some reason, at this point in his mania, my father had been fixated on the weather. I scanned the pages for any indication of a date, so I could try to map the progress of his deterioration, and perhaps learn where his murderous instincts had arisen.

I settled back against the uncomfortable seat as I read. Parts of it were much like a diary; he had recorded a conversation with John and a list of dull, everyday tasks such as approving the lunch and dinner menus. My heart leaped and I suppressed a sudden sob. My mother used to oversee the menus before her disappearance. I could see her now in my mind's eye, her dark head bent over Mrs Armitage's writing as she scrawled an amendment in her flamboyant, loopy script. She would sit back in her chair, hold the menu up and scrutinise it, then give a little huff of approval before ringing for the maid to take it back to the kitchen. I could smell the lavender on the handkerchief she kept tucked into her cuff and feel the touch of her lips against my forehead as she kissed me goodnight.

My eyes stung and I turned to the window, blinking, forcing the tears back. As I struggled to control my breath, there was a rustle of fabric and suddenly Anna was sitting beside me. She gave my shoulder a gentle squeeze.

'I don't know what you were reading,' she said, 'but maybe now is not the time. Wait a few days until you feel more settled.'

I turned to her, dashing the tears away with the back of my hand. 'It's one of my father's journals,' I said, my voice cracking. 'I thought there might be something – some clue – to explain…'

I broke off and hung my head, closing my eyes. Anna squeezed my shoulder again. 'Would it help to talk about it?' she asked. 'I won't ask for any private information. Share what you are comfortable with.'

The floodgates opened. I told her about my mother's disappearance and the changes that my father had undergone, both after that and after the War. 'I was hoping there would be something to explain what happened to him. Something to tell me why…'

'…Why he wants to kill you,' she finished, her voice soft and full of understanding. I looked at her and nodded.

'We were always so close before he went away to war,' I said. 'If we had been at odds, it might have made more sense.'

'I haven't seen my parents for a long time, either,' she said after a brief pause. 'I chose the life I have, and they turned their backs on me. For some reason, it did not matter to them that I was doing something useful.'

'I'm guessing you were not doing what they deemed useful,' I said, and she nodded. She looked wistful but not upset and I reasoned that she had had time to reconcile herself to the situation.

'I wrote and told them I was comfortable and what I did was valued, but they never responded. At the time it hurt. They made me feel like a disappointment, even though I was doing something far more valuable than I ever would have, had I remained at home.'

'That is why you want me to see the world like this,' I said, indicating my clothes. 'You are right. When my father is found and returned to St Bernadette's, I will have to go back to my normal life. There will be more talk of marriage, which does not appeal in the slightest.' I wrinkled my nose in distaste, making her laugh.

We lapsed into silence. It was starting to get dark now, so I opened the journal and turned the page towards the window, keen to read for as long as I could. Anna folded her hands and stared down at them for a while, then she got up and swung herself back to the other seat.

From the writing, it was clear to see that this had been the point when my father's mania had become all-encompassing. As the sun dipped below the horizon and it became too dark to see, I put the journal away and closed my tired eyes, thinking about what I had read. He was still recording the weather but had started talking about mythological creatures as though they were real. It was odd, because I had no recollection of him mentioning anything on the subject, even in the dark days before my uncle's orderlies wrestled him into the secure carriage and drove him away.

The roads were less bumpy now and I found myself dozing, only jerking briefly into semi-wakefulness when the carriage hit a rut. After my conversation with Anna, I felt a great deal better about the understanding we had reached. She was older than I had first thought, I realised, perhaps nineteen or twenty. No wonder she was so poised and confident. I wished she would tell me what sort of work she did. Travelling around in disguise sounded exciting.

I was awakened by a hand on my arm, and I opened my eyes to find Anna gazing into my face with a serious expression. The carriage was in darkness, the only light a faint glow from the lamps outside. 'We've slowed down,' she whispered. 'I am not certain what is going on. Have you anything you can use as a weapon?'

'Not even a hatpin,' I whispered back.

Anna quietly slid down the window in the door next to her. I heard her catch her breath and she reached out a hand to me.

'Viktor, look at the fog.'

Chapter 11

I went cold. Pulling my coat more closely around me in a fruitless attempt to stop the shudders coursing down my spine, I peered into the darkness. It was clear why Henri had slowed the horses to a walk. We were surrounded by dense, swirling fog, tendrils slipping into the carriage and snaking around us.

'Henri, are you all right?' Anna called in a low voice.

His muffled voice floated back to us. 'Yes, Mademoiselle, all is well. This fog, it came from nowhere.'

'Is it usually this foggy around here?' I asked. In Dover, sea fog was part of daily life.

'I have never seen anything like this before,' Henri said. 'Bring your bags and join me up here, if you please. I may need some assistance.'

He reined in the horses. Anna and I grabbed our bags and jumped down from the carriage. I remembered to give Anna my hand so she could clamber up beside Henri. I was about to follow her when we heard a sound that chilled us to the bone.

From somewhere in the distance, came a long, mournful, quavering howl which crept towards us through the fog, its sinister ululations fading away into silence before a second creature lifted its voice in response. All at once, the air was thick with a cacophony of yowling, wailing cries.

Henri stared wide-eyed into the fog, craning his neck forward as far as he could. 'Quickly!' he exclaimed. 'We must keep moving.' He leaned across Anna and extended a hand to me. I gripped it and hauled myself up to the driver's box. He handed me the reins and turned to fiddle with the lamp to his right, removing it from its bracket. 'You must drive,' he told me, then jumped down, holding the lamp. 'I will walk ahead with the light, to keep us safely on the road.'

I had never driven a carriage before, but I could ride. Shoving my bag between my feet, I gripped the reins, trying to remember what I had seen John do when he had brought the carriage around for me. Embarrassment rose in my throat as I realised how little attention I had paid, and I fumbled around, trying to find a comfortable way to hold them. Anna leaned over and whispered, 'You can do this,' into my ear.

Just then, the howling began again, sounding nearer. It swelled and pitched, ebbed and intensified until our ears were ringing. We froze, listening as it died away once more, ending with a strange throaty noise I couldn't identify.

'I do not like this,' muttered Henri. He looked at me. 'Please keep them straight, Monsieur, unless I say so.'

'I will,' I assured him, sounding far more confident than I felt. My hands were shaking. As Henri moved away, I noticed that Anna's expression matched Henri's, grim and alert.

Anna and I shifted around on the driver's box to get comfortable, pulling one of Henri's blankets across our legs, we started inching our way along, the journey punctuated every now and then by the howling. It increased in volume the further we went, as though we were driving straight for them, but the fog was like a velvet drape, and we could see nothing.

'How much further is Vieil-Moutier, Henri?' Anna asked after a while.

'Less than an hour,' he called back. 'I believe we are not far from Lottinghen. I can walk from there to Vieil-Moutier in perhaps thirty minutes.'

Anna pulled the blanket more closely around her legs and shivered. She muttered something beneath her breath which I didn't catch, then we froze again as another howl shattered the night.

Henri was right. A short while later, we passed through a small village. It was hilly here. The tree-lined road meandered a little before turning left and dropping down a long slope. Part-way down, the fog suddenly vanished. We had not driven out of it into clear air; one moment, we could scarcely see Henri up ahead of us, the next, the fog was completely gone, the night had opened up around us and the glow of a faint moon peeped out from behind scudding clouds.

Puzzled, Henri shone the lamp around, staring at the trees which we could now see looming overhead. He urged us back into the carriage, a concerned look on his face.

'I think all is well now,' he said, 'but I want to get us to safety as soon as possible. Hold on to the straps, as the road can sometimes be a little bumpy here.'

We reached for the leather straps next to the windows as Henri climbed back onto the driver's box and urged the horses into a trot. Their hooves sounded far louder on the road than before, as though the fog had muffled them. I silently urged them onwards, desperate now to be out of the night.

We soon turned a sharp bend to the right and pulled up outside a long, low house. The door opened and a young man of around Henri's age appeared with a lamp. Henri jumped down from the driver's box as the man came over. They embraced, then Henri gestured towards us. The other man glanced over and nodded. Anna and I gathered our bags and stepped down from the carriage, Henri hurrying forward to give Anna his hand.

'Jacques, may I present Mademoiselle Anna and Monsieur Viktor Stenberg,' Henri said. 'This is my good friend Jacques Granet.'

Jacques bowed over Anna's hand and shook mine. 'It is a pleasure,' he said in a deep, rich voice. 'I will prepare somewhere for you to sleep. You may have to share a room, I fear.'

'We would be happy to do so,' Anna smiled. 'It will be like when we were children all over again, won't it, Viktor?'

'It will indeed,' I said. 'Thank you very much for your hospitality, Monsieur Granet. We are very grateful to you.'

'Please, come inside. And call me Jacques,' he added. 'Henri, I will join you in a moment and help you with the horses.'

Henri thanked him and started leading the horses around the far end of the house as Jacques ushered us into the kitchen, where a welcoming fire was blazing in the hearth. The room was large and square, with a door leading to the yard outside. A battered oak table dominated the space, and the walls were lined with a variety of utensils, pots, and bunches of dried herbs, which wafted their soothing aromatic scents around us as we sat down and accepted the wine Jacques offered. Anna drank with a little more enthusiasm than was strictly appropriate for a young lady, while I, still unaccustomed to the concept of 'being a man', had to keep reminding myself to do likewise.

Satisfied that we were comfortable, Jacques excused himself and went out into the yard to help Henri with the horses. A waft of manure whisked around the room as the door opened and closed.

At once, Anna whipped off her hat and leaned back in her chair. 'Ugh!' she complained. 'These clothes are so uncomfortable!'

'Is this how you usually travel?' I asked, indicating the outfit and raising an eyebrow. 'It is hardly a practical dress for a stowaway.'

Her warm, rippling laugh made me smile. 'I have stowed away a couple of times,' she said, 'but it was an emergency measure when plans did not work out as hoped, or messages were delayed. I once crossed the Channel wedged between two enormous trunks in the luggage hold. In all honesty, I am still not sure how I managed to get away with it.'

'It would never have occurred to me to do that,' I admitted.

'You would be surprised at how creative you become when your life depends on it,' she quipped, then, as my face fell, she put one hand to her mouth, looking horrified. 'I am so sorry,' she said. 'That was thoughtless.'

I took a deep breath and swallowed a couple of times, trying to ease the restriction which had arisen in my throat. 'No need for apologies,' I said. 'I have to face up to it at some point, and the sooner I do, the better it will be for me.'

Relieved, she leaned over and patted my hand. 'You are quite right,' she said, 'and that is the kind of thinking which will get you through this.'

'My father was recording the weather back in Dover,' I said, in part to change the subject and in part because I was interested in Anna's opinion. 'He mentions storms and freak events like that awful period we had in '62 where it was cold and wet almost every day and the harvests were poor.'

'I remember,' Anna said, her face grim. 'I saw a lot of people who were badly affected.'

'He talks about the size of hailstones and the damage they caused, both around town and in places like London,' I went on, thinking back to the scrawl I had been deciphering. 'There is also a section about fog. Will you have a look?'

Anna immediately drew her chair close as I pulled the journal from my pocket and turned to the correct page. As she bent her head over the words, her eyes lit up with keen interest. I watched as she worked her way through the first page, then pointed out a section on the next.

"Tonight, I was working in my study with the window ajar, when I noticed a creeping fog. It did not carry with it the scent of the sea, as it usually does; there was a strong acrid smell which awakened my interest. I could determine nothing from my window, so I went out into the road, the better to observe. To my amazement, when I went some little distance from the house, I saw that the fog was localised in that area. The remainder of the road was completely clear. I walked up and down for a time, trying to understand. The fog looked like typical Dover fog. The only remarkable features were the odd smell and the fact that it only covered my house. I decided to look at it from all angles, but as I approached the corner, John and Parsons appeared and started urging me back inside. I resisted, trying to explain my actions, but they refused to listen and laid hands on me. John insisted there was no fog, and as I stopped struggling with them and started to correct him, I saw, to my shock, that he was quite correct. The fog had vanished without a trace."

When she had finished reading, Anna sat still for a few moments before slowly turning her head to me. 'Do you think it might be the same fog that arose in the street the other day?'

I shook my head, biting my lip as my stomach began to churn. 'I remember that night well. We thought Father was hallucinating. After all that has happened in the last couple of days, though, I am not so sure.'

'We were not hallucinating,' Anna murmured, looking back at my father's writing.

'This is what concerns me,' I said. 'Suppose something has been happening and only he could see it?'

'It doesn't explain his hostility towards you, though,' Anna pointed out, and I sighed, slumping back in my chair.

'No,' I agreed. 'But what if we have done the wrong thing by putting him into St Bernadette's? If that decision has somehow contributed to his condition, I will never forgive myself.'

'How much of that decision was left to you?' Anna asked. 'Wasn't it made by a doctor?'

'My uncle, yes.' I thought back to that horrible night, the terror and confusion which had gripped me, the days and nights I had spent wide awake and exhausted from crying as I tried to find some sense in the nightmare that my life had become. I recalled rattling around in my four-storey townhouse, unable to settle to anything, unwilling to socialise, too tired to walk far. I remembered the servants' pity and tenderness as they cared for me; Cook preparing all my favourite foods for weeks, Mrs Armitage gently squeezing my fingers whenever we were alone, Eliza almost tiptoeing around me, concern etched across her pretty freckled face. It had taken me so long to drag myself back from the helplessness, the guilt, the fear, and confusion. I tried to explain it to Anna, but it was difficult to put into words and I fell silent.

'Does he say why he was recording the weather?' Anna asked after a while, turning a couple of pages. She stopped and stared at one page for a moment before hastily going on to the next.

'Not that I have found so far. His writing has taken a while to decipher. It is almost unrecognisable as his.'

The door opened at that point, making us both start. I put the journal into my bag as Jacques and Henri walked back in. Henri went straight to the fire and held his hands out to it. Jacques brought him some wine, then bustled about with a pan of thick broth brimming with vegetables and herbs. It was the second time in my life that I had seen a man cooking and I watched fascinated, my thoughts straying to Arthur every now and then. I hoped my message would reach him. It would be sent on the night ferry; perhaps it had already left.

We were all grateful for Jacques's hearty broth and for the huge chunks of bread he warmed for us. There was more wine, although I was careful not to have too much, and the two men proved to be amusing companions. Jacques, to my surprise and relief, asked very few questions, but I found relaxation impossible. The bizarre experience of turning up unannounced at someone's home and being welcomed, fed, and given a room for the night was alien to me, yet it paled into insignificance next to the nagging doubt that grave errors had been made in my father's care.

Anna, too, seemed pensive. She joined in the conversation with wit and intelligence, but once or twice, mistranslated something. What I had seen of her French so far told me that she was every bit as fluent as myself, possibly even more so. She made light of it and accepted Henri's gentle teasing, but I suspected she had misheard because her mind was elsewhere.

As we settled down in the comfy room Jacques showed us to, each curling up in a narrow bed with a beautiful quilt, I wondered what she had been thinking about.

Chapter 12

The next morning, I was awake with the birds after a restless night. I lay listening to them for a while, mulling over the fractured dreams which had punctuated the little sleep I'd had. One had been a strange combination of details from our journey: wolves howling and Anna punting us along the road in a large soup pan while Henri walked beside us reading aloud from my father's journal.

That snapped me into wakefulness. I could see Anna was still asleep, her dark hair spread over the pillow and all but her eyes and nose invisible beneath the quilt. Leaning down to my bag, I slid the journal out and turned the pages as quietly as I could until I reached the section we had been looking at the previous night. Anna's expression had changed at one point. Perhaps she had seen something which held some sort of significance for her. Was that what had distracted her after our meal?

I found the page we had looked at together and turned over the next couple, trying to recall how many she had looked at. There was another page of closely written weather observations with the words running one into another, then a page of random scribbles and sketches. My father was no artist, but I recognised the rosemary he had drawn. The other plant, however, was unfamiliar to me. There was something in one corner which looked like a crest. Perhaps he had been copying buttons from his army uniform. It was quite small, and the detail was impossible to make out, apart from what appeared to be a snake in the shape of an S on one side of a shield. Next to it was a quote.

'I had a dream, which was not all a dream.

The bright sun was extinguish'd, and the stars.

Did wander darkling in the eternal space.'

I recognised it instantly. It was the beginning of Byron's poem 'Darkness'. My father and I had shared a love of the great poet, and I remembered my surprise at seeing Byron on Arthur's shelf. Could this have prompted Anna's reaction, and, if so, why?

Frustrated, I put the book away and was just thinking about finding some water for a wash when Jacques knocked on the door to tell us there was a jug of hot water waiting outside in the hall for our toilette. I called out my thanks and when his footsteps had faded away down the stairs, and I could hear him singing a folk song in the kitchen, I opened the door to retrieve the jug. Anna was stirring now, so I went over to the washstand and filled the bowl. I did the best I could with the few things I had with me, then hurriedly dressed and started fiddling with the cursed cuff buttons. Anna groaned, threw back the covers and trudged over to the washstand.

By the time we made it downstairs to the kitchen, Jacques and Henri had almost finished their breakfast. They both looked at us as we walked in, and chuckled, but were kind enough not to comment. There was bread, cheese, some cold meat and rather bitter, but strong, coffee. The two of us tucked in gratefully and once Jacques was satisfied we had all we needed, he and Henri went to deal with the horses and carriage. As soon as they were gone, Anna got up and went over to the shelves, taking the lids off jars and peering inside.

'What are you doing?' I asked.

'Looking for some honey to sweeten this coffee,' she said, indicating her cup.

I left her to it and took out my father's journal again, turning the pages as I munched on the bread. It felt so strange to be left to fend for myself; at home, Parsons would have waited by the sideboard in the dining room, ready to step forward and serve me if I required anything. Here, I could just lean across the table and take whatever I wanted. I wasn't restricted in the amount I could eat by the iron prison of a corset. It felt wonderful, and I added it to my mental list of positives.

'Did your father draw a lot?' Anna asked. She had given up on the search for honey and had come to stand behind my chair. I was staring at the sketches again, uncertain if this was just a page of random thoughts and scribbles.

'Hardly ever, that I saw,' I said. 'Yet these journals are full of little sketches.'

The two men came back at that point, so I slid the journal into my pocket, fishing out some coins to pay for our lodgings and food. Jacques looked affronted.

'Please, Monsieur, there is no need,' he said firmly. 'I am always delighted to see my good friend here,' and he clapped Henri on the shoulder. 'It has been a pleasure to make your acquaintance and I would never dream of asking a friend to pay for their time beneath my roof. You will always be most welcome here.'

'In that case, my friend,' I said, remembering to hold out my hand as I put the money away, 'I thank you most sincerely for your kind hospitality towards my sister and myself. I hope I will be able to repay you one day.' Jacques shook my hand and clapped me on the back. As he looked at me, I saw something flit across his face, as though he had, for a split second, seen through my disguise. My heart skipped a beat, and I felt my cheeks flush, but by then Jacques was releasing my hand and turning to bid Anna farewell. As I watched, I found I was sorry to be leaving the safety and security of Jacques's house.

We went outside and waited for Henri to bring the carriage around. Now that it was daylight, I could see we were at the edge of a hilly plateau. There were a few houses clustered near the road, but there was only one other beyond Jacques's. The church was almost opposite, a plain, unadorned building quite unlike the gothic grandeur I was more used to. Behind Jacques's house, the land sloped gently upwards, and I could see it was crammed with crops of all kinds. The air was sweet and gently tinged with pine from the forest on the hills. I looked around with pleasure, drinking in as much detail as I could.

I turned to Anna and offered my hand so she could climb into the carriage. She accepted with a smile and, when she had turned away from the two men, gave a little wink which made me smile back.

Jacques and Henri were still standing by the house and were deep in conversation. As I turned away from Anna to look at the view again, I spotted Jacques taking something from Henri which looked like money. At once, I felt guilty, even though Jacques had been most insistent that we owed nothing. I fixed my eyes on the view again. Their arrangements were none of my business. I couldn't help but wonder, though, and wonder I did, as the horses began carrying us on the next part of the journey.

I wondered all the way to Hesdin, our next stop, which was in a rather impersonal coaching inn run by a motherly woman named Louise, and Alexandre, her giant of a husband. They fawned over Anna as if she was a little china doll and I had to admit it was amusing to see her next to Alexandre, who towered over me by several inches. Anna's head barely reached his chest. She tolerated their attentions with good humour, although her expression by the end of the evening suggested it had started to wear somewhat.

Anna's behaviour fascinated me. The previous night, she had been what I had come to think of as her 'normal' self, if such a thing even existed, chatting freely despite her distraction. Here, though, she simpered and fluttered, her eyes cast downwards, modesty personified. I had watched in astonishment at first, but as the evening unfolded, I realised she was like a chameleon, gauging people and giving them what they expected to see in her. I was so engrossed in watching the changes in her mannerisms and speech pattern that I was disappointed when the lateness of the hour dictated that we should retire for the night.

The next day, when we left Hesdin on our way to Doullens, Louise gave us a basket full of bread, cakes, cheese and even wine. Anna, Henri, and I ate like royalty that day, as Henri stopped at one or two villages along the route to pick up some supplies from markets and traders. Anna and I wandered around, looking at the stalls. Anna produced a purse from somewhere and bought some pastries, and I even found a half-decent hat for a reasonable price. As I handed over the francs, I was aware of Anna's eyes on me.

'Where did you get those?' she asked. I could see a smile playing at the corners of her mouth and there was a look on her face I had not seen before. She looked approving.

I shrugged, trying to look casual. 'The bank was near the telegraph office in Calais,' I said.

Anna laughed. 'We are quite a pair,' she said. 'Each with our secret supply of money. Well done. You are rather good at this survival game.'

'I wish you would tell me what work you do,' I blurted. The longer I spent with Anna, the more intriguing she became. 'You were so different with Henri and Jacques than you were with Louise and Alexandre. It was like watching two different people.'

Anna sighed. 'You would never believe it, so I would prefer you to see me working first and explain later. Does that make sense?'

I said it did, but I was not sure I understood. How could I find out anything if she refused to tell me? I had not seen her doing anything which I would describe as work, but was that because there had been nothing to see or because I was too naive to spot it? Was she a spy, or something to do with the government, perhaps? I racked my brains for other possibilities but came up with nothing. Frustrating though it was, I understood her reticence. She understood why I felt unable to divulge my real name or details about my family and the least I could do in return was offer her the same courtesy.

I continued to read my father's journals, trying to work out if they were in any sort of order. The state of his writing gave me a rough guide, but in one or two, it was almost as though he had used the journals simultaneously. Much of it made no sense to me. In one, he ranted about evil monsters who were all around us, watching. He wrote page after page about ghosts, interspersed with scribbled sketches of what looked like fairies, some with bat-like wings and jagged teeth. There was also a long section, about a third of one of the books, about Byron. It began as a summary of his life and achievements, with which I was already familiar, but soon descended into a chaotic collection of half-thoughts and wild speculations about the poet's death. He wrote about Augustus Darvell, the character from Byron's 'Fragment of a Novel' as if he were a real person, and there were a few short paragraphs about various public figures whom he believed had the power to transform themselves into wolves. I had to put them to one side on occasion, for the depth of his mania was both terrifying and upsetting to read.

Instead, I focused on whatever I could see out of the window. There were tiny single storey cottages, sweeping expanses of fields and crops, roadside shrines. In one or two villages, there were mansions right next to the road, contrasting sharply with the abject poverty all around us. Not half a mile from a shabby group of dilapidated cottages and a run-down farm was an elegant Georgian house with five attic gables and ten windows stretching across its upper floor. I thought back to the places I had walked past in Dover, the bodies curled up in doorways and figures leaning against walls, huddled in groups. I tried to focus on something positive, but there was little to see – it was either trees, fields, ridiculous wealth, or poverty. We were travelling according to Henri's timetable, so there was little opportunity to stop other than to rest the horses. I had the feeling that Henri had been shaken by the strange experience with the howling and the fog that first night on our way from Calais. Whenever we stopped for the horses, it was always for the shortest possible time. Henri would hover nearby in a manner which reminded me very much of Mrs Armitage on our shopping trips, when I wanted to look at something, but she was keen to return to whatever tasks she had left undone at home. It made me nervous, and I wished there was more to distract me. All I had were my father's journals.

The evening wore on and beyond the glass was darkness. I tried to sleep, but it was too cold and uncomfortable. I shifted around, trying to stretch my cramped limbs and aching back.

'For heaven's sake, will you stop?' Anna's voice cut through the darkness. 'You have been squirming around for most of the evening.'

'I am tall!' I retorted. 'You can stretch your legs far more easily. I hope we get there soon. Why on earth did we not simply take the train? The station was right next to the ferry port.'

'I told you that you would have to become accustomed to doing things my way,' Anna shot back. 'I suppose you have always travelled on velvet cushions with plenty of little luxuries to keep you occupied.'

That stung and I felt my anger and frustration rise. 'What if I have? I can no more help my upbringing than you can yours,' I snapped. 'Do you feel better when you say these things to me? Does it help you somehow?'

Anna said nothing and, emboldened, I continued. 'I am certain that you yourself are no stranger to luxury travel and frivolous distractions, either. You have no right to judge me. The difference between you and I is nothing more nor less than planning. You plan to travel this way. I did not even plan to leave my house.'

A long and heavy silence hung between us as the carriage wheels clattered and rumbled over the uneven roads, jolting both of us into even greater discomfort. I had made up my mind. As soon as we arrived at Amiens, or sooner, if I could make the necessary arrangements, I would take the train back to Calais and draw a line under this ridiculous escapade. I had been away for days. Surely my father would have been discovered by now. I would find a good hotel in Calais, send word to Arthur, and then spend the rest of my time in France drinking good coffee, eating delicious pastries and reading whatever I could find in the hotel which was not my father's journals. I would not tell Anna of my intentions. What business was it of hers? I sighed. Every time I thought we had reached an understanding, she did something like this, driving another wedge into the abyss between us.

'Viktor,' Anna began, her voice hesitant. I started, as she had been silent for so long that I thought she had fallen asleep.

'Please don't,' I said, my tone sharper than I had intended. 'Don't.'

I heard Anna take a breath, then Henri reined in the horses, and we rumbled to a halt. Looking out of the window, I saw we had, finally, reached our destination. I immediately grabbed my bag and almost fell out of the carriage, staggering a little as my legs protested. Anna got out of the carriage on the far side and walked around to join me, her bag in one hand.

Henri had jumped down from the driver's box and was hugging a short woman in a plain brown dress with a white apron tied over it. A younger man, of perhaps Anna's age, appeared from the building beyond and joined the embrace, then hopped up onto the box and drove the carriage past the house and into a yard at the back.

The woman looked at Anna and myself, her face creased in a warm smile. 'Welcome, welcome,' she said, beckoning to us to follow her. She turned and headed back into the house, ushering us into a cheery kitchen where two children were playing with a dog in front of the fire. As soon as they saw Henri, they left the dog and ran to him shouting, 'Cousin Henri!' in delighted voices. The girl was about ten years old, and her brother a year or two younger. Henri enveloped them both in a bear hug and was quickly towed over to the hearth to join in their game. As he tried to stop the dog from leaping up to lick his face, he introduced his aunt Renée and his cousins Fleur and Michel. Renée greeted us with a kiss on both cheeks and urged us to sit by the fire, where a couple of wooden chairs were draped in blankets. We did so, watching as Renée bustled around the kitchen humming a folk song, setting out bowls and bread. The kitchen smelled of polished wood and stew and my mouth was already watering. As I watched, I realised I had not heard Henri tell his aunt anything about Anna and myself, yet here she was with food at the ready for her unexpected guests. *It is almost as if we are not unexpected at all*, I mused, but soon dismissed the ridiculous notion. Unless she had a crystal ball, how could she possibly have known her nephew would turn up with a couple of strays in tow? Henri clearly had a group of very generous and accommodating friends, I thought, turning my travel-ravaged brain towards more simple pursuits, such as eating and watching the children play.

'How has your journey been?' asked Renée. 'Are you cold? Henri, if you need more blankets, take some from the chest before you go and let me have them back next month.'

'It has been rather cold,' Anna said, 'but we have been able to stay in some lovely, welcoming places.'

'We are very grateful to you for your kindness in taking us in,' I said. 'I do apologise that we have been rather sprung on you.'

'Not at all, not at all,' Renée said with a broad smile, ladling steaming stew into the bowls. It was loaded with vegetables, chunks of meat and thick, aromatic gravy. I closed my eyes and breathed in deeply. For a moment, it smelled like home.

Anna tucked in straight away and Henri and I were not far behind. Renee sat opposite Henri, peppering him with questions about his journey, which he answered between mouthfuls. She shooed the children up to bed, then set a pot of coffee brewing on the stove, another tantalising aroma which soon filled the room. I leaned back in my chair and let out a contented sigh.

'You will leave for home in the morning?' Renée asked Henri, who nodded.

'Yes, as early as possible,' he said. 'I promised Mother I would be home by sunset tomorrow.'

'I spoke to a man from Amiens earlier today,' Renée remarked. 'One of the neighbourhoods has become caught up in the most dreadful situation.'

Henri rolled his eyes and reached for more bread. 'What has happened now? I have never known such argumentative people!'

'This is serious,' Renée said, her expression earnest. She leaned forward over the table and caught Henri's hand as he picked up the bread. 'You must make sure you are there by sunset and go prepared. I will give you what you need.'

'Prepared for what?' Henri asked.

Renée let go of Henri's hand and sat back, looking at the three of us. 'To protect yourselves,' she said. 'There is a vampire in Amiens.'

Chapter 13

For a moment, no one spoke. It was I who broke the silence.

'I beg your pardon... but did you say 'vampire'?'

'I did,' said Renee. 'It is causing quite a commotion.'

I was flabbergasted. 'Forgive me, Madame,' I said, trying to keep the incredulity from my voice, 'but there is no such thing.'

I heard Anna catch her breath and felt the heat rise in my cheeks. Renee pursed her lips and gave me a scornful look. 'You think so, eh?' she said. 'Well, then, tell me this. If there is no such thing, why is the grave of Louis de Vaux disturbed, and what is attacking people?'

All eyes turned to me, and I stared back. Anna looked uncomfortable, and I saw her exchange a glance with Henri, as if to apologise for her stupid brother's ill-manners. I had to say something.

'Please forgive me if I have committed a faux pas, Madame,' I faltered, my throat suddenly feeling dry and constricted as embarrassment gripped me. 'I have never heard vampires being spoken of in this way. I am familiar with Dr Polidori's work, and Lord Byron's, of course, but-'

Renee raised her eyebrows. 'Stories!' she exclaimed. 'Those were stories!'

The door opened then and the young man who had taken the horses walked into the kitchen and kicked off his boots. He went to the fire to warm his hands, then introduced himself as André, pausing as he noted my embarrassment, Anna's discomfort, and Henri's puzzlement.

'Have you told them about the vampire, Mother?' he asked, crossing to the dresser for a bowl and joining us at the table. He helped himself to the stew and reached for some bread. He broke a piece off, dipped it into the stew and took a bite, then, gesturing with the remainder, he said, 'Henri, do you know Monsieur Courbet? He deals in cloth, I believe.'

Henri nodded. 'I know him. My mother sometimes uses his shop in town. What of him?'

'He passed here on his way to visit some relative or other,' André said. 'Mother and I were just returning from the market, and we met him on the road. He mentioned he was from Amiens. Mother asked him how the town did, and that was when he told us.'

'What did he say?' asked Anna. She leaned forward, watching André intently, her eyes flashing with interest.

André smiled at her. 'It is fascinating, no? I am almost inclined to join you so I can see for myself,' he said with a chuckle, as his mother tutted and shook her head at him. 'It seems that an old gentleman, Monsieur de Vaux, passed away at the beginning of last month. He was laid out at home and buried a week or so later. The day after the funeral, a young girl was attacked by a creature which bit her neck before running off into the cemetery. Her father went to investigate and found the earth on the old gentleman's grave had been disturbed.'

'It does not necessarily mean it is a vampire,' Anna observed. 'An animal could have disturbed the soil. That can happen with fresh graves, I believe.' André nodded.

'Indeed, Mademoiselle, you are correct,' he said, 'but rumours are spreading like wildfire.'

'Monsieur Courbet said some of the local men have formed groups and are patrolling the cemetery,' Renée said. 'It seems the mayor wants to have the body dug up, but de Vaux the younger won't hear of it. He's written off to Paris for someone to deal with the matter, Monsieur Courbet said.'

'Monsieur Courbet is very well informed,' Anna observed. Her tone was light, but her expression was pensive.

Henri chuckled. 'Ah, Mademoiselle Anna, old Courbet is a terrible gossip,' he said. 'If there is even a sniff of a rumour within five miles of him, you may be certain he will hunt it down like a dog with a rat.'

'Do you think it is likely to be true?' asked André. 'The more I think on it, the more curious I am becoming.'

'True or not,' Renée said, 'rumour or not, you will go prepared, Henri. I have garlic for you. I would never forgive myself if anything happened to you. Your mother would never forgive me, either,' she added.

'Who are the de Vauxs?' asked André. 'I don't think you have ever mentioned them, Cousin.'

Henri shrugged. 'They are rather out of my social sphere,' he said. 'I know them only by reputation. They are one of those grand old families who sneer at what they call New Money.'

I knew people like that in Dover. The Harcourt-Fyfes had five daughters and were terrible snobs. They had moved to Dover a year or so previously and had made some unpleasant remarks about me behind my back, believing that I, the daughter of a soldier, had airs above my station. Dear Elizabeth had overheard them and been quick to point out that the soldier of whom they were so scathing was the second son of a baronet and had chosen to serve his country on the battle lines rather than retreat to a distant estate. After that, all five had been overly solicitous, which was even worse than the insults.

'Was there much disturbance at the grave?' Anna asked. I noticed her voice was different again but could not quite pinpoint what had struck me about it. André gave a shrug.

'Monsieur Courbet did not mention anything else,' he said.

'No, he did not,' Renée said, getting up and casting a warning glance at André. 'Now, Mademoiselle, perhaps you would like some more bread?'

Anna blushed at this blatant attempt to divert the conversation. 'I apologise, Madame,' she said, lowering her eyes demurely. 'I am afraid I am rather fascinated with the subject, thanks to Dr Polidori and Lord Byron.' I blinked. Not once had she given even the slightest indication that that was the case, even when we had talked about some of the strange things in my father's journals. Had my reaction to those things perhaps made her reluctant to discuss them with me? Were those even her true thoughts, or was it simply another facet of whatever character she was now playing? To my surprise, I felt a sudden surge of jealousy rise in me, which I struggled to subdue. I recognised it, and it left a bitter taste in my mouth. Elizabeth and I had often discussed it, as it was something which affected us both. The need for approval. A part of me, which I preferred to ignore, wanted Anna's approval. It longed for us to develop a proper friendship, rather than the fragile companionship of convenience we had established. I did not want Anna to prefer discussing such things with André. I wanted her to discuss them with me.

Renée's frown softened into a benevolent smile. As she turned away to fetch some more bread, I saw an arch expression flit across Anna's face and the corners of her mouth twitched. Did she enjoy her deception? Was anything about her real, or just a carefully constructed façade?

'Perhaps it is time to read something less sensational, eh?' Renée said as she returned to the table with more bread. André and Henri immediately helped themselves, but I declined with thanks. I was not accustomed to eating large amounts of food and was already feeling uncomfortable. Anna accepted a small slice of bread to accompany the last few mouthfuls of her stew. She nodded at Renée and dipped her head in a becoming manner which made her look much younger.

'You are right, Madame,' she said. 'I must curate my reading habits more severely in future. It must have been such a thrilling and unexpected conversation, though,' she added, with an earnest smile. 'Nothing so exciting ever happens to me!'

'I do wonder what will happen,' Renée admitted. 'It's unheard of to demand that a grave be opened. I feel sorry for the family. Can you imagine, André, what your father would say if someone wanted to do that to your grandpère?'

André had just taken a bite of bread and almost choked at his mother's words. He began to cough, and Henri thumped him on the back until it subsided. 'Where is Uncle Claude?' Henri asked. 'I thought he would be here.'

'He went to our neighbour Guillaume, to help with the lambing,' Renée said. 'Guillaume was short-handed for some reason and Claude offered to help. He should be back tomorrow if all goes well.'

Conversation then turned to England and our travels so far. I was tired and kept my answers as brief as I could without appearing rude or abrupt. I did not want to add to the impression Anna had made with her over-enthusiastic desire for gruesome details about the vampire incident in Amiens. Plus, I wanted to retire so I could read through the section of my father's journal where he had mentioned Byron and Augustus Darvell. Although I was once again irritated with Anna, I could not help but be intrigued that people would still think vampires existed. Perhaps my father had had thoughts on the subject. If so, they might be recorded in one of the journals I had with me. There was also something about the question Anna had asked which was playing on my mind, but I could not work out what it was. I needed some time to sit in silence and think.

Eventually, the opportunity came. Renée glanced at the clock on the mantelpiece, tutted softly, then disappeared out of the kitchen. We heard her going upstairs, there was the sound of a chest being opened and closed, then footsteps overhead. I took a sip of the wine Renée had pressed on me, feeling my eyelids growing heavy. Anna nudged me with her foot and I jerked into wakefulness, almost spilling the contents of the glass. Feeling self-conscious, I fixed my eyes on the fire, looking at the patterns on the glowing logs. Henri, André and Anna chatted easily about Amiens and what we could expect on the remainder of our journey, but I registered very little of what was said. All I wanted was for Mrs Armitage to walk through the door and tell me all was well, that it was now safe for me to return home. I blinked back tears and was grateful for the distraction when Renée bustled into the room and, after making sure we all had everything we needed, shooed us off to bed like a pack of naughty children.

'I hope you will not mind sharing a room,' she said to Anna and I as she led us up the stairs.

'Not in the slightest,' Anna replied. 'It will be just like when we were children, won't it, Viktor?'

It was the line she had used on Jacques. Two could play at that game, I thought. 'Indeed, it will,' I said. She shot an amused glance at me, but I was in no mood for humour and a small, petty part of me felt satisfaction when the smile faded from her lips.

Our room was simple but comfortable, the beds piled with blankets and beautiful patchwork quilts. We thanked Renée for her kindness and bade her goodnight. Anna listened to her footsteps heading along the landing to her own room, then sat on one of the beds and turned to me, her face serious.

'Why are you so angry?'

She sounded genuinely curious, and I sat in silence for a moment, wondering whether I would answer. Eventually I looked at her and saw her flinch. My expression must have been more hostile than I realised, and I struggled to compose myself. She was right, though; I was angry. I was angry and frightened. And in the midst of all the friendly, welcoming people I had met over the last few days, I had never felt so alone in my life.

'All the people we have met on our journey welcomed us with open arms,' I said quietly. 'None of them so much as blinked an eye at the thought of unexpected guests. And how have you repaid them? With lies and deception!'

'It's not like that,' she began, but I interrupted, my patience wearing thin.

'What is it like, then?' I demanded. 'Tell me. What is it like? Has anything you have said to me been the truth, or am I just another mark to be taken in by your web of lies?'

Her mouth fell open and I saw temper flare in her eyes. Perhaps earlier, or last night, it might have bothered me, but at that moment, I did not care. I took off my jacket and, turning my back on her, fished in my bag for my petticoat, which I had been sleeping in. I shrugged out of the shirt and pulled the petticoat over my head, then examined the shirt to see if it would stand another day's wear. It was serviceable, so I hung it on the back of the chair next to my bed, along with the trousers and jacket. Anna was still sitting on the other bed, staring at me, as I slid under the blankets and pulled them up to my chin.

'You think I spend my time lying to everyone?' Anna asked.

'No,' I said, 'I do not think it, Anna, I know it. I have seen how you behave with people. You show them whatever they want to see. Including me.'

She was silent for a minute or two. 'I am sorry you feel that way,' she said at last. 'I have never had occasion to think about how I appear to others because I travel alone.'

I snorted into the blankets, surprising myself at my ill manners. With no one watching my every move, there was no need to suppress my feelings as I usually would. It was liberating in a way, but it also made me feel sick to my stomach. I was not confrontational as a rule, but with Anna, it seemed it was hard to be otherwise.

'You're right, though,' she admitted. 'I do adapt my behaviour according to the situation I am in. With Henri and Jacques, it was relaxed and fun. Louise and Alexandre wanted someone to mother and Renée's fascination with the sensational has its limits when it comes to young ladies.' She gave a soft, rueful laugh. 'If you had asked those questions, I am sure she would have reacted very differently.'

'Maybe so,' I said shortly. I was musing over my own behaviour and realising that I, too, made subtle changes, depending on who I was with and where I was. Had I been too harsh? I was becoming tired of second-guessing my own reactions, tired of trying to figure out who and what Anna really was. I was also tired of the carriage, of travelling, of living off people's good natures. I resolved that, as soon as we reached Amiens, I would arrange to send money to pay every single person with whom we had stayed.

'Viktor, please,' Anna said. 'Don't be like this. Do you feel like I am shutting you out? Is that it?'

'I know nothing about you,' I shot back. 'How would I know if you were shutting me out? I have to take every word of yours on trust, but I would be very surprised to find you have told me the truth even once.'

I heard a quiet intake of breath and guessed I had touched a nerve. I was surprised at how bad it made me feel.

'Look.' Anna tried again. 'I am alone most of the time. My work is solitary in nature. You must understand what it is like, being a young woman, travelling alone. At times, I have to be one thing and show the world another to keep myself safe.' She raised an eyebrow. 'You should appreciate that, at least.'

'Are people trying to murder you, too?' I asked pointedly. She gave a sigh of frustration.

'People do not usually want to murder me,' she said with exaggerated patience. 'However, from time to time, I do encounter unpleasant characters whose intentions towards me are less than honourable. Have you ever struggled to get people to take you seriously?'

I gave a bitter laugh. 'My parents didn't even tell me the details of my father's treatment.'

'I share those same frustrations,' she said. 'I have a… a special skill, let's say, which means I can help people, yet even those who ask for help have to be persuaded that I am capable of providing it. That is what life is for women. An endless parade of people who have to be persuaded of your worth. It's exhausting.'

'Why do you do it, then?' I asked.

She looked at me and smiled, then shrugged. 'There are not many people who can do what I can,' she said. 'I see it as a calling. It's challenging and exhausting, yes, but it's also fascinating and rewarding, and I always learn something. Plus, I like helping people.'

'If that's true,' I said, 'then I wish you would help me.'

'With what?' she asked. 'I look at you and see a remarkable young woman who is observant and intelligent. You have adapted so well to these circumstances. You don't look like you need help.'

'If what you said about being alone is true,' I said slowly, 'then you will understand how alone I feel. Isn't it rather foolish to be alone when we could have friendship instead? I have said before that I don't want to feel I am constantly annoying you, but I don't want to feel annoyed by you, either. I'm in the dark about everything, and while I might have dealt with that differently back in Dover, here, I just feel lost.'

I had to stop, for my throat was constricting with the sobs which threatened. I had not intended to say any of those things, but my speech made Anna get up and come and sit on my bed. She reached out a hand to me, and after a moment's hesitation, I took it.

'I know you're sceptical,' she said. 'Believe me, I don't blame you. If I were in your position, I would be the same.' She paused and looked down at our clasped hands. When she raised her eyes to mine again, her expression was earnest. 'Please will you do something for me?' she asked. 'It's important, so don't feel you have to answer straight away.'

Intrigued, I pushed myself up onto my elbow and looked at her. 'What do you want me to do?'

'My employers are based in Paris,' she said. 'I will need to go and see them. I would very much like you to come with me.'

I stared at her. Whatever I had been expecting, it was not this. 'Who are they?' I asked. 'Why would I want to meet them? Why would they want to meet me?'

She bit her lip as she looked at me, and I could tell she was trying to decide how to word something. 'I expect you have already guessed that my work is unusual,' she said. 'I am not a seamstress, or a milliner, or a nanny, or housemaid. Thank heavens,' she added. 'We are always on the lookout for exceptional people. You may have the qualities they seek.'

'What qualities?' I demanded.

'Let's talk about it in the morning,' she said, brushing my question aside. 'I need to give it some thought, and for now, there is only so much I can tell you. It's something I think you would be rather good at, and it would give you a rare opportunity for the kind of independence you could only dream of.'

I blinked. 'You really are the most frustrating person,' I sighed, sinking back onto the pillow.

'I didn't lie about Byron, though,' she said. 'I have read everything he wrote.'

'Prove it,' I said with a little smile. I should have pressed her to tell me about her employers, but I was far too tired.

Anna laughed softly and squeezed my hand, then started reciting 'From Anacreon'. I closed my eyes, enjoying the familiar words, and drifted into sleep still holding Anna's hand.

Chapter 14

My stomach was full of butterflies when I awoke and for a moment, I thought I was going to be sick. I rolled onto my back and lay still, eyes closed, trying to breathe slowly and deeply. The nausea passed after a few minutes, and as it receded, I replayed my conversation with Anna. I was puzzled. What did she think I could do? How could she see it when I was not even aware of it myself?

'Are you all right?' Anna asked from the other side of the room. I looked over and saw her leaning up on her elbow, a concerned expression on her face.

'I felt rather sick when I awoke,' I told her. 'It's passed now.'

'Good,' she said. 'Will you tell me if it comes back? I know Henri is hoping to be home by sunset, especially with all this vampire business going on, but if we need to stop between here and Amiens, then we will.'

As she spoke, I suddenly knew what it was about her demeanour the previous night which had struck me. It was authority. Her voice had become business-like, her words clipped and efficient as she questioned André. The question had suggested a depth of knowledge on the subject that I did not possess, in spite of also having read both Polidori and Byron over and over. What had she learned from them that I had missed?

I pushed back the blankets, catching my breath as the chilly air hit me. 'I think I would rather just keep to Henri's schedule,' I said. 'I feel better now. It would not be fair to Madame Martin to keep Henri on the road for another night when she is expecting him.'

Anna nodded and gave a little smile, then pulled a blanket around herself and went off to find some water for the washstand. I heard her soft footsteps padding along the landing and down the stairs, then Renée's voice floated up from somewhere outside the window. Wrapping myself in one of the blankets, I went to open the shutter.

It was a bright, cheerful day. Birds chorused merrily in the trees nearby and there was a hubbub of clucking in the yard below, where Renée was feeding chickens. I watched as they scurried after her, diving for the corn as she spread several handfuls around the yard. There was a small metal trough in one corner and she emptied the remainder of the corn into it, tucking the empty bowl under one arm as she watched the birds for a moment or two. She looked happy, I thought. Contented with her lot. I envied her.

Anna returned a couple of minutes later with a steaming jug. We relished the warm water and hurried into our clothes as the goosebumps rose on our skin, reddened from a vigorous drying with the rough towel Renée had laid out for us. Anna helped me with my hair and cufflinks, then asked me to lace her corset. I remembered doing the same for my mother and had to swallow hard to stop the tears.

The beautiful morning had affected everyone, and breakfast was full of laughter. Claude had not yet returned from the lambing, and Renée told Fleur and Michel to run across to Guillaume's after they had finished eating, in case more help was needed. I was surprised to find I was hungry after my unpleasant awakening, and Renée nodded in approval as I piled my plate with her delicious food.

'It is good to see a young man with a hearty appetite,' she beamed. 'Eat up, eat up! There is plenty more. I will put together a basket for you for the journey, Henri.'

'Thank you, Aunt Renée,' Henri said between mouthfuls, as Anna and I added our own thanks. As we were finishing, Renée went over to a shelf and came back with a small package. She handed it to Henri.

'You may think me a silly, superstitious woman,' she said, 'but please take this, if only to humour me.'

"I would never dream of humouring you,' he told her. 'Especially not for showing how much you care. What is it?' he asked.

'Seeds,' Renée said. 'For protection. Against the vampire.'

'Seeds?' Henri repeated. 'What do I do with them?'

'You sprinkle them on the ground,' Anna said quietly before Renée could answer. 'The vampire will be compelled to stop and count them, giving you the opportunity to escape.'

Renée turned and gave Anna a long, appraising look which raised a gentle, becoming blush. 'Well,' she said, a little taken aback. 'You know your folklore, young lady.'

The conversation stalled just long enough to be awkward, then Henri hugged his aunt and thanked her again for her hospitality and for the seeds. 'I shall be sure to defer to Mademoiselle Anna's superior knowledge, Aunt Renée, so you need have no fears for my safety,' he added.

The atmosphere relaxed and Renée's eyes filled with tears. 'You are a good boy,' she beamed. 'Now, Henri, see here.' She indicated a pile of blankets and a large, cloth-covered basket. 'There are some extra blankets and food for you all. You will be passing this way again next month?'

'As always,' Henri smiled. 'Thank you, Aunt Renée. I will return everything when I next see you.'

There was a fond farewell, Henri surrounded by his cousins, his aunt watching with a smile. Anna and I, standing to one side, exchanged a glance and found we were both misty-eyed. I missed the affection I had enjoyed from my parents just a few short years before, and it was horrible to think I might never experience that feeling again, with my mother gone and my father now a stranger to me. Anna took a deep breath, then stepped forward to say her own goodbyes, and I followed suit. As we set off, I opened the window and, looking back, saw the family standing at the side of the road, waving. I leaned out and waved until we turned a corner and they disappeared from view.

Sinking back onto the seat, I started stacking my father's journals on the seat beside me. The contents of my bag were a terrible mess, so I emptied it, then spent a while folding and repacking as best I could on the bumpy road.

101

As I pulled out a blouse, a journal landed on my lap. It had a large ink stain on the cover and I frowned.

'Another journal!' I exclaimed, holding it up. 'One of my blouses was wrapped around it. I knew my bag was overdue for a tidy!'

'Would you like to go through it by yourself, or can we look at it together?' Anna asked.

I thought. She had been sweet and kind to me all morning, and the atmosphere between us had settled. I had not felt on edge once and was even philosophical about the journey ahead of us, determined to view it in as positive a light as I could. Yet Anna could change in the blink of an eye, and I was under no illusion that the awkwardness between us was over. Still, we had to start somewhere.

'Let us look at it together,' I said, and Anna smiled. 'I will put the rest of my things away. Should we have the other journals to hand, in case he mentions anything we've seen in one of the others?'

'Good idea,' she said. 'Pass me those stockings and I'll roll them up for you.'

Between us, we dealt with the rest of my belongings, then I handed Anna the journals and sat next to her, opening the new one. The writing was almost illegible, and we both peered at it, trying to decipher the words. There were countless tiny drawings, the detail lost in ink blots when he made them too small for his pen nib to deal with. I recognised a dragon and fairies, different types of clouds, a Tudor rose and what appeared to be a sketch of the back of our house as seen from the garden. I turned the pages, my heart sinking as I saw more of the same on each one. None of it made any sense, and after a while, seeing how distraught I was becoming, Anna gently took the book from my hands and placed it, and all the others, back in my bag.

'We can look at them later,' she said, moving across to the other seat and stretching her legs. I did the same, fixing my eyes on the view. The weather was holding, and the sun was pleasant, but it could not disguise the monotony of field after field after field. The endless green was punctuated by impoverished dwellings clustered close together by the road as if seeking warmth from one another. It was the children which affected me the most, standing barefoot in the road and staring as we went by, their clothes sometimes little more than rags. I sat in silence for a long time, my mind wrestling with the things I had seen in my father's books. I was more impatient than ever to reach Amiens. Hopefully, when we arrived, word would be waiting for me from Arthur. Was it now safe for me to return home?

Was that really what I wanted?

The question was so unexpected that I caught my breath. Anna glanced over, but said nothing, returning her gaze to the expanse of fields beyond the window. My mind was racing. Where had that thought come from? Of course I wanted to go home. I wanted to be somewhere comfortable and familiar, with people I knew.

Yet part of me did not. Part of me loved the freedom, which was both terrifying and exhilarating in equal measure. Part of me delighted in the absence of my corset. A large part of me loved the freedom of movement trousers gave me, the anonymity I could enjoy in my disguise. There was a niggling feeling in my stomach which told me I should be arranging my journey home regardless of what the situation was in Dover, but was that just more of my conditioning? It was what everyone would expect of a well-brought up young woman, but was it what I wanted to do?

I mulled over that question for hours, curled up in my seat under one of Renée's blankets, which were warmer and softer than Henri's. Anna had fallen asleep, her head drooping forward, and as we rattled along, I gave serious consideration to the adventure I was having. Anna had called it a once-in-a-lifetime opportunity and I had to admit she was right. Would I be foolish to give it up, or was it more foolish to maintain my disguise? What would happen if someone realised that I was not all I seemed?

We stopped for lunch and sat on the grass at the side of the road, watching the horses drinking from a stream and occasionally giving each other a nuzzle before dropping their heads to crop the grass. I turned my thoughts to Anna's words from the night before. It was intriguing to think I might have qualities that would interest her mysterious employers, but I could not for the life of me imagine what they might be. She had not said a word about it all morning, either, which did not surprise me. As we set off again, I considered whether I should raise the subject, but decided against it. After a while, my eyes closed.

It was dark when I awoke, and Anna was leaning forward, looking out of the window, her face close to the glass. 'We're almost there,' she said, her voice taut. I yawned and sat up, surprised at how long I had slept.

'Are you all right?' I started, but she cut me off with a terse, 'Yes, of course,' which made her sound far from all right. Was she, perhaps, more nervous about the vampire than she would admit? I had been so wrapped up in my own thoughts that I had forgotten about the vampire. I looked out at the gaslit streets. We turned a corner and I saw a river to our left, a row of small, neat houses on our right overlooking the water. Henri took us down a road which led away from the river and past more terraced houses. Every now and then, I thought I saw a swirl of fog, but whenever I tried to focus on it, there was nothing there.

After a few minutes of rumbling along cobbled streets, the horses' hooves echoing off the buildings around us, Henri turned right and started driving up a hill, then reined in the horses and stopped. I reached automatically for the door handle, but Anna caught my hand. 'Wait a moment,' she said, peering into the gloom.

Puzzled, I looked out of the window and saw we were on a narrow hill with houses on both sides. I opened the glass and leaned out into the cool night air. There was a strong smell of dung and farmyards, which confused me, but I had no time to think about it. I could see a small knot of men approaching, carrying lanterns. One held what looked like a pitchfork, and as they came closer, I could see the lamp light glinting off blades. My heart began to pound in my chest and, biting my lip, I closed the glass and sank back into my seat.

'There's a group of men out there,' I hissed.

Anna, her face pressed to the glass on the other side of the carriage, waved me into silence. 'I know. I need you to follow my lead, Viktor. This is important. Can I rely on you?'

Fear seized me in its icy grip for a moment. 'What's going on? Do you know them? Are they going to hurt us? Why isn't Henri driving on?'

'Shh!' Her voice was sharp. 'Whatever happens, just play along.'

Before I could say anything else, a man appeared at Anna's window and peered into the carriage. I gasped and recoiled as the door was yanked open with unnecessary force. The man squinted into the darkness at me. He was thin and gaunt, wearing rough clothes and with the smell of horses about him. He looked from my face to Anna's, his expression a mixture of relief and confusion.

'You are the one who was sent?' He addressed me in a heavy regional accent. 'You are from Paris?'

As I opened my mouth to reply, Anna leaned forward. 'My name is Mademoiselle Anna Stenberg. It is I for whom you have been waiting. I presume you are here on behalf of Monsieur Guy de Vaux?'

My jaw dropped in stunned surprise before I realised what I was doing, but fortunately, the man was focused on Anna. De Vaux? Not the de Vaux at the heart of the vampire scandal, surely? Why was he expecting Anna?

The man's expression had shifted into disbelief. Whatever he had been expecting, I realised, we were not it. He stared at Anna for a moment, then took a step back. He looked across at me, then back to Anna. There was a moment of silence, then he began to laugh, a thick, ugly, snorting sound with a slight hysterical edge to it. The other men clustered around him peering in at us as though we were a sideshow exhibition at a circus. Lanterns were thrust towards us, casting dancing shadows around the inside of the carriage and across the gawking, puzzled faces. I could hear Henri challenging them and ordering them to step back, but they paid him no attention. There was more laughter. I stared across at Anna, trying to work out what was going on. Why was Anna saying she had been sent from Paris when we had just travelled from England?

Henri appeared on my side of the carriage, startling me when he opened the door and leaned in. He looked angry. 'Do you wish to descend here, Mademoiselle?' he whispered. 'I am not certain what these men are doing. I can take you elsewhere, if you prefer.'

'All is well, Henri, thank you.' Anna's voice was reassuring. She stood, held out her hand and he helped her to climb down into the street. I scrambled after her, heart pounding against my ribcage. All seemed far from well, as far as I was concerned, and I had no idea what Anna was doing. She walked around to the other side of the carriage where the men were gathered, and as I followed, I noticed something. Her entire physicality changed. She carried herself with pride and confidence, her head high and her step the self-assured stride of a man rather than the measured elegance of a young woman. Something about her made me stand to my full height as I followed her. As I drew near to the men, I saw I towered over most of them, so, to hide my fear, I took advantage of my height for once. I thought back to Arthur's advice and tried to reproduce his stance, my feet planted slightly apart, and my hands clasped in front of me. One or two of the men glanced up at me, eyes narrowed. I focused on Anna, hoping they would do likewise.

The man who had stared in at us was now leaning against the carriage looking Anna up and down. I took a step forward so I was close behind her, and stared down at him. He was several inches shorter than me, and his lip curled as his uncertain gaze flicked towards me and then back to Anna.

'Where is the person who is being sent for Monsieur de Vaux?' he demanded. 'Is he travelling in a different carriage?'

'Perhaps you did not understand what I said.' Anna's voice was pleasant, but there was a hard edge to it.

'You are the one who has been sent?' He gave another snort of unpleasant laughter. 'But you are a woman.'

As I bristled with indignation, Anna continued to stand in front of me, the picture of calm. She said nothing, and I wondered why she was not demanding that they fetch de Vaux. No doubt he would ensure these ruffians treated her with respect.

'They would not send a woman, Gérard,' one of the other men said. 'This must be his secretary.'

'Or his whore,' another man chortled. As he spoke, he thrust his lantern forward, and I saw he was even shorter than Gérard. A chorus of hoots and jeers echoed around us, and a window opened a little further up the hill. A man leaned out.

'Keep the noise down!' he shouted. 'Honest, hard-working folks are trying to sleep!'

'What would you know about being honest or hard-working, Alain, you fool?' One of the men picked up a stone and hurled it in Alain's direction. I heard it smack against the wooden windowsill before falling to the ground. Alain withdrew, slamming his window shut, which prompted more jeers and insults before the men turned their attention back to Anna and myself.

'When is your employer coming?' Gérard looked down his nose at Anna and the others joined in. 'Why didn't he travel with you?' 'Yes, where is he?' 'Monsieur de Vaux is waiting!' All the while, they closed in, jostling each other as they pressed nearer, taunts and insults loud in my ears. Anna reached back and gave my fingers a quick squeeze before withdrawing her hand.

'Are you sure it is safe for you to be out at this hour, gentlemen?' she asked.

That gave them pause and they gaped at her for a moment. 'What do you mean?' demanded Gérard, frowning.

'Have you the necessary protection to keep yourselves safe from the vampire I have heard of?' Anna's voice was calm and reasonable. 'I can assure you, I have.'

'What protection?' The short man pushed forward, his face obviously red even in the weak light from the lanterns. He leaned close to Anna and it was all I could do to stay in place and not reel backwards from the foul stench of his breath. How Anna stayed there, unflinching, was beyond me. I noticed the other two men had stopped smiling and were glancing around uncomfortably as if they expected to see the vampire standing there ready to pounce. One held his pitchfork at the ready and the other had a knife. I shivered. My legs were trembling and I was glad no one could see my hands. Even with my fists tightly clenched in my pockets, they were shaking violently.

'Come on, woman, what do you mean? What protection?' The red-faced man reached out a filthy hand and I was shocked to see him actually prod Anna's arm. Henri, standing just behind me, uttered a curse and lunged forward, but the man caught his arm and swung him round and away from us. Henri staggered backwards and fell against the wall of the nearest house.

The men laughed. 'Go on, Joubert!' one of them shouted, and Joubert glanced round at him with a horrible leering laugh. He made a rude gesture, which set them all laughing again, their hooting and braying making my head ache as I struggled not to panic. Windows started lighting up here and there, and one or two opened, shadowy heads appearing as annoyed neighbours tried to work out what had woken them. I was certain that someone was standing in one of the shadowy recessed doorways a little further up the hill. Why were they just standing there? Why weren't they coming to help?

'Somebody do something,' I muttered under my breath in desperation. The lanterns were casting strange leaping shadows across the sneering, hostile faces, turning them into alien, distorted masks. The men were loud and offensive, but I could also see they were afraid, and I did not know what to do. Should I step forward and lend my voice to Anna's, without knowing exactly what was going on, or why she was here? I did not want to inadvertently make things even worse.

As I agonised over what to do, I noticed a tiny movement at the corner of my eye. Looking to my right, towards where Henri was still leaning against the wall, catching his breath, I saw a thick fog surging forward as though being blown by a gale, yet the night was perfectly still. A familiar acrid stench enveloped me even as the floating tendrils stretched towards the men, billowing round them in a sudden explosion of energy. As one, they all yelled and staggered backwards away from the carriage, ending up in the middle of the road. The horses neighed in fright and Henri, rubbing the back of his head, ran over to try to calm them.

The four men had all fallen silent as they stared in confusion at the thick circle of fog all around them. Anna glanced at me and took my hand, and together, we approached, our steps slow and cautious, until we were standing right next to the wall of swirling fog which completely surrounded the four men in its midst. Anna paused for the briefest of moments, then we both stepped through and joined the men.

'This cannot be natural...' one of the men breathed. I thought it was the unpleasant Joubert, but the voice was muffled and distorted. I was not paying much attention, however. I was fixated on the fact that I had begged for someone to do something and at that very moment, the strange fog, with which I was now so familiar, had arisen around me.

Around me.

Could it be? I shook my head, trying to ignore the obvious thought that was screaming at me. It was impossible. It was fog. Why was I thinking of it as some kind of sentient being?

The half-remembered image of the creature within the fog arose unbidden to my mind, even as I saw before me, between myself and the men, a clawed hand appear from the depths of the swirling clouds. Humanoid fingers stretched out towards them and, as one, the men shrank away with raw cries of fear. This was the closest I had been to the creature and I could see the serrated edges on the claws, the hairless, desiccated skin stretched taut over wiry muscles and slim bones.

We could all hear the sound of breathing coming from the depths of the fog, ragged, snarling breath. It grew louder as one of the men fell to his knees, eyes glued to its talons even as the creature began to emerge more fully from its billowing shroud into the centre of the circle. Anna was staring at it too, but her expression was one of fascination rather than of fear. She alone had neither cowered nor fallen back when the fog appeared, and now she gazed into its depths with a rapt expression. The creature was approaching her, its tall, slender form resolving itself in the weak lantern light. Its skin was the colour and texture of fallen leaves and looked impossibly thin. From where I was standing, I could not make out its expression, but I could see Anna's as she lifted her eyes to it. They widened and she looked up at me.

'Viktor!' she urged, indicating the creature with an almost imperceptible tilt of her head. I froze, realising what she meant. I had to try. If it would diffuse this awful situation, I had to try.

As the creature raised its arm, claws extended, I cried out, 'No! Please don't hurt them!'

There was a rush of air and the fog started to whip around us, yet there was still not a breath of wind. Gérard was crying, racked by huge, gasping sobs. He sank to his knees, and the tang of urine mingled with the creature's own stench. Joubert was clutching at his neck, eyes staring in terror. There was a clang as the pitchfork fell to the ground. From somewhere beyond the circle of fog, I thought I heard running footsteps,

109

Anna was watching me in delighted amazement as the creature paused and turned its head to regard me. I could see the glint in her eye and the little smile dancing at the corners of her mouth.

'Gentlemen,' I said, in a voice which sounded far more confident than I felt. 'I trust this is sufficient indication of Mademoiselle Anna's credentials? May I presume that this is the last we will see of such unbecoming behaviour?'

It sounded ridiculous even as I said it, but the men were too focussed on the creature to notice. Taking strength from their fear, I continued, pretending I knew far more than I did. 'Mademoiselle Anna is here to assist you. That fact alone is testimony to her skill and ability.' I glanced at Anna, hoping this was true. 'It is disappointing that you required a demonstration. You, the very people who will benefit from those skills.'

'Who are you?' quavered the man with the knife.

'Shut up, Matthieu!' hissed Joubert.

'My name is Viktor,' I said. 'I am Mademoiselle Anna's assistant.'

I flicked my gaze to Anna to see her reaction to this spur-of-the-moment invention, but she looked as serene and unflappable as always, as though this was simply a routine part of her day.

'What is that... that...thing?' Joubert's voice was strangled and seemed to jerk from his throat as if trying to escape. His fingers worked at his neck, and I saw he was playing with a crucifix on a chain.

'There are more things in heaven and earth,' Anna quoted, her voice full of authority. That sent a wave of mumbling rippling through the little cluster of men, even as I registered suddenly that she had changed her voice again and now sounded like gentry, in accent, vocabulary and phrasing. 'May we now proceed, gentlemen, to address the issue I am here to deal with?'

'Make it leave.' Joubert turned a half-petrified, half-furious gaze onto us, his voice laced with terror. Anna gave a small nod and looked at me.

Panic rose in my throat, and I thought for a terrible moment that I would vomit. My heart rattled in my ribcage so loudly that I feared Gérard, who was closest to me, would hear it and realise I was a fraud. What if I could not control this creature, whatever it was?

Yet, it had come to me when I had needed help and had stopped when I asked it to. What on earth was it? Some kind of protective spirit, able to materialise when it sensed danger? If it was, then perhaps it could be persuaded to leave once the danger had passed.

I took a deep breath and looked at the fog. It had stopped swirling around and simply hung there motionless in a thick circle around us.

Stepping forward to where the creature stood poised, half in and half out of the still tendrils, I stood facing it, shaking like a leaf. 'I thank you.' My voice sounded as though it was coming from somewhere far away and I took a deep breath, struggling to maintain my composure. 'I thank you for your care and your protection. The danger has now passed.'

Nothing happened.

The creature regarded me through dark, unfathomable eyes and its head tilted slightly to one side as though it was listening. I could feel the men's eyes boring into me. The silence roared in my ears as I gazed at the motionless wall of fog.

'You are free to go where you will, with our gratitude,' I continued. 'If you permit, I will call upon you again should we require your protection.'

The fog hung there, as still as the creature. I was running out of ideas. This had been a horrible mistake and now Anna and I would be at the mercy of these awful people. Henri could not fight off four men. I had no idea of Anna's capabilities, but I knew my own limitations very well. For a fleeting moment, I wished I had insisted on remaining in Calais. What on earth was I thinking? And who *was* Anna Stenberg?

All at once, the fog started to swirl around us like a hurricane, spinning faster and faster until my eyes could follow it no longer and I backed away dizzily towards Anna, who caught my arm, holding me tightly. The air around us changed, thickening, solidifying, growing heavier, as though I could reach out a hand and touch it. The maelstrom of fog reached a crescendo and started to rise upwards, forming itself into a great column around us. The creature seemed to sink back into it as though into a pool of water, disappearing from sight. I could hear voices, hooves, shouting, the whistling of the rushing fog, yet still there was no whisper of a breeze. Footsteps, a slamming door, a scream, more shouting. One of the men, Joubert, I think, cried out, wordless, incoherent noises.

With a whoosh, the fog vanished, leaving us frozen in place in the street. Two of the men ran away.

Chapter 15

For a long moment, no one moved or spoke. I stood there, petrified. Had I made things worse than they already were? The men were frozen just as I was, eyes wide, mouths hanging open. Gérard was cowed, but Joubert's lip curled, and his fists clenched and unclenched as he stared at me with undiluted hatred. I feared he might strike me, but he remained where he was, and I realised his terror was stronger than his anger. It was clear he would be no friend to me.

Unbidden, a remark of my father's popped into my head, a comment from years before. 'Frightened, angry men are volatile and unpredictable,' he had said. I recalled the moment clearly, for it had been one of the rare occasions that he had spoken of his time in the Crimea as one of the ill-fated Light Brigade.

Racking my brain to try to recall anything Arthur had taught me about fighting, I cast a sidelong look at Anna. She was still standing tall, her calm, composed demeanour unshaken. I tried to do the same, but my efforts were feeble in comparison. It was fortunate that the men's attention had shifted to Anna.

'Henri.' Anna raised her voice, her authoritative tones echoing off the buildings. Henri was standing between the horses, an arm around each neck, murmuring in low soothing tones. He looked up.

'Oui, Mademoiselle?'

'What arrangements have been made for our accommodation?'

'Monsieur de Vaux made a room available.'

Anna looked at Joubert. 'Where will I find Monsieur de Vaux?'

Before Joubert could answer, we heard footsteps from further up the hill. A moment later, a tall, slim, aristocratic looking man appeared out of a gate just beyond us on the right-hand side of the road. He was dressed in a dark smoking jacket, and I guessed this was de Vaux. He hurried towards us, pausing when he spotted Gérard on the ground. Beyond him, hovering next to the gate, stood one of the men who had run away. A lantern trembled in his hand, casting eerie patches of light and shadow onto the ground and walls around him.

'I am Guy de Vaux,' the newcomer said, in a quiet, refined voice. 'I understand there was some trouble on your arrival and for that, I offer you my sincere apologies. It should not have happened. If those men were members of my household, I would deal with them appropriately.' He glared at Joubert, who met his eyes steadily for a moment before looking away. De Vaux dropped his gaze to Gérard, who seemed oblivious to everything, arms wrapped round his knees, face buried. 'My housekeeper has prepared a room,' de Vaux continued, looking up at me. 'I did not realise there would be two people, however.'

Anna smiled and held out her hand, which de Vaux took and bent over with elegance. 'I am Mademoiselle Anna Stenberg,' she said. 'It is I whom you have been expecting. I apologise that I was unable to advise you that my brother would be accompanying me in order to assist with the case. It was rather a last-minute decision, was it not, Viktor?'

She turned to me, smiling, and I found my voice, agreeing. De Vaux nodded and offered his hand. I stepped forward for the handshake, remembering, at the last moment, Arthur's instruction to grip firmly. De Vaux clasped my hand and bade both of us welcome.

'I feel it may be more appropriate, Monsieur, if alternative accommodation could be found,' Anna said, to my surprise. De Vaux raised a quizzical eyebrow and Anna continued. 'In my experience, impartiality is everything in cases such as yours.'

De Vaux thought for a moment, then nodded. 'I understand. As I said, we are not prepared for two. Joubert,' he said sharply, turning to him, 'please go round to Madame Archambeau in the Rue Saint-Martin and see if she will provide rooms.' He looked back to Anna and myself. 'She sometimes takes in young gentlewomen. I am sure she will make an exception for you, young man.'

My heart lurched as he said this, for it had not once occurred to me that I might have to sleep apart from Anna.

Joubert stared at de Vaux for a long moment, and I thought he was going to refuse. Then he nodded, dipped his head in what I supposed passed for a bow in his mind, and went off down the hill. He was still clutching his crucifix.

De Vaux turned his attention to Gérard. 'What is wrong with him?' he asked.

Anna glanced at me before replying. 'I am sure you understand that, in the kind of work I undertake, strange things can often happen,' she began, pausing when de Vaux shook his head.

'Forgive me, Mademoiselle, my knowledge of your work is somewhat limited. Perhaps you would do me the honour of joining my family and myself for some refreshment after your journey? There is much which needs to be said, and it would be more comfortable to do so inside.'

'Indeed,' Anna agreed. 'However, this gentleman has experienced quite a fright. Perhaps the other gentleman might be willing to see he reaches home safely.'

De Vaux nodded. 'Michel, take Gérard home.' His voice was suddenly hard, and I saw he was not a man to be crossed.

Michel, still lurking by the gate, hurried over and jerked Gérard to his feet. Gérard gaped at him as if he had no idea who he was. Michel put an arm around Gérard's shoulders and was about to start propelling him up the hill when de Vaux said quietly, 'And Michel, I trust that for the duration of Mademoiselle Stenberg's investigation, you will see to it that everyone – and I mean everyone – shows her and Monsieur Stenberg nothing but the utmost respect. Have I made myself clear?'

I saw Michel's lips tighten in the lantern's soft glow and he nodded at de Vaux. 'Perfectly clear, Monsieur,' he muttered, then turned and led Gérard away. De Vaux watched their retreating backs for a moment, then gestured towards his house. 'Shall we?'

'I will remain here with the horses, Mademoiselle,' Henri said.

'Thank you, Henri.' Anna smiled at him. 'I am glad they have calmed.'

'I will send out my maid with refreshment for you, Monsieur,' de Vaux said. 'Some hot soup and bread, perhaps? You must be chilled. Have you blankets? And a crucifix?'

Henri assured him he had all he needed, and that soup and bread would be very welcome. De Vaux then led Anna and myself up the hill to a beautiful detached town house which looked at odds with the more modest modern houses on either side. It was square with ornate chimneys and a single attic gable overlooking the front garden. De Vaux led us through the wrought iron gate and along a path lined with pretty flowerbeds to a heavy oak front door. As we approached, the door swung inwards, letting warm candlelight flood out into the dark evening. A young man peered out, his expression concerned.

'Papa?'

'Ah, Armand. Run and tell Cook to prepare some soup and bread for Mademoiselle Stenberg's driver and ask Sylvie to serve the refreshments.'

Armand nodded and hurried along the hallway, disappearing through a door at the far end. He was around my age, perhaps a little older, tall and slim like his father, with dark hair and intelligent brown eyes. He looked wary, watchful. Our little welcoming committee had been on edge, and I wondered how far that discomfort rippled through the community. It was certainly providing me with a distraction from my own troubles.

De Vaux showed us into a beautifully appointed parlour that had an understated grandeur which reminded me very much of my grandfather's estate. A maid appeared to take our coats and hats, and as we handed them over, a woman rose from one of the velvet armchairs by the fire and came to greet us with a warm smile. She was attractive and elegant in her mourning clothes, but I could see the same exhaustion etched into both her face and de Vaux's. There were dark smudges under her eyes, and her cheeks were gaunt and hollow.

'I am Catherine de Vaux,' she said in a clear, sweet voice. She appeared to be some years younger than de Vaux, and I could see Armand in her. They had the same oval face and dark hair, although Catherine's eyes were a startling, brilliant blue. 'Welcome to Amiens. I am only sorry that your visit has been prompted by such an unpleasant reason.'

Anna introduced us and the two of them shook hands. Madame de Vaux turned her gaze to me and I bowed, raising her fingers to my lips. They were soft and warm, scented lightly with lavender. Hands which reminded me of my mother's. I pressed my lips together and forced myself to concentrate. The long journey and the stress of the last few days were catching up with me, and I realised I was exhausted. I hoped Madame Archambeau would agree to take us both in so I could stay close to Anna, but at that moment, I would have fallen gladly into any bed offered to me.

Catherine de Vaux returned to her chair by the fire and indicated two others. Anna and I sat and looked around the room. Elegant ornaments graced the shelves and sideboard, and a vase of spring blossoms stood on a small table next to a pair of glass doors, which appeared to lead outside to the garden behind the house.

'This is a delightful room, Madame,' I said. 'I imagine it must be glorious in the summer, with the doors flung wide to let the fresh air in.'

Catherine de Vaux smiled softly. 'Thank you, Monsieur Stenberg, how kind you are. And you are quite right. This is, perhaps, my favourite room.' She glanced at her husband. 'Is Sylvie bringing the coffee, Guy?'

'Yes, my dear, everything is in hand.' Guy de Vaux crossed the room and stood next to Catherine's chair, leaning down to drop a kiss on the top of her head. She smiled and reached up to take his hand. De Vaux settled himself on the arm of her chair, to my surprise, and was about to speak when there was a soft tap on the door. 'Come!' he called, and the door opened to reveal a young dark-haired boy of around ten. 'Ah, Aubine, my son, come in.'

Aubine, who was a smaller, slightly wider version of his older brother, gave us a nervous grin and went to stand next to his father, who introduced us. Aubine turned admiring eyes to Anna.

'I didn't know women were vampire hunters!' he exclaimed. Catherine flushed.

'Aubine!' she chided. 'You know better than to be so impolite.'

The boy ignored her. 'You will help us, won't you?' he asked Anna. 'Please, Mademoiselle. Everyone is saying terrible things about Grandpère Louis, and they aren't true!'

Anna leaned forward in her chair, her face serious. 'I will do everything in my power to help you and your family, Aubine, I give you my word.'

Impressed, Aubine nodded and lapsed into silence, evidently satisfied. De Vaux reached out to place a hand on his son's shoulder and I was touched by the simple act of love and support.

'Perhaps you could give us a brief understanding of your difficulties, Monsieur de Vaux,' Anna suggested.

De Vaux closed his eyes for a moment and took a deep breath. I thought of how many times he had been forced to tell this story, and felt for him.

'It is difficult,' he began. Anna nodded.

'Take your time,' she said. 'Don't try to ascribe meaning or logic to anything. Just give me the bare facts as you see them.'

Catherine looked up at her husband and squeezed his hand. He took another deep breath, set his lips and began speaking in his beautiful, refined voice. 'My father Louis died on the seventh of last month. He had been unwell for some time with a wasting illness. After he passed, he was laid out here in the parlour, and his funeral took place the following week.'

'Where is he buried?' Anna asked.

'The de Vaux family plot is in the Cimitière de la Madeleine.' De Vaux indicated towards the street. 'It is close by. The main entrance is in the Rue Saint-Martin, perhaps five minutes' walk from Madame Archambeau's house. You can also reach it by means of a path which runs along the edge of the Bernier farm opposite, a little further along the road from here.'

'A farm?' I repeated, puzzled. Catherine smiled.

'The de Vaux family used to own all the land in this area. Over time, it was parcelled up and sold off, and the Bernier family chose to establish a farm on the land they bought. I believe there is some old family tale that the Berniers had a long-standing disagreement with the de Vauxs and Bernier set the farm up as revenge for some wrong which had been done to him.'

I nodded. That, at least, explained the stench of dung I had noted earlier.

We were interrupted by the arrival of Sylvie the maid, who appeared and asked us to be seated in the dining room. She escorted us across the hall to another beautiful, elegant room, then vanished, reappearing with a large tray and followed by a footman similarly laden. Armand followed him in, helping with the door before taking his seat. Sylvie, a small, slim girl with blonde curls peeping out from beneath her lace cap, served us quickly and efficiently, then withdrew, leaving de Vaux to continue with his story. He formally introduced Armand, who was regarding us with a guarded, watchful expression.

Silence fell for a few moments as we all ate and drank. Anna caught de Vaux's gaze, nodding in encouragement. He sighed and continued.

'The funeral went as well as one would hope, but the following evening, as we were about to retire, there were terrible screams from outside in the street. We rushed out and were just in time to see Louise, the daughter of the farmer Bernier who lives opposite, running into the farmyard towards her house. I sent one of my men over to enquire after her health and Bernier came back with him to tell me that Louise had been attacked in the cemetery by a creature which had tried to bite her neck. Between us, we gathered some men and went to investigate.'

De Vaux paused and took a sip of coffee, then set the cup aside and went over to the sideboard to pour himself a glass of wine from a beautiful glass carafe on a silver tray. He took a long draught before continuing. 'We made our way around the cemetery. You will see, tomorrow, that it is quite large, roughly rectangular in shape, and the de Vaux plot is close to the centre. It took a while to reach it. We saw no sign of disturbance, no one running around or playing practical jokes. I expected that the attacker was long gone, and that we would make a round of the paths and then leave it to Bernier to speak to the police in the morning.'

His voice quavered and he drained his glass. 'As we approached the family plot, I could see straight away that something was wrong. One of the wreaths was lying in the centre of the path and another was on its side next to my father's grave. The men saw it too, and stopped, so I could go on alone.'

He looked at Anna, desperation in his eyes. 'The earth on my father's grave had been disturbed,' he said, keeping his voice low. I glanced at the door, surprised that he was worried about his servants eavesdropping.

'Disturbed?' Anna set her coffee down on the table next to her and shifted in her seat so she could face him. 'In what way?'

'There was a hole dug in the earth right above the coffin.' De Vaux paused. 'As though something had pushed its way up from beneath the ground.'

'A hole?' Anna was frowning, I noticed.

'Yes, perhaps this size.' De Vaux put his glass down and indicated the dimensions of a hole about a foot wide and two feet long.

'How deep was it?' Anna asked. 'Was the coffin visible?'

De Vaux shuddered. 'No, thank God. The earth was piled up on either side, but it did not seem to go down more than a foot or so.'

Anna looked thoughtful. She picked up her coffee and sipped, then said, 'I see. What happened next?'

De Vaux explained that some of the men had fled, shouting 'Vampire!' and since then, the most terrible rumours had been circulating around the area. Reports had been made to the Sûreté, not only by Bernier, regarding the attack on his daughter, but also by a number of people who lived nearby, all terrified that the late Louis de Vaux was going to murder them in their beds. De Vaux had been visited the following afternoon by the mayor, Gaston Frossard, and Inspector Jean Escoffier of the Sûreté. The three men had examined the grave together and Frossard had demanded that it be opened and whatever lay within be 'dealt with', as he had put it. De Vaux, furious at the insinuations against his father's good character, argued against such an unspeakable course of action.

'As far as I am concerned,' he finished, 'vampires are nothing but superstition. I could not believe I was having such a ridiculous conversation, particularly with educated gentlemen in positions of authority. But there had been an attack. We agreed that the cemetery should be patrolled, and Escoffier put together two groups of men who alternated. However, after a week or so, nothing had happened and Escoffier put a halt to the patrols, claiming he needed the men elsewhere. Bernier took it upon himself to find his own men, and now there are two or three groups taking it in turn.'

He paused and looked at Aubine. 'Son, it is time for you to bid us goodnight.'

Aubine's expression darkened, but he stood, set aside his plate, and said his goodnights. There was a hug for each of his parents, a bow for Anna and I, and a fond hair ruffle from Armand. As the door closed behind the boy, de Vaux continued with his story.

'Mayor Frossard remained adamant that my father's grave needed to be opened. Inspector Escoffier, I could tell, was unconvinced, but caught between the public and Frossard. He struggles enough as it is to obtain the funding he needs to police Amiens properly, and that crook Frossard refuses to hand it over.'

Catherine de Vaux nodded in agreement. 'We have long held suspicions about Frossard's ethics, Mademoiselle. We suspect him of taking bribes, although there is no evidence of any wrongdoing.'

'What has this to do with the vampire?' Anna asked. Her eyes were alight with interest, and I suspected that she, like myself, was trying to take the various pieces of the puzzle and fit them together.

'Guy recently announced his intention of running for mayor at the next election,' Catherine explained. 'Since then, Frossard has been acting strangely. He has always been rather difficult to get along with, but lately, he has been quite unpleasant.'

De Vaux nodded. 'It would not surprise me to learn that Frossard had one of his men vandalise my father's grave in an effort to discredit me. He wants to hang on to his position and I suspect one of the main reasons for that is my desire to properly fund our police.'

At this point, Armand, who had been sitting silent and thoughtful, spoke up. 'He has to be taking bribes,' he said, his voice earnest. 'What other reason could there be for blocking progress, for not wanting a fully funded police force protecting our streets? If Frossard is taking money from one of the criminal elements in Amiens, he'd have the perfect reason for keeping things as they are, which means he has to fight off anyone who might challenge him in the elections.'

'Guy's policies are popular,' Catherine added, 'and he has a good chance of being elected, we think. Frossard's insistence on the exhumation is so extreme that it must surely be a crass attempt to undermine the good name of the de Vauxs.'

Anna nodded in understanding. 'This is an interesting insight,' she observed. 'How did my employers come to hear of your plight?'

De Vaux explained how he had written to his brother in Paris, asking for advice. 'Charles is very practical and intolerant of anything fanciful, and I knew he would come up with something sensible. However, instead of agreeing with me that the whole thing was ridiculous nonsense, he contacted a friend who has an interest in ghosts and suchlike. Supernatural things, you know. Shortly afterwards, I received an anonymous letter, advising me that an agent would come to investigate and act as mediator.'

Anna inclined her head and I supposed that this was a perfectly normal chain of events to her. 'Tell me, Monsieur,' she said, 'did anyone, at any point, suggest that your father's grave had been dug by an animal?'

De Vaux looked down at his manicured fingernails. 'They might have done, had it not been for whatever – whoever – attacked Louise Bernier.' He spread his hands in a gesture of helplessness. 'Mademoiselle, I appeal to you. I do not believe my father could possibly be a vampire, but the combination of his illness, the attack on Louise and the disturbance of the earth on his grave have all painted a very bleak picture and I do not know what to do. The people in this neighbourhood are good Christian people, but they are still susceptible to the kind of hysteria Frossard seems to be instigating.'

Just then, there was a knock at the front door, and I heard footsteps in the hall as someone went to answer it. Low voices murmured and a moment later, there was a tap on the dining room door. De Vaux called, 'Come in!'

The door opened and Sylvie stepped in. 'Monsieur Joubert says Monsieur and Mademoiselle will be welcome at Madame Archambeau's house. The driver is waiting outside with the carriage.'

'Very good, Sylvie.' De Vaux nodded at her. 'I trust the driver was taken care of?'

'Oh yes, sir. Cook warmed some of the vegetable soup and I took it out to him, with some bread and coffee, as you instructed.'

'Thank you, Sylvie. Please ensure our guests' coats are waiting for them.'

The maid nodded, bobbed a little curtsey, and left, closing the door behind her with a soft click. De Vaux patted his pockets, withdrew a small, flat case and handed Anna and myself his card.

'I would like to return in the morning, if I may, Monsieur,' Anna said. 'I must view the grave and walk around the cemetery to understand the layout. I will need to speak with the Bernier family, as well as Mayor Frossard and Inspector Escoffier.'

'I can arrange an appointment with the mayor and Escoffier,' de Vaux said. 'I will send a boy round to Madame Archambeau's when they confirm. Would, say, ten o'clock suit?'

'Yes, thank you, Monsieur, it would suit me well,' Anna said. Sylvie returned with our coats and hats, helping Anna with hers while I shrugged into my overcoat and held out my hand to de Vaux, who took it with a look of both gratitude and relief.

'Thank you,' de Vaux said. 'You have no idea how much this means to the family. We have all been beside ourselves.' He turned to Anna and bent low over her hand. 'I will speak to the employers of the men who troubled you earlier, and I give you my personal assurance that there will be no repeat of such behaviour.'

'I appreciate that. Thank you.' Anna turned to leave the room, then paused and looked back at de Vaux. 'In my experience, vampires usually target members of their own family when they are roused from their grave. They yearn to return home, you see. Yet Louise Bernier is not connected to your family in any way, is she?'

De Vaux looked startled, but recovered himself and shook his head. 'No. The only connection between our families is past history.'

'And Louise is the only person who has been attacked?'

'Yes, to the best of my knowledge.' His expression darkened. 'I am certain that people would not hesitate to inform me if a second attack took place.'

Anna nodded, her expression sympathetic. 'I fear you are right, Monsieur.' She turned to Catherine and Armand, who were now standing together in front of the fireplace. 'I fully appreciate how you must be feeling, but please try not to worry. I will not permit an exhumation to proceed unless I see very good cause.'

Catherine nodded and Armand pressed his lips together, his eyes bright with tears. The sense of loss and grief which hung over the family shifted into sharp focus. I added my own condolences, and assurances that we would do all we could to assist them.

Sylvie was hovering in the hall as we left the dining room, but de Vaux shooed her away and escorted us to the door himself. 'Once again, my thanks,' he said as we stepped out into the cool night air.

I was about to follow Anna down the path when something struck me and I paused, turning back, thinking over de Vaux's description of events. 'Monsieur,' I said, 'there is something which puzzles me.'

Anna stopped and turned. In the soft light from the hall, I could see her eyes were warm with approval and, emboldened, I regarded de Vaux, who looked apprehensive.

'What is it you wish to know?' he asked.

I waited for a moment before I spoke.

'What was Louise Bernier doing in the cemetery?'

Chapter 16

De Vaux stared at me, a frown creasing his forehead. Shadows from the hall lamps fell across his profile, making his expression suddenly lupine. His lips tightened into a thin line.

'I am sure I have no idea,' he said, then bade us goodnight once more. Anna inclined her head and I bowed, then we turned and made our way along the path to the road, where we could see Henri standing with the horses. As we approached, he hurried over to us.

'Mother of God, I was so worried,' he said, his voice low and urgent. He cast a glance towards the house. 'Was everything all right in there?'

'You are a good friend, Henri.' Anna gave him a warm smile as he helped her climb into the carriage. 'Monsieur de Vaux has manners and was embarrassed by the welcome we received. All is well. He gave us a good outline of the issue and tomorrow, we start investigating.'

As I settled into my seat opposite Anna, I glanced across at the de Vaux house and noticed that the front door was still open. Someone was silhouetted against the gentle glow of the lamps beyond, and I realised, from his build, that it was Armand, watching us. I debated whether or not to acknowledge him as Henri guided the horses in a neat half-circle to face back down the hill. Deciding it was too dark for him to see me, I turned instead to Anna as Henri urged the horses into a brisk trot.

'I do hope you don't mind that I have appointed myself as your assistant,' I said in a low voice. 'It was the first thing which occurred to me.'

Anna smiled. 'But you thought of something on the spur of the moment, and something that is entirely plausible,' she pointed out. 'You have a good brain and quick wits, Viktor. It will be useful to have a second set of eyes in this case, especially yours.'

Relieved, I thanked her, glad she could not see me blushing in the dim light.

We sat in silence for a moment or two, watching the houses flash past as we trotted down the Rue Saint-Martin, then Anna spoke again. 'You rather threw de Vaux when you asked why Louise Bernier was in the cemetery.'

'He knows, I think.'

'He either knows or suspects,' she agreed. 'There was certainly something he left unsaid.'

'Are there many occurrences like this?' I asked, unable to contain my burning curiosity any longer. 'Vampires, I mean. I thought they were fictional, the creatures of folk tales, but I can see I shall have to reassess.'

Anna chuckled. 'They are real enough. You would be surprised. I know I was at first.'

'And they are all real vampires?' I was struggling to comprehend this. 'Undead creatures which drink human blood?'

'Some are, yes,' Anna replied. 'Some are ordinary people with unusual illnesses which make them believe they are vampires. The world is full of interesting creatures, Viktor. Only a handful of people have the ability to see them and even fewer know how to interact with them.'

'You are one of those few?'

She nodded. 'I was born with the ability to see them. I have studied them for years. There are many different kinds, found in all sorts of places, each with its own set of rules of engagement, if you like. You cannot stake a forest spirit as you can a vampire, and turning your pockets inside out protects you from neither, although it will prevent you from falling victim to pixies. The most important thing is being able to identify each species and know how to engage with it. Violence is always, *always* a last resort. Negotiation comes first. Quite often, they are only reacting to something we humans have done to upset their environment.'

I stared across at her, squinting in an effort to make out her expression. Was she making fun of me? 'These are all fairy tale characters, surely?' Even as I said it, I could hear the uncertainty in my voice. She sounded so matter-of-fact, as though she was discussing the attendees at a dance. 'Are you telling me they actually exist?'

'It's a lot to take in,' she replied, 'and it's late. You must be as exhausted as I am. Let us meet Madame Archambeau and see our accommodation. We can talk more tomorrow.' She paused. 'Well, now you know what my work entails, and why you really needed to discover it yourself, rather than having me tell you. What do you think of it?'

I huffed out a long breath as my tired brain began to mull over what I had seen in the last couple of hours. 'I am torn between believing every word you say and thinking I am caught up in some kind of hoax.' I stifled a yawn.

The carriage slowed to a halt and Anna peered out. 'Ah, here we are,' she said, side-stepping my comment. Henri jumped down from the box to assist Anna and as I climbed down after her, I looked up at the house. It was sizeable, although not so large or grand as de Vaux's, with three windows along the top floor and one either side of the central front door, all with delicate lace curtains. To our left, a wide archway led to somewhere behind the house, a yard or stables, perhaps. There was a soft glow beyond the drapes on the ground floor, and someone was playing a sweet, gentle waltz on a piano.

Henri busied himself with our bags and, to my surprise, started to unstrap the large trunk from the back of the carriage, which I had thought belonged to him. As he did so, Anna climbed the three steps leading to the front door and rang the bell. The piano music stopped, and the silence which followed seemed deeper than any I had ever experienced before. I gave a little shudder, but, hearing footsteps, pulled myself together and tried to stand tall. A moment later, the front door was opened by a maid not much older than myself, with honey-coloured hair and a sprinkling of freckles across her nose. As she greeted us in a light, sweet voice, I noticed a tall dark-haired woman behind her, who stepped forward.

'Mademoiselle Stenberg?' she asked as she reached the door, her voice husky and low. 'I am Christine Archambeau. Welcome!'

The maid moved discreetly to one side, busying herself with our coats and hats as Madame Archambeau extended a hand. Anna took it, smiling.

'It is a pleasure to meet you, Madame. We are both very grateful to you for your kindness in allowing us to sleep here tonight at such short notice.'

Christine Archambeau returned the smile, her hazel eyes twinkling. 'It was no trouble at all. The rooms are usually ready, and it did not take us long to freshen them, did it, Céline?'

The maid, who was hanging up our coats and hats, turned and beamed at her mistress. 'No, indeed, Madame, we were very efficient, weren't we?'

Christine gave her a fond smile, then looked back to Anna, the smile fading. 'I understand from Joubert that there was some trouble when you arrived? I trust it will not follow you here.'

I blushed and cast my eyes down to the polished wooden floor, but Anna launched into a very brief description of events, her voice calm and confident. Christine listened, a tiny frown creasing her brow. She rolled her eyes when Anna explained how we had been greeted and opened them wide at the mention of the fog creature but refrained from speaking until we had been ushered into an elegant parlour and settled before the fire. We both leaned towards it, hands held out to the dancing flames, as Christine gave Céline instructions about refreshments and sent her off to the kitchen, then directed Henri to a room upstairs.

'I trust that Monsieur de Vaux's hospitality was not lacking?' she asked suddenly, as if the thought had just occurred to her.

'He was keen to make amends for our unpleasant experience,' I told her. 'Something light will more than suffice, thank you, Madame.'

Anna nodded in agreement, and Christine excused herself to amend Céline's orders. I leaned back in the armchair, taking in my surroundings. There were some beautiful landscape paintings, rich velvet curtains of a deep, vibrant blue, a walnut writing desk in one corner, a large, well-stocked bookcase and the usual assortment of chairs, sofa, and occasional tables. A vase of daffodils blazed cheerfully on top of the writing desk, and I spotted a copy of Voltaire, open and face-down, beside the fireplace, as though someone had been reading whilst lying on the rug before the fire. It was a welcoming, peaceful house and I took a deep breath, feeling my muscles relaxing. Out in the hall, I could hear heavy footsteps mounting the stairs, and guessed Henri was taking the trunk up to our room.

After a couple of minutes, Christine came back into the parlour, sweeping past us with a subtle waft of rose water, and settled comfortably into the armchair next to Anna's. She made light conversation about the weather, our journey and the delights of Amiens until Céline appeared to announce that supper was served. We rose and followed Christine into an equally beautiful dining room, papered in deep red and half-panelled in dark wood. Céline had prepared cheese, warm bread and what proved to be an excellent red wine, which she served unobtrusively, moving between us with silent, well-practiced steps. She was very solicitous of her mistress, I noticed with approval, anticipating her needs almost as though there was some form of psychic communication between them. Christine was clearly the sort of mistress my mother had been, I thought, recognising the tender concern on Céline's face as she watched Christine. I had seen the same look on the faces of our own staff.

Once Céline was satisfied that her mistress had all she needed, she curtseyed and left the room. As the door closed behind her, Christine leaned forward, her fingers toying with the stem of her wine glass. She was seated at the head of the table, with Anna on her right and myself on her left. Due to the lateness of the hour, she had already supped, but took a small chunk of bread and a thin wedge of cheese.

'Now we are alone, I would like to know more about this strange creature you speak of.' She eyed me curiously. 'Joubert says it obeys you.'

For a moment, I panicked. 'It will not be a threat to you, Madame,' I reassured her hastily, hoping my voice sounded more confident than I felt.

'The creature can sense when my brother is in danger,' Anna chipped in. 'He treats it with great respect and it, in turn, respects his wishes.'

'And that respect is why those fools are still alive, I am guessing,' Christine murmured, more to herself than to us. I did not know how to reply, and paused, a piece of bread half-way to my mouth. Christine's expression was thoughtful, and she regarded us with narrowed eyes. I hoped she was not going to ask us to leave or, worse, request a demonstration. For some reason, I was more tired than I had been on any of the previous few evenings. Perhaps it was the knowledge that I was safe and could afford to relax. Perhaps it was because I could guess at the quality of the bed awaiting me upstairs, and that I was guaranteed to have a comfortable night. As Christine's silence lengthened, despair rose in my throat. The little piece of bread was suddenly a leaden weight in my hand. If I tried to eat it, I knew it would stick in my throat.

Anna, too, had stopped eating. It seemed an age before Christine's face relaxed and she smiled, eyes twinkling again.

'Come now, do not look so concerned! I am not going to ask you to leave. I am sure you understand that I must know who and what I am welcoming into my home.'

'Of course, Madame,' Anna said, and I was surprised to hear the relief in her voice. 'Believe me, we do not wish to cause trouble for anyone. We are, after all, here to help.'

'Ah yes de Vaux's unfortunate situation.' Christine nodded and took a sip of her wine. 'It has rather taken our circle by surprise, I can tell you.'

'I can imagine,' I said. 'You socialise with the de Vaux family, Madame?'

She smiled. 'Yes, I often spend an afternoon with Catherine, Guy's wife. She is a talented pianist, and we play together now and then, although I am nowhere near as good as she. You have met her?'

We said we had met the whole family and she nodded. I asked for her opinion of the vampire rumours, eager to hear what this intelligent, well-educated woman made of something so bizarre and unreal. The bread was delicious and comforting, the cheese full of flavour, and I was starting to feel drowsy, although that might have been the effects of the wine. I tended not to drink at home and only had the occasional glass of punch or champagne at balls or parties.

Christine frowned. 'It is a strange case,' she said. 'Louis de Vaux was a lovely old gentleman. He had been unwell for some considerable time, and he was advanced in years. Sometimes, if he was well enough to descend to the parlour, or even outside, Catherine and I would play cards with him in the afternoon. I find it very hard to believe there is anything in this vampire story. There needs to be far less focus on that and more on the ruffian who attacked poor Louise Bernier. As for the damage to Louis's grave, surely it must have been an animal?'

'I will go and see it for myself in the morning, Madame,' Anna told her. 'Unfortunately, I suspect that any clues will have been lost by now, and I will need to look further afield within the cemetery for other tell-tale signs of activity.'

'There was a terrible fuss over the desecration, as you can imagine,' Catherine commented, taking a small bite of cheese. 'Guy was beside himself when it was discovered and was all for calling in the police. Then Bernier started talking about vampires and the men refused to let Guy anywhere near the grave because they thought he was attempting to hide evidence of his father being a vampire.' She shook her head. 'It seems that once Mayor Frossard became involved, and Inspector Escoffier, poor Guy had no chance of restoring the grave. It has been hard on him, as you can imagine.'

I nodded in sympathy as Anna picked up her wine glass and took a sip. 'I will need to see the grave in the morning, Madame. We are due to meet with Monsieur de Vaux at ten, and it would be helpful to have seen it before then. Will there be time, do you think? As I understand it, the cemetery is not far away.'

'Not far at all. My garden backs onto part of Bernier's farm, which, in turn, adjoins the cemetery.' Christine indicated a direction which would take us beyond her house and further along the Rue Saint-Martin. 'At most, it is perhaps a five-minute walk from here to the main gate.'

'Ah, convenient indeed.' Anna flashed a satisfied smile. 'It will give me ample time to look around,' she said. 'I will just need directions to the grave site.'

'I will ask my son François to escort you,' Christine said. 'He was one of the first to volunteer when Monsieur Bernier asked for help with patrols. I was torn between pride and concern. Personally, I would rather he was not involved, because I worry so much whenever he goes out.'

'He is out tonight?' I asked, helping myself to more bread and wondering where my appetite had come from.

Christine nodded. 'Yes, his group is out until dawn.'

'Monsieur de Vaux said the police removed their patrols,' Anna observed. Christine sighed and nodded.

'Such a terrible fuss at first, although nothing has happened since, and people are at least starting to calm down now. There were demonstrations in town during the first week or so, once word got out, and the rumour mill has been working very hard ever since.' She gave a rather unladylike snort and winked at us. 'Honestly, we think we are in an advanced and enlightened society...'

I chuckled softly and Anna smiled. 'I have a different viewpoint, Madame,' she said. 'Once, I thought very much as you do... that such creatures are figments of the imagination. It was only when I had come to terms with the fact that I could see and communicate with otherworldly beings that I came to fully appreciate just how many mysteries the world holds.'

Christine regarded Anna, fascinated. 'You really are an intriguing young woman. I am looking forward to knowing you better,' she said.

'May I ask what precautions the patrols are taking while they are in the cemetery?' Anna asked, and I saw a sudden cloud pass over Christine's expression. She gave an elegant shrug.

'You know what men are, Mademoiselle,' she sighed. 'I do not know about the others, but the men who patrol with François seem to be terribly superstitious. They have crucifixes, I understand, and each has a weapon, of course. François has a cudgel,' she added. 'I would not permit him to acquire a gun.'

I saw a frown flit across Anna's brow, gone almost as soon as it appeared. 'François is still quite young, I take it,' she said.

'He is seventeen, more or less a man, yet I still see him as my little boy,' Christine said. She smiled, but kept her lips pressed together, and the smile did not quite reach her eyes. 'He is my only child and I know the day is fast approaching when he will need to strike out on his own. I would delay that day forever, if I could.'

'We all fly the coop eventually, Madame,' Anna said, her voice gentle. 'He is truly fortunate to have a caring mother who will not hold him back.'

Christine nodded and took a sip of her wine, struggling to compose herself. When she spoke again, her voice was a little shaky. 'De Vaux is an influential man in Amiens, you know. Did he tell you he is running for mayor?'

'He did,' I said. 'Do you think there is some political motivation behind all this?'

Christine shrugged again. 'I have no idea, Monsieur, although from what I have heard from Catherine these last weeks, I would not be surprised. It does seem like a targeted campaign, does it not?'

'On the face of it, yes,' Anna agreed. 'What is Mayor Frossard like?'

'I do not know him well. I see him occasionally at social events. He was once a popular mayor, but in the last few years, his policies, and his derision for the poor and needy have lost him a lot of support, especially his attitude towards the police. That particular issue has raised its head again recently with all the fuss about patrols in the cemetery. Catherine thinks Frossard is genuinely concerned that Guy will be elected, and that he is somehow behind this vampire business. Frossard certainly has the most to lose. Yet at social gatherings, it is hard to read him. He is always on his best behaviour. Any conflict is hidden behind the mask of manners.'

'If the human element is the strongest suspect,' I said slowly, feeling my way through my thoughts, 'why do you need Anna?'

Anna looked across at me, her expression unreadable, and I suspected I had made an error, although I was not sure how, or why. 'Just in case,' she said quietly.

Christine shifted in her seat, her gown rustling. She picked up her glass and took a long draught, then looked at our plates. 'Do you have enough to eat? Shall I ring for coffee?'

We assured her that we had more than enough food, but coffee would be delightful. Christine rose and crossed the room to ring the bell. As she was returning to the table, the door opened and a young man entered the room. He was a little shorter than me, and his resemblance to Christine was striking. They both had straight, well-sculpted noses, hazel eyes, and a similar jawline.

'François!' Christine exclaimed. 'Has something happened? Why aren't you on patrol?'

The young man smiled, a sheepish expression on his face, and gave a stiff little bow. 'Joubert came to complain about our visitors and told me you were both staying here, so I excused myself for a while to come and meet you.'

Christine gave him a fond smile, introduced us, then indicated the chair next to me. François loped over and sat, reaching for some cheese and looking with open fascination at Anna and myself. Céline appeared and Christine asked her to bring coffee.

'Of course, Madame,' said Céline. She looked over at François. 'Will you be requiring anything, Monsieur François?' she asked.

'He needs a plate,' Christine said, chuckling, and headed for the sideboard, but Céline protested as she hurried over.

'Sit down, Madame, I can take care of that for you,' she said, bustling about with crockery and napkins. Christine smiled and returned to her chair. Céline laid out a plate, glass and knife for François and handed him a napkin, then curtseyed and went to fetch the coffee.

François reached for the bread and cut himself a chunk, then looked across at Anna. His cheeks had a warm glow. 'How does one become a vampire hunter?' he asked.

'François!' Christine's eyes widened. 'Please! You know better than to be so indelicate.'

'Oh Maman, I am certain you are just as curious as I am,' retorted François. Christine tutted and huffed a little, but her eyes gave her away. Anna laughed.

'Do not worry, Madame,' she said. 'I am asked all the time. The answer is rather uninspiring, I fear. One has to possess certain innate abilities, be aware of them and able to control them, and demonstrate them in front of the right people at the right time. I assisted an influential man in Paris several years ago, and he introduced me to the people who are now my employers.'

'You assisted him?' repeated François. 'With a vampire?'

'My specialism is vampire relations and politics, yes,' Anna explained. 'My role is primarily that of a negotiator.'

'Will you have to negotiate with old Monsieur de Vaux?' François speared a piece of cheese on the end of his knife.

'That depends on a number of factors.' Anna's voice became more business-like as she explained. 'Firstly, I have to determine whether there is a vampire at all, and if there is one, who it is. Often, there is no vampire, and I find myself helping humans to work through issues. But in cases where there are undead... Sometimes, they are roused by human activity, which requires mediation to resolve. Sometimes they rise because of other factors, which can be more complicated and usually more dangerous. That, fortunately, does not happen very often. You would be surprised at how many times I am asked to investigate something and find that a grave has been disturbed by animals.'

'This is fascinating!' François leaned forward with a boyish enthusiasm which I found rather charming. 'Maman, you were absolutely right to invite them to stay!'

'Oh François....' groaned Christine, her cheeks flushing. Anna and I did our best to conceal our smiles, but all four of us ended up bursting out laughing. After that, the already congenial atmosphere became friendly and relaxed. Céline served coffee in the parlour and built up the fire, while we settled ourselves, chatting easily. Christine invited us to use her first name, and we returned the compliment. I was relieved, for it felt odd to be addressed as 'Monsieur' by someone old enough to be my mother. I caught her looking at me once or twice, fearing she could see through my disguise, but if she did, she gave no indication and called me Viktor as if it was the most natural thing in the world.

François fired questions at us, which I let Anna answer for fear of revealing my lack of knowledge. In return, he told us a little about the patrols, barely disguising his disappointment that he had not, as yet, seen a vampire. 'I know my mother would prefer me to stay at home with her,' he said, giving her a little smile, 'but I believe I have a duty to my community and should do what I can to assist, now I am of an age to do so.'

Anna nodded approvingly and François beamed. I realised that he, like myself, needed such approval. As the conversation unfolded, and there was no mention of Monsieur Archambeau, I looked at the photographs in the room, all of which were of Christine and François alone. It struck me that Christine might be widowed.

'What precautions do you take?' Anna asked. I wondered if she ever got the answer she hoped for from any of the people she helped. It seemed she was destined to be disappointed on this occasion also, for François turned a puzzled expression to her.

'Precautions?'

'What would you do to protect yourself if you encountered a vampire?'

He considered. 'I confess I have only my club. I never really expected to see a vampire. I hoped I might; but they are only in books, after all, are they not? I think we are looking for a dog, Mademoiselle Anna. Or a fox, perhaps.'

'But what of the attack on Louise?' Christine asked, bringing us back once again to the crux of the issue. Anna nodded.

'Indeed,' she said. 'That cannot be explained away so simply. Do the other men share your opinion?'

'Some do, yes.' François took a sip of coffee. 'One or two are very vocal about the entire thing being the work of Monsieur de Vaux's enemies but will not – or cannot – say who those enemies might be. Others think de Vaux is behind it, as a way to make the police look bad and throw a spotlight on his policies about police reform. There are suspicions about both of them, of course, but nothing definite. I think if we had that information, the entire situation could be resolved in no time.'

'Only the damage to the grave,' Christine insisted. 'What about poor Louise?'

François looked across at her, cup half-way to his lips. 'Why do you think the two things are unconnected?' he asked, sounding genuinely curious. 'She was clearly in the wrong place at the wrong time, was she not? She must have disturbed whoever was responsible for the damage to Monsieur de Vaux's grave, so they attacked her to add weight to the vampire rumour. That is what the men I patrol with were talking about earlier. Some believe it, including myself. Some don't.'

Anna looked thoughtful. 'Have you ever seen dogs or foxes in the cemetery, François?'

He rolled his eyes. 'There are always dogs in the cemetery. Bernier's sheepdog spends half its time roaming around the graves when it should be earning its keep on the farm. I have seen a few others in these last two weeks, too, although I think they were strays. They looked rather thin and kept their distance from us.'

'When you next go out on patrol, please take some mustard seeds with you,' Anna told him. François frowned.

'What for?'

'Vampires have a compulsion to count anything small like seeds, or knots in a piece of string. It distracts them, hopefully long enough for you to get away.'

François wrinkled his nose, a scornful expression on his face, but under Anna's serious gaze, he wilted. 'Is that really true?'

'I would not suggest it otherwise.' Anna regarded him over her coffee cup. 'I have already had my authority questioned tonight. I am not in the habit of making myself look foolish.'

François reddened. Christine opened her mouth to apologise, but François spoke first, his tone sincere. 'Mademoiselle Anna, please forgive me. I meant no disrespect, and I will do as you say.' He glanced at the clock on the mantelpiece and drained his cup, setting it carefully on a table. 'I should get back to the cemetery. I will ask Céline for some mustard seeds before I go. Goodnight, Mademoiselle Anna. Goodnight, Viktor.' He gave each of us a formal little bow, even Christine, and went to the door. 'Sleep well, Maman, and try not to worry.'

We bade him goodnight and wished him luck on the patrol. He nodded, then turned and left the room, closing the door behind him with a soft click. Anna looked at the clock and smiled at Christine.

'It is late, and we have much to achieve tomorrow,' she said. 'With your permission, we will retire for the night.'

'Let me show you to your rooms,' Christine said. She led us up the stairs and opened the door to a neat, clean, functional bedroom which had a connecting door to a room beyond. 'As you are brother and sister, I thought this might suit you,' she smiled. 'Your luggage is there, and I regret that I neglected to ask for the key to your trunk so Céline could unpack for you.'

'What a delightful room!' Anna looked about her with obvious pleasure. 'This will suit us perfectly, will it not, Viktor?'

'Indeed it will,' I agreed. 'Thank you, Christine…and please do not worry about the trunk. We can deal with it ourselves.'

Anna twinkled at me and I wondered if she was thinking, as I was myself, that I had never had to unpack my own trunk in my life.

We said goodnight to Christine and after the door had closed behind her and her soft steps had faded away, we wandered around the two bedrooms, one of which overlooked the Rue Saint-Martin and the other the yard behind the house. Anna claimed the front room for herself, and I happily settled into the other. I peered out of the window, but could see nothing in the darkness, so I drew the drapes and turned my attention to the important issue of nightwear. I suspected Céline would come and wake us in the morning. If she did, she would see immediately that I was not a boy. I laid out my few possessions on the floor at the foot of the bed and sat there staring at them. Anna came in through the connecting door and stood watching for a moment.

'What are you doing? Are you all right?'

'How can I maintain this disguise overnight, Anna? Céline will see I am a girl!'

'Ah!' Anna turned and went into her room again. I heard the sound of the trunk being opened, there was some rummaging, and a moment later she was back. Her arms were full of fabric, which she thrust at me with a pleased look on her face.

'What's this?' I automatically held out my arms to take the items.

'Your new wardrobe,' she said. 'I always have a trunk waiting for me wherever I go, so it was easy enough to send a message asking Henri to add some men's clothing for you. I suspected you might end up coming with me.'

'Henri?' I stared at her, confused. Anna paused for a moment, a little flush blooming in her cheeks. She bit her lip and sighed softly.

'The people I work for have a network of agents worldwide,' she said. 'Most of the people working for them do not have the abilities I have, so they serve the organisation by acting as facilitators for those of us who go out into the world and interact with the various otherworldly creatures we spoke of before. Henri manages transport and accommodation in this area, for example, and there is a man in Paris who deals with clothing. Another deals with documents and tickets.'

'Henri knew who you were all this time?' I felt the rug being pulled from beneath my feet once again and glared at her, the hurt showing on my face. 'Were any of the people we stayed with actually who they said they were, or has it all been one great big deception?'

Anna sighed. 'Please don't be like that! Of course they were who they said they were. They know Henri, and that he works for an organisation which sometimes requires accommodation for people, but they do not know why, or who any of their guests are. They just know there will be no trouble, and a generous payment for their discretion.'

'So 'Renée really is Henri's aunt?' I persisted.

'Yes. She is. Now, look at what I have brought for you.'

Anna reached for one of the garments, pulling it from the tangle and holding it up for inspection. It was a gentleman's nightshirt, a very good quality one, too, I noticed. Distracted, I pawed through the clothes, discovering a new suit, several shirts, a couple of neckties and a more casual outfit. I held one of the shirts against myself and found it was enormous. Anna bit her lip, cocking her head to one side as she regarded me.

'We might need to adjust one or two of these,' she murmured, smiling. 'Either way, it gives you some options. There should be a nightcap in there, too, which will help to disguise your hair.'

'Does Henri know I am a girl?'

'He may have guessed, but it really doesn't matter,' Anna said, dismissively. 'Henri has worked for the organisation for some years now and he is discretion itself.'

'I am guessing that the story about his mother was a fabrication.' My voice was more sullen than I had intended and Anna rolled her eyes.

'Please, try to see it from my perspective. I don't even know your name. We encountered each other by chance that night in Dover. You could have been anyone.' She paused and smiled at me. 'Yet...it seems we are a good match, does it not? I can deal with vampires, and you have a strange creature which materialises out of fog to protect you. I think my employers will be very interested. You're observant and intelligent, speak French as though you live here, and are far more willing to embrace change than most girls of your class. You are also very strong. Think of everything you have been through these past few days.'

As I gaped at her, my cheeks flushed red, she continued to regard me thoughtfully, that soft smile playing at the corners of her mouth. 'Yes,' she said. 'I think you might make a superb operative. Would you like to do this kind of work, do you think?'

I gaped at her, not sure what to say. 'I don't really understand what it is you do,' I managed. 'It certainly seems interesting…'

At this, Anna collapsed in a fit of giggles. 'Come,' she said, reaching for the suit and shaking it out. 'Let us hang these in the wardrobe. We are both tired and we have a long and busy day ahead of us.'

We chatted about the case as we dealt with my new clothes, but Anna refused to give an opinion about what had happened, as there was not enough information and she had not yet seen the grave itself. My logic told me that François was probably right, and the culprit was a dog, but even as I thought it, I kept reminding myself that vampires really did exist, and a sliver of doubt insinuated itself into my rock-solid argument.

I donned my new nightwear and pulled the cap over my hair as far as possible. I doubted Céline would be fooled, but perhaps my height and the unlikeliness of a girl going about dressed as a man would be enough to prevent her from looking too closely or questioning anything. All the same, after Anna had retired to her own room, leaving the connecting door open, I lay awake for a long time, mulling over the events of the day. The more I thought about it, the more I realised that the world held far more wonders than I had ever imagined, and I fell asleep excited for the coming day, no matter what it brought. As I drifted off, I thought back to the question I had asked de Vaux.

What *had* Louise Bernier been doing in the cemetery?

Chapter 17

The following morning, we awoke early. As I forced my eyes open, I could hear Anna already moving around in the next room. Céline tapped on my door gently and I croaked a 'Good morning' as she placed a jug of water on the washstand and opened the curtains. She then went into Anna's room, and I heard the two of them talking about what a beautiful day it was and whether we would prefer breakfast downstairs or in our rooms. Anna decided we would eat downstairs.

I snuggled under the blankets for a little longer, trying to absorb every moment of bliss in this comfortable bed. I had slept well, untroubled by dreams, and would have been happy to remain where I was for the rest of the day.

Anna poked her head around the door frame and regarded me. 'Hurry up!' she urged. 'We have much to do this morning and we are seeing de Vaux at ten, remember.'

I gave a dramatic sigh and dragged myself from the bed's warm embrace. As I hurriedly washed, standing to one side of the window, I peered out into the stark morning sun. As Christine had described, the green fields of the Bernier farm beyond the end of the garden stretched off to the right, back towards the Rue Beauchamp. In the other direction, off to the left, was a line of tall evergreens, which I guessed must be part of the boundary of the cemetery. From somewhere not far away, I heard a cow lowing.

Christine was already seated in the dining room when we entered. She smiled as we took our seats and rang a little silver hand bell that lay on the table in front of her. Céline appeared with coffee, pastries, bread and cheeses, which she served with a cheery smile. She was just cutting cheese for Anna when François walked in, groomed and smiling. He gave us another of his formal little bows, then slipped into the seat next to his mother and reached for the coffee.

'Maman says you wish to inspect the grave, Mademoiselle Anna,' said François. 'I will be happy to escort you. I can also explain how we have been organising the patrols, if it would be useful.'

'Extremely useful!' Anna smiled at him. 'Thank you.'

François smiled back, his whole face lighting up. Again, I mused on how attractive he was. I would be happy to spend time in his company.

Anna caught me looking at François and flashed the tiniest of winks at me. I felt my cheeks redden and turned my focus to my coffee cup. For a fleeting moment, I had completely forgotten that I was disguised as a boy.

Breakfast over, we set off for the cemetery, François leading the way and pointing out various houses as we walked along the Rue Saint-Martin. 'That is the home of Madame LeBrun. Our neighbour says she is a witch and keeps a toad in a box by her bed,' he announced cheerfully, indicating a small, shabby cottage on the opposite side of the road. It had a single window overlooking the street and a battered front door which was badly in need of replacing. 'She's not a witch, of course, and I have never seen her with a toad, but she does talk like this...' He began to impersonate the high, rasping tones of an elderly woman so precisely that Anna and I were soon reduced to fits of laughter. Emboldened by our reaction, François launched into an impersonation of Guy de Vaux, which was uncannily accurate. This brought us to the cemetery gates, and all three of us fell silent as we approached.

The cemetery was beautiful in its poignancy. Elegant carved mausoleum tombs stood in regiments, with avenues passing between them. There were some which almost resembled churches, so grand were they, while others, more modest, consisted of a headstone surrounded by a low fence or iron railings. Anna asked some questions about the layout of the cemetery, and

François paused to point out several features which were obscured by the tombs, or the shrubbery, or both, in the case of the path which led out of the cemetery and along the edge of the Bernier property. The cemetery was rectangular, with a stretch of the Rue Saint-Martin forming one of its long sides. We walked around for a few minutes, Anna stopping now and then to listen, or to examine a particular grave, or to write something in a notebook she pulled from the small, neat bag she carried. All at once, she looked across at François and asked him to take us to the de Vaux grave.

'This way,' he said, indicating. We followed him along the paths, Anna still looking around her. I tried to keep track of the direction and the number of corners we rounded, but soon had to admit to myself I was horribly lost. Following François's confidant strides, I turned my attention instead to Anna. She was still looking around her, although what she was seeing, I could not tell. Her gaze was focused, and her expression fixed, eyes darting everywhere, recording all she saw. She was paying particular attention to the less elaborate graves, I noticed, slowing occasionally to peer at them.

'We are heading towards the Bernier farm, are we not?' she asked suddenly. François looked at her with admiration, nodding.

'Yes, Mademoiselle, you are correct. And the de Vaux plot is just around this next corner.'

The grave was not as I had expected it. Seeing the grandeur of the de Vaux house, I had imagined that their final resting place would be one of the larger mausoleum-style vaults. However, François stopped next to a square plot surrounded by a low fence of ornate cast-iron railings about two feet high. A statue of an angel, wings folded, hands extended as if in prayer, graced a tall square column in the centre of the plot and was surrounded by eight understated gravestones proclaiming dates of birth and death for various members of the family. Louis de Vaux's grave, with its new white marble headstone, was front and centre, the angel appearing to be blessing him from above. To my surprise, all were simple lawn graves. I had expected a ledger stone, or a grave kerb, perhaps, with its centre filled with gravel or a graceful stone vase for flowers, yet all I saw were gentle mounds of neatly trimmed grass.

All except for de Vaux's, of course. The sexton had replaced the turf after the funeral, but the disturbance had knocked much of it away and the once-neat squares of grass now lay in a jumble amid the earth from the hole which had been dug in the centre of the grave. Anna stood silent for a moment, head bowed, then hitched up her skirts and climbed over the railings. François averted his gaze from her ankles, and I confess I gaped. It would never have occurred to me to do something like that if I had been wearing skirts. Following, I leaned over and looked at the ravaged grave, biting my lip. Anna glanced up at me and was about to say something when we heard a loud shout. Turning, I saw a stocky man with a long, dark beard and broad, powerful shoulders, who had paused at the end of the path and was glaring at us. François looked over and gave the man a friendly wave.

'Bonjour, Monsieur Arnal,' he called. 'This is Mademoiselle Anna Stenberg and her brother Viktor, here to investigate the vampire!'

The man frowned and stomped heavily along the path towards us. 'What are you doing to that grave?' he demanded. 'Do you know whose grave it is?'

Anna glanced at me and rolled her eyes before turning to Arnal with a charming smile. 'Good day to you, Monsieur,' she said. 'You are the sexton, I presume?'

'I am.' Arnal stared down at the grave. 'What are you doing?'

'As Monsieur Archambeau just said, I am investigating this matter on behalf of the de Vaux family,' Anna replied, a little edge creeping into her tone. 'I am glad to make your acquaintance, Monsieur. Perhaps you can answer some questions for me.'

'You are the investigator from Paris?' Arnal's eyes widened. 'Forgive me, Mademoiselle, I did not mean any disrespect to you.' He held out a hand, and when Anna took it, he raised her fingers to his lips. 'Please, ask me anything.' Turning to me, he bowed. I nodded and did likewise. François, I noticed, had moved back a little, his expression dark. Arnal had not acknowledged him, nor had he taken any notice when François had introduced Anna and myself. My heart went out to him. No longer a boy, but not quite a man, hovering uncertainly between two worlds. It was something with which I was very familiar, now more than ever.

Anna sat back on her heels next to de Vaux's grave and looked up at Arnal. 'I would be interested to hear your thoughts on this matter, Monsieur.'

Arnal snorted. 'My thoughts? I think you are wasting your time, Mademoiselle.'

'Why, Monsieur?' There was genuine curiosity in Anna's voice.

Arnal chuckled and stroked his beard for a moment. 'I do not believe in vampires,' he said. 'They are creatures of story books, are they not? I am not sure what it is that you do, Mademoiselle, but with the greatest respect, it seems to me that you are chasing fantasies.'

Anna smiled. 'I hear that a lot, Monsieur, and I sincerely hope you will not see the evidence which will prove you wrong. Believe me, it can be extremely unpleasant, especially when the vampire is angry.'

Arnal narrowed his eyes and was silent for a moment. 'What are you telling me? You have seen… a vampire?'

'Seen them, spoken with them, negotiated with them and, on a couple of unfortunate occasions, destroyed them.' Anna dismissed that with a wave of her hand. 'But we are not discussing my qualifications, Monsieur. What do you think happened here?'

Arnal suddenly looked uncomfortable. 'I have my opinions, Mademoiselle, but the subject is hardly fitting for -'

'Oh, please,' she interrupted, with a flare of impatience. 'I am not some delicate little flower, Monsieur. I travel the world dealing with cases such as this. There are few things I have not seen, believe me. I cannot help this community if you keep information from me.'

Arnal blinked, then took a long, deep breath. 'Well,' he began. 'Some years ago, there was a similar occurrence in a different part of Amiens.'

'Another vampire?' Anna asked, with interest. 'No one has mentioned this to me.'

'No, no,' Arnal said, his expression darkening. 'It is not discussed. By anyone.' He lowered his voice, glancing around as if he feared being overheard. 'Some years ago, something almost identical happened in another graveyard in Amiens.'

'Almost identical?' I asked.

Arnal nodded. 'On that occasion, graves were not only dug up like this one, but...' He broke off, shaking his head. 'Bodies were removed.'

I felt a wave of nausea wash over me and even Anna blinked, a glimmer of repulsion flickering across her face before her expression settled once more into what I now realised was a mask. Whatever emotion she was experiencing was carefully concealed. 'Removed,' she repeated. 'Can you elaborate?'

'I would rather not, Mademoiselle.' Arnal took a step back and folded his arms across his broad chest. 'It was a terrible thing to happen.'

'You were the sexton then?' I asked. 'You found them?'

He nodded, lips tightening beneath his beard. 'I had never seen anything like it, and I hope I never will again.' He looked at us, this time including François. 'You are young, and while I do not doubt, Mademoiselle, that your travels have shown you many things, believe me when I say that whatever else may be in the world, the worst monster of all is man.'

I glanced at François and saw him watching Arnal with a frank curiosity, his eyes bright with fascination. Turning back to Anna, I saw she looked much the same, but with a distance about her which suggested she was turning things over in her mind.

'You believe a man was responsible for that atrocity?' I asked.

Arnal nodded. 'I heard someone in Paris had confessed to the crime. It never happened again, I am glad to say, until now.'

'Paris?' Anna looked interested. 'I will contact my employers and request information. If anything surfaced in Paris, they should know of it. How long ago was it?'

Arnal considered. 'Almost twenty years now. I have not thought of it in a very long time.' He looked down at the grave, shaking his head again. 'Monsieur de Vaux was a good man,' he said, his voice tinged with sorrow. 'A godly man. This is a terrible thing.'

'Viktor,' Anna said. 'Come and look at this, brother. What do you see?'

Taking a deep breath, I climbed over the railing and crouched on the opposite side of the grave, marvelling once again at how easy movement was when one was not trapped inside a corset or hobbled with layers of petticoats.

Anna pointed at the disturbed earth. The hole was roughly as de Vaux had described it, right in the centre of the grave.

Heart pounding, I made a show of peering at it, trying to calm my racing heartbeat. What did she expect me to say? All I could see was a hole dug into a grave. Think, I told myself. Observe. Take your time.

'The hole is quite shallow, only a foot or so deep, as Monsieur de Vaux said.' I spoke slowly, trying to buy myself some time, and looked at the bottom of the hole. 'It does look as though something dug down, rather than up, though.'

Anna tilted her head to one side. 'What makes you say so?'

I frowned, unable to repress a shudder as I thought about what lay just a few feet beneath me. 'Surely the earth would have been far more disturbed than this if a man had pushed his way out of a coffin.'

Arnal harrumphed and François let out a low whistle. Anna sat back on her heels, a proud smile on her face.

'You have a good mind, my dear brother, and I always value your insights,' she said. 'Monsieur Arnal, can you recall if there were any dogs in the cemetery around the time of Monsieur de Vaux's burial?'

Arnal gave a wry smile. 'There are always dogs in the cemetery, Mademoiselle. That mangy cur of Bernier's for one. If it was not for what happened to Louise Bernier, I would dismiss the entire thing as the work of a dog.'

'Were there paw prints around the grave?' Anna asked.

'By the time I was summoned, Mademoiselle, people had been in there. If there were paw prints, I never saw them.'

Anna nodded. 'I understand.' She stood and shook out her skirts, then climbed back over the railings to join François on the path. Arnal and I followed. Anna held out her hand to Arnal, who took it and bowed.

'I hope you get this business cleared up quickly, Mademoiselle,' he said. 'I don't begin to understand what you do, but if you can help to settle matters, a lot of people will be very grateful.'

Anna gave him a warm smile. 'I can assure you I will do everything in my power to assist, Monsieur. Now, I do not want to keep you from your duties...'

She left the hint hanging as I offered Arnal my hand. He clasped it and nodded, then acknowledged François briefly, more as an afterthought for appearances' sake, I thought, than anything else. He walked off along the path, turned a corner and disappeared from view. In the serene, still air, I could hear his firm steps fading into the distance. As they did, Anna went back towards the grave, taking a small object from her bag. She fiddled with it briefly, then leaned over the railing and started waving it about. I realised she was sprinkling seeds around de Vaux's grave.

Anna shook the last few seeds from what I now saw was a simple twist of paper and smiled at us. 'This is merely a precaution, you understand. I am seeing nothing as yet to convince me of the presence of a vampire. I need to examine this place thoroughly.'

François and I both nodded. 'What would you be looking for?' François asked. 'There must be things we patrolmen should be looking out for.'

'As my brother pointed out, if a body had left this grave, the earth would be much more disturbed,' Anna explained. 'It is also common for there to be a spate of attacks, not just one isolated one. Usually, the vampire's family are the victims, yet Louise Bernier is not a member of the family. I take it there has been no other activity in the cemetery?'

'Activity?' François looked puzzled.

'More disturbed graves,' Anna said.

'Ah.' François shook his head. 'No, Mademoiselle, nothing that I am aware of.'

Anna pursed her lips, then cocked her head as a distant clock chimed the quarter hour. 'We must hurry if we are to meet with Monsieur de Vaux at ten,' she said. 'François, please could we trouble you to escort us to the de Vaux house by the most direct route?'

François looked delighted. 'It would be my pleasure,' he said, bowing slightly. 'Please come this way.'

Anna paused for a moment next to one of the mausoleum tombs opposite the de Vaux plot, looking at something, then turned her gaze back to François and thanked him. He led us through the maze of mausoleums, past stone crosses and grieving angels, past graves loaded with fresh flowers and memorials whose floral tributes had long since died, giving them a forlorn, neglected feel. We left the cemetery by a small, discreet side entrance which led into a narrow road. François pointed to our right, where a hedge lined the route, tall and overgrown.

'That is the Bernier farm,' he said. 'Look, there in the hedge is a gate. If you need to visit them in the future, you can take a short-cut to the house through the fields. Today, though, I will show you to the door.'

Anna nodded and when we reached the gate, she paused, looking into the field at the cows and sheep. I marvelled once again at the incongruity of a farm, even a tiny one like this, in the midst of a town. It must be so odd to live alongside the noise and bustle, not to mention the stench.

François set a brisk pace, and as we approached the end of the road, the hedge gave way to the side of a barn, which in turn gave way to a row of small cottages. At the end of the road, François turned to the right, leading us down a steep road with houses on both sides. A couple of minutes later, we found ourselves standing outside the De Vaux house, and I began to understand where everything was in relation to the cemetery. A carriage stood outside the house, a bored-looking coachman regarding us with a disinterested expression.

'Thank you for your assistance, this morning, François,' Anna smiled. 'You have been a great help, and I appreciate it.'

He beamed, looking suddenly younger and somehow vulnerable. 'It was my pleasure, Mademoiselle,' he said. 'I hope the rest of your day goes well, and if I can assist you again, please send someone to the house. I shall be there helping my mother today.'

Anna thanked him again and assured him she would send word if she needed him. He bowed and set off down the hill towards the Rue Saint-Martin, humming a jaunty tune. We watched him go, then went to the front door and rang the bell.

As its clanging died down and we waited for Sylvie's footsteps to approach along the hall, Anna caught my arm and pulled me close. Startled, I leaned down so she could murmur in my ear.

'Let me do the talking,' she said softly. 'It would not surprise me if one of the men we are about to meet is our vampire!'

Chapter 18

Sylvie greeted us warmly and relieved us of our coats and hats, then led us along the corridor to de Vaux's study. As she approached the door, I noticed her fussing with her uniform, straightening the neat cap and smoothing the already pristine apron. Anna caught my eye and raised an eyebrow.

Sylvie was about to knock when Anna said quickly, 'How have the gentlemen been this morning?'

Sylvie started and stared at her, then shook her head, looking uncomfortable. 'Not good, Mademoiselle,' she whispered, then tapped at the door before Anna could engage her further. A creeping dread crawled up my spine and I was relieved that Anna was going to be handling this discussion.

De Vaux bid us enter. He rose from behind a grand walnut desk as Sylvie opened the door and ushered us inside. 'Mademoiselle and Monsieur Stenberg, Monsieur,' she announced.

There were four other men in the room, all of whom were getting to their feet and regarding us with varying degrees of interest and hostility. Sylvie busied herself setting out chairs for us. De Vaux asked for coffee and Sylvie curtseyed and vanished, closing the door silently behind her.

'Good morning to you both.' There was relief in de Vaux's voice and the tension in the room was obvious. 'I trust your accommodation was comfortable?'

I nodded and Anna assured him we had had a most pleasant night. De Vaux flashed a quick smile which did not reach his eyes, then turned to the four other men to introduce us.

Inspector Jean Escoffier of the Sûreté was in his early forties, I guessed, six feet tall, stout, rugged and reminiscent of Arthur. He shook hands firmly, eyeing me with interest, then bent to kiss Anna's hand with great aplomb. 'I am delighted to make the acquaintance of someone who undertakes such interesting work,' he said to her as he straightened. I shot a hard glance at him, but to my surprise, he seemed genuine, with no malice or sarcasm evident in his expression. Anna nodded, a soft smile on her lips.

'A pleasure to meet you too, Inspector. My employers always encourage good working relationships with the local law enforcement, and I trust we will be able to work alongside each other in this case.'

Escoffier took in every detail of her deep blue gown, the neat coiffure, her elegant poise, and graceful hands. 'I look forward to hearing more about this work you do,' he remarked as he sat down again, flipping the tails of his coat as he did so. For a moment, I was reminded of my father and wrenched my attention away from Escoffier's keen grey eyes. De Vaux was introducing Mayor Frossard.

Frossard was probably around fifty but looked considerably older. He was some inches shorter than me and made it clear that this did not please him in the slightest. His waistcoat buttons strained across his girth as he extended a hand to me, and as I shook it, I could have sworn I heard the buttons creaking against the fabric. He turned to Anna with open hostility. 'Monsieur, Mademoiselle,' he said in clipped, nasal tones, his dark, beady eyes narrowed. 'I trust this unfortunate business can be concluded as swiftly as possible.'

Anna regarded him. 'Indeed, Monsieur. Provided everyone assists me and holds nothing back, of course.' Frossard shifted from foot to foot and did not meet her gaze. He rubbed his bulbous nose. 'I still feel this is a waste of time. The grave must be opened!'

'You have proof, Mayor Frossard, that Monsieur de Vaux is indeed a vampire?' Anna asked, her voice sharp. 'I would be glad if you would make that evidence available to me at your earliest convenience, then, particularly if you wish the matter to be resolved promptly.'

Frossard opened his mouth but only a strangled sound emerged, and he closed it again with a snap. Anna raised an eyebrow, waiting, eyes fixed on Frossard, who crumpled under her gaze and looked away. *He has nothing*, I thought. *He is all bluster and no substance.*

A small, wiry white-haired man in his sixties, with gold-rimmed pince-nez, rolled his eyes and stepped forward. 'I am Père Michel Grondin,' he said before de Vaux could introduce him. 'I also have little understanding of what exactly you are here to do, Mademoiselle, but if it prevents an unnecessary exhumation, then I will give you as much assistance as I am able.'

Frossard snorted at the priest and threw himself back into his chair with ill grace. The fourth man let out an exclamation of frustration. He too was in his forties, but where Escoffier was neatly groomed, his hair slicked back, collar pristine and trousers pressed, this man was crumpled and shabby. He was wiry and lean, deeply tanned, and when de Vaux hastily interjected with an introduction, I was not surprised to learn that this was Maurice Bernier, father to the unfortunate Louise.

'We must dig up that body!' Bernier exclaimed, and I heard a note of desperation in his voice, a tightly strung hysteria.

'I have been to inspect the grave site this morning,' Anna told him. 'At this stage, I cannot see any reason to believe there is a vampire, nor to insist upon an exhumation.'

'We need to know the truth before we are all murdered in our beds!' Frossard spun round in his chair to face Anna.

'That is not the vampire's way,' Anna replied, her voice calm and pleasant, dripping with scholarly authority. 'The vampire's mission, if you will, is to seek humans and drink their blood. Very few vampires of my experience actively seek to kill off their food supply.'

Bernier gave a dismissive snort and folded his arms, looking Anna up and down. I saw the tiniest smile flit across her face.

'Tell me, Monsieur le Mayor,' she said, 'if you believe you are likely to be murdered in your bed, perhaps you would be so kind as to explain what has happened to make you think that way. How many murders have there been since the attack on poor Mademoiselle Bernier?'

Frossard opened his mouth to retort, then closed it again, staring at Anna. She persisted. 'How many of the patrolmen have been attacked? After all, they are conveniently placed for a vampire, are they not, sitting right next to its resting place for hours on end?'

No one answered, and for a minute or two, the room was full of movement. Pursing his lips, his already ruddy face taking on a deeper hue, Frossard shifted in his seat for a moment, then snorted and turned abruptly to look out of the window. Escoffier got up and moved to the fireplace where he stood with arms folded, one hand up at his mouth. From where I was sitting, it looked as though he was concealing a smile. Père Michel sighed and shook his head, and returned to his seat, fingers twitching on his knees. Anna and I took the opportunity to settle ourselves into our own chairs. As I sat, I glanced at de Vaux, whose hands were clasped in front of him on the desk, knuckles gleaming white through the skin.

'As mayor,' Frossard began, finding his voice, 'I have a duty to the people to ensure they can go about their business safely. This issue has caused widespread concern and, in some cases, hysteria. People are afraid. Some of them have long memories and certain old stories are being dredged up again.'

'And I am sure you are doing your part by providing Inspector Escoffier with all the resources he needs to police this case effectively,' I said, then caught myself when I noticed Anna's expression darken a little. Escoffier coughed, a twinkle in his eye. However, when he spoke, his pleasant, mellow voice betrayed no humour whatsoever.

'We are seeing an increase in reports from people claiming to have been followed by a strange creature,' he remarked. 'Including a giant bat, just yesterday. There is also a noticeable rise in hoaxers running around in sheets, scaring people.'

'Ridiculous,' muttered de Vaux under his breath. Frossard turned on him.

'You may think it ridiculous, Guy, but look at the amount of trouble you are causing with your stubbornness! I feel we have a justifiable reason for requesting an exhumation, and the fact that you are so set against it suggests you are afraid of what we might find inside that coffin!'

De Vaux shot to his feet with such force that his chair fell backwards, landing with a thump on the thick carpet. His nostrils flared and he looked suddenly wolfish. 'How dare you, Gaston!' he hissed, fury in every syllable. 'How dare you sit in my house, piling slur after slur on my dear father, whom you knew well!'

Frossard started to reply, but de Vaux thundered on. 'You, who has sat at our table, you who played cards with my father! You, who withholds funds from the police!'

'Guy.' Escoffier moved towards the desk; hands held out in a calming gesture. 'This is not helping.'

Frossard's face turned an alarming shade of purple and he was about to retort when there was a loud knock on the door, which opened to admit Sylvie, laden with a tray of coffee. Armand appeared behind her, having clearly opened the door for her. He took in the scene: his father, snarling and hurt, leaning over his desk, Frossard scowling back, Escoffier watching them both with narrowed eyes, while the rest of us looked on. I gave Armand a sympathetic smile and nod, but he ignored me. He stared at us all with a look of disgust, then closed the door with a loud bang, making Sylvie jump. The cup she was setting on the sideboard rattled in its saucer.

De Vaux seemed to slump. He turned and righted his chair, then sank into it. There was silence while Sylvie served the coffee. Although clearly nervous in the strained atmosphere, she almost flew round the room. I had never seen drinks served with such speed, particularly by someone whose hands were shaking so much. She handed the final cup to Monsieur Bernier, collected the empty tray and practically ran out into the hall.

The moment the door closed behind her, Frossard set his coffee on de Vaux's desk. 'Don't bring up this funding nonsense,' he hissed. 'I won't tolerate you using these baseless slurs on my office as a smokescreen to hide the truth about your father!'

'Indeed?' De Vaux narrowed his eyes. 'I think it more likely that you are focusing on my poor father in order to divert attention away from your own activities, Frossard.'

'Gentlemen!' Père Michel said, a note of impatience in his voice. Both men ignored him. I noticed Escoffier open his mouth to speak, then think better of it. Bernier was gaping at the scene, clutching his cup.

'Have you any idea how much it costs to put extra police officers in place?' Frossard demanded.

'I know how much I could spend to provide a properly funded, first-rate police force,' de Vaux spat back.

Frossard's face twisted into a sneer. 'I grow bored of your tedious rhetoric, de Vaux. Extra police would not be required if you would simply agree to the exhumation and end the matter once and for all. Do not attempt to lay this difficulty at my door. Unless, of course, that is what this is about.'

Anna was sipping her coffee, apparently paying little attention to what was happening. At first, I was puzzled about why she was not taking command of the room, impressing them with her knowledge, but I suddenly realised that was not the point here. She was letting them talk, reveal things, demonstrate their relationships. I leaned back in my chair, fascinated, wondering what she was finding out, and which way the conversation would turn next.

'If I may.' Père Michel's voice rang out sharp and clear and everyone froze for a moment, responding to the unmistakeable authority of a man accustomed to addressing large crowds and guiding people through their greatest challenges. He peered at us all, myopically disdainful. 'The Church's view is that the human body is sacrosanct. I do not need to explain that to a room full of good, church-going Christians. You are also aware that the Church frowns on exhumation unless there is a very good reason. In this particular case, I am extremely uncomfortable and would prefer some form of solid evidence to persuade me that exhumation is the correct course of action.'

De Vaux threw a look of gratitude at the priest, but I noticed that Père Michel did not meet his eye. Bernier had lapsed into sullen silence, coffee all but forgotten in his rough hands. De Vaux looked at Anna and when he spoke, his voice was tentative.

'Mademoiselle Stenberg? What have you discovered so far?'

Anna raised an eyebrow. 'Having only arrived late last night, I am sure you will not be surprised when I tell you that, as yet, I have insufficient evidence to offer an informed opinion either way.' She eyed them all. 'Usually, in genuine vampire cases, humans have disturbed their environment in some way, which triggers a reaction or retaliation. Such matters can generally be resolved satisfactorily by negotiation, but I have yet to see anything to suggest there is anyone here to negotiate with.'

Frossard gave an indignant snort, Bernier muttered something unpleasant sounding under his breath and Père Michel leaned forward a little, looking thoughtfully at her, cup half-way to his lips. De Vaux sat back in his seat, a flicker of triumph on his face.

'I see,' Escoffier said and, looking at his intelligent expression, I believed he did. 'What are your initial thoughts?'

Anna finished her coffee and leaned forward to set the cup on de Vaux's desk, but Escoffier moved to her and took it from her, placing it on the desk himself. He stepped back with a small bow, and I noticed his eyes never left Anna's face. Feeling a smile threatening, I busied myself with another mouthful of coffee, waiting for Anna to gather her thoughts.

She began to speak, and as she did, I realised all five men were hanging on every word, eager to see which of their individual agendas she favoured. She began to list her observations; insufficient disturbance of the grave itself, no further attacks, no sightings from any of the patrolmen. 'All of this is highly irregular if a vampire is responsible,' she concluded. 'I have taken the liberty of sprinkling some seeds around the grave to act as a deterrent, just in case, but — '

Frossard interrupted with another unpleasant snort. 'Ridiculous!' he spat. 'Have you forgotten about the attack on poor Mademoiselle Bernier? Surely that is evidence enough! What do you want, the entire town to be drained of blood?'

Anna turned and fixed him with a cold stare. After a moment, he wilted and when she continued to stare silently at him, he shifted in his seat and eventually mumbled an apology.

'It is that kind of language which fires people up and causes hysteria.' Anna's voice dripped disdain. 'I suspect it would not be hard to pinpoint the source of most of the issues you are having with rumours and panic.' Frossard looked indignant, but Anna held up a hand and he froze, mouth open like a floundering fish. 'One of the most unpleasant things which can happen in a case like this involves the graves near the suspected vampire. On occasion, the vampire itself digs into them and creates more of its own kind. I noticed, Monsieur le Mayor, that your family tomb is just opposite the de Vaux plot.'

Frossard's eyes opened wide and his jaw dropped. 'What...what are you saying?' he breathed, his voice suddenly strangled and hoarse.

'I would have thought that was obvious.' Anna leaned forward, her eyes two shafts of ice, boring into him. 'If there is a vampire, and if it is minded to create some companions, your own family members could be at risk.'

Frossard looked horrified. 'But...but...that has not... no graves have been disturbed...' he stammered.

'Precisely my point.' Anna looked round the room. 'Gentlemen, I am not ready to offer an opinion, but I will say this. Nothing I have seen or heard thus far has convinced me that we are dealing with a vampire. I should have an answer for you by Friday at the latest. Inspector Escoffier, what provisions have been made for the likelihood that a human element is at work here?'

Escoffier flashed Anna an approving look. 'I regret that nothing specific has been put in place as yet for that eventuality.'

'Oh?' Anna cocked her head. 'Yet surely that would have been seen as the most natural explanation?'

Escoffier gave an elegant and very Gallic shrug. 'Monsieur le Mayor had a different view and requested that we proceed according to his instructions,' he said. 'Since then, we have been far too busy dealing with the unrest the rumours have caused, alongside our normal day-to-day duties.'

Frossard once again started spluttering and stammering in indignation, and this time, I noticed a slight frown on Bernier's face as he stared at the back of the mayor's head. Père Michel rose and took his empty cup to the sideboard, setting it down quietly. 'Gentlemen,' he said, 'Mademoiselle Stenberg speaks sense. We need to set aside personal differences, and political ones,' he added, looking pointedly at de Vaux and Frossard. 'Surely men in our positions should be working together for the good of the town and its people. This is a strange and unusual set of circumstances, and we must all remember that if we seek God's counsel, He will guide us.' He fixed a disapproving eye on Frossard. 'We are the figureheads of society, gentleman, not a gaggle of hysterical young women...your pardon, Mademoiselle,' he added hastily, as Anna turned to him with raised eyebrows. 'Now, please excuse me, but I am due to meet with the bishop shortly. If you need me, Monsieur and Mademoiselle Stenberg, you may find me at the Church of Saint-Leu, on the opposite bank of the River Somme.'

De Vaux rose and rang the bell behind his desk. Anna thanked the priest for his insights and de Vaux came round the desk to shake his hand. Sylvie appeared and escorted Père Michel from the room.

Frossard took this as a cue and rose to his feet, folding his arms across his belly as he looked down at Anna with distaste. 'Mademoiselle, I shall be aggressively pursuing an exhumation on Friday,' he announced without preamble. De Vaux went white. 'And –'

'As I said,' Anna interrupted in a cold, businesslike voice I had never heard before, 'I should have sufficient information by Friday to provide you with a definitive answer, Mayor Frossard. If you choose to pursue anything, please ensure you pursue it within the law.'

Frossard's eyes bulged, and he gaped for a moment, turning purple once more. I saw de Vaux recover sufficiently to raise an appraising eyebrow, and Escoffier turned away on the pretext of examining the painting above the fireplace. Frossard made a few strangled noises in his throat, then recovered his voice and, with much fuss and a good deal of stammering and bluster, was also escorted out. Escoffier waited until the front door had closed behind him, then left the fireplace and came to sit in the chair next to me. 'Guy, you must stop aggravating him,' he said. 'His policies frustrate us all, believe me.'

Before de Vaux could answer, Anna spoke. 'What exactly would Mayor Frossard have to gain were he behind this whole incident?'

De Vaux blinked at her for a moment, and it was Escoffier who answered. 'Monsieur de Vaux has, in my humble opinion, an excellent chance of being elected as mayor,' he said. 'I have been made aware of rumours of…irregularities…in the mayor's office, but as yet have no firm evidence which would enable me to investigate. All I can do is watch.' He sighed. 'If the rumours are true, Guy will definitely be elected and Frossard's personal losses will be considerable.'

'Ah,' I murmured. 'It is more about what he will lose than what he stands to gain.'

'Precisely.' Escoffier gave me an appraising look.

'All I want is justice for my girl,' Bernier said suddenly, making me start a little. I had almost forgotten him, sitting in his rough, workman's clothes, uncomfortable and out of place in this fine room. 'You see that, don't you, Mademoiselle? All I want is justice. This delay is unacceptable. Whoever, or whatever hurt her, I want there to be consequences. The police have found nothing to suggest a human attacked my Louise, and now you say there may be no vampire, either.'

'No one has been apprehended, Monsieur,' I said quietly. 'That is not the same as saying a human was not responsible for the attack.'

Bernier considered this for a long moment, then nodded. 'Yes, Monsieur Stenberg, that is a good point. Well, I see that all I can do is leave the matter in your hands.'

Anna smiled warmly at him, nodding in understanding. 'I give you my solemn word, Monsieur Bernier, that I will bring this matter to a conclusion, whatever it may be. If there is a human at work here, and punishment is appropriate, that is what I will pursue.' She paused for a moment, then said, 'I will need to speak with Louise.'

'Please attend us at your convenience, Mademoiselle,' Bernier said. 'The maid can fetch me if I am in the fields.'

Anna nodded and Bernier excused himself. De Vaux rang for Sylvie, and Bernier gave us an awkward bow before the door closed behind him. Escoffier huffed out a long breath, leaned back in his chair and stretched out his long legs, looking at de Vaux, who had slumped forward, elbows on the desk, head in his hands. 'Guy?'

De Vaux sighed. He looked exhausted, and I realised the strain he was under. Anna, too, regarded him with sympathy as she got to her feet. Both men immediately stood, and I did the same.

'May I ask what trouble there has been generally in Amiens over this matter?' I asked Escoffier. 'You mentioned reports of hoaxes earlier.'

Escoffier nodded, his face grim. 'We have had a few people outside the city hall and my office, complaining about the lack of police, about the fact that no one has been arrested for the attack on Mademoiselle Bernier…They don't care that there is no evidence. The girl saw so little that we have nothing to work with. As time passes, the number of demonstrations has fallen, although the men are being run ragged by time-wasters. You will notice there are fewer people on the streets around here than one might expect, and those who are out are moving much more quickly than they usually would. People are not pausing to speak to neighbours. Many do not seem to be leaving their houses at all, and there are quite a number of terrified servants running errands.'

I nodded. 'I see… thank you, Inspector.'

Anna gave her hand to de Vaux, then Escoffier, who lingered over it far longer than was strictly necessary. Anna tolerated his attention patiently, bestowing a sweet smile on him when he finally straightened. He reached into his pocket and passed his card to her. As an afterthought, he gave one to me and shook my hand. 'I will be happy to discuss anything to do with the case,' he told Anna. 'Should you need my assistance, please send for me at once. No heroics.' He addressed this to me, and I inclined my head.

'Of course not, Inspector.'

De Vaux rang the bell, then came around the desk to shake Escoffier's hand. 'You are a good friend, Jean.'

Escoffier clapped him on the back and told him to bear up, that the matter would soon be resolved, but we all knew that the outcome might not be to de Vaux's liking. Until Anna and I managed to work out who or what had attacked Louise, the threat of exhumation still hung over the family, the taint of vampirism following them and their servants as they tried to go about their daily routines.

Sylvie fetched coats and hats and showed us all out. Escoffier bowed and set off at a smart pace down the hill towards the Rue Saint-Martin. Anna watched him go; her expression thoughtful.

'You did not ask much of de Vaux today,' I observed in a low voice. 'Or of any of them, really.'

'That was not my original intent. Sometimes, though, more can be learned by letting men talk,' Anna murmured. 'What did you make of that, Viktor?'

I considered. 'Escoffier is a smart and capable man. Practical, too, but clearly hampered by this funding issue which keeps cropping up. He and de Vaux dislike Frossard, and Frossard appears to dislike everyone. I also got the impression that Frossard is very afraid of something, and Bernier is angry and helpless.'

'An excellent appraisal,' Anna said, giving me a quick smile. 'I am inclined to agree with everything you said. Yet you have not answered the most important question. Was our vampire in that room?'

161

Chapter 19

I let the question rattle round in my head for a few moments before answering. 'No.'

Anna raised an eyebrow. 'Oh?'

I took her arm and we moved away from the de Vaux house. 'None of those men would get their hands dirty,' I said. 'And Bernier is Louise's father. Why would he attack his own daughter?'

'Perhaps the answer to that lies in her reason for being in the cemetery.' Anna pursed her lips.

'You think she was doing something she should not, and Bernier was trying to...what? Frighten her into not doing it again?'

Anna chuckled. 'Viktor, she was in a cemetery late at night. Of course she was doing something she should not.'

The idea of wandering round a cemetery, the night still and silent around me, sent a shiver down my spine and part of me could not help admiring Louise. I had spent my entire life doing my best to conform, to be what my parents wanted, what my family expected. Our position in society made that far more difficult; there was always some tedious gossip ready to murmur behind her fan about 'the baronet's granddaughter'. I imagined what those women would make of me if they could see me as I was now, dressed as a man and standing to my full height in a French street, accompanied by a mysterious young woman who spoke to vampires and spent some of her time disguised as a pickpocket. A faint smile played on my lips as I pictured Mrs Armitage's look of horror, but the image brought with it an almost physical pain as I thought of home.

'I need to send a telegram to my uncle,' I said suddenly. 'He must be so worried, even if Arthur managed to find him and give him some reassurance.'

Anna nodded. 'Yes, you should. Why not do that now? I will call on the Berniers and arrange a time to speak with Louise, and I must also contact my employers about that old incident which was mentioned.'

'Do you think it relevant?'

She shrugged. 'Not to the case itself, but it will be useful as an overview of the community and how they react to such things.'

I nodded and we arranged to meet at Christine's for a late lunch. Anna crossed the road and went into the Bernier yard, and I continued down the hill, turning left at the bottom, enjoying the cool, crisp morning and the cheery spring sunshine which turned the nearby river to a sparkling ribbon of diamonds.

Amiens was a pretty cathedral city and I wandered around for a while, enjoying the novelty not only of my surroundings, but also the manner in which I was experiencing them. By the time I had reached the shops, I had perfected my walk and, although I still had a few nerves about my hair giving me away, none of the noticeably few people I saw gave me more than a brief, disinterested glance, the same as any other stranger they passed on the street. I bought a couple of books, a new hat to replace the cap, a pen, some ink and a journal of my own. I also treated myself to a larger travel case and some new undergarments, hovering outside the gentlemen's outfitters for a while before summoning the courage to enter. The proprietor Monsieur Levesque, an older gentleman with thinning grey hair and an impeccable suit, accepted that I was shopping for myself for the first time because my valet was unwell, and guided me through the process like a benevolent uncle. When the thought hit me, I immediately asked him for directions to the nearest telegraph office and he took me to the front of the shop, pointing out a couple of landmarks.

'You may wish to avoid the area around the mayor's office, Monsieur,' he commented as we returned to the counter. He began wrapping my purchases with deft, well-practised moves which I found fascinating. 'There has been some trouble these last couple of weeks, sadly.'

I feigned surprise and innocence. 'Oh?'

Levesque sighed and shook his head. 'The level of foolish superstition in this town is quite remarkable. There are people creating a terrible fuss about vampires, would you believe? Vampires! In these enlightened times!'

'I have heard tell of a vampire in Amiens,' I remarked. Then a thought struck me. 'Although it happened a long time ago, did it not?'

He paused in his work, startled. 'You have heard about that? My, but bad news does have swift wings, does it not?' He shook his head, the leaned forward over the counter and lowered his voice, even though there were no other customers. 'The incident you refer to happened almost twenty years ago now. It was no vampire, young sir, it was a man.'

Remembering his own words, I decided to adopt a sceptical viewpoint. 'I hardly imagined it would be an actual vampire, Monsieur, unless one had somehow managed to step out from the pages of a book!'

Levesque gave an enthusiastic nod. 'Indeed, indeed!'

I asked what exactly had happened, but at that point, another gentleman entered the shop, and the opportunity was gone. I thanked Monsieur Levesque, paid, and asked for everything to be sent to Christine's, addressed to Monsieur Stenberg. Levesque bowed, gave me a warm smile, and assured me that it would be taken care of. I left the shop, musing over the new fragment of information I had gleaned. The previous vampire incident had happened almost twenty years earlier which would make Frossard thirty years old at the time. I considered his unpleasant sneering and his ghoulish insistence on an exhumation and shuddered. Was the attacker on the mayor's payroll, a cog in the mechanics of smearing a political opponent?

My musings paused as I noticed the telegraph office just ahead, and hurried in, mentally composing a note to my uncle. I said nothing of where I was staying, just that I was safe and with a friend. I did not ask about my father. I told Uncle Geoffrey I would collect messages from the telegraph office, and spent a few minutes arranging it with the clerk. I also sent a message to Arthur, thanking him for his kindness and reassuring him that I would compensate him appropriately on my return to Dover.

As I wrote those words, however, something in my belly gave an uncomfortable lurch and it struck me that, strange though my situation was, and with the constant fear of discovery hanging over me, I was enjoying myself. I was doing something useful, although my sense of accomplishment was wildly out of proportion to my actual actions and the amount of help I could provide. I thought back to my life in Dover, the endless tedium of days spent in ladylike pursuits, hurrying past shops I could not linger in, being driven everywhere, being the wallflower at dances. This strange set of circumstances in which I now found myself was exciting. Would that change in time? Would the tiny part of me which currently yearned for the familiarity of home increase as the days passed? Would I come to resent the kind of rootless existence Anna seemed to have, or might I find myself?

A sudden hubbub snapped me out of my reverie, and I looked around, realising I had wandered unconsciously and had lost my bearings. Ahead of me, I could see an imposing, elegant building, the French flag dancing on its roof in the light breeze. Like many of the buildings I had passed in Amiens, both modern and older, its cream stone façade gleamed in the spring sunshine. An untidy knot of people clustered near the main doors, shouting up at the windows. I caught Frossard's name, and, curious, joined a small crowd of a dozen or so passers-by who had paused to watch what was going on.

There were fourteen or fifteen protestors, their voices echoing off the building as they shouted for Frossard to show himself, to reassure them about the vampire, to explain the ineptitude of the police. I wondered idly where the police were based, listening to the comments of the people around me as the crowd of onlookers grew.

'Are they still making a fuss about this vampire nonsense?' demanded an elderly woman, peering around the people in front of her to look at the protestors. 'How ridiculous. Time to let it drop, now.'

One or two people near her murmured their agreement, but the man to my left, who was wearing an immaculate dove-grey suit, tutted audibly, glancing over at her as though he smelled something bad. I could not resist asking, 'You disagree, Monsieur?'

He turned a frown on me. 'Everyone forgets a girl was attacked,' he said in a curt, clipped voice.

'No one has forgotten.' A young woman standing just in front of us turned around and glared at us. 'Perhaps if the police did their job and arrested the man responsible, all this vampire talk would go away.'

'The police are doing their best,' called a man somewhere behind me.

The elderly woman snorted. 'Their best! Ha! If this is their best, I hope we never see their worst.'

'We see their worst every day!' another woman retorted.

'It's Frossard's fault for spending the taxes on whores!'

'How do you know he spends the money on whores?'

'My sister had washing stolen a few weeks ago, and the police did nothing.'

'What was that girl doing out so late, though, eh? And in a cemetery, of all places?'

'Young girls these days…'

The comments and arguments whirled around me, and I was suddenly thrown against the man in the suit as a scuffle broke out somewhere behind us. People tried to move out of the way, others were sent flying as the unseen combatants grunted and scrabbled. I decided it was time to move on. It would not do to be arrested, especially whilst disguised as Viktor. Holding on to my new hat, I started to shoulder my way through the jostling throng of bodies, tripping over feet, being shoved and elbowed, losing my balance and staggering into people, with panic rising in my throat. It had not taken long for the crowd to expand from a handful of observers to an unwieldy emotive throng of thirty or more. I finally broke free of the press of bodies, moving away quickly as I spotted a couple of policemen approaching from the opposite direction. Two or three uniformed guards had come out of the building and were gesticulating at the protestors.

There was a small café nearby, so I decided to go and sit for a while to regain my composure. I took a window seat, ordered a café au lait and waited for my heart to stop pounding. The experience had unnerved me, and my hand shook so badly when I lifted the cup that I had to set it down again. It rattled against the saucer, and an elderly gentleman sitting at a corner table lowered his newspaper to peer at me. I fixed my gaze out of the window, feeling horribly self-conscious and awkward, cheeks flushing in embarrassment. People hurried past with anxious, watchful expressions. No one dawdled. There was an unsettling air of urgency which did little to soothe my frazzled nerves. After a few minutes, my breathing slowed, and my hands steadied sufficiently to allow me to drink my coffee without fear of slopping it into the saucer.

From somewhere nearby, a clock chimed the hour, and I realised I needed to return to Christine's for lunch. I finished the last of my coffee and left some coins on the table, tipped my hat to the waiter as he emerged from behind the serving counter and went back outside into the sun. All seemed quiet now, and when I reached the corner from where I could see the mayor's office, the crowd had dispersed.

I paused, trying to get my bearings, but I had been so distracted when I reached this part of town that I was uncertain which direction I needed to take. I stopped an elderly gentleman and asked him the way to the Rue Saint-Martin. With very bad grace, he pointed out the road I needed. I bowed and thanked him politely, but he dismissed me with a supercilious shake of his head and stalked off, looking very like a heron wading through a river in search of fish.

I stared after the unpleasant man for a moment, then set out for Christine's, enjoying the walk. No one paid attention to me, although a couple of girls of about my age, walking with a woman who I suspected was a governess, paused to turn around and stare at me. At first, I panicked, thinking they had seen through my disguise, but when I saw one of them giggling and peeping at me from beneath lowered lashes, relief made me bold, and I decided to have a little fun. Being careful of my hair, I removed my hat and gave her an elaborate bow, then quickly walked off. Behind me, I could hear giggling and a smile rose to my lips.

The rest of the walk was uneventful, and I found my way easily enough. As I approached Christine's, I could hear raised voices. At first, I did not recognise them, but as I drew level with the end of the house itself, slowing my steps, I realised it was Christine and François in the parlour, arguing. Curious, although feeling horribly guilty, I stopped before I reached the parlour window, and leaned against the house, making sure I would be out of sight if either of them glanced over at the window. I pretended to go through my pockets for something as, holding my breath, I strained my ears.

'Why bring this up now?' I was shocked at the defeat and harshness in Christine's voice. 'Your father has been dead these past nine years. Why all these questions?'

'I want the truth, Maman,' François said, the same hard edge making his voice almost unrecognisable.

'Truth? What truth? What are you talking about?'

'I want to know who I really am!'

'What on earth do you mean?' There was bewilderment in Christine's voice.

'I think you know exactly what I mean, Maman.'

There was a silence, then Christine said, 'Enough of this nonsense, François. I will not tolerate being spoken to in this manner.'

'Why did you pause?'

'What?'

'Why did you pause before you replied? Were you trying to decide which lie to tell me?'

'How dare you?' Christine cried. 'I have no idea what has come over you, young man, but while you live in my house, you will keep a civil and respectful tongue in your head.'

There was a long silence, and I was about to make my way into the house when François said heatedly, 'I don't know what has come over me, either.'

Another silence. I shifted from foot to foot, trying to determine whether they had left the room, and if it was safe for me to walk past the window. Perhaps Christine was working out what to say. I considered whether François was struggling with issues to do with becoming a man. Thinking back to some of my own difficulties after my mother vanished, I felt a rush of sympathy for him. It is difficult to become yourself when you have no one beside you to show you how to go about it.

Even as the thought processed itself, another sped after it. If François was asking about his late father because he wanted to know who he was, that, surely, would have been a reasonable discussion between mother and son, a chance to look back over old memories. Yet this conversation was the opposite. My heart leaped as it suddenly struck me. Was François suggesting his father had not been a good man, and that Christine had pretended he was? The only other thing I could think of, that she might have cause to lie about, was terrible. Was there some doubt about François's parentage?

I huffed out a breath, shocked at the direction my mind had taken. Christine was the picture of respectability, and it was very wrong of me to even think something so awful of her.

Pushing away from the wall, I went to the front door, knocking loudly before opening it, and calling a cheerful, 'Bonjour!' as I entered. There was a slight pause, then Christine appeared in the parlour doorway to my right, her expression strained, but a welcoming smile curving her lips. I bowed politely, noticing as I did so that the smile did not quite reach her eyes.

François slunk out of the parlour behind her, gave an awkward nod in acknowledgement, then excused himself and went along the hall towards the kitchen. A few moments later, the back door to the yard opened and closed and silence fell.

Recovering herself, Christine said, 'A parcel arrived for you, Viktor. Céline has left it on the table in your room.'

'Thank you, Christine,' I smiled, taking off my coat.

'How did you find Amiens?' she asked.

'Very pleasant indeed!' I replied with enthusiasm. 'There were some protestors outside the mayor's office, though. I was caught briefly in a crowd of onlookers.'

'What were they protesting about?' she asked, beckoning me to join her in the parlour. I followed her and took an armchair by the fireplace while she rang the bell for Céline.

'The lack of police action in Mademoiselle Bernier's attack,' I told her. She sighed.

'The police did plenty in the first few days, as far as I am aware,' she said, 'but there was simply no evidence. The trail, as they call it, was cold almost from the outset. That is why people are so frightened, I think, and these ridiculous vampire rumours are not helping in the slightest.'

'The attacker was lucky that Louise saw so little,' I observed.

'Have you spoken to her yet?'

I shook my head. 'Anna is arranging a time for us to see her.'

Christine nodded. 'Gentle discussion with you two may release a memory she has been unable to recall,' she said, hope in her voice. 'Your approach must be so very different to that of the police. Perhaps thinking about things from a completely fresh angle will trigger something.' She sat in the chair opposite me. 'When there are no clues and a grave has been disturbed, some people are bound to start thinking outlandish thoughts, are they not?'

I nodded. 'It seems so. People want answers and will look wherever they have to in order to find them, no matter how outlandish or unlikely.'

Christine smiled then, a proper, warm smile which set her eyes twinkling. 'So wise for such a young gentleman,' she said. 'You sister must greatly value your input into her work.'

I flushed, but she was being sincere, so I smiled and muttered something vague and polite. Céline appeared and Christine gave orders for luncheon, and I excused myself to go and wash. As I mounted the stairs, the two of them were heading for the kitchen, Christine saying something about ordering vegetables.

Céline had made my bed and the window was open to let the cool spring breeze air the room. I gazed out over the yard and the trees beyond for a few moments before going to the table to unpack my goods. Céline brought me a jug of hot water for washing, and told me to leave the items on the table so she could put them away for me while we were having lunch. I thanked her and when she had gone back downstairs, carefully washed my face and hands. The conversation between Christine and François was replaying in my head, along with something else. It was something Christine had said the previous day which suddenly struck me as odd, but all I could summon was a feeling of discomfort, not the actual words themselves. I dried myself on the fluffy towel by the washstand, trying to retrieve some tiny clue from my memory as to what we had been talking about, but whatever it was, it remained elusive.

Keen to see if Anna had returned, I tidied my hair, making sure it was tucked well into my collar, and went downstairs. Her coat and hat were not hanging in the hall, so I decided to sit down in the parlour to wait for lunch.

As I opened the door, François was hunched over the writing desk with a bundle of papers in his hand. He whipped round as I took a step into the room, a furious expression on his face which made me pause, my greeting frozen on my lips. He immediately tried to soften his expression, battling to smooth it into something more neutral, but with little success.

'I did not mean to disturb you…forgive me,' I said quietly, taking an uncertain step back towards the hallway. 'I was wondering if my sister had returned yet.'

'Oh!' His face lit up a little, although not as much as I had come to expect at the mention of Anna. 'She went to the cemetery to do some more investigating. Luncheon will be about half an hour, so we could walk round and collect her, if you like? I wasn't doing anything important,' he added. As he spoke, he stuffed the papers into one of the desk drawers almost without looking at them, closing the drawer with unnecessary force. One of the knickknacks wobbled and he automatically put up a hand to steady it.

'I would be glad of your company,' I said. I wished there was a way to get him to reveal something about what I had overheard without giving myself away as an eavesdropper. 'Let me get my hat.'

As I pulled on my coat, François jogged down the hall to let Christine know we were fetching Anna. He looked at me as he returned. 'New hat? Suits you well. Makes you even taller.'

I gave a little bow. 'Thank you. The height issue is a little unfortunate, though, is it not? It is not like I needed to be any taller.'

He took his coat from a hook and slipped it on, laughing, suddenly very different from the boy I had interrupted in the parlour. 'There is nothing wrong with being tall, you know. I'd be happy to have some of your extra inches!'

We ambled along the road to the cemetery gate. Whereas Arthur had a purposeful, 'don't-mess-with-me' stride, François had a more relaxed lope, and I had to slow my steps a little so I did not march off and leave him trailing in my wake.

We entered the cemetery and found Anna almost at once, heading towards us. She had a small notebook in her hand and was making notes as she walked. 'Ah, perfect timing!' François grinned, bowing to her, and I noticed how much his face had lit up. He seemed to be searching for a little excitement, and now I was learning to appreciate and enjoy the adventures I was having, I could understand how he felt. This would probably be the most exciting time in our lives. François was just a little more open and enthusiastic about how much he was enjoying the chance to be involved in Anna's investigation. 'Céline is serving luncheon soon, Mademoiselle.'

Anna smiled. 'My stomach has just been telling me I should go and eat something,' she said. 'Before we go, Viktor, come and look at this.'

She turned and led us back the way she had just come, stopping beside another recent grave in a grassy plot similar to the de Vauxs'. The turf had not yet been replaced on this one, and the three of us gazed down at the neat mound of bare earth.

'What am I looking at?' I asked.

Anna indicated. 'This burial took place a few days after Monsieur de Vaux's. Look at the dip in the centre.'

I looked where she was pointing and saw there was indeed a shallow indentation in roughly the same place as the hole above de Vaux's coffin. 'I see it,' I said. 'It's very different to de Vaux's.'

'Yes!' Anna beamed, her eyes shining. 'Can you think why that would be?'

The obvious answer was that someone or something had disturbed de Vaux's grave, but not this one. Yet somehow, I did not think that was what Anna was looking for, so, trying not to panic at being placed on the spot in this manner, I turned the matter over carefully in my mind.

'It is evident that something has intentionally dug into the earth of de Vaux's grave. Here, though, it looks to me as though the earth has sunk. Perhaps because the soil used to fill the grave has settled?'

'Explain.' Anna gave me an encouraging smile and I took a deep breath, my cheeks reddening and heart thumping. Hoping I was not making a fool of myself, I spoke slowly, my thoughts feeling their way.

'The earth used to fill a grave will not be as compacted as the surrounding earth, will it? As the soil in the grave settles, it is bound to shift around, which might cause an indentation such as this.'

'Excellent!' Anna regarded me with pride, very much the teacher praising her student. I smiled, relieved that I was somehow on the right track, even though I had no idea what I was doing. Anna bent her head to her notebook to jot something down.

François looked at me with awe, his voice full of admiration. 'I would never have thought of that,' he said. I gave him an awkward smile, hoping he would not want to delve deeper into my reasoning. To my relief, he turned his focus to Anna.

'Have you had a productive day so far?' he asked, sidling over and peering at her notebook. As he drew near, Anna finished what she was writing with a flourish of her pencil, snapped the book shut and whisked it out of sight in the little bag she carried. Disappointed, François instead offered her his arm, which she took, but instead of making for the cemetery gates, she instead directed us further along the path and towards an area full of moss-covered memorials. She led us off the path and we picked our way through the grass, pausing next to a vault tomb. Releasing François's arm, Anna stepped close to the stonework, peering at it.

'Look at this,' she said, indicating.

At first, I did not understand what she meant. I squinted at the engraved marble cover stone, taking in the name, and the dates of birth and death of the person interred beyond it. Yves de Montfort had been just twenty-nine when he died in 1823 and I wondered what had happened to him.

Glancing at Anna, I saw she was watching me intently, the little frown line deepening between her brows as I remained silent. Heat rose in my cheeks and my heart began to pound as I scanned the mossy stone. What was I missing? The name meant nothing to me. Biting my lip, I looked at every tiny part of the stone, desperately trying to imagine what Anna would see. But there was nothing, just a scattering of moss in the centre of the stone, through which the engraved letters were just visible.

I stepped back, looking at the entire building, and was about to concede defeat when something about the next cover stone made me pause. This was identical to that of Yves, but the moss was growing differently across its surface.

'The moss,' I said, thoughts falling into place.

'Yes?' Anna leaned forward, intent.

'It grows differently on these two stones. Here, on this one, it covers the entire stone, but on this one, belonging to Yves, it is only growing in the centre, over the engraving.'

Anna's eyes glinted and she gave me a nod. 'What does it tell you?'

From the corner of my eye, I caught François shaking his head, confusion on his face. 'It's like there is something on the stone, preventing it from growing at the edges.'

She bit her lip. 'Look at the edges, Viktor, really closely. Compare them to the other stone.'

Puzzled, I did as she asked, flicking my gaze between the two. Suddenly it hit me.

'The moss has been brushed away from the edges on this stone. I do not see anything which is holding it in place, either. Yet the other stone clearly has mortar around it. The moss is growing on that, also.'

Anna was nodding at me in satisfaction. 'Meaning?'

'Meaning this stone is not secured. It can be moved.'

François caught his breath, and a chill gripped me, sending a ripple of goosebumps over my body. Leaning forward, I peered at the stone belonging to Yves de Montfort. 'There are patches of discolouration around the edges,' I said.

Something brushed my sleeve, making me start. François joined me, his eyes fixed on the faint, slightly yellowish patches. 'It looks as though there was lichen growing there,' he said finally, straightening.

I stared at the stone, imagining the occupant of the tomb sliding it into place, long, pale fingers whispering over its surface, dislodging the lichen. A shiver coursed down my spine and instinctively, I turned to glance around us. The cemetery was unnaturally still. The air hung, unmoving and empty of birdsong. All I could hear was my own breathing and the rush of blood in my ears as my heart rattled against my ribcage.

'This is where the vampire is?' I whispered. Anna nodded. She was busy treading the grass flat and sprinkling seeds around our feet, and I stepped backwards, drawing François with me, careful we did not tread them into the ground.

François's face was white, and he allowed me to steer him backwards away from the vault. The excitement was gone, his mouth agape, eyes wide with horror. The two of us watched as Anna took a little bottle of clear liquid and sprinkled a few drops in an arc in front of the cover stone.

'What is that for?' François's voice cracked slightly, and he cleared his throat, repeating the question.

'Holy water will also give the vampire pause, providing it is of a clan which is susceptible. Some clans are not.'

'They have clans?'

'Clans, factions, a Supreme Council. Their communities are as complex as ours. There are wars over territory. They fight over individual clans' reactions and responses to humans. Sometimes they fight over prey.'

I blinked at her. 'Prey?'

'They are hunters. Never forget that.' Her tone became business-like, her speech clipped and crisp. 'They may be erudite, learned and compelling, but at their core, they are hunters. Ruthless and untiring.' She slotted the little bottle back into is place in her bag and ran her fingers over the other contents, pausing at one briefly before moving on to the next. Eventually, she sat back on her heels and nodded in satisfaction. 'This will hold him until I can speak with him,' she said.

'Speak with him?'

Anna got to her feet and gripped François's arm. 'I know it is a lot to take in,' she murmured, 'but I need you to try, François. I always speak with the creatures I discover. How am I to understand their difficulties, their situations, if I do not?'

He gaped at her, and she released him, then picked up her bag. Almost automatically, he offered her his arm, which she took, and the two of them walked ahead of me back to the main path. I kept glancing behind me, half-expecting to see Yves de Montfort materialise and start counting the seeds. He did not.

'Do you expect him to confess to attacking Louise?' I asked curiously.

Anna threw a smile over her shoulder. 'No,' she said. 'I do expect him to know what is happening in this cemetery, though. I simply have to persuade him to tell me.'

François actually caught his breath. Anna looked up at him and murmured something in a soothing tone, to which he replied with a brief nod. I confess that the thought of Anna standing in the cemetery conversing with a ruthless, otherworldly hunter, was alarming. Yet if the entire matter could be cleared up after one simple conversation, then so much the better.

As we reached the path, I realised I envied François. We were so similar, he and I, both on the cusp of adulthood, straddling that uncertain chasm between it and childhood, simultaneously both and neither. He might be struggling, but he had Christine to love and guide him, whereas I was alone.

Even as the thought crossed my mind, I recalled Eliza and Mrs Armitage, and a pang of guilt seared through me, bringing unexpected tears to my eyes. Loving and sweet as they both were in their own way, they were not, and never could be, my mother.

I took a deep breath, trying to compose myself and turn my thoughts back to the vampire and the case. I took in the serene landscaping, the silent rows of tombs and memorials, the sentinel trees and protective wall of shrubs insulating the sleeping dead from the bustling world of the living. Despite the drama playing out along the paths between the rows of tombs, it was a peaceful place.

My thoughts were interrupted suddenly by a movement in a bush some distance away and I stiffened, focusing on it. Was that a figure amongst the foliage? I blinked a few times and frowned, peering into the depths of the shady greenery to try to decipher the ragged shadows and make something solid from them. Had someone been watching us?

I stayed like that for several moments, staring at the spot, but whatever I had seen – if, indeed, I had seen anything – had gone.

Chapter 20

'What is it?' Anna called. She and François had paused to see what I was doing. Casting one final look at the foliage, I went to join them.

I described what I had seen. 'Just a vague movement, though. It was probably my imagination.'

Anna looked thoughtful and I saw a frown pause on François's brow for a moment before he smoothed it away. 'Would you like me to investigate?' he asked. I shook my head.

'If there was anyone there watching, they will be long gone now.'

François looked shocked. 'But what of Mademoiselle Anna's safety?' he pressed. 'If someone is watching her, they may mean her harm!'

Anna patted his arm. 'I am grateful for your concern, François, but it is unnecessary, I can assure you.'

François set his jaw stubbornly. 'What if there is another attack? Should we not be guarding that vampire's tomb?'

Anna smiled up at him. 'The movement of the trees does catch the eye sometimes. I noticed it myself while I was working. Viktor is right, François. If someone was watching, they will have fled the moment they realised he had spotted them. You will be chasing your tail. Also,' she added, 'I do not fear an attack. I have a number of skills and am more than capable of defending myself. Monsieur de Montfort will not hurt me.'

François's eyes widened at this, but he lapsed into silence, his expression set and moody, annoyed at having his concerns brushed aside. He said nothing more during the short walk to Christine's, and excused himself as soon as we were inside, running up the stairs into his room. Anna and I exchanged glances but made no comment. Instead, we remarked on the delicious aroma of bread wafting towards us from the kitchen, and as we finished hanging up our coats, Céline appeared at the far end of the hall, looking flustered.

'Please forgive me, I did not hear the bell,' she exclaimed.

'Do not worry yourself, Céline, because we did not ring it,' Anna soothed. 'We returned with Monsieur François and were just commenting on how delicious luncheon smells!'

Céline relaxed a little, but I noticed her casting an uncomfortable glance towards the parlour. 'Thank you, Mademoiselle Anna,' she said, dragging her gaze back to us. 'It will be ready in just a moment, if you would care to be seated in the dining room.'

She moved past us and tapped on the parlour door. Christine bade her enter and the maid announced luncheon, reappearing a moment later, closing the door softly behind her. She smiled and ushered us along before her into the dining room, then returned to the kitchen. Anna and I settled ourselves comfortably. Christine entered the room in a rustle of skirts, taking her place at the head of the table and smiling at us both.

'I do hope you have had a productive day?' she said, reaching for the water jug.

'It is certainly proving enlightening,' Anna commented. 'Christine, would it be a terrible inconvenience to you and Céline if Viktor and I joined the cemetery patrol this evening?'

I blinked at this, and Christine looked taken aback. 'Is that necessary?' she asked.

'I cannot hope to resolve matters, or even have a clear idea of what might be happening here without experiencing the cemetery at night.' Anna spoke in a matter-of-fact way, but I saw her eyes were alight with interest as they watched Christine, who had folded her hands in her lap and was sitting serene and still. I wondered why she was not mentioning the vampire, but presumed she did not wish to alarm Christine.

'Then I have no problem whatsoever,' Christine replied. 'I will ask Céline to prepare some coffee for you to take, and perhaps a blanket would be welcome?'

I nodded, smiling, as Anna said, 'That is very kind, and will be much appreciated, I can assure you!'

François joined us at that point, looking fresh and groomed and more like himself. He bowed and joined us at the table, only to leap to his feet almost at once as Céline's footsteps approached along the hall. He opened the door for her, and she smiled her thanks to him as she manhandled a large tray over to the sideboard. She began laying out dishes as François took his seat, and served us all with her usual efficiency. Anna, I noticed, steered the conversation away from the investigation and we were soon engrossed in a discussion about poetry and books, which lasted for the remainder of the meal. Afterwards, Anna and I excused ourselves and retired to our rooms, where we brought each other up to date on what we had discovered. Before going back to look around the cemetery, Anna had arranged to see Louise Bernier at four o'clock. She listened to my description of the scene in town, nodding, her eyes distant, her mind working.

'Interesting,' she said.

'There is something else, too.' I told her about my sudden recollection that Christine had said something which jarred, and which still eluded me. Anna thought back, shaking her head.

'Nothing struck me,' she said. 'Don't try too hard to remember, though. It will probably come to you tonight as you are lying in bed.'

'As I am wandering around a cemetery, you mean,' I corrected her with a smile.

'I should probably have warned you about that.' She eyed me. 'How do you feel about it? You need not come, if you prefer.'

'And miss the opportunity to see a vampire with my own eyes?' I retorted. 'In addition, we will be with the patrol. A vampire cannot take on all the men at once, surely?'

'Vampires are fast, Viktor, faster than you can fathom.' She paused, then lowered her voice. 'We must be cautious, especially now we know there is indeed a vampire in that cemetery. There is something odd about this entire affair.'

'What makes you say that?'

'One person has been attacked, and not badly, either, as far as I am aware. Scaremongering aside, there have been no other sightings within the cemetery itself, apart from one or two of the patrolmen, who occasionally think they see something in the trees. There is never anything there when they check.'

I listened, fascinated. 'This is unusual?'

'Very!' she said. 'There is usually a spate of attacks at the beginning, focusing on the deceased's family. After that, they widen out into the community. Our vampire has not followed this pattern, which is highly irregular. Where does he feed? Why have we heard nothing of other attacks? The sightings Escoffier mentioned are typical of hysteria and wild imaginations, not of an actual vampire. If a vampire does not wish to be seen, they will not be seen. We should be seeing reports of mysterious injuries with no apparent cause, or of people taking to their beds with bouts of weakness and fatigue. Yet we are not.'

'The only person to be attacked is Louise Bernier,' I mused. 'She is not a de Vaux, and none of the de Vauxs have been attacked, have they?'

'If they have, they are keeping it to themselves,' Anna said. 'That is something we must bear in mind, Viktor. Frossard certainly appears to have a motive to hurt de Vaux, but equally, de Vaux has good reason to engineer something to make the police look ineffective. Also, we cannot lose sight of the fact that this may well be a completely new breed of vampire, one that my organisation has not yet encountered.'

'I had no idea there were different types,' I said. 'Why did you not tell me?'

Anna sighed. 'I thought you already had more than enough to consider. I was going to determine what we were dealing with and then instruct you accordingly.'

'And as we have yet to meet Monsieur de Montfort, you do not know which one to tell me about.'

'Exactly.'

'I understand.'

'I was musing over something Christine said,' Anna remarked. 'About my approach being different to that of the police.'

'I remember! She said we might help Louise unlock some hidden memory.'

'I hope we do, too,' Anna said. 'I feel Louise is somehow key to all this.'

'Perhaps she was simply in the wrong place at the wrong time.'

'You raised the pertinent question yourself,' Anna said. 'You asked what she was doing in the cemetery, remember. Have you heard anything about that from anyone yet? I certainly have not. Yet someone must know what she was doing there. Young girls do not wander round in cemeteries at night, in my experience. Well, not unless they are up to something.'

I stared at her, realising what she meant. 'You think she was meeting someone?' I whispered. Anna shrugged, shaking her head.

'I have no proof of anything yet,' she murmured. 'But that is the only reason I can think of for her to be where she was in the middle of the night.'

'If leaving a victim unscathed is not typical of a vampire, we need to consider other options, do we not? Was she robbed?'

'No one has mentioned it. Perhaps we will find out later.'

'It could be an important point in working out whether she was a target or not,' I said thoughtfully.

We had a little time before we needed to head to the Bernier farm, so Anna excused herself to write up some notes and pen a letter to her mysterious employers. I unlaced my boots, removed my jacket and took my journal, pen and ink to the table, along with some of my father's journals. I wrote down every snippet of information I could recall, all my observations and questions and thoughts. After a moment's consideration, I turned to a fresh page and jotted down what I could recall of the confrontation between Christine and François, hoping it would jog my memory and shove the elusive fragment into the light, where I could capture it.

Notes written, I sat back in my chair and looked at my father's journals. Part of me wanted to spend the rest of the day poring over them, but another part was reluctant to even open one. I pulled the pile towards me and spent a few moments neatening the stack, realising that whatever else I did that day, I would not be returning to the tragedy of my father's ravaged mind. I grabbed the books and stuffed them back in my bag, shoving it well out of sight beneath the bed. Instead, I pulled my own journal towards me, turned to the back and began to write to my uncle, explaining a little of what had happened since I had left home. I downplayed most of it, knowing he would be horrified if he learned the full extent of what I had dealt with, but even so, I had soon filled three sheets of paper and was not even half-way through the story.

Anna tapped on the connecting door and poked her head in. 'Are you ready to go and speak to Louise?'

'Let me put my boots on,' I said, stuffing the journal into my pocket. I hurried into my outdoor clothes as quickly as I could and, after letting Céline know where we were going, the two of us set off along the Rue Saint-Martin. Once we were well away from the house, I told Anna about Christine's and François's argument. She listened, but when I had finished, she shrugged.

'We need to focus on the case,' she said. 'One thing you will learn is that people have complex lives, and it can be so easy to be distracted by them. Observe and file the information, by all means, but do not lose sight of the reason we are here.'

I nodded, chastened. 'I did not think it was connected to the case,' I agreed. 'I suppose it struck a chord with me because François and I are quite similar in some ways.'

'Perhaps a little.'

'I think he just wants someone to notice him,' I said. 'In the cemetery this morning, Arnal completely ignored him. I get that all the time from adults. You must, too, being a woman.'

Anna gave a tight nod, her lips thinning. 'Yes, indeed. All the time. That is why I am happy to tolerate François. Plus, it is actually rather useful to have someone asking questions. It helps me to think more creatively.' She squeezed my arm. 'You and François have a different view than I, and your questions are helping me to see the case more objectively. I usually focus on finding supernatural answers, but in this case, I suspect your input will be just as valuable as my otherworldly skills.'

We turned left into the Rue Beauchamp and climbed the hill until we reached the archway leading into the Bernier farmyard. As we walked through the open gates, I marvelled once more at its location, a verdant, if less than fragrant oasis in the midst of the jumble of houses. The farmyard was compact and square, with sheds to our left and in front of us, and the farmhouse to our right. Anna lifted her skirts and as we picked our way through the hay and dirt which lay scattered across the yard, I thought of the de Vaux family watching their land being sold off piece by piece, ending up with a farm in what must once have been their parkland. The ill feeling between the de Vauxs and the Berniers must have run deep.

A dog started barking somewhere within the house in response to Anna's knock, and a moment later, someone within hushed it. The door opened to reveal a stout grey-haired woman in her fifties, wearing a plain black dress. She looked us up and down as Anna introduced us, at which her eyes widened, and her mouth fell open.

'Oh! You are the vampire hunter!' she exclaimed. 'Come in, come in! I will tell the master you are here. Come, come!'

Like a mother hen, she bustled before us along an unlit passage whose floorboards protested loudly beneath our feet. We were shown into a dim parlour with a small, square window overlooking the street. I glanced out, noticing that I could see the de Vaux house almost opposite. The maid invited us to make ourselves comfortable, then fussed her way out of the room and back along the hallway, taking Anna's calling card with her.

The Berniers' parlour was not in the best state. It was clean enough, but the furniture was shabby, and threadbare cushions slumped, limp and colourless, in the corners of the armchairs. Knitting was strewn across the sofa, part-way through a row, as though suddenly abandoned. Anna sat in a chair next to the fireplace and I stood next to her, leaning on the mantelpiece.

After a few minutes, we heard footsteps as someone creaked along the corridor. Maurice Bernier, in his rough, dirty workman's clothes, entered the room and greeted us formally, bending over Anna's hand and returning my bow. He sat heavily in one of the armchairs and picked at a darn on the worn lacework which covered its arms.

Before any of us could speak, there was a light tap at the door and the maid appeared with coffee, which she served with a great flourish and much unnecessary fuss. I looked up at her to smile my thanks and saw worry in her eyes. She was trying to create a good impression, I realised, and then I thought back to some of the comments about Louise I had heard in Amiens, and what Anna herself had intimated about the girl. The family was clearly struggling against those rumours just as much as the de Vaux family was with the taint of vampirism. Reputations were at stake here. Family reputations.

'How are you, Monsieur Bernier?' Anna asked in a soft voice.

Bernier snorted and his cup rattled in its saucer as he leaned forward. 'How should I be, Mademoiselle, when my daughter is attacked and the police cannot find the culprit, and when everyone seems determined to protect the one responsible? You tell me... how should I be?'

I bristled, but Anna did not react, as though she had been expecting something of the sort. She gave Bernier a sympathetic nod. 'I understand your frustration completely, Monsieur, believe me. There is a great deal of frustration in Amiens generally concerning the actions of the police, is there not?'

Bernier nodded. 'It is as you heard this morning. I do not know what Frossard may or may not be doing, but something is not right, and who listens to a man such as myself when he has a problem?'

'Please be assured that I do not seek to protect anyone or anything, Monsieur Bernier,' Anna said. 'My role here is to uncover whatever truth there is to be found. I wish to ensure that I am in possession of all the facts before I reach a conclusion. In my experience, relations between humans and vampires can be fraught with all manner of complications, and great care must be taken with any negotiation.'

'You have concluded that there is a vampire?' Bernier suddenly became more animated. Anna held up a hand, and he paused.

'Monsieur,' she said, her voice soft, yet firm. 'As yet, I have made no conclusions. I have insufficient information. I cannot state categorically that a vampire attacked your daughter, yet neither have I anything to conclusively prove that a human was responsible.'

Bernier slumped, huffing and looking away, disgruntled.

'I know you need answers,' Anna said, 'and I know how frustrating it is when no one can tell you anything. I beg just a little more patience whilst I investigate, and I promise I will have an answer very soon.'

There was a silence, broken only by the muted ticking of the clock. For a few moments, during which my heart thumped against my ribs, I thought Bernier was going to ignore Anna. The silence yawned between us like a chasm, then Bernier spoke. His voice seemed too loud for the room and my hand shook a little.

'I am not a grand gentleman like de Vaux,' Bernier said in a gruff voice, 'but I love my daughter, and want justice for her. I know what people are saying about her, about my family. I know. I understand why you are taking the approach you are and thank you for it. Although I still believe Louis de Vaux is somehow responsible, I see why you are being so cautious in your investigation. It is...reassuring. It means you will do what is right.'

Anna smiled at him. 'I appreciate that, Monsieur Bernier. Thank you.'

Bernier nodded and turned his attention to his coffee, ducking his head a little, but his eyes were bright with tears. We were saved from another lengthy silence by the sound of more footsteps approaching, and a moment later, the door opened to admit Louise Bernier and her mother, followed by the maid, who went round topping up our cups and then poured two fresh cups, placing them carefully for the two women before leaving the room.

Louise was around my age, and extremely attractive. Petite and slight, she had long russet brown ringlets, and her oval face was pale and drawn. As I rose from my chair, setting my cup down on the table, I imagined her dark eyes were usually bright and shining, but at the moment, they were dull and slightly puffy, with shadows beneath. The poor girl looked as though she had not slept for days.

'Ah, Louise, come and sit down, ma chère,' said Bernier, indicating an armchair by the window.

'Yes, Papa,' the girl said in a soft, musical voice. She nodded to us both self-consciously as Bernier introduced us, then slipped into the chair with an easy grace I immediately coveted, glancing out at the late afternoon sun as it gleamed off the windows of the houses opposite. Smiling nervously, Madame Bernier came forward to shake our hands. She looked very like her daughter, small and trim, with curly chestnut hair and hazel eyes.

'My husband told me about the sensible and level-headed manner in which you operate, Mademoiselle,' she said, pressing Anna's hand, 'and I cannot tell you how reassuring it is for all of us. I do not begin to understand what it is that you do, but I thank you for your care.'

Anna gave her a tender smile, murmuring reassurances.

Madame Bernier nodded, looked at the coffee pot and the liquid which remained in our cups, and quickly excused herself to see about a refill. As the door closed behind her and her footsteps retreated in a chorus of creaks, Anna settled in her seat. I remained standing for a moment, intending to lean against the mantelpiece, but Anna caught my eye and indicated the chair with an almost imperceptible tilt of her head. Cheeks flushing, I pretended to fiddle with my collar and cravat for a moment before sitting down and taking up my coffee.

'How are you, Mademoiselle Louise?' Anna asked, turning to the girl.

Louise gave her a weak smile. 'I am better, thank you,' she said. 'I am still having unpleasant dreams, though.'

'Understandable.' Anna nodded sympathetically. 'You have had a terrible experience.'

The girl bit her lip and looked out of the window again, with a little shudder.

'Will you tell us what happened?' Anna asked gently. 'I am sorry to make you go through it all again, but it is important I know everything, so I can help you. Take your time. I know how hard this is.'

Louise flushed deep red and the hand holding the cup trembled a little. Anna waited patiently, an encouraging smile on her face. After a few moments, Louise began to speak, her voice so soft that I could only just catch her words.

'I was just inside the cemetery, not far from the end of our field,' she said. 'All at once, I heard a rustling sound, and suddenly I was seized, and felt a mouth at my neck, trying to bite me.'

'Were you bitten?' Anna asked, looking at Louise's neck. I followed her gaze but could see no obvious sign of injury above the high collar the girl was wearing. Louise shifted in her seat and raised her hand to her neck, tugging the collar a little higher.

'My skin was not broken. I had a little bruising, nothing more.' The relief in her voice was clear.

'And you were not robbed?'

'I did not have anything with me to steal,' Louise said. Anna nodded. That answered one question, at least.

I took a sip of coffee. 'How did you get away, Mademoiselle?'

'He pushed me away from him,' she said. 'I fell, and whoever it was disappeared into the trees.'

'What exactly did you see?' Anna leaned forward, her eyes keen with interest and coffee half-way to her lips, all but forgotten. 'Think carefully, and don't rush. Did you smell anything, hear anything?'

Louise bit her lip and turned her gaze onto her coffee. 'It was dark, and I did not have a lamp with me. I saw very little, Mademoiselle Stenberg, just a man wearing something white and shapeless, like...like a shroud.'

Anna glanced at Bernier. 'Was Monsieur de Vaux buried in a shroud, Monsieur, do you know?'

Bernier's face darkened. 'According to his son, he was not, but who can trust a word that man says? You would have to speak with the undertaker to be sure.'

Anna nodded and, setting her coffee down, slipped her notebook and pencil from her bag and made a note. I watched Bernier carefully, starting to understand how damaging this entire episode would be for de Vaux's reputation as a man of honour.

'What did you see in the cemetery before he grabbed you?' Anna asked. 'Did you see anyone moving about, or hear something strange?'

Louise shook her head. 'No, Mademoiselle, I saw nothing at all. I wish I had.'

Anna made another note, then paused, her pencil resting on the page as she turned something over in her mind. She scribbled several lines of incomprehensible scrawl.

'What did he smell like?' Anna turned her attention back to Louise, who blinked at her.

'Smell like?' she repeated.

'The dead have a particular smell. Think for a moment and tell me what you recall.'

Louise frowned and I saw genuine confusion on her face as she turned the matter over in her mind. She did not speak for a couple of minutes, at one point closing her eyes as though running over the entire incident. When she did answer, she spoke slowly. 'I hadn't thought of this until now, Mademoiselle, but it didn't smell of...of death. It didn't seem to smell of anything in particular.'

'Interesting,' Anna said. 'You are doing so well, Louise. Now, you told me he said nothing, which is to be expected, but one thing I am curious to learn is what his hands felt like. Were they warm, or cold? Can you recall?'

Louise's hands trembled violently, and the cup clattered against the saucer. Her father rose swiftly and took it, setting it on the table next to her, then giving her a reassuring nod, squeezing one of her hands. Closing her eyes, Louise took a deep breath and Maurice Bernier sat down again, concern etched across his face. We waited as Louise collected her thoughts.

She opened her eyes wide a few moments later, turning her gaze to Anna. 'His hands were warm, Mademoiselle!' she exclaimed, a spark of life in her voice that I had not heard before. Her forehead crinkled as she tried to process the memory. 'They were warm,' she repeated, almost to herself.

Anna nodded and I could see her eyes were bright with excitement. Before she could say anything, Louise gave a low cry. 'Oh! Mademoiselle! I have just remembered something else, too... his breath, against my neck, and his skin... all warm!' She stared at us. 'It wasn't a vampire at all, was it?' she whispered. 'It was a man, a living man!'

Bernier choked on his coffee and set the cup down with a bang, turning to stare at his daughter. 'You are sure?' he asked.

To her credit, Louise did not immediately answer but sat in contemplation for a moment, her gaze distant. When she spoke, her voice was stronger. 'Yes, Papa, I am certain,' she said. 'I can remember his breath particularly. It was hot.'

Bernier's face darkened so much at this that I feared he would make a scene, not that I could blame him. Perhaps sensing the same thing, Anna rose and asked him if she could have a word in private. Bernier struggled to compose himself, giving her a puzzled look, but got up and invited her to step across the hall into his office. I watched with some indignation until Anna shot me a glance, darting her eyes towards Louise. I stared back until a flash of comprehension hit me. I understood why she was getting Bernier out of the room and hoped Louise would answer the question I had to ask her. I could not help thinking I should have been the one to speak with Bernier. That question would have been far better coming from Anna.

The two of them crossed the hall into the office, leaving both doors open as Madame Bernier had not yet returned and Louise and I were therefore without a chaperone. I could hear the low murmur of their voices, although not their words. Louise retrieved her coffee with steadier hands and turned her gaze out of the window as she sipped. It was a beautiful afternoon, and I suspected she was torn between a desire to enjoy the sun and a fear of leaving the house. Knowing it was a man, and not a vampire, who had attacked her would be little consolation.

We sipped our coffee in silence for a few moments, then, not wanting to make it too obvious, I murmured, 'You did incredibly well, Mademoiselle. Your memory is excellent, and every detail you recall will help my sister so much.'

She smiled with a little more confidence. 'Thank you, Monsieur... you are at Madame Archambeau's I understand? If I should remember anything else, should I send word to you there?'

'Yes, indeed, it would be most helpful,' I said. 'One thing does puzzle me, though, Mademoiselle.' I lowered my voice and leaned forward, even though I was across the room from her. 'May I ask why you were in the cemetery in the first place? That might help clear up some other issues my sister has uncovered.'

Louise caught her breath and froze. I had touched a nerve. She stared at me with what looked like blind panic for a moment, then her expression shifted to something between sullen and defiant.

'I was searching for one of the dogs.' Her voice was so soft I could barely catch the words. 'It had got out of the field, and I didn't want it running round the cemetery. Monsieur Arnal is always complaining to Papa about it, and they argued last time.' She did not sound convincing.

'You were searching for a dog?' I repeated, trying not to let my disbelief show. 'Did you have a lantern with you?'

'No,' she said, sounding puzzled. 'Why?'

'The cemetery is large,' I pointed out. 'How were you going to find him without a light?'

She pursed her lips. 'I did not take a lantern because I thought he was in the field, and I know my way around the field, even in the dark.'

'I understand,' I said. 'How did you know the dog was missing at that time of night?'

This time she looked like a startled rabbit. 'I went down to the kitchen to get some water and he was not there,' she said after an over-long pause.

'So, you went looking.' I nodded, still not certain I believed her. I had a sudden flash of inspiration. 'So, no one could have known you would be in the cemetery at that time.'

'I do not understand.' Her eyes were wide.

'I am trying to make sure you were not targeted deliberately, Mademoiselle,' I replied, waiting for her reaction.

I was not disappointed. It was clear that the thought had not occurred to her at all. She pressed her lips together into a line and seemed to retreat into herself. With all the focus on the rivalry between de Vaux and Frossard, I doubted if it had occurred to anyone other than, perhaps, Bernier. What had he made of his daughter's night-time wanderings? Perhaps Anna was finding out.

As we sat there in strained silence, Anna and Bernier reappeared. 'We must take our leave, brother,' Anna said, and I nodded, setting aside my cup.

Anna looked to Louise, eyes warm and kind, not reacting in any way to the girl's shaky, weak flicker of a smile. 'Thank you, Mademoiselle Louise. You did very well to remember what you did, and I am sorry again for having to ask you to relive it. I trust you will feel a little stronger tomorrow. Please rest assured that I will do all I can to find out who is responsible. I have a very good success rate.'

It was meant to be reassuring, but if anything, Louise looked worse now than she had earlier. She was almost grey, and I could see her hands trembling even from where I was standing. The maid appeared behind Madame Bernier and a few pleasantries were exchanged as we donned our coats. I took my hat, bent over Madame Bernier's hand and shook her husband's. Louise gave us a stiff little nod, but although she rose from the chair, she remained next to it, and I heard the springs creak slightly beneath her weight as soon as we had left the room.

Monsieur and Madame Bernier accompanied us to the door, she standing just inside while he crossed the yard with us, solicitously pointing out areas for Anna to avoid stepping. As we reached the gates and he shook hands once more, he said suddenly, his voice low, 'I'll tell you something, Mademoiselle. She did not mention it, but Louise had gone to look for one of the dogs.'

Anna nodded. 'I see, Monsieur Bernier. It had escaped?'

Bernier rubbed his chin. 'It happens now and then, if a door is left open, or we are dealing with the animals. Sometimes they go off and do their own thing, as dogs do.'

'It is fortunate that Louise noticed, given how late it was.' I smiled at Bernier. 'She is extremely observant, and her memory today was impressive, especially under such trying circumstances.'

He peered at me, and I kept my expression bland and neutral until he looked away. 'You seem like good people,' he said. 'Make sure my daughter gets justice.'

'Monsieur, you have my word,' Anna said. He paused and looked at her for a moment, then, realising that was as much as he could hope for, he nodded and without another word, went back to the house. Anna and I went out onto the street and paused for a moment, looking at each other.

'That was illuminating,' Anna said, her eyes sparkling with enthusiasm.

'Now we know why Louise was in the cemetery,' I observed. Anna chuckled.

'Well, we know why she says she was there, which is not the same thing.'

I took a deep breath, considering this, looking up at the beautiful deep blue of the sky and the soft clouds scudding past. All at once, something caught my eye and I squinted at the gable window in the de Vaux house, where a candle was burning, despite the early hour and the brightness of the day. 'Odd,' I said softly. Anna glanced up, and then swiftly, turned her attention elsewhere. She took my arm, guiding me along and pointing out shapes in the clouds which I could not make out at all. Once we had crossed the road and walked a little way up the hill, she paused and, holding on to me, reached down to fiddle with one of her boots. As she straightened, she whispered, 'Ha!'

'What?' I muttered. 'What's going on?'

'Look at the Bernier house. The window above the parlour.'

I did so, catching my breath. In the window was a single lit candle.

'It cannot be a coincidence,' I murmured, turning my gaze back to Anna.

She nodded thoughtfully. 'Well, well, well. That must have been what Louise was watching for. Did you notice how often she glanced out of the window?'

'Oh!' I breathed. 'Are we presuming that one window is Louise's bedroom, perhaps, and the other is a convenient lookout point for one of the de Vauxs? If so, it means Armand...'

'It's likely,' she agreed. 'Louise Bernier and Armand de Vaux... I would be surprised if there is anything formal between them, though. Something tells me that neither father would be pleased if they found out.'

'There is no love lost between their families, is there?' I thought of the two men's bitter comments, and all at once, I found myself feeling sorry for the two young people. If Anna's suspicions were correct, they had found in each other something I never expected to have myself, and to be unable to express that happiness must be unbearable. It would certainly explain why Louise was sneaking around the cemetery.

'Do you believe Louise was out looking for a dog?' I asked.

'I think she was out looking for something,' Anna said slowly. 'I'm just not convinced that it was a dog.'

Chapter 21

Anna stood staring at the de Vaux house for a moment, the little tell-tale crease in her forehead as she considered this new information. I relayed in full what Louise had told me about her reason for being in the cemetery, and without warning, Anna marched towards the house, her stride purposeful. I hurried after her as she went to the front door and rang the bell.

'What is going on?' I exclaimed as I joined her on the step. She hushed me as footsteps approached, and a moment later, Sylvie opened the door.

'Is Monsieur Armand at home?'

I blinked at Anna's forthright approach and lack of preliminaries. Sylvie's eyes widened and her words of greeting froze on her lips. She flushed red.

'I think he has just gone out on an errand, Mademoiselle.' Her tone was not challenging, but it was sufficient to make Anna raise an eyebrow and draw herself up to her full height.

'I wish to speak with Monsieur Armand as a matter of urgency.' Anna reached into her bag for a card, which she presented to Sylvie. 'Will you please see that he receives this as soon as he returns, Sylvie, and ask him to call upon me at Madame Archambeau's?'

Sylvie nodded and curtseyed, looking confused as Anna turned away from the door. I nodded to Sylvie, then strode after Anna. She turned to the right, heading up the hill, and I realised that she was intending to walk through the cemetery. I was surprised at the pace she set until I caught up with her and saw her lips pressed together in a thin line. She did not speak, so I hurried alongside her, a little breathless, until we were back within the cemetery grounds. Arnal was tidying weeds along one of the side paths and we nodded to him as we passed. Shortly afterwards, Anna slowed down.

'Armand is actively avoiding me.'

'It seems so. Surely, he can't be involved, though? Maligning his own grandfather?'

Anna shrugged. 'We know nothing of their relationship. He may have been badly treated by de Vaux, for all we know.'

'Think about what Christine told us. She certainly did not give me the impression that there were any difficulties in the family.'

'Every family has its difficulties.' Anna gave me a look.

'Something which would damage not only your father's career, but your own reputation alongside it, and that of your mother and brother, too? Something which would make you malign your own grandfather to the point of people wanting to exhume his body?'

'It does sound extreme when you put it like that,' Anna conceded, 'but we cannot afford to become emotionally involved. We need to keep a clear head. Let us return to Christine's and consider everything we have learned so far. With any luck, young Monsieur de Vaux will appear shortly.'

We walked through the silent rows of marble, pausing to examine the de Vaux plot when we reached it. Anna leaned over the railings and, not knowing what she was looking at, I turned my attention back to our surroundings. All at once, I spotted a figure standing behind a large vault tomb at the far end of the path, peering out at us. I gave a cry and grabbed Anna's arm. The figure vanished and as I started running, I could hear footsteps pounding along somewhere up ahead, in the direction of the main gate.

'Was it Armand?' Anna gasped as we ran, looking in all directions, trying to spot the fleeing figure.

'It was impossible to tell. He moved so quickly that I did not get a good look. All I could say for certain is that he had dark hair.'

'Could be anyone,' grumbled Anna.

We rounded a corner and hurried along another path, seeing nothing. Another corner. Nothing. Another. An elderly woman in full mourning paused in the act of placing flowers in a stone vase, turning towards us in fright. We slowed, knowing our quarry was long gone, and that he had evaded us by leaving the path.

'Forgive us, Madame, we did not mean to alarm you,' I said, giving her a deep bow. 'You did not happen to notice someone, a young man, perhaps, running this way just now?'

She wrinkled her nose as if we smelled unpleasant. 'Such disrespect!' she exclaimed. 'How dare you disturb me in this manner!'

We apologised sincerely and retreated to the end of the path. Anna stopped when we were out of sight of the grieving woman and took a deep breath. 'That was unfortunate.'

I agreed, craning my neck to see if there was any flicker of movement between the silent tombs. Everything around us was still, and the mausoleum tombs prevented me from seeing very far in any direction. Letting out a frustrated grumble, I looked at Anna. She was frowning again. Before I could say anything, she caught my arm and started to hurry back the way we had come.

'Where are we going?' I exclaimed as I stumbled along beside her.

'Back to the de Vaux house. I want to speak with Armand.'

We reached the road leading to the Rue Beauchamp and as we passed one of the gates leading into the Berniers' fields, I spotted a man kneeling beside it, a bag of tools at his side as he tinkered with the hinges.

'Excuse me,' I called, and the man looked up. 'Did a young man just run past you?'

The man looked up and touched his cap, then shook his head. 'Apologies, Monsieur, but I have seen no one.'

Thanking him, we continued along the road and were soon standing outside de Vaux's gate. As I stood trying to catch my breath, I marvelled at how fresh Anna seemed. Until recently, I would never have contemplated running around in such a manner, and it was not something which would have been approved of in my social circle, or in my family.

'What are we doing?' I asked. 'Do you think Armand might be here already?'

Anna blew out a long breath, then straightened her coat and patted her hair. She did not reply, but opened the gate and marched along the path, and I realised the depth of her frustration and annoyance.

As we approached the front door, it opened to reveal de Vaux himself. I blinked in surprise, which increased when he beckoned to us to enter the house. My heart began pounding as I stepped into the hall. It was unheard of for the gentleman of the house to open his own front door. Had something happened?

De Vaux ushered us into the parlour with a marked lack of ceremony. He bade us sit and went to stand by the mantelpiece. For a moment, the only sound was the soft whisper of fabric as de Vaux fiddled with his cufflinks. If possible, he looked even more drawn than he had earlier.

'I understand you called for my son.'

My eyes widened at the lack of courtesies, but I could tell that whatever was going on, we were past that. Anna nodded.

'We did.'

'For what reason?'

Anna raised an eyebrow. 'I am trying to make sense of what is happening, Monsieur de Vaux. In order to do so, I must speak with everyone involved.'

A humourless smile stretched de Vaux's lips. 'My son is not involved. I cannot see what he would be able to tell you.'

Anna inclined her head. 'You would be surprised at the insights one can glean from people who claim they were not involved in something. Quite often, they saw something from an upstairs window, or happened to be in the right place at the right time.'

'That is as may be, but I can assure you Armand will have nothing useful for you.'

'I will be the judge of that, Monsieur.' Anna's voice was sharp, and I saw de Vaux flinch. 'I suspect I have just wasted time chasing your son around the cemetery, time which would have been far better employed in actual investigation. If he is in the house currently, I would be grateful if I could speak with him to find out what he was doing in the cemetery just now.'

De Vaux looked genuinely puzzled. 'As far as I am aware, he is out on an errand for my wife,' he said, a note of doubt in his voice.

'Unless the errand involved watching us in the cemetery, Monsieur, I suspect that Armand has a rather different agenda,' Anna remarked. I glanced at her, curious, because I hadn't seen enough of the silent watcher to identify him as Armand.

De Vaux regarded us both for a moment, then moved towards the door. 'Please excuse me,' he said. 'I shall ask Sylvie to bring coffee.'

Anna nodded and de Vaux left the room, closing the door behind him with a click which sounded unnaturally loud in the strange, tense atmosphere. I shuddered a little and shifted on my chair. Anna got up and went to the window. Her frustration was battling with that fascinated glow I had seen when the fog creature manifested, her eyes shining with the thrill of the chase. I was confused and could not help feeling de Vaux was right. If there had been some sort of assignation between Armand and Louise, then he could not be the attacker. Yet... where had he been when Louise was attacked? Could he have seen something he was unable to reveal without giving himself away? I whispered this to Anna, who nodded.

'Could this be key to the investigation?' I asked.

'Maybe, but try not to jump to conclusions.' She smiled at me.

'If he was doing nothing wrong, why run away? If he wanted to see what was going on, why not simply ask? No one would have thought anything of it, surely?'

'We must remember the family is grieving, Viktor. Grief presents in many ways, not all of them logical.'

That gave me pause and I lapsed into silence, listening to the ticking of the mantelpiece clock and the chirruping of a bird outside. Suddenly, the parlour door opened, and Catherine de Vaux entered the room, looking apologetic. 'Please forgive me,' she began as we shook hands, 'I was in the garden and have only just been made aware of your arrival. Please, do be seated. Sylvie will bring coffee in a moment.'

We did so, Anna assuring her that no offence had been taken. Catherine nodded, looking relieved. 'Guy is not himself, and with matters about to come to a head... thank you for understanding.'

'I have seen it often, Madame,' Anna said, her expression softening, and I realised how deeply she cared about the people she helped. 'You are all under enormous pressure, trying to deal with something you have never encountered before. If you were taking it all in your stride, I would be extremely concerned for you.'

Catherine nodded and plucked at her skirt with long, slender fingers. I recalled Christine saying she was a pianist. 'Guy tells me you are looking for Armand,' Catherine said, a spot of colour appearing on her cheeks. 'Can you tell me why?'

'I am trying to assist you and your family, Madame,' Anna replied. 'I need to discover what everyone knows, what they have seen, what they believe, what they think is going on. I need to speak with your son to find out why he is spending so much time in the cemetery watching me.'

Catherine stared hard at Anna, her colour rising. 'I beg your pardon?'

'That is why we are here,' I explained. 'We called earlier and were told that Armand was running an errand for you, but just afterwards, he was in the cemetery, watching us, and ran off when we tried to approach him.'

A frown creased Catherine's brow and for a moment, she looked as exhausted as de Vaux. My heart went out to her as she struggled with some inner emotion. 'That does not sound like Armand...'

'People do strange things when they are grieving, Madame,' Anna said in a soft, gentle voice, reaching out to lay her hand over Catherine's. 'We have not lost sight of the terrible loss you have suffered.'

The woman's face blanched at this, and she reached into her sleeve for a small lace handkerchief, her pale skin stark against the black fabric. Dabbing at her eyes, she apologised again. 'I have no idea where Armand is. I did not send him on any errand, so I have no idea why you were told that I did. I shall speak with the servants.'

'They told us what they were instructed to tell us,' Anna said. 'I do not believe they have done anything wrong.'

Catherine de Vaux regarded Anna, tucking the handkerchief back into her sleeve. Her eyes were red-rimmed, and she seemed to sag as she said, 'Armand cannot be involved in this, Mademoiselle Stenberg. I am sure you will dismiss my words as the ravings of a fond mother, but please believe me when I say Armand and his grandfather Louis had a wonderful relationship. Towards the end, when Louis could no longer rise from his bed, Armand spent hours with him, reading to him, or talking or simply sitting holding his hand. I cannot believe he would be involved in anything which maligned his grandfather so much.'

Anna reached out and took Catherine's hand again. For a moment, I thought the woman would pull away, but she did not. She looked earnestly into Anna's eyes, and when she spoke, her voice quavered with the tears that threatened. 'Please do all you can to find out what is happening. We are all devastated. Armand is not himself; Aubine barely leaves his room. The servants are whispering amongst themselves, and I cannot set foot outside without people pointing and muttering behind their hands wherever I go. Please help us!'

Anna gave her a warm smile. 'Be assured Madame, I will do everything I can to bring the truth to light,' she said. 'But Armand needs to understand how suspicious he looks. He should not be sneaking around the cemetery, especially if he has nothing to hide.'

'What could he possibly have to hide?' Catherine asked. She tried to make her tone light and airy, but her voice cracked as she spoke, and I could not help but think she knew more than she was saying. She was a mother protecting her child, and I could not blame her. If she knew about Louise, it was an extra burden she was carrying.

Anna and I remained diplomatically silent, and Catherine glanced at the door, murmuring something about the coffee.

'Do not worry, Madame,' Anna said. 'Viktor and I should return to Madame Archambeau's now. I do need to speak with Armand, however. I hope you will explain why, and request that he attends me as soon as possible.'

Catherine nodded. 'I will speak with him. I understand that you cannot help us unless we help you.'

Anna smiled; all traces of her earlier frustration gone. 'I do appreciate it, Madame, thank you. Now, we must take our leave. Please give our regards to Monsieur de Vaux.'

A little flush appeared on Catherine's cheeks again, but she said nothing. Eyes bright with tears, she nodded, pressing her lips together, and rose to ring the bell. When the door opened a few moments later, I was surprised to see a tall, slender man in livery, who bowed and awaited orders. Catherine was as surprised as I. 'Laurent, where is Sylvie?' she asked.

'Forgive me, Madame, but the Master has sent her on an errand.' Laurent's face was impassive. 'How may I serve you?'

'Please escort my guests to the door,' Catherine said as Anna and I got to our feet and offered her our hands. Catherine's was clammy and trembled slightly, but when I looked into her eyes, she seemed calm and composed and I marvelled at her strength.

Laurent escorted us to the door, closing it quietly after us. There were three women standing on the corner at the bottom of the road, one weighed down with a large bundle of laundry and the others in drab, shabby dresses. As we emerged onto the street, one of the women glanced over, then stared, and the others turned to see what she was looking at. The three of them exchanged glances, then hurried off. A cart clattered past, the clopping hooves echoing off the houses, but otherwise the area was silent. Anna slipped her hand through my arm and guided me up the hill.

'Let us walk back through the cemetery,' she murmured. 'Just in case anything exciting might be occurring. I would also like to glance over the de Montfort vault.'

I was surprised to see a couple of families in the cemetery laying wreaths. They all looked nervous, men and women alike, glancing around them as if expecting to be pounced on at any moment by some terrible creature. I asked Anna if we should say anything to them, but she shook her head. She looked tired, which scared me a little and forced me to acknowledge that I, too, needed to get some rest after our energetic day.

Arnal was lurking, pretending to weed, but mainly staring into the bushes and watching the mourners. We stopped briefly, but he had nothing to report.

The day had been uneventful, he said, and he was looking out for anyone acting suspiciously. Anna thanked him and we continued on our way, passing through the main gate onto the Rue Saint-Martin. I rang the bell when we arrived back at Christine's, and Céline let us in, solicitously offering coffee as she hung up our coats. Anna asked if she would mind serving it in our rooms, and she smiled.

'It is no trouble at all, Mademoiselle. Do you need anything else?'

'No, thank you, Céline. Coffee will be fine.'

Céline curtseyed and went off down the hall. Anna glanced at the silver tray on the hall table and frowned.

'No indication that Armand has called yet,' she muttered. 'I was hoping there would be a note from Henri, too. I have him running some errands for me.'

'Oh?' We mounted the stairs and went into my room, as it was the closest. Anna perched on my chair while I sank onto the bed and unlaced my boots.

'Henri is dealing with some letters for me,' she said. 'There will be no answers until tomorrow, of course, but I was hoping he might have updated me on his progress.'

'I hope I will have the opportunity to check the telegraph office tomorrow,' I said. 'I really want to hear something from my uncle, whether it is reassuring or not.'

'Understandable.' Anna threw me a warm smile. 'I do hope it's good news, when it arrives. You deserve that, after what you have dealt with.' She looked at me for a moment, head tilted as though appraising me. 'You ask good questions, Viktor. I am impressed with the way you have managed to fit in with my work so well. You do not demand explanations like most people do, which surprises me. Is there a reason for that?'

I blinked. 'I rarely demand anything,' I said, 'and you have made it clear we will discuss things at some point. I have not consciously avoided asking, or anything. We have simply been focused on the case.'

'I think my employers will be impressed with you. I am, and they trust my judgment. Have you given any thought to whether you would like to do this kind of work?'

I shook my head. 'There has been no time. Plus, you said you have certain skills – the ability to see creatures. I cannot, so surely I would not qualify anyway?'

'You mentioned you were born on a Saturday,' Anna said. 'Did you know people born on that day are often possessed of extraordinary gifts?'

'What kind of gifts?'

'The Sight, for example. Some can move objects with their minds. I once met a woman who could control the weather. Her brother could read minds.'

I stared. 'I cannot do anything like that, Anna!'

'Yet there is something special about you. The creature in the fog. I don't quite understand it yet.'

'You and I both!' I shook my head. 'Nothing like this has ever happened to me before. I am not sure how to explain it, even to myself.'

Anna nodded. 'Don't try. It will exhaust you, and I would be willing to guarantee that whatever conclusion you reach, it will be the wrong one.' She chuckled. 'You look so puzzled.'

'I am!'

'The explanation is out there somewhere. I expect one of my colleagues will possess the right skills to help you find it. I hope that when you have had a chance to consider, you will agree to come and meet my employers. What are your initial thoughts about what I do?'

'I find it fascinating,' I said with enthusiasm. 'The problem is that I feel I have only half the story. About you, I mean, and your employers. I understand the basics, but even those are hard to deal with.'

'Recruitment is undertaken in a very particular manner. All I can do is recommend people, which is why I can't give too many details at this point. You have all you need to know.'

'I did not mean specifically,' I said. 'I was thinking more of the existence of vampires. How does one learn about such things? Had I discovered a vampire back in Dover, for example, how would I go about researching it? There must be books, but where?'

'There are. Specialist books, rare and hard to track down.'

'And I am sure your employers own a copy of every single one,' I said lightly. She smiled and nodded.

'Indeed. Some of them were written by members of the organisation.'

At that moment, with the weight of my father's journals pressing on my heart, I would have given anything to look at the collection. My mind flitted back to some of the strange things he had written about. Would such books help to shed light on some of the creatures which inhabited my father's mania? More than anything, I wanted to break through the impenetrable darkness with which he had surrounded himself and find out what I had done to make him so determined to end my life. A little shudder rippled through me, and Anna looked at me, concerned.

'Is something wrong?'

'I was thinking of my father.'

She nodded. 'You are safe. Try not to dwell on it too much. You are bound to hear from your uncle soon, so try to keep it at the back of your mind until then. In the meantime, you have the case to keep your thoughts busy!'

'You are right. I do not want to spend my time thinking about that part of my past. We need to find François and get him to do some of his funny voices. It will make me laugh.'

As Anna was chuckling at the memory of François and his impression of the old woman, Céline arrived with our coffee, and the next few minutes were taken up with small talk and cups. As the door closed behind her and I sipped the warm, refreshing brew, I said, 'What do you have planned for tonight?'

She looked thoughtful. 'Not a great deal. Observation of this kind is usually just that. I like to sit back and see where people take themselves, as you saw earlier. If they forget you are there, they reveal so much more. Occasionally I steer the conversation if it is veering too far off course, but much of the time, I let things play out.'

I could see the logic in her approach. 'Tell me, what do you see in this case which I cannot?'

'It is too clumsy, for one thing.' She sipped her coffee, considering. 'Vampires may be creatures of terror, yet they have a certain elegance in their actions and motives. I see none of that here. Also, and this is an unpleasant thought, for which I apologise, Louise would have been injured far more severely by a vampire. Even if it was interrupted just as it grabbed her, it would have had a taste of her before vanishing.'

I frowned, thinking back to Louise's words. 'There was nothing to suggest that the attacker moved unusually fast.'

'No. She saw little. What I did not share with anyone was that I expected her to see nothing whatsoever.'

I stared at her, processing her words. 'Of course,' I breathed. 'A vampire would have moved too fast for her to see it.'

Exactly. Yet she describes someone in white.'

'But you would be able to see it?' I pressed, curious about Anna's strange abilities. She nodded.

'I can see them even when they move. The gentleman in Paris whom I helped – remember? I helped him avoid death.'

I sat and gaped at her, coffee forgotten, as she added, 'It was lurking in the shadows in a rather unpleasant part of the city. In fact, it was similar to the way I met you.'

Images of that night leaped to my mind and I shuddered, remembering the cloying stench of the fog clinging to me. 'That collection of books you mentioned,' I said, 'might one of them contain something which would help me to understand my father's condition? He does seem to be fixated on unusual creatures. It was easy to dismiss when I believed those creatures were figments of his imagination, but now I am not so sure that we – my family, I mean – have done the right thing by him. If there is anything in the world which might help him, I need to investigate it.'

'I cannot promise, but I do think our library is a good starting point. You will also be able to talk to other agents, all of whom have different specialisms. Just because I do not know what your fog creature is, it does not mean it is new, or unknown. Some of my colleagues have been working on cases for forty years or more. They have a true wealth of knowledge between them. Will you come with me when I return to Paris?'

I considered. Once the investigation was complete and I had received word from Uncle Geoffrey that my father had been found and returned to St

Bernadette's, I should return home and leave Viktor behind forever, to be dismissed as a brief aberration in my usually faultless behaviour. Yet something was stirring inside me, something frightening and exciting, something which tugged at me and drew me further away from the claustrophobia of what awaited me when I returned to Dover. I took a sip of coffee, then smiled at Anna.

'Yes,' I said. 'I will.'

Chapter 22

Dinner that evening proved a lively affair, with both François and Christine on good form, entertaining us with amusing local anecdotes and stories about their neighbours. I gathered that, although they seemed to live quietly, they had a good social circle thanks to Christine's late husband, Franck. He had been a popular and successful businessman and had left her a significant allowance, much of which she channelled into charity work, whilst the bulk of his fortune was held in trust for François when he came of age. He had been a good deal older than Christine, and had died of pneumonia several years before. They were the kind of family with whom my parents would have socialised, although my grandfather sneered at what he termed the 'mercantile classes'. Yet Christine was equally as refined, educated and elegant as my mother, moving easily from subject to subject once the conversation drifted away from local affairs. I liked her very much and was fascinated by her descriptions of the work she undertook to better the condition of women and girls in the poorer areas of Amiens. It did not surprise me that she had extended her philanthropy to offering accommodation to well-bred young ladies.

François was amusingly excited about the prospect of Anna and myself joining the patrol. He chattered about the men with whom he patrolled, mentioning one named Christophe quite often, I noted. There was a very funny interlude where François showed off some of his impressions, including one of Arnal which made Anna laugh so much that tears ran down her cheeks and she was forced to excuse herself to splash some cold water on her face. I was relieved to see her laughing, because Armand had not called upon her and she was annoyed. She had waited in the parlour, growing increasingly irritated, and by the time we had to go and wash before dinner, her mood was foul. She sat and scribbled in her notebook as the minutes ticked by, and when Céline came to announce dinner, she stood and left the room without a word. I apologised to Christine and François, then followed Anna upstairs, not daring to speak. She went into her room and closed the connecting door with a sharp click, leaving me staring at it, uncertain how to handle this new aspect of her personality. I sighed as I washed my hands. Every time I began to feel comfortable with her, something happened.

Fortunately, when Céline rang the dinner bell and Anna opened the connecting door to see if I was ready, her mood had lifted. I said nothing, letting her lead the conversation as we went down to the dining room, but she was her usual self once more. She had, at least, heard from Henri, for which I was extremely grateful, and by the time we were seated at the table, her dark mood seemed well behind her.

Christine sat at the head of the table, an indulgent smile curving her lips as she listened to her son's antics. At one point, she reached out to smooth one of the lapels on his coat. François bore this fussing with much comedic eye-rolling, sending Anna into another fit of giggles which took some time to subside. I avoided catching her eye for a good few minutes while she shook silently in her seat across the table, trying to control herself.

Even Céline joined in as she was serving, and watching her laughing with Christine, I was reminded again of the relationship my mother had enjoyed with our own staff. Christine looked extremely handsome in a gown of rich chestnut brown; her eyes bright with merriment. Every now and then, the gentle aroma of her rose water wafted over me, making my heart lurch with loneliness. My mother had had a dress in a similar shade and in Christine, there were many subtle echoes of her which were both comforting and agonising at the same time.

After a while, once Anna was able to string sentences together without collapsing in helpless laughter, the conversation turned to darker matters. François listened to Anna, rapt, his eyes full of admiration.

'Viktor and I will remain in the background,' she said, catching my eye, and I realised her words were mainly for my benefit rather than educating François. 'We shall be extra pairs of eyes and ears to assist the patrol. If something should happen, we can remain near the de Vaux grave, if necessary, while the men go off to investigate.'

'Why would you do that?' A little frown creased François's brow. 'Wouldn't that be where the danger is?'

Anna smiled. 'In some cases, yes, you are right. However, there is a theory I hope to test.'

François peppered her with questions, but Anna refused to elaborate, and Christine eventually had to ask him to stop. She looked with interest at Anna. 'There is one thing about which I am curious, Anna. You are the investigator, yet your intention is to act as an observer?'

'There is always much to learn from observation.' Anna smiled.

'Indeed,' agreed Christine with enthusiasm, but I noticed her casting a glance of concern at François and imagined the expression on my mother's face if I had told her I was going to sit in a cemetery to watch for a vampire. I was surprised that François had not alluded to de Montfort once, but given Christine's thoughts on the patrols in general, I could see why he was being as reticent as we were. Her look spoke volumes.

'Perhaps I should be your escort, Mademoiselle Anna,' François said suddenly. 'If there is likely to be danger to you...'

'Thank you, François, but Viktor will be doing that.'

He flushed, suddenly looking much younger, and looked across at me. 'Apologies, Viktor, I meant no disrespect.'

I assured him no offence had been taken, desperately wanting to communicate to Anna that I would feel much safer with François at our side. However, François seemed determined to plead his case and Anna eventually relented. 'Very well,' she said. 'However, if something occurs and you need to look into it, that is what I expect you to do.'

'Oh, of course, of course!' he exclaimed, beaming.

'This is a serious matter,' Anna added, and François's face fell a little at the implied criticism. 'It needs to be resolved as soon as possible. There is no room for either ego or heroics.'

François nodded, subdued, and looked down at the table. His nostrils flared as he did so, and I recalled the look on his face in the cemetery when Arnal had ignored him. The slight must have stung. I resolved to have a quiet word with him later if I could.

Once dinner was over, we retired to the parlour and played a hand of cards, then Christine excused herself to write some letters. Anna, François, and I went to our rooms to prepare what we needed.

Anna grumbled quietly about well-meaning boys for a couple of minutes until I felt obliged to challenge her. 'It would be good to have someone beside us who actually is a boy. I swear you forget sometimes I am not.'

'If I do, it is a testament to your disguise,' she retorted, throwing a cushion at me through the connecting door. I laughed and ducked, then grabbed the missile and sent it hurtling back towards her. The lighthearted game continued for a couple of minutes, then Anna tossed the cushion onto her bed, sat down, and buttoned her boots, manipulating the button hook with a fluid dexterity which was mesmerising to watch.

'Is there anything you wish me to do tonight?' I asked.

'I would like you to simply watch and listen.'

I nodded. 'For anything in particular?'

She mused. 'There is a possibility that Armand might be sneaking around, if he has a way of leaving the house unobserved.'

'Unless he is very clumsy, he will have the advantage over us,' I observed. 'It will be impossible to spot him in the dark.'

'I suspect he wants to know what is going on,' Anna said. 'You are right that he will have the advantage of darkness, but I think he will hide nearby so he can hear what is being said. Otherwise, what will he learn?'

'If he wants to know so badly, why not ask?' I leaned against the doorway, watching as she went to her dresser and sat before the mirror, pinning her hat into place.

'Remember what I said about grief,' she said. 'It makes people do all sorts of strange things.' She darkened. 'Like ignore requests to call on people.'

'There must be a good reason for it,' I said. 'The de Vauxs want the matter resolved, so surely they would have insisted he attend you.' I paused as something occurred to me. 'They did not even send a note. Maybe they did not think you would expect him tonight.'

'Whatever the reason, it is frustrating.' She repositioned her hatpin, then peered at her reflection. 'I hope we do not arrive at the cemetery to find out something else has happened.'

I shook my head. 'No, they would have sent for you immediately, surely.'

'Not if they discovered that Louis de Vaux has indeed risen as a vampire,' she said. 'We do not know de Montfort or his intentions.'

I could not think of a suitable response to that one and lapsed into silence as Anna pulled on her gloves, smoothing the fabric over the backs of her hands. She flipped open a small square case on the end of her bed and checked the contents, then latched it shut.

'Ready?' she asked.

I took a deep breath. 'Yes.'

'I will handle de Montfort,' she said. 'I will need you to remain behind me while I do. At a distance. If I give you an instruction, I need you to follow it without hesitation or question. It is vital that we discover the extent of his involvement, if, indeed, he is involved at all. The sooner we obtain that information, the better.'

'Do you think he is involved?'

She sighed, shrugging elegantly. 'It is likely, but not inevitable. If anything should happen tonight, while we are present, I will be more inclined to believe there is a human element behind this.'

'It would be the height of foolishness to do anything while you are there.'

Anna grimaced. 'You would be amazed at the theatrics I have seen. People think they will not be believed, so they put on a show, which serves only to muddy the waters. In this case, though, everything seems clumsy. It lacks the vampire's usual finesse. I am surprised the attacker was seen, yet ultimately managed to escape detection. Of course, that could just be luck on his part.'

'Or carelessness on the part of a vampire attacker?'

'Vampires are never careless.'

As I rolled that around in my head, a thought struck me, and I struggled to shape it into something coherent. 'One thing we need to consider,' I said. 'We are focussing on Frossard because he seems to be the only one with anything significant to gain. We have also been working on the assumption that the damage to the grave happened before the attack on Louise, have we not? What if it was the other way round?'

'You are right. It could easily have been staged in order to deflect attention away from the attack on Louise and towards a potentially innocent man. I will be very interested to see what happens tonight.' Anna picked up her case. 'Come, let us go and see if we can have a conversation with Monsieur de Montfort.'

We descended the stairs and met Céline, who handed Anna a note. 'This just arrived for you, Mademoiselle.'

It was from de Vaux. Short and to the point, it read, 'Sincere apologies. Armand did not return home until dinner time. I have requested he attend you in the morning.'

Anna left the note on the hall table. 'I wonder what time they have dinner?' she mused.

As Céline helped me into my hat and overcoat, Anna handed François and myself a small twist of paper. I nodded, keeping my face as blank as I could so François did not realise I was as clueless as he was.

'Mustard seeds, François, as I explained before,' Anna told him. 'Should the need arise, sprinkle these behind you as you retreat. The vampire's compulsion will force it to stop and count, giving you time to escape. I will be watching and will do the rest.'

I made a mental note as I slipped the twist of paper into my overcoat pocket, sincerely hoping I would not need it and musing about what 'do the rest' actually entailed. François regarded his as though it was a holy relic, tucking it into his waistcoat pocket with great reverence, his ashen face serious. The three of us left the house and made our way along the Rue Saint-Martin to the cemetery's main entrance, treading the paths with slow, quiet steps. The night was cool and a watery moon peeped out from behind silvered clouds, casting a thin, ethereal glow across the tombs and gravestones as we passed. In the distance, a dog barked, which set off a short chain reaction of answering barks and howls. As the cacophony ebbed away, the silence closed in around us and I shuddered, pulling my collar closer around my neck, and glancing about, very aware that I had no weapon. François was alert, walking alongside us and turning every few paces to look back the way we had come. Anna appeared completely unruffled, her steps even and measured, and when I squinted at her, I could see her eyes glittering as she cast them this way and that.

As I walked, I noticed a few wisps of mist trailing round my calves and ankles, but when I slowed, trying to focus on them, they vanished, only to reappear a few moments later once I had continued along the path. Was the fog creature waiting nearby, watching in case of need? Despite Anna's assurances, was I still in danger?

Were these delicate tendrils of mist a subtle warning?

Chapter 23

The three of us left the path and Anna led us back to the de Montfort vault. We halted a little way off and stood, listening to the sounds of the cemetery at night. There was a light breeze, and the leaves were whispering. Usually, it would have soothed me, but tonight it was unsettling, raising the hairs on the back of my neck and sending shivers coursing through me. Anna knelt and rummaged in her bag, removing something, then handed the bag to me with a little nod. I hefted it, thinking I could clutch it to my chest like a shield, or hold it in both hands to swing upwards at an attacker.

'Now what?' whispered François after a few tense minutes, during which nothing whatsoever happened.

Anna waved him into silence with an impatient flick of her hand, and he instinctively stepped a little closer to me. Together, we stared at the vault, and I found myself willing something to happen, terrified though I was.

It did not take long. There was a sudden grating sound which made all three of us start and catch our breath. François took a couple of steps back and I froze, but Anna stepped forward calmly. She was holding a sharp wooden stake behind her back, gripping it tightly, the pointed end resting against her elbow out of sight.

The most extraordinary thing happened.

The cover stone moved, tilting inwards with a soft grating sound. It vanished into the dark space beyond, and I thought I caught a glimpse of a long, white finger. All at once, there was a quiet whooshing of air and a blur of movement around the opening, stirring Anna's hair as she stood watching. Suddenly, in front of us, there stood a tall young man, his long, dark hair gleaming like ebony in the moonlight. He was impeccably dressed in fashions from forty years earlier, his chiselled features austere, his dark eyes glittering as he glared at us. François staggered back several steps, but I could not move. I stared at the creature, fascinated. Whatever I had expected, it was not this.

Yves de Montfort took a step towards Anna, then his gaze dropped to his feet, and he stared at the ground for a long moment. His hands were trembling, I noticed, and when he dragged his gaze up to Anna's, it seemed to take a great deal of effort.

'What is the meaning of this?' he hissed.

Anna inclined her head. 'I am Mademoiselle Anna Stenberg, representative of the Order of Guardians,' she said. 'I request audience with one Yves de Montfort.'

The vampire bared his fangs at her and seemed to be fighting the urge to drop to one knee, his eyes flicking so rapidly between Anna's face and the ground that I was amazed he was able to focus on either. 'I am he. What does the Order of Guardians want with me?'

His tone was harsh, but beneath it, I could sense a voice every bit as beautiful and compelling as he himself was. I moved forward, instinctively, and his gaze shot to me, halting me in my tracks, pinning me to the spot with its depth and intensity. Anna stepped to the side, towards me, throwing out her arm. De Montfort let out a soft, sensual chuckle. His eyes raked me, narrowing in curiosity, but they returned once more to the seeds at his feet.

Anna lowered her arm slowly, shifting a little, and I guessed she was keeping me in the corner of her eye. 'Monsieur de Montfort, I come to you for assistance, if I may.'

He raised an eyebrow. 'Indeed?'

'There has been an attack in this cemetery. A vampire is being blamed. Yet while I detected your presence here, I feel the attack was too clumsy and unrefined for one of your kind.'

He frowned darkly. 'A vampire is being blamed, you say. You mean... I?'

'No. A recently deceased gentleman, whose grave shows signs of disturbance, is currently being blamed.'

De Montfort drew himself up to his full height, nostrils flaring. 'There are no vampires here other than my clan, Mademoiselle. Tell me of this attack. Why, in your opinion, was it clumsy?'

Anna ignored the sardonic tone and gave him a brief description of the case. De Montfort was clearly offended. As he listened, he leaned back against the vault, toying with his lace cuffs. As Anna finished speaking, he shook his head and scoffed.

'I can assure you this was not my doing,' he said firmly, all traces of sarcasm gone. 'You are right, Mademoiselle. There is an inelegance in this which tell me no vampire would have been responsible.'

'Yours is the only clan here?'

'There have been de Montforts here since the cemetery was built.'

'Are there young in your clan?'

'It is decades since I enjoyed the speed of a newborn. Yet not even the youngest among us would be so careless as to allow ourselves to be seen in the way you describe. Vampires have finesse. What you describe is not the work of a vampire. If you asked me for my opinion in this matter, I would say a human is responsible, not one of us.'

Behind me, François caught his breath sharply. I stared at de Montfort, drinking in every aspect of his appearance. I had expected something very different to this erudite, well-spoken man with his immaculate clothes. Even his scent was alluring, a musky hint of spice. A strange yearning overcame me suddenly and I blinked, shaking my head to clear it. When I looked back at de Montfort, both he and Anna were watching me with interest. Uncomfortable, I shifted my feet and drew myself up to my full height. De Montfort, perhaps expecting an attack, did the same, and I was surprised to find he was much taller than me. Anna diverted his attention.

'In recent days, has anything you have seen in the cemetery seemed odd, or out of place?' she asked. De Montfort laughed.

'Mademoiselle, I have had no need to feed for several weeks. This is the first time I have risen since my last...meal.' He smiled disarmingly and I was startled by the depth of my desire to go to him. It took all my focus to remain where I was and I balled my hands into fists in my pockets, nails digging into my palms.

Anna nodded, looking thoughtful. 'May I ask if there are others in your clan to whom I might speak?'

'You wish to accuse us in turn?'

'Monsieur, you are clearly familiar with the Guardians, so please do not pretend you do not know our methods. Have I, at any point during this conversation, accused you of anything?'

De Montfort chuckled wryly. 'Please, Mademoiselle, calm yourself,' he said, his voice suddenly honeyed and soothing. Anna shook her head.

'Please, Monsieur, do not try that tactic with me. It will serve only to delay my investigation, and, for the most part, I seem to be immune anyway. You would be wasting your time.'

A look of irritation flickered across de Montfort's face, and he parted his full lips for a moment, the sharp points of his fangs glittering in the soft light. After a moment, his alabaster features smoothed, and he inclined his head. 'Indeed. Forgive me, Mademoiselle. My dealings with the Guardians are scant and occurred many years ago. I forgot how many of you are immune to compulsion.' His gaze slid inexplicably to me, then back to Anna. Behind me, I could hear the sound of François's laboured breathing as we both stared at this creature, this killer, this monster.

Anna chuckled softly as de Montfort continued. 'I regret, Mademoiselle, that I am the first of my clan to have risen in some time.' He nodded towards the vault. 'Our feeding requirements are similar. I expect them to rise soon, but I am the first.'

'May I solicit your assistance?' Anna asked bluntly. 'There are reputations at stake in this case…'

De Montfort shuddered and held up at hand. 'Please, do not use that term.'

Anna nodded. 'Forgive me, a slip of the tongue.'

'How can I assist you?' De Montfort looked doubtful. 'I know nothing.'

'It would be helpful to know if anyone is hiding in the cemetery,' Anna explained, 'but it is a large space, and anyone in hiding will easily avoid human searchers in the dark.'

'You wish me to sniff around the cemetery for you?' De Montfort looked appalled.

'Your senses are far more sophisticated than ours, and you have the gift of preternatural speed.' Anna was her usual unflappable self. 'Please, Monsieur. If you are innocent of this attack, I need to be able to protect you from those who would seek to destroy you.'

His eyes widened as he considered Anna's words. He gave a begrudging nod. 'I understand. For the sake of my clan, I will look, but you will need to attend to this first.' He indicated the ground with an elegant shudder and Anna immediately scuffed through the seeds, grinding them underfoot. De Montfort took a step forward and let out a long breath. 'Holy water does not work on my clan,' he murmured, then was gone, a blur in my vision. I wheeled round with a soft cry, trying to follow his movements, but nothing remained except a tiny, lingering hint of his scent.

Anna was staring at me, her mouth open, her eyes full of astonishment. She started to say something, but de Montfort suddenly reappeared beside her. I started and fell back a step or two, as did François.

'I see no signs of anyone in the cemetery other than a group of men who are standing near the grave of the suspected vampire,' de Montfort said quietly.

'Is there anything about the grave which should concern me?' Anna asked.

De Montfort smiled wryly. 'Yes, Mademoiselle. You should be concerned about the men standing around it.'

'Why?'

He shrugged. 'Because they do not understand anything.'

Anna nodded slowly, as though she had been expecting this.

'I must go,' said de Montfort. 'Do not worry, Mademoiselle, I will do nothing to disturb you, and if I can be of assistance again, please call upon me.' He eyed her narrowly, his gaze roaming over her. 'I have no doubt you will know how to do so.'

'I do indeed,' she replied.

He chuckled. 'Of course, you do.'

And then he was gone. I followed the blur as it vanished, earning another sharp, searching stare from Anna. As the colour rushed to heat my cheeks, she blinked and reached for her bag. I handed it over silently.

François let out a long, shuddering breath behind me, making me start. For a moment, I had forgotten him entirely, and guilt curdled in my stomach. I turned and put my hand on his shoulder.

'Are you all right, François?'

He nodded, although his pale skin was evident even in the dim light. 'I am,' he said, his voice cracking. Clearing his throat, he shuffled awkwardly. 'Are we going to the grave now?'

'Yes,' Anna said. 'But please, do not mention de Montfort. I do not believe he is involved, and it is now my duty as a Guardian to ensure he is not wrongfully harmed. I must have your word on this, both of you.'

François nodded, looking serious. 'I understand, Mademoiselle, and you may rely upon me.'

'Thank you, François. Viktor?'

'Of course,' I said quietly. 'I will say nothing.'

'Good. Now, we must go to the de Vaux grave and see what the patrol is doing,' Anna said, her tone brisk and business-like. 'François, please, will you lead the way?'

He nodded and the three of us moved away from the de Montfort vault and back towards the path. As we walked, Anna took my arm and slowed her pace a little, lengthening the distance between ourselves and François. She leaned in and whispered, 'You could see him, couldn't you?'

I frowned. 'Well, yes, of course I could. He was standing right in front of me.'

'I meant when he moved.'

'Oh! No, I saw only a blur.'

She gripped my arm, making me start and turn to her. Her eyes were sparkling. 'Viktor, no one else can see that.'

I blinked, my jaw dropping. 'François didn't see the same thing?'

'I should think it highly unlikely. Your eyes followed de Montfort. François's did not.'

'What does that mean, Anna?'

She pulled me down to whisper in my ear, 'It means I was right about you!'

François turned back at that point and, seeing us so far behind, paused until we caught up. My mind was bubbling with Anna's revelation. Did I actually have some strange, otherworldly ability after all?

We turned left along another path and in the distance, I could see the glow of a cigarette. As we drew near to the de Vaux plot, François called out in a low voice and immediately, there were muffled whispers and the scuffling of several pairs of feet. 'Who's there?' someone demanded in a loud, hoarse whisper.

'It is I, François. I have brought Mademoiselle and Monsieur Stenberg, the investigators.' François kept his voice low as we walked up to four men who were standing ready to fight, peering at us in the dim moonlight. They relaxed as soon as they could see us, although I noticed they kept their weapons to hand. François introduced us properly.

The four patrol men – Jean, René, Matthieu and Christophe – shook hands with both of us. It was difficult to determine ages, but they all seemed to be at least thirty, and Jean around fifty. Something about his bearing made me suspect he either was or had been a soldier, especially when he sheathed the sword he was carrying. Matthieu, who I recognised from our unpleasant welcome committee, sat down, his back against the railings of the de Vaux plot. As he did so, I saw the faint glint of metal in his hand and remembered the knife he had been waving the previous night. Christophe and René had cudgels. I was relieved that nothing had happened since the attack on Louise. If they happened across anyone in the cemetery, someone was bound to be injured.

'There is nothing to report, Mademoiselle,' said Christophe. 'As usual.'

Jean scoffed. 'You sound like you are sorry about that,' he grumbled. 'Surely having nothing to report is what we all hope for.'

Christophe started to protest, but Anna waved a hand to silence them. They broke off mid-sentence and stared at her. Christophe took a final drag of his cigarette then dropped it and ground it under his heel.

'My brother and I will share the watch with you tonight,' Anna said quietly. 'We will keep out of your way, so behave as you normally do. There is one change I would like you to make, however. Do you patrol around the cemetery on a regular basis, or at random times?'

'Every two hours from ten,' René said.

'And this is widely known to be your practice?'

The four men looked at each other. 'I suppose so,' Christophe said. 'We have never made a secret of it.'

'In that case, I would like you to make one change, please,' Anna said. 'I would like you to patrol in a few minutes' time, and then again at around half past ten, and then at random intervals. Human observers will now be familiar with your usual habits, so let us change things. It may be that nothing happens, but I would still ask for you to remain cautious, just in case.'

The men listened, nodding now and then, casting glances around us. Christophe took out his cigarette packet, but everyone, myself and Anna included, declined with thanks. He took another for himself, the flare of the tinder box briefly casting an eerie orange glow over his face.

Anna spent a few minutes answering questions about what she did, then chatted about preventative measures and handed out more paper twists of mustard seeds, which the men pocketed, looking bemused. René pulled a small silver necklace from inside his collar. 'Got a crucifix,' he said. She nodded approval.

'That is good, but you should be aware that not all vampires fear the crucifix.'

René looked startled and Christophe nudged him. 'I told you your prayers would not help you!'

Anna looked at Christophe. 'I see Matthieu has a knife…you have a stick?'

Christophe patted it. 'This has never failed me yet, Mademoiselle,' he assured her. She nodded.

'Do you know how fast vampires move?'

Christophe gaped at her and ran a hand through his hair while he considered this, then caught himself and chuckled. From where I was standing, I could see the little frown and the raised eyebrow as Anna regarded him thoughtfully.

'Why are you laughing?' she asked.

'Ah, Mademoiselle, you jest with us!'

'What makes you say that?'

'Because in spite of what is happening here, I still do not believe we have a vampire in Amiens,' Christophe said frankly. Matthieu scoffed.

'Oh, Christophe,' he said. 'Are you still clinging to your view that there is no such thing as a vampire?'

Christophe shrugged. 'I have never seen one,' he said. 'I have only read of them in books. Fiction books, yes? Books which someone made up. Not real!' Matthieu snorted with derision and Christophe continued. 'But you, Jean, you were a soldier. Yet you fear these creatures of the imagination!'

Jean bristled and his hand rested on his sword hilt. 'You know my opinion, my friend, he said testily. 'It is hardly a subject to be discussing at the present moment, is it?'

'Why is that?' asked Anna, interested. 'Given the circumstances, I would consider this to be the perfect time.'

The men fell silent and Anna let it hang there for a while, stretching and growing around us. Eventually she said, 'Gentlemen, I am here to help. And despite what you may or may not think, I am here for your entire community. We have seen for ourselves today the different ways in which people's fear and anger are showing. The more you tell me, the better placed I am to discover what is happening, and the sooner life can return to normal. Please tell me anything you know which will help. It is important.'

Jean gave a heavy sigh and shifted from foot to foot, his discomfort obvious. 'It is...er... it is unsuitable for delicate ears, Mademoiselle.'

Anna gave an impatient exclamation. 'I am not some shy, retiring flower who faints at the merest thought of a scary creature,' she said, enunciating clearly, the irritation in her voice obvious. 'Treating me as such will only annoy me and prevent me from undertaking my work to my fullest capability. I have opened coffins, gentlemen. I have seen what lies within, and I have dealt with them as the circumstances dictated.'

I gaped at Anna before I could stop myself. It seemed that every time she opened her mouth, I learned something new. The men, too, were staring at her.

'Dealt with them?' Jean asked.

'Driven a stake through their heart and cut off their head.'

Matthieu caught his breath and Jean murmured, 'Ah.'

Silence fell as that little nugget of information was digested and I regarded Anna with open admiration. That would disqualify me from working for her employers. Whatever my skills, there was no way I could do such things myself.

'Please explain to me, Jean, exactly what is so unsuitable for my delicate ears,' she said, a touch of humour in her voice. Jean turned away and looked down at the ground, his profile catching the moonlight. I could see a wry smile on his face for a moment before he looked back at her, and his expression was lost in shadow.

'It was perhaps seventeen or eighteen years ago,' he said. 'One of the graveyards was defiled, but not like this.' He gestured to de Vaux's grave. 'It was far more unpleasant. A man was eventually caught doing something similar in Paris and admitted he had been responsible for the atrocities here also.'

Christophe joined in at this point. 'I was a young man at the time. I remember my father talking about it. It was shocking and stayed with people for a long time.'

'This man was very sick,' Jean continued, nodding at Christophe. 'Worse, he was a soldier. He had been stationed here briefly with his regiment.'

'He had terrible impulses,' Christophe chimed in, warming to the subject. 'I won't go into detail, but he dug up graves with his bare hands.'

'This is why I believe we are dealing with a human, and not a creature of fantasy,' Jean said.

'If that is the case, Monsieur Jean,' I said quietly, 'what are you afraid of?'

Jean turned his face towards me, and I peered at him, trying to make out his expression. 'I have been in war, young man,' he said. 'More than once, I have seen things I cannot explain.'

Anna nodded. 'Thank you, gentlemen. I have already sent to Paris for further information regarding this case, but your personal insights are extremely useful. Now, can you tell me how many people have been wandering around this grave? I know it is many days since the attack on Mademoiselle Bernier. Has anyone attempted to preserve footprints or paw prints in the area?'

The four men exchanged glances and René shook his head. 'I have not seen anyone doing such a thing, Mademoiselle.'

'Is that important?' Matthieu asked. He was still sitting by the grave, keeping a distance from the rest of us. Perhaps he felt uncomfortable about his behaviour the previous night. Part of me sincerely hoped he did.

'It is important if we are to determine whether a human or a dog is at work here,' Anna remarked. 'Or something else entirely.'

The men looked uncomfortable and there was some shuffling of feet and unnecessary checking of weapons. François, who had been standing next to me, listening with great interest, cleared his throat.

'I think...' he began, but René spoke over him.

'As far as I know, Mademoiselle, no one has even given a thought to such things,' he said, ignoring the dark look François gave him. 'Everyone immediately started shouting 'vampire' and no one seems to have given much thought to anything else.'

'Who was the first to suggest it was a vampire?' I asked.

Christophe shrugged. 'I would imagine Bernier,' he said. 'I was not there, so I do not know.'

Jean was nodding. 'Seems likely,' he said. 'Bernier is a superstitious farmer, after all.' There was an edge to his voice. Where did his sympathies lie? He had been a soldier, and soldiers have their fair share of superstitions. The other men agreed with him and made a couple of derogatory comments about Bernier, then Matthieu added, 'Mind you, it could easily have been that old fool Frossard who cried 'vampire' first.'

That prompted a few remarks about Frossard and his failings as mayor, which ranged from the already familiar policing issue, to being too fat, and serving inferior wine at events. Once it reached that level, Anna gently suggested the men should go off on their first patrol of the night. They agreed and a quick discussion ensued about who would take which direction. As they were about to separate, Christophe asked François if he wanted to join them, for which I felt a rush of gratitude. The other three had completely ignored him.

François said he would and offered to check the far end by the main entrance. Christophe took the opposite end, with René, Matthieu and Jean starting from various points in between. 'That should make it a more thorough check,' Christophe observed. 'Make sure you go home when you get tired, though, François. You were part of the patrol last night, weren't you?'

'I was, but I am happy to do my part,' François assured him. Christophe nodded and turned away. All five of them melted into the shadows, leaving Anna and I alone by the de Vaux plot. We took up position next to a large marble monument on the opposite side of the path and about twenty yards along. A beautiful statue of an angel with outstretched wings stood atop the monument, and we huddled together in the shadows, peering between the rows of quiet tombs, straining our ears for any unusual noise.

'And now we wait,' Anna breathed next to my ear, making me jump. 'Will we have a long, dull night ahead of us?'

At first, it seemed that her hopes were answered. The men returned from their patrol with nothing to report and some time passed where the only matter of interest was counting the number of different sitting positions in which I could get a cramp. Matthieu and Jean exchanged some more comments about Frossard, some of which I struggled not to laugh at. René joined in occasionally, but François sat in silence, listening, and Christophe, who appeared to be deep in thought, paced about restlessly in a manner I soon began to find unnerving. He looked for all the world like he expected our mysterious target to appear at any moment and was ready to wrestle him to the ground.

Half past ten came and the men split up again, this time leaving René at the grave. Christophe disappeared as soon as he had been allocated his portion of the cemetery, and I felt more relaxed once he had gone. François, who had not been given a specific route this time, seemed uncomfortable at being left with René, who made no attempt to speak to him. After a few minutes he slunk off along the path to do his own thing. I watched him go, nudging Anna to get her attention. She nodded.

'Better he shows initiative in that manner than remain here glowering,' she murmured. 'The more spread out we are, the greater the chance of spotting anything unusual.'

René wandered up and down the path, smoking a cigarette and swinging his cudgel. Anna lapsed into silence, and we sat huddled in our blankets, the coffee long gone. A moth fluttered past my face, making me jump, but beyond that, there was only the sound of a gentle breeze ruffling the nearby leaves, and the sound of René's footsteps. At one point, I thought I heard a faint scratching noise, but as soon as I caught my breath and focused, it had gone. The moonlight cast a gentle glow over the marble forest and the clouds occasionally gave the impression of figures darting here and there as their shadows danced across the cemetery.

Anna gave a soft sigh and leaned her head on my shoulder. 'How are you holding up?' she whispered, her breath tickling my ear.

'Cramp,' I muttered, shifting as quietly as I could into a more comfortable position, teeth gritted as my calf muscle twitched.

Anna made a sympathetic noise as I massaged my leg. An owl hooted somewhere in the distance, startling us, and a couple of dogs barked in response from the direction of the Bernier farm. Silence settled over the cemetery like a blanket. Even the sound of René's footsteps seemed muted somehow.

All at once, René gave a yell, threw down his cigarette and bolted along the path away from us towards the side of the cemetery which backed onto the houses along the Rue Saint-Martin. He vanished into the shadows as Anna leapt to her feet and reached down to pull me up. I caught my breath as I put weight on my cramped leg.

'What is it? What did he see?' Anna was muttering under her breath, eyes searching the shadows. All at once, she stiffened. 'There! A flash of white, between the trees, look!'

She was off at once, following René. I hobbled along more slowly as my leg muscles started to work themselves out of their knots. My heart was pounding, although whether from fear or excitement, I could not tell. Running footsteps sounded to my right as I reached the end of the path and François appeared from the direction of the main gate. 'What's happened?' he demanded. 'Are you hurt?'

'Cramp,' I hissed. 'René saw someone in the trees and Anna went after him.' I pointed. 'Over there.'

François was off immediately, setting a swift pace I had no hope of matching even without my stiff, protesting muscles. Ahead, I could hear shouting. René was the closest, but I could hear Matthieu and Jean not far off. Christophe had taken the main gate area on this patrol, and I guessed he would join us soon enough. Anna had vanished into the darkness, so I half-ran, half-stumbled my way along, peering all around me, alert to every tiny shiver of leaves and swaying of branches.

I found Anna staring into the foliage. She gripped my arm. Together we stood unmoving, listening, eyes straining to make sense of the different shadows. 'I thought I saw something,' she hissed. 'Maybe I was mistaken. Let's find René.'

'Where is François?' I asked.

'I haven't seen him. He must have gone in a different direction.'

There were shouts I could not pinpoint, and Anna slowed, head cocked to one side as she listened. The voices echoed strangely off the gravestones and vaults. We started running, keen to catch up with René. I squinted into the gaps between the tombs, searching the shadows for threats. The thumping of my heart kept pace with the pounding of our feet as we passed memorial after memorial with no sign of anyone. We rounded a corner and set off along another path, when a strange, otherworldly, and almost animalistic cry cut through the air somewhere behind us.

I froze, grabbing Anna and almost pulling her off her feet. The hairs on my arms and down the back of my neck rose as goosebumps shuddered down my spine. The sound was inhuman, chilling the blood in my veins. It sounded like no animal I had ever heard before.

'What was that?' I quavered, unable to keep the fear from my voice. 'Was it…a vampire?'

Anna's voice was grim. 'Where are the men?'

'I don't know. François went ahead of me. I couldn't keep up with him.'

Anna gave a soft tut under her breath and we slowed, listening to the echoing voices and trying to work out where they were coming from.

'That noise was not human, surely?'

Anna was silent for a moment, and the voices died away, leaving our footsteps sounding unnaturally loud all of a sudden. Even the owl and the dogs were keeping their own counsel now. The graves rose on either side of the path, threatening in their stillness. When Anna spoke, I had to lean in to catch the words.

'No. No, it was not.'

Chapter 24

The path we were on was the long side of a rectangle which enclosed a large area cramped with gravestones and mausoleum tombs. The de Vaux plot was along one of the short sides. Anna and I reached the opposite end with no sight of any of the men. A creeping sense of panic rose in me, and I fought to control it, staring all around us until Anna gripped my arm and murmured reassurances that I was not convinced she truly felt.

'Let us leave the path,' I urged. 'We are too exposed here.'

'We are never going to solve this if we spend all our time hiding, Viktor! That is not how this works!'

'But I have no weapon!'

'Then stay close!'

'We don't know where the men are!'

'I am trying to find them. Come!'

'Surely, we will just be running in circles, Anna! They are bound to come back to the grave…would it not be better to wait there?' I took advantage of my height to lag back as she tugged at my overcoat. She stopped and faced me hands on her hips.

'If this is going to work, you have to trust me!' she hissed. 'Don't you understand what is at stake? An exhumation is traumatic for everyone involved, believe me. I have to find out what is going on before any more lives are ruined!'

'I'm sorry,' I said, contrite. 'I am doing my best…'

She started to say something else, but just then, we heard voices and the unmistakeable sound of scuffling footsteps and loud, aggressive swearing. I was glad Anna could not see me blushing. The moon swung out from behind a cloud at that point and ahead of us along the path, we saw a little knot of men approaching. As they drew near and headed towards the de Vaux grave, Anna came back to life, grabbed my arm and hurried after them, pulling me along with her.

When we caught up, I could see they had someone pushed to the ground between them. We ran over as René produced a lamp from next to the grave, lighting it and holding it out towards the man so we could see his face. I caught my breath.

It was Joubert, the unpleasant, foul-smelling man from the previous night.

'What are you doing here?' demanded Anna.

Joubert hawked up something unpleasant and spat, causing Matthieu to aim a kick at him. 'Don't be so foul in front of the lady, you dog! Why are you here? This is not your patrol night.'

'*You* are part of the patrol?' I could not keep the surprise from my voice and Joubert glowered up at me. I quavered for a moment, then remembering Anna's words, I drew myself up to my full height and stared him down.

Joubert gave me an unpleasant instruction in his surly voice and this time it was Jean who reacted. He moved with a speed and grace which reminded me of Arthur, shifting behind Joubert and dropping to one knee. The moonlight glinted on the blade he held at Joubert's throat and from where I was standing, I could see his profile silhouetted against the lamp's warm glow.

'What are you doing, you scum?' he snapped. 'Come on, speak up, or I swear to God, you will regret it.'

'I regret nothing,' Joubert snarled, teeth clenched.

I heard Anna beside me, hissing out a long quiet breath. 'You are not on patrol tonight. Do you usually visit the other patrols?'

'He never has before,' René muttered. Joubert said nothing, but his hard eyes glittered in the lamplight as he glared at us.

Anna knelt down so she was on Joubert's eye level. 'You are not on patrol, and you do not normally spend time with the other patrols. Yet here you are.'

She paused for a moment and when she spoke, her voice was flint. 'Who sent you?'

'How do you know someone sent me?' Joubert sneered after a brief pause.

'You do not strike me as someone who would do something from the kindness of his heart, Monsieur Joubert.'

Jean chuckled and tightened his grip on Joubert, who caught his breath and struggled as the knife pressed harder into his skin.

'Who sent you?' Anna repeated. 'I know your type, Joubert. It must be someone with deep pockets.'

Joubert shot her a look and I saw she had touched a nerve. An inspiration struck me.

'Someone like Mayor Frossard, perhaps.'

Joubert shifted a little in Jean's grip. 'What would you know of Mayor Frossard?'

'Is that it?' demanded Jean. 'You are in Frossard's pay? You scum. What the hell are you doing here? Checking on your handiwork with de Vaux's grave?'

'That was not me!' For the first time, Joubert sounded afraid. 'I had nothing to do with it and I will not be blamed!'

'Then talk to me.' Anna leaned forward. 'Mayor Frossard has a strong motive for damaging Monsieur de Vaux's reputation, and here you are, sneaking around with no good reason…You look very, very suspicious, Monsieur Joubert, and people are desperate to find someone to blame for the attack on Mademoiselle Bernier.'

'No!' At this, Joubert pushed at Jean's arm and struggled. René and Matthieu immediately piled on top of him. When they paused, panting and grunting with the effort, Joubert said, 'It wasn't me! I will not take responsibility for any of this! I did not attack that girl!'

'Did you disturb Monsieur de Vaux's grave?' asked Anna. 'Because the more I think about it, and the less you tell me, the more likely it seems that I have found the man behind this entire sorry mess.'

'No! No! I swear! I did nothing! Frossard wanted me to watch you, that's all! To watch you and tell him what you did!'

Anna chuckled, a hard mirthless laugh which spoke volumes about what she had experienced before. 'For what purpose?'

'He did not tell me why!'

'Come now, Monsieur Joubert, you must have some idea. What did he specifically tell you to look out for?'

'Nothing, Mademoiselle, I swear to you! None of this is anything to do with me! He said he wanted to make sure things were done properly!'

Anna laughed. 'How would he know whether I do things properly?' she asked. 'He has no knowledge of how I work, or what my work involves.' She leaned in, and I saw the men's grip tighten on Joubert. 'So, Monsieur, what are you going to tell him when you report to him?'

'I have nothing to report!' Joubert exclaimed. 'Tonight, like every other night, nothing has happened! I cannot tell him anything because what is there to investigate?'

'There is you, Monsieur.'

Anna's voice was full of quiet menace and a chill shot down my spine. It affected Joubert, too, because the bluster began again, but this time there was a note of genuine fear in his voice. 'No, no, Mademoiselle, please! I swear to you I have nothing to do with what happened! Yes, I work for Frossard, but this is the first time he has asked me to do anything connected to the vampire! I swear it!'

'What kind of work do you usually do for him?' I asked, burning with curiosity.

'I deliver messages,' Joubert said. Matthieu scoffed again.

'Deliver messages, indeed! Along with bundles of francs!'

I huffed out a breath, but Anna said, 'That is a police matter and does not immediately concern us, Monsieur Matthieu. If you know anything, I suggest you take it to Inspector Escoffier in the morning.'

She turned her attention back to Joubert. 'That noise we heard a while ago. The strange, inhuman cry...what was it?'

Joubert stared at her, and I could see genuine confusion and fear on his face. 'I do not know, Mademoiselle.'

'It could not have been him, Mademoiselle Anna, more's the pity.' René shook a cigarette loose from its pack and handed them round. Jean refused, but Matthieu took one. 'I heard the noise when we were chasing this dog. It could not have come from him.'

Anna let out a frustrated exclamation. 'I had better not have been wasting my time with you, Joubert,' she said. 'Are you working alone, or have you a confederate?'

'If Frossard has sent someone else, Mademoiselle, he did not tell me,' Joubert said, his voice sullen.

Anna was silent for a moment, then she looked at the three men. 'You know where Joubert lives, I take it?'

'Yes, indeed, Mademoiselle. And where he works.' Jean tightened his grip again and this time, Joubert let out a whimper which made René chuckle and Matthieu snort in disgust.

'Good. Then let him go.'

'What?'

'Let him go. We have more important things to deal with than Mayor Frossard's messenger.'

Jean opened his mouth to protest, but at that moment, we all heard approaching footsteps. René spun round, Matthieu leapt to his feet, and Jean relaxed his grip on Joubert, lowering the knife but keeping one hand on the man's collar. Anna, too, leaped to her feet and I froze, eyes darting from shadow to shadow, heart hammering.

'There you are!'

I relaxed and let out a long breath as François's voice reached us. A moment later, he appeared at the edge of the lamplight, slowing down as he saw Joubert. 'It was him?'

'François!' I exclaimed.

René muttered something under his breath and Matthieu gave an exasperated sigh. Jean tightened his grip on Joubert again, but I noticed he kept his knife hand ready. Anna beckoned François closer, and he came to stand next to her, staring down at Joubert with distaste.

'Monsieur Joubert is on his way home,' Anna said meaningfully, nodding to Jean. The man scowled, and with very bad grace, released Joubert, shoving him away and getting to his feet, blade still ready. Joubert rolled over out of the way, scrambled to his feet, and ran. We all watched him go, and I wondered if any of the men were questioning the sense of Anna's decision.

'Where were you?' I asked François.

'I heard a noise,' he said. 'A horrible noise... like some kind of animal. Did you hear it too?'

'We did,' Anna nodded.

'It came from somewhere quite near me. At least, I thought it did. Things sound different in here. So, I went to see if I could find what had made it.'

'On your own?' I asked, shocked. François shrugged.

'I didn't think about that,' he said. 'I heard it, I reacted. I found nothing.' He rubbed his chin, and I noticed his hand was filthy.

'What happened?' I asked, nodding at it. He looked, frowned for a moment, then gave a rueful smile and wiped it on the seat of his trousers.

'Tripped over something and fell flat on my face,' he said. 'So... Mademoiselle, what do we do now?'

Anna considered. 'Where were you when you heard that noise?'

François waved in the direction of the main entrance. 'Over there.'

'And you saw nothing?'

'Not a thing. I did not hear the noise again, either, nor anything that sounded like an animal moving around. I heard some shouting, so I came back. The lamplight helped.'

Anna nodded. 'I suggest we continue with the original plan. Patrols at random times, as we discussed.' Hopefully, we have had our excitement for the night, such as it was, but listen out for that noise again.'

'May have been a fox,' Jean said. 'They do sometimes make odd noises.'

'That was no fox!' Matthieu exclaimed. 'It sounded like a human voice.'

'Like no human voice I have heard in my life,' Jean retorted, 'not even in war!'

'Wait a moment,' François said suddenly, staring at them. His voice was unusually sharp and, for once, all three of them paid attention.

'What?' asked René.

François held up a hand, looking all around, and at first, I thought he had heard something, so I did the same. When he spoke, though, his words filled my heart with dread.

'Where is Christophe?'

Chapter 25

There was a pause as we peered into the shadows. Jean was the first to speak. He looked at Matthieu.

'Wasn't he with you?'

Matthieu shook his head. 'No. Once we reached a fork in the path, we went off in different directions, like we always do. I have not seen him since.'

'Has anyone seen him?' There was a note of concern in René's voice.

No one had. Panic rose in my breast, as the men started looking around us in earnest. Jean drew his sword and I saw Matthieu's knife in his hand as he cocked his head, listening to the night.

'Perhaps he is still patrolling,' Jean said, but he did not sound convinced. Anna was not convinced, either.

'That was a great deal of shouting to miss,' she said, her voice grim. 'We need to find him. How many lamps do we have?'

There were two others next to the de Vaux grave. René retrieved and lit them, passing one to Matthieu and one to me. I gripped it, my heart thumping painfully against my ribs. 'Jean and I will follow the direction Christophe took,' René said, nodding at him. 'Matthieu, you take the opposite direction.'

'Circle round,' Anna told them. 'Stay together. Shout for help if you need it, or if you see anything. Viktor and I will search this large central area in front of us. And above all,' she added, 'please be alert. That is paramount and could be the difference between life and death.'

They blinked at her, faces set and eyes wide, the seriousness of the situation suddenly striking home. We split up and started searching. François, who was glowering at René again, paired up with Matthieu, footsteps pounding along the path as they called out for Christophe. Anna and I plunged into the sea of marble, squeezing between mausoleum tombs and following narrow, overgrown paths between them, swinging the lamp this way and that. Christophe's name echoed around us, bouncing off the stone. We ran along one path, then another and another, the shadows bouncing and stretching and looming, overgrown shrubs snatching at our hair and clothes with thin, gnarled fingers. The central area was avenue after narrow avenue of tombs, the marble stark, foreboding and threatening in the bobbing lamplight as Anna dragged me along, our breath ragged.

'Christophe!' she shouted, making me start so violently that I almost dropped the lamp. She slowed her steps, trying to control her breathing while we strained our ears, but there was no answering shout. All we could hear were the men, calling for their comrade.

I set the lamp down by my feet and leaned over, panting. As I did, I noticed tiny tendrils of fog dancing through the grass and straightened up with a little gasp. If Anna noticed, she did not comment, taking my arm and continuing on our hunt. I tried to keep an eye on the fog, but once we started moving, it seemed to dissipate, and I realised it was simply fog. Focus, I told myself. You cannot afford to be distracted now.

We burst out from beneath a straggling rhododendron onto the main path and were about to run around the end tomb and start along the next path when there was a sudden yell from somewhere at the far end of the cemetery in the direction of the Bernier farm. Both of us skidded to a halt and I gripped Anna's arm. 'Are they shouting 'Stop!'?' I asked, straining my ears as other voices joined in and the words became indistinct.

'Yes. Hurry!'

We turned right along the path, ran past the fork which led off to the de Vaux plot to our right, and pounded along in pursuit of the voices. 'They're moving,' I gasped. 'Over there now!'

Anna muttered a curse under her breath as we rounded a corner and tore along another path. The shouting was ahead of us now, and I could just make out a bobbing light flickering in the gaps between the tombs. As we neared, I saw the men had left the path and were in the shrubbery next to the wall, waving their lamps around. All four were shouting at once, their voices a cacophony I could not decipher.

'What's happened?' Anna demanded as we reached them. 'Have you found Christophe?'

'I saw something white moving through these bushes!' Matthieu exclaimed. 'It was around here somewhere, but now there is nothing!'

'What kind of thing?' Anna asked. She moved off the path and joined them, pushing through the branches. I shone the lamp towards the wall beyond. It was perhaps eight feet high, covered in ivy, with slight bulges here and there where the roots of the trees next to it were starting to undermine the foundations. François and Matthieu were just beyond my lamp light, shining their own lamp away from us, their eery silhouettes casting distorted shadows in every direction as the lamp swung to and fro. Suddenly, René, who was staring up at the wall a little further along to our left, gave a sharp cry, and we all ran over to him.

'Look there!' he hissed, pointing upwards.

Above us, caught partly on the top of the wall and partly on a branch overhanging it, was a strip of something white which fluttered very slightly in the breeze.

'What is that?' asked Jean, but as he spoke, François nimbly scaled the tree, inched his way along the branch and reached out a hand to the white object.

'It's a piece of cloth,' he called down, pulling it free and peering at it. 'From... from a petticoat, I think.'

'A petticoat?' Anna repeated blankly. 'Let me see.'

François tucked the fabric into his pocket and swung himself down from the tree, landing gracefully next to us. He handed her the fabric and she turned it over in her hands. It was indeed a strip torn from the hem of a petticoat, a plain, practical one with simple scalloped edging. It was something that Eliza might have worn. Something Louise might have worn.

I glanced at Anna and saw her frowning, the little ridge between her brows as she studied the fabric.

'It's not a piece of shroud, is it?' Matthieu asked, his voice betraying his nerves. Anna shook her head.

'I think François is right. This is part of a petticoat,' she mused.

'A woman?' exclaimed René. 'We are looking for a woman?'

'No,' Jean cut in. 'We are looking for Christophe. Why have we not found him? What is going on here?'

'We should get back to the grave,' Anna said suddenly. 'This is a distraction. Something must be happening elsewhere.'

She rolled the material up and passed it to me. I slid it into my pocket and watched as she cut a notch into the tree trunk. 'What is that for?'

She looked at me. 'To mark the place.'

I felt stupid and nodded without comment, falling in alongside her as the six of us made our way back to the path, turned left and hurried along towards the de Vaux plot. René, Jean and Matthieu were muttering under their breath to each other about why a woman was in the cemetery and all I could think of was Louise.

It made no sense, though. Would Louise really have come back to the cemetery after everything that happened? Yet Anna had said she thought Louise was the key. Had we been on the wrong trail all the time? Was Armand nervous because he was trying to shift our attention away from Louise? That would certainly explain his clumsy attempts to spy on us. But what had this to do with Christophe? And where was he?

We reached the branch of the path and turned along it towards the de Vaux plot. All of us were walking quietly, alert to the slightest noise. I kept starting, as the swinging lamps made shadows catch the corner of my eye. Suddenly, Jean stopped dead, one hand up, sword brandished.

'Listen,' he breathed.

There was the unmistakeable sound of footsteps approaching.

'Hide!' Anna hissed, and we quickly ducked off the path, guttering the lamps and slipping into the shadows between the tombs, ears straining to work out where the footsteps were coming from. Minutes passed and the footsteps grew louder. 'He's coming towards us,' Anna muttered. 'Stay calm. I am ready.' She held out her hands and I saw that she carried not only a knife, but also a long, sharpened stick. I was crouching behind her, as she peered around the end of the tomb and looked along the path. Suddenly, she leaped up and was gone. 'Stop!' she shouted.

There were exclamations from the men as they, too, sprang into action, leaving their hiding places, weapons ready. I leaped out too, still clutching the lamp, and found myself facing an extraordinary tableau.

Anna was pointing both knife and stick at a man who had frozen in front of her with a cudgel raised in defence. Jean, René and Matthieu were ranged around Anna, and the moon was hiding amongst the clouds, so the man's features were lost in shadow. François was somewhere behind me, and I was relieved that he had decided not to attempt any heroics.

'Stop!' the man exclaimed. 'It's me! What are you doing?'

'Christophe?' René's voice was bewildered. 'Christophe? Is that you?'

'Of course, it is me, you fool,' Christophe grumbled. 'What is the meaning of this? Did you catch him?'

'Catch who?' demanded Anna, lowering the stick but not the knife. 'Did you not hear us all calling for you, man? Why did you not answer?'

'The man in white,' Christophe cut in. 'The man in white! He ran this way...did you not see him?'

'No,' said Anna shortly, lowering her knife. She tucked the pointed stick into her waistband. 'Where were you, Christophe? Why did you not respond when you heard us calling your name?'

'I was chasing the man in white,' Christophe said defensively, lowing his cudgel. 'He went off over there somewhere.' He waved an arm vaguely in the direction from which we had just come and fiddled with his shirt collar. René lit the lamps, enveloping us in their warm glow, then folded his arms and glared at Christophe. Jean, too, did not look happy.

'What are you doing?' René asked. 'We have been running around this place looking for you? Why did none of us see you?'

Christophe shrugged. 'It is a big place.'

René leaned in and peered at him. 'Your shirt is inside out, man! What have you been doing? Playing dress up? Huh? What is going on?'

This raised a chorus of comments from the other men and Christophe's protestations became more and more feeble against their onslaught. Eventually Anna stepped in. Facing Christophe, she looked up at him, her eyes two glittering shards of flint.

'You know how suspicious this looks.' She eyed him. 'You vanish, someone is running around the cemetery, and we find a piece of petticoat caught in a tree. Now. You either tell us exactly what you have been doing, or I send for Inspector Escoffier.'

Christophe scowled at her and folded his arms. 'Escoffier and his men should be here anyway,' he retorted.

'Why is your shirt inside out?' Anna asked. 'Either you tell us, or I will describe what I think has been happening here, and you can tell me if I am right or not.'

The man scoffed, but wilted somewhat when he realised the others were standing staring at him with undisguised annoyance. Anna waited for a moment, then said, 'François, please could you go and fetch...'

'Wait!' Christophe exclaimed. 'Let us not be hasty, Mademoiselle...'

'Stop blustering, man, and explain. I do not believe for a moment that you have been chasing a man in white.' Anna's voice was hard, and she made no attempt to disguise her irritation. Christophe slumped a little and cast a glance over his shoulder as though he feared being overheard.

'All right, all right,' he said, his voice weary. 'I assure you, Mademoiselle, I am nothing to do with all this.' He waved his hand towards the de Vaux grave. 'I have...er...I have been...er... '

'Just say it,' René snapped, taking a step forward. I saw Matthieu half in the shadows, arms folded, shaking his head, and realised how concerned they had been for Christophe. If he had been trying to put on some kind of show for Anna's benefit, it had backfired badly.

Christophe sighed heavily and rubbed his chin. 'I took advantage of the patrol to meet someone,' he said.

'A woman?' René asked.

'Of course, a woman!' Christophe shot back. 'Please… do not tell my wife.'

Anna stared at him. 'You have been using the patrols to meet your mistress in a cemetery?' she said slowly, distaste dripping from every syllable. Christophe shifted from foot to foot and rubbed his chin again.

'It was easy,' he said. 'The patrols were always at regular times, so we arranged that she would wait in a particular place when her duties were done, and I would look for her there every time I passed on patrol.' Jean gave a snort of derision and Christophe added hastily, 'It is not every patrol, nor every night!'

'That makes it *so* much better,' René snorted, and Christophe winced at the sarcasm.

'I think we can all agree that you have wasted our time, Christophe,' Anna said. 'Viktor, may I have the fabric, please?'

I delved into my pocket and handed it over. Anna took it and unfolded it, displaying it for Christophe to see. 'I expect this looks familiar?'

Christophe peered at it and shrugged. 'What can I say, Mademoiselle, I was not looking…'

René uttered an infuriated exclamation, stepped forward and grabbed Christophe's collar, raising a fist. Christophe yelped and dropped his cudgel, raising his arms defensively. 'Yes! Yes, it is hers… it must be.'

'Where do you think we found this?' Anna asked, waving it at him. He stared at her for a moment, then I saw the penny drop and he nodded towards the tree.

'She was going to go over the wall over there somewhere, so that is the only place it could have been,' he said.

Anna nodded and passed me the fabric. 'That wall backs onto the houses along the Rue Saint-Martin,' she said. 'Very few of their courtyards have access to the street. What is she going to do, hop over the walls until she finds one which does?'

Christophe shrugged again and I felt my own irritation rising. 'I do not know, Mademoiselle.'

Anna snorted. 'We are wasting time. There was no 'man in white', was there?'

His face fell and he scuffed a foot on the path. 'No.'

'We have wasted time and energy on you, Christophe,' Anna snapped. 'I am used to people putting on a show when I am investigating, thinking they have to provide some kind of spectacle, or prove their experiences are real. I am used to people hijacking my investigations because they choose not to believe, or have something to gain from doing so. I thought I had seen it all.' She looked him up and down. 'I have now.'

Matthieu snorted with laughter and René released his grip on Christophe, shaking his head. Jean tutted under his breath and said something unsavoury. The group dynamic had been shattered. François and I stayed silent. This was not François's usual patrol group, and I was glad he had chosen to hold his tongue. This was not his battle, nor mine.

They answered my question almost as I thought it. Jean exchanged a look with René and said, 'Go home, Christophe.'

'What?' Christophe shot him a startled look. 'Go home? But...'

'How can we trust you?' demanded René. 'We have been out here for the good of the community and you have been running around with some woman! We cannot trust you to support us, Christophe. Jean is right. You should go home.'

'Mademoiselle Anna may have solved the case by the morning anyway,' Matthieu chipped in, and I rolled my eyes at the sycophantic praise, especially coming from him. Yet deep down, I really hoped he was right, and something about tonight would fall into place and give us the answers to the many questions buzzing around inside my head. As fascinating as the experience was, I knew I was running on nerves and excitement, and that could not go on indefinitely. I itched for the dawn to come so I could sleep for a few hours and then go to the telegraph office to see if I had had word from Uncle Geoffrey. I hoped Arthur had been able to contact him to let him know what I was doing, but even so, I still worried for his safety. Could I go home now?

Did I want to go home?

Once again, that question pushed its way to the forefront of my mind and I shook my head a little to clear it, knowing it was important to focus on the matter in hand. Christophe was still staring at everyone, and I heard François behind me chuckling softly. No one spoke. Anna stepped to one side and stood with her back to the de Vaux grave, leaving the men to deal with Christophe themselves.

It did not take long. Christophe tried protesting again, but was met with stony silence, all three of them simply looking at him. René's fingers were twitching, and I half-expected him to throw a punch, but he remained unmoving. After several minutes, Christophe threw up his hands, turned and stomped off down the path, turning left at the end towards the side entrance by the Bernier farm. Matthieu muttered a curse beneath his breath, took out his knife and a stone and started honing the blade, leaning up against one of the mausoleum tombs. René kicked at the tufts of grass overhanging the path, swinging his cudgel. Jean simply stood, his military discipline showing, one hand resting on his sword hilt, the other at his side. Anna was standing with folded arms and a dark scowl on her face. François was just beyond the light cast by the lamps, but I could make out folded arms and see his eyes glittering.

'You are satisfied that you have done the right thing, gentlemen?' Anna asked.

René huffed. 'What else could we do?'

'I am inclined to agree. His antics have muddied the waters, and I do not expect anything else to happen tonight, unless someone turns up to enquire what all the shouting was about.'

'Unlikely,' Jean said. 'No one is inclined to be a hero in this matter. I suspect most people, if they heard, will have pulled a pillow over their head, and prayed loudly to drown us out.'

Anna nodded. 'Let us hope so. We could do without further distractions tonight. Hopefully, that will be the end of the show. Let us have a rest and take stock, then we can start a fresh round of patrols. Agreed?'

'Sensible.' Jean settled himself on the ground. He reached into his pocket and brought out a small silver flask which he handed round. Matthieu and René accepted, Anna, François and I all declined with thanks. I was pleased to see Jean including François, but he still kept his distance, remaining just at the edge of the lamplight. René guttered two of the lamps and the shadows thickened once more, plunging François into almost complete darkness, but he remained where he was as René returned the lamps to their hiding place and took out his cigarettes. He lit one, then wandered up and down the path, smoking, lost in thought.

After a couple of minutes, Matthieu muttered, 'Damn fool.'

'He was gone for quite a long time three or four nights back. Do you remember?' Jean said. 'We thought nothing of it.'

'Why would we?' Matthieu asked. 'We thought he was doing what we were doing, just being more thorough. And all the time...'

'It's done,' Anna said quietly. 'Don't dwell on it. This is not over, and you must not distract yourselves with irrelevancies. We found no sign of whatever made that noise earlier, remember.'

'Could it have been Christophe?' François asked suddenly. 'If he was...you know...'

René and Matthieu laughed. Jean, however, looked thoughtful.

'You hear all kinds of noises on the battlefield,' he said in a low voice. 'All of them come from men. Not all of them sound like men.'

'What did you think of it?' asked Anna, giving him an appraising look. 'Human?'

Jean shrugged. 'I would not like to say.'

Matthieu sniggered and muttered something about Christophe's sexual prowess which made René and Jean laugh, albeit reluctantly on Jean's part. I knew, from seeing my father after he returned from the Crimea, that Jean was seeing ghosts, and shuddered.

A distant clock struck midnight and Anna chuckled drily. 'Only midnight,' she observed. 'An eventful evening, eh, gentlemen?'

'Too eventful,' Jean murmured, and she nodded.

'What do you think about making another round of the cemetery?' she asked. 'Christophe should be gone now. François, might you take his place for this one, please?'

François said he would, and the duties were agreed upon. Jean and François would take the Bernier end and the main gate respectively, while René and Matthieu started at either end of the path we were now on, all moving in a clockwise direction. Anna and I remained at the grave, for which I was grateful. Now that the excitement was over, I realised I was exhausted, my thoughts dull and my eyelids starting to droop. I flopped down onto the grass and leaned against the tomb opposite the de Vaux plot, trying to stay awake. Anna, by contrast, was alert and sharp. She leaned over to gutter the lamp René had left us, giving me a glimpse of her biting her lip with a frown on her face before she plunged us into darkness. I wanted to ask her a dozen questions, but I knew I was too tired to put my thoughts into words and focused instead on staying awake.

We sat in silence for some time, listening to the clock chiming the quarter hours. The cemetery was silent, peaceful, and I dozed off once or twice, waking when my head fell back against the marble behind me. Once when I awoke, I saw Anna had lit the lamp once more and was scribbling in her notebook. She had her bag beside her, and I could see the long sharp stick poking out of the top of it. My eyes started closing again and I let them. It was too much of an effort to fight sleep any more.

I awoke when the men returned. They had nothing to report and seemed satisfied that all was as it should be. Anna, too, sounded relieved.

The rest of the night was uneventful. The men patrolled again, and when they returned just after three o'clock, Jean looked at me and smiled. 'You look like you need your bed, sir.'

I felt heat creep into my cheeks. 'I am fine, Monsieur.'

René chuckled. 'You should go and sleep. Both of you. Nothing will happen now. It will start to get light soon enough.'

Anna stretched and nodded. 'Never say never, Monsieur. I half expected something to happen during the night. However, I need to be able to think clearly tomorrow and do not wish to lose too much of the day to sleep, so perhaps Viktor and I should return to Madame Archambeau's. Will you send word when your patrol finishes, to confirm all is well?'

'Of course,' René replied. Matthieu nodded.

'I can. I have to pass that way,' he said.

François let out a frustrated sigh. 'I can tell them when I return home,' he said pointedly, and Matthieu nodded as though the possibility had not occurred to him. I rolled my eyes and gave him a sympathetic smile, but he did not respond. I bit my lip, wondering if I should say anything, but my sluggish brain had switched off. It was all I could do to rise to my feet and shake hands with the men as we prepared to take our leave. René gave us one of the lamps, which I took, managing to remember to offer Anna my arm. François told us to go through the yard behind the house and use the door into the kitchen, and to help ourselves to any food and drink we wanted. Anna thanked him and tucked her hand into my arm. Together, we made our way slowly through the cemetery, peering down the narrow paths between the mausoleum tombs out of habit. There was no sign of de Montfort.

'How are you?' Anna asked as we reached the main gate and emerged onto the Rue Saint-Martin.

'Exhausted.'

'It's hard at first. It gets easier.' She paused. 'You did very well.'

'I did almost nothing.'

'You did not panic or run away screaming. You stayed with me every step of the way, Viktor. I am impressed.'

I considered this. 'I was scared, though.'

'If you had not been scared, I would doubt your sanity.' She chuckled. 'This is not about fearlessness. This is about justice and doing the right thing. It is not easy. I have been terrified so many times, especially in the beginning.'

'You hide it so well.'

'I have to.'

I nodded. 'I understand that. It makes you almost impossible to read.'

She did not respond until we had reached the arch leading to Christine's yard and I thought I had made some terrible error of judgment. However, when she stopped, and I turned to shine the lamp on her to see what was wrong, she was smiling.

'This is another of your qualities I like,' she said. 'You accept me for what I am, even though you have only the vaguest concept of what that actually is. I don't mean to shut you out, Viktor, and I am sorry for the times when it seems as though I do. To do this work, one needs to erect walls, and unfortunately, mine are designed to keep everyone out, because that is how I function, how I survive. It is not intentional. I hope you can understand.'

'Yes,' I said. 'I understand completely. Some people enjoy finding the cracks in people's façades so they can bring the walls down. You cannot afford to let that happen. Let one person in, and it opens the gates to all.'

She reached out and squeezed my hand. 'I can't wait to introduce you to my employers,' she said. 'Come, let us heat some milk before we sleep. I am chilled in spite of Christine's blankets.'

We each had a blanket wrapped around our shoulders, but they had done little to ward off the cold. Tiptoeing into the yard, we let ourselves into the lobby as quietly as we could, then went through into the kitchen, where the warmth enveloped us in its embrace. We huddled by the stove for a few minutes, then Anna went to fetch some milk while I took a pan from the dresser.

While we waited for the milk to heat through, I tried to order my thoughts, but they flitted around in chaos. We took our drinks to the parlour and curled up in the armchairs. As I sat there, the beaker of milk cupped in my cold hands, I found myself glancing across at the writing desk and my thoughts immediately settled on the conversation I had overheard between François and Christine. All at once, I was desperate to see what François had been looking at in the desk, that sheaf of papers, the newspaper clipping I recalled in Christine's hand. I shook my head. Anna had told me not to get distracted, but the more I tried to push those thoughts away, the more they persisted. I told Anna, who regarded me for a moment, brow furrowed in thought.

'I know you said I should not distract myself,' I murmured, 'but the entire conversation is proving to be a distraction.'

'Viktor, you are proposing to rifle through our host's private papers!'

My face fell. I had not thought of it like that, but she was right. What on earth was I thinking? 'I'm sorry,' I said, flushing scarlet. 'I am tired, and my mind is all over the place.'

'Don't worry,' she said. 'It can sometimes be difficult to work out what is important and what is not. Christophe and his romantic liaisons, for example. That wasted so much valuable time.'

'Do you think we can work out what is going on before Frossard starts the exhumation proceedings?' I finished my milk, set the beaker down and stifled a yawn, snuggling further under my blanket in the comfortable chair.

Anna placed her beaker on the table next to her and leaned back in the chair, closing her eyes. 'It is not a question of whether we can, Viktor. We must.'

I gave the writing desk one final look before closing my own eyes. Sleep on it, I told myself. If it is still foremost in your mind when you wake, find a moment to have a quick look and then it can be forgotten. Anna is right. The stakes are too high.

Even as I itched to cross the room and look through the desk right then and there, I felt myself drifting into sleep. There was something else, too, right on the edges of my fading consciousness. It was partly connected to that elusive comment of Christine's, which I still could not recall, but there was something else now, too, something which had happened during the patrol. Vague images flitted around my mind, but every time I tried to reach for them, they vanished like the tiny tendrils of fog which had danced around my ankles in the darkness.

Chapter 26

'Viktor? Viktor, wake up!'

I blinked, confused, as a face loomed over me. Startled, I sat up, wincing as my muscles creaked in protest. My head was heavy, and I dragged myself into wakefulness, surprised that I did not feel more refreshed. The room was still quite dark, and Christine smiled down at me as I took in the armchair, the blanket wrapped round me, the buttoned overcoat I still wore. Embarrassed, I stared up at her as she placed a hand on my shoulder, the soothing aroma of her rose water surrounding me.

'Don't get up. I am so sorry to disturb you, but there has been a development in the case. Your sister needs you.'

'A development?' I rubbed my eyes with the heels of my hands and waited for my dull brain to catch up. 'Something has happened?'

Christine looked grim. 'I am afraid Louise Bernier has been attacked again.'

'What?' My jaw dropped and my heart skipped. 'How? Is she…'

'She is unhurt, just badly frightened, as you might imagine. François ran back to find Anna.'

For the first time, I registered that Anna was not in the room and sat bolt upright, shoving the blanket away. 'Do I need to go to her?' I asked. 'Is she at the Bernier farm?'

251

'No, she is in the dining room,' Christine said. 'You both had a full day yesterday, followed by a busy night, from what I hear. You have had almost no sleep. I insist you have some food before you go anywhere today.'

She moved to the window and opened the curtains, letting soft early morning light flood the room and banish the shadows. Smothering a yawn, I levered myself onto the edge of the seat, catching my breath as something twanged painfully in my neck. Christine wandered to the fireplace and fiddled with one or two of the trinkets, then went to the writing desk and did the same. Seeing her standing there, tall and elegant in her pale blue morning dress, hair neatly pulled back in a heavy chignon, I thought of my conversation with Anna a few hours earlier. Would violating her privacy achieve anything other than satisfying my curiosity? I had to control it, or it would cloud my vision. It was none of my business.

I realised Christine was talking and apologised for missing her words. She smiled. 'You poor dear boy, you must be exhausted,' she said. 'I hated having to wake you. You looked so peaceful. Come and have some food while François explains what happened.'

We went out into the hall, where I paused to shed my overcoat and glance at my reflection in the mirror to make sure my hair was behaving. A few strands had worked themselves loose, so I tucked them away, hoping Christine had not noticed. Rolling my stiff shoulders, I followed her into the dining room.

It was a hive of activity. Céline was setting out plates as Anna, pale and drawn, poured glasses of water. François, who was rather grey after two consecutive nights without much sleep, was standing next to my chair, loading bread rolls from a tray into a basket. He nodded at me, looking serious.

'Did you get any sleep?'

'A little. I am not sure what time it is.'

'Just after five.'

I groaned. 'We should have stayed in the cemetery.'

'I wish you had,' he said, leaning past me to put the rolls in the centre of the table before taking the chair next to mine. I caught a faint waft of Christine's rose water as he did so and all at once, part of that elusive comment wavered at the edge of my memory. It was definitely something she had said, and I was certain we had been here in the dining room when she said it. The substance of it, though, still eluded me and I forced myself to pay attention to François. Céline put a platter of cold meats and cheese on the table, then went round with the coffee pot as François explained what had happened. As he spoke, Anna's expression grew darker.

The men had been patrolling and everything appeared to have returned to its usual peaceful state when all at once, they had heard terrible screams from the far end, near the Bernier farm. They had all immediately headed in that direction. 'I got there around the same time as Matthieu,' François said. 'René found her. He said she came tearing around a corner and collided with him. Then there was more screaming. Jean got there just before Matthieu and myself. I think he thought René was harming her at first, because he drew his sword. She was clinging to René, though, saying something about Louis de Vaux grabbing her throat and telling her to leave.'

'What was she doing there?' Christine asked. There was a note in her voice which sounded almost like despair, and I found myself in sympathy with her. Anna, however, looked angry.

'An excellent question,' she said, her voice sharp. 'But this time, the attacker spoke to her?'

'She said it was old Monsieur de Vaux.'

Christine looked deeply troubled. 'How could it be Monsieur de Vaux?'

'She knew him?' I asked. 'That seems unlikely, given the difference in status.'

'We all knew him,' François shrugged. 'We saw him at church on Sundays. Before he became ill, he would sometimes read the lesson.'

Anna helped herself to a roll and a slice of meat, taking tiny bites as her mind worked. 'Did she say why she was there this time?'

'No, Mademoiselle Anna, and I did not hear anyone asking, although they may have done before I got there.' François reached for a roll, and I saw Christine, sitting to his left at the head of the table, blanch slightly as he did so. My heart skipped and I watched her, worried she was ill. She caught my eye and flashed a small, quick smile before picking up her coffee and taking a sip. I turned my attention to François, who was slicing his roll in half. His nails were filthy, and I suppressed a smile, suspecting that was what had caught Christine's eye. Thinking back to her fussing over his lapel, it was easy to imagine her fussing over his nails also.

'Where is Louise now?' Anna asked.

'René and Jean took her home. Matthieu went back to the grave and I came to fetch you.'

'She was shaken but unhurt, like before?'

'As I understand it, yes.'

Anna gave a small, brisk nod. 'Did anyone mention sending for the police?'

'Not that I heard, Mademoiselle, but I am sure Monsieur Bernier would do so, like last time.'

Christine gave an almost inaudible sigh. 'Poor girl,' she murmured. Anna raised an eyebrow.

'Indeed,' she said quietly, 'and I truly feel for her, especially as I will have to ask her some hard questions and will not accept any of the lies she has previously told us.'

'Lies?'

'About what she was doing wandering around a cemetery at night,' I explained. 'I am not sure anyone believes she was out looking for a dog.'

'If they did, they won't after today,' François observed. Christine gave him a reproachful look. 'Oh, Maman, you always want to believe the best of everyone. Surely even you can see how this looks?'

Christine frowned. 'Of course, I can see what it looks like,' she said with a tiny flash of anger. 'And that is what saddens me. Even if she was telling the truth about looking for the dog, her reputation has been tarnished, and will follow her around forever. And if she was lying, well, I wish things could be different, so girls do not constantly find themselves in this sort of position.'

I recalled the charity work she undertook and guessed she saw a great many women and girls who had followed their hearts and, as a result, paid the price society demanded. Thinking about it from that perspective made me consider my own situation, and the respectable marriage I would eventually make. Even the thought made me shudder. Anna glanced across at me, a look of concern on her face, and I smiled reassuringly, finishing my bread and draining my cup. Anna, Louise and I were all so similar, I realised. Each of us was trying, in our own way, to escape the confines of the lives society and our families had mapped out for us. Anna had succeeded. Louise, it seemed, was destined to fail. I chose not to consider where I fell on the scale. Anna and Louise both had their places in the world, whereas mine was currently in flux. What would become of me was anybody's guess.

We raced through the rest of the meal and ran upstairs to splash water on our faces. Christine and Céline hovered in the hall as we hurried into our coats, Christine trying to dissuade François from going with us. 'Anna and Viktor need to work, my son,' she chided. Anna shook her head.

'It would be better if François does accompany us,' she said. 'The police will wish to speak with him about what he heard and saw. If they can do so while we are at the Berniers', then so much the better. It means they will not need to come here and disturb you.'

Christine nodded, one hand toying with the buttons on her cuff. 'It would be useful,' she admitted. 'Do you think the police will need to speak with myself or Céline? I was intending to go into town this morning.'

Anna looked surprised. 'I cannot imagine why they would. Neither of you were involved.'

Christine flushed pink. 'I thought they might need me to corroborate François's story, but the other men will be able to do that, won't they?'

'Of course they will,' François grumbled, wrapping a scarf round his neck. 'Please stop making a fuss, Maman. I shall simply tell them what I saw and heard, offer opinions if they ask, and see if there is anything else I can do to be of assistance. Now, we really must go.'

The three of us stepped out into the chill morning air and I thrust my hands into my coat pockets as we hurried along the Rue Saint-Martin. The sky was ablaze with soft pastel colours, the last of the night's shadows fading. A coal merchant drove past, his horse's hooves clopping loudly, and there were signs of life in many of the houses we passed. Two or three women were scrubbing their front steps, another was emptying a bucket of water into the gutter. An old woman with a heavily lined face, a pipe clenched between her teeth, was setting up a chair next to her front door, sinking into it and staring up and down the street as she puffed. She took some knitting out of a bag at her waist, unrolled what looked like a part-finished stocking and began working on it, eyes fixed on us as we hurried along. By the time we reached the corner and turned up the hill to the Bernier farm, I was out of breath and struggling to conceal it. My legs trembled with the unaccustomed activity, and I was glad of the coffee and food Christine had insisted upon, as I felt light-headed.

We paused at the corner for a moment, as Anna murmured something to François which I did not catch. He nodded and ran off up the hill, crossing the road. Anna and I continued at a slightly slower pace, and I watched as François bounded up the de Vauxs' path and rang the bell. My thoughts would not organise themselves, and as we crossed the Bernier yard and Anna knocked at the door, my head was a chaotic mess. Taking a few deep breaths, trying not to sound like I was about to expire, I forced my tired brain to focus on the case and hoped Anna would not call on me to say anything intelligent. Or, ideally, anything much at all.

The Berniers' house was a blur of activity. I could hear some of the farmhands chatting in the sheds around the yard and somewhere nearby was the rattle of milk churns. One of the cows lowed and another answered, which set the dogs barking, and a man's voice yelled at them to be quiet. The door was opened by the maid, her face grey and pinched. She offered us a muted greeting and showed us into the parlour, where Louise was lying on the sofa, covered with a blanket. Josephine Bernier sat next to her, wearing a wrap over her day dress, holding her daughter's hand. Maurice Bernier, dressed for work, stood next to the mantelpiece, gazing down into the fire. When we entered the room, all three of them started and turned to face us.

'Thank you, Julie,' said Josephine quietly. 'Please bring some coffee and ensure there will be sufficient when the police arrive.'

'Of course, Madame.' Julie curtseyed and left the room. As she closed the door behind her, I caught another glimpse of her drawn, worried face and wondered what had been said so far.

Bernier waved us into the armchairs, and we sat, Anna's face grim as she regarded Louise. 'Thank you for coming,' Bernier said. 'I understand you had only left an hour or so earlier to get some sleep, so I appreciate it.'

Anna nodded at him, turning with businesslike efficiency to Louise. 'Are you hurt?'

Louise shook her head, her face crumpling. She burst into tears and Josephine pulled a handkerchief from her sleeve, mopping at her daughter's face with gentle, tender movements. Anna moved towards her and laid a hand on Louise's shoulder.

'May I look?' she asked. 'To make certain?'

Louise hiccupped and nodded, struggling free from the blanket so she could unbutton the collar of her blouse. Anna started to lean in and paused. 'This is what you were wearing?'

Louise glanced up at her, a look of panic flashing across her tear-streaked face and gave a barely imperceptible nod. Josephine's eyes narrowed and Maurice Bernier threw his daughter a hard look. They know she is lying about the dog, I thought. What is going on here?

Anna said no more, but leaned down to inspect Louise's neck, looking up at one point to ask for more light. Maurice turned up one of the lamps and Anna gently tilted Louise's chin, peering at her skin. 'Bruising, nothing more. Not even a graze,' she said, relief in her voice. 'I expect it will be tender for a few days, but it will fade soon enough.'

She returned to her chair and looked at the Berniers. The atmosphere was different to our previous interview. There was a tension in the air, as though something unseen was hanging between us, known, but unmentioned. Anna let a silence stretch around the room. It lasted only a few moments, but it was enough to set Josephine fiddling with the handkerchief and Maurice to shuffle his feet, while Louise's trembling hands fumbled with her buttons.

'I think it sensible to wait until the police arrive,' Anna said. 'Louise will then only have to explain things once and we investigators will all have the same information.'

Josephine nodded. 'Thank you for your consideration, Mademoiselle. That is kind.'

'I have been in this situation many times, Madame,' Anna said. 'My greatest concern is always for the victim.'

Julie appeared and served us with steaming coffee. The interruption eased some of the tension in the room and the business of accepting hot milk in our drinks occupied several minutes. Once or twice, I caught the Berniers exchanging a glance above their daughter's head. Louise kept her eyes cast down towards the floor, and although she accepted a cup, did not touch it. She was sitting more upright now, leaning against the cushions, blanket wrapped tightly round her waist and legs like a shield. Her hands trembled as they cradled her coffee, and I felt a pang of pity shoot through me. Whatever her situation was, she must be desperate if she had chosen to venture back into the cemetery so soon after what had happened. And for the same thing to have happened again… was it simply an unfortunate coincidence, or could Louise be the target, as we had discussed before? I sipped my coffee and tried not to shift around in my seat, willing the police to hurry.

The relief in the room was evident when we heard a knock at the door. Bernier straightened and tried to dust off his grubby work jacket, while Josephine rose, leaving her wrap on the sofa next to Louise, whose eyes were the size of saucers. Anna and I set our cups aside, listening to the footsteps creaking down the hall. It sounded like three or four people were approaching. The door opened and I blinked in surprise.

I had expected to see Escoffier, but it was de Vaux who was ushered into the room, followed by Armand, and behind him, François. De Vaux looked even more gaunt than he had the previous day and Armand was white, his skin pallid against the deep black of his mourning clothes.

Bernier had taken a step forward, but on seeing de Vaux, he froze, staring at him in confusion. 'Why are you here?' There was genuine puzzlement in his voice as he looked from de Vaux to Armand, and then to Anna. François stood by the door, hands behind his back, looking on with interest. I realised what Anna was intending and hoped it would not backfire.

De Vaux looked at Anna, who nodded in greeting. 'I asked Monsieur de Vaux and Armand to join us, Monsieur Bernier. A discussion needs to occur and it involves all of you.'

The Berniers greeted the de Vauxs with a certain amount of reserve, the exchanges clipped and polite, the handshakes brief. As the de Vauxs seated themselves, Anna looked at François.

'Thank you, François, for your assistance,' she said. 'May I request that you return home? You need to sleep, and I will not require any further assistance that Viktor cannot provide.'

His face flushed red for a brief moment and his lips tightened, but he nodded. 'That is good advice, Mademoiselle. I am glad to have been of service to you.' He bowed stiffly, turned and left the room, closing the door behind him. The floorboards protested as he passed, and as the front door opened, we heard the clatter of hooves somewhere nearby. A cool early morning breeze snaked its way beneath the parlour door and as I felt it cling to my ankles, I found myself almost missing the layers of petticoats, which startled me into wakefulness. I was surprised Anna had sent François away when he would also need to speak to the police.

Men's voices rose in the yard outside, calling for grooms. A dog barked and a woman, Julie, perhaps, shouted at it to be quiet, which had no effect whatsoever. A couple of minutes later, Julie appeared.

'Inspector Escoffier, Monsieur,' she announced as Escoffier strode into the room, halting when he saw the little assembly before him. We started another round of greetings as Julie curtseyed and hurried off, returning with a tray laden with coffee and pastries. She circled the room, serving in an unobtrusive manner as Escoffier settled into a chair and regarded us with interest.

'Thank you for coming, Inspector,' Bernier said, relief and gratitude in his voice. 'Can you believe that it has happened a second time?'

Escoffier turned his gaze to Louise, looking thoughtful, and the girl quailed under his scrutiny. Anna watched with narrowed eyes. The Inspector reached into his pocket and withdrew a small notebook and a pencil. Seeing this, Anna spoke.

'I believe a discussion needs to take place, Inspector, which will serve to resolve some of the issues affecting Monsieur de Vaux's unfortunate situation,' she began. Bernier interrupted her with a snort.

'Unfortunate situation indeed!' he scoffed. Anna turned to him, her eyes flashing.

'You do not consider it unfortunate, Monsieur Bernier? I would say that no matter how you examine it, from Monsieur de Vaux's viewpoint, it is extremely unfortunate. Either his beloved late father is a vampire, or his beloved late father's grave is at risk of being dug up for no reason. I would class both of those things as extremely unfortunate. Wouldn't you?'

De Vaux caught his breath and Armand seemed to crumple in his chair, the cup frozen half-way to his lips as he stared at Anna. Escoffier looked at Anna appraisingly, while the Berniers' discomfort was palpable. Josephine gave a soft gasp, clutching at Louise's hand, while Maurice Bernier lowered his eyes to the hearth and murmured a vague apology.

'Tell me about this discussion, Mademoiselle,' Escoffier invited. Anna acknowledged this with a graceful inclination of her head and rose, tapping her fingertips together as she regarded the faces before her.

'I have gleaned a lot of information from what I have seen and experienced so far,' she said. 'Firstly, I would be grateful if Mademoiselle Bernier could tell us what happened. Once I have heard, I would like to give you my opinion of what I believe has happened here. Anyone who has knowledge of the situations I describe may feel free to correct me if I should make a mistake with any detail. Do you all find that acceptable?'

I looked around the room at the watchful, wary faces and excitement bubbled within me. Was this the moment when we would discover our vampire? Was it Armand? Hardly daring to breathe, I waited for Louise to start speaking.

When she did, at Anna's gentle prompt a moment later, her voice shook. She spoke so quietly that Escoffier, who was sitting the furthest from her, got up and came to stand just behind Josephine at the end of the sofa, looking down at the girl with an encouraging half-smile, nodding now and then. The essence of her story was identical to that which we had already heard. She had been in the cemetery when suddenly she was grabbed from behind, the attacker tried to bite her, then she heard Louis de Vaux's voice in her ear.

'What did he say?' Escoffier asked, making notes.

'He said, 'Leave this place,' Inspector,' Louise whispered, shuddering.

'What makes you so certain that it was Monsieur de Vaux's voice you heard?' Escoffier paused, regarding her, pencil poised over the notebook. Louise turned wide, frightened eyes to him, tears spilling down her cheeks.

'I know his voice, Inspector.' She sobbed, and Josephine handed her the handkerchief. Mopping at her face, Louise continued. 'He would say good day whenever we met, and I saw him in church. I know his voice.'

Escoffier nodded and made a note. 'What happened then?'

Louise closed her eyes and shook with silent sobs for a moment. Bernier set his coffee down and went to stand with his hands on her shoulders. She leaned back against him, her fingers plucking at the blanket. 'He pushed me,' she whispered. 'He pushed me, and I fell. I turned to look but he was gone.'

'Where exactly were you when this happened?' Anna asked. 'On the path?'

A bright spot of colour bloomed in Louise's white face. 'I was amongst the tombs, Mademoiselle.'

'So it would have been simple for this person to avoid being seen.' Escoffier made another note. 'I have to ask you, Mademoiselle: what were you doing in the cemetery this time? Surely what happened before was sufficient reason to confine your visits to daylight hours only?'

Bernier bristled. 'What are you insinuating?' he demanded, stopping as Escoffier held up a hand.

'If this matter is to be brought to any sort of conclusion, Bernier, you must understand that I need all the details, no matter how small, how irrelevant they seem. Or how embarrassing they are,' he added, with a pointed look at Louise. She lowered her gaze to her tightly clasped hands. Armand's eyes were fixed on her, but she had not once looked his way. Was that to disguise love, or fear?

Armand looked tense and awkward as he stared at Louise, shoulders hunched. I shifted a little in my chair and he glanced my way, reddening when he realised I was watching him. For a brief moment, I held his gaze. The pallor and slightly hollowed cheeks gave him a romantic, Byronesque appearance. If Louise was captivated by him, I could understand why.

Louise took a deep breath and murmured something so quietly than none of us caught it and Escoffier had to ask her to repeat it. She pursed her lips and said, 'I was after the dog again.'

'Forgive me, Mademoiselle, but I do not think there is a single person in the room who believes that,' Anna said. I caught my breath, shocked at her bluntness, as did Louise, whose mouth fell open. The two young women stared at each other in silence, and the fact that Bernier made no protest told me Anna was right. The dog story may have been just about plausible once, but twice?

Louise burst into tears and Armand shot to his feet. 'Enough of this!' he exclaimed. 'Can't you see how upset she is?'

'Armand!' de Vaux protested, frowning. 'Sit down!'

Armand remained standing. De Vaux set down his coffee and turned to face his trembling son. 'Sit down, boy!' he hissed through gritted teeth. 'Do you hear? Sit!'

Still Armand ignored him. 'You are right, Mademoiselle,' he said, his voice low.

'Armand?' De Vaux stared in open-mouthed confusion. 'What is this? What are you saying?'

'There was no dog,' Armand said, his voice low. Louise started and gasped.

'Armand, no….' she breathed.

'What is this?' demanded de Vaux, springing to his feet with sudden energy and turning to face his son. 'What could you possibly know…of…'

His already pale face turned a worrying shade of grey. He reached for the back of the armchair, staggering a little, and eased himself back down onto the seat, staring at his son.

Anna gave Armand an earnest, encouraging nod. 'This needs to be said. It has muddied the waters long enough.'

'What is going on?' exclaimed Josephine, just as Maurice snapped, 'What the hell is this? What are you talking about?'

Armand quavered but raised his chin, and his voice, when he started to speak, was quiet but firm. 'There was no dog, Monsieur Bernier. Louise went to the cemetery to meet me.'

'What?' Both Bernier and de Vaux were open-mouthed now. Bernier recovered first, rounding on Louise. 'What is this? You disgrace our family by running around with a boy...with *that* boy... in a cemetery, of all places? Have you no dignity, no sense of what is right and proper?'

'Papa...I...' Louise protested weakly, but Bernier thundered on, reducing the girl to tears almost immediately. Josephine sat unmoving next to Louise, face white, lips set. Her gaze had settled somewhere in the mid-distance, as if she was replaying conversations in her head, looking for the tell-tale signs she had missed.

De Vaux had crumpled, it seemed. Slumped forward, he rested his elbows on his knees, head in his hands. 'Why, Armand?' was all he said.

'If I may.' Anna cut through Bernier's rant, and he stopped in surprise. 'This investigation is already on an incredibly tight timescale. If I cannot resolve it by the end of the day, Mayor Frossard will begin pursuing an exhumation tomorrow. I either need to produce a vampire, or the people or person responsible for the attack on Louise and the damage to Monsieur de Vaux's grave. As matters currently stand, I can do none of those things and I am running out of time. By maintaining your secrets, you are seriously impeding the investigation and I must now insist on the full truth being disclosed.'

Armand shuffled his feet, a bright spot of colour staining his pale cheeks. 'You are right, Mademoiselle, and I sincerely apologise for my part in it,' he murmured.

'You went to the cemetery to meet each other. Why that night? The night of your grandfather's funeral?' Anna was all business now, and Armand bit his lip before answering.

'I know how it must look. Especially considering how much I loved my grandfather.' De Vaux snorted and Anna frowned at him. Armand swallowed. 'We arranged to meet that night because I wanted some comfort. I thought if we were discovered, Louise could say she was hunting for her dog, and that I had been sitting by my grandfather's grave and met her on my way back home.'

De Vaux exclaimed in disgust and Josephine turned her head away from us towards the back of the sofa. Bernier's hands were clenching and unclenching, and I hoped he would control his anger. Louise was so white that I feared she might faint. My own stomach was twisting itself into knots in the oppressive atmosphere and I longed for the truth to come out quickly so we could escape to the sanctuary of Christine's friendly, welcoming home.

'When the appointed time came, though, I could not bring myself to go,' Armand said, his cheeks flushing red. 'In the days before the funeral, all I wanted was comfort, but afterwards...I needed to be alone. So, I did not go to the cemetery that night. When I awakened the following morning and heard what had happened, I was devastated. I might have been able to prevent it had I been there.'

'How do we know that this is not just another of your lies?' Bernier demanded. 'If you have violated my daughter - '

'I would not, sir! How dare you!' Armand stepped forward, eyes blazing. 'I love your daughter, and respect her - '

'Respect? What would you know about respect?' I was shocked to see Bernier turn and spit into the grate. 'Forcing her to run around a cemetery at night like some common whore!'

'He did not force me!' Louise raised her voice in protest, struggling to free herself from the confines of the blanket tucked around her. 'I wanted to be with him to offer what comfort I could...'

'And you know what the entire neighbourhood is saying about the kind of comfort Louise Bernier offers?' shouted Bernier. I started, slopping coffee into my saucer. 'Do you have any idea what it will be like when you start going out again? Do you have any idea what it is like for your poor mother when she goes into town, seeing the fingers pointing, and the sneers, and the looks of disgust? Can you even begin to imagine what it is like?'

Louise burst into deep, racking sobs, her body convulsing with each. 'But Papa, it was not like that...'

'It does not matter what it was like!' Bernier shouted. He was shaking with frustration and fury, hands balled into fists. 'It does not matter; do you not see?

You have brought shame on this family. Everyone believes you have no morals, and that will follow you around for the rest of your life!'

'Maurice, please,' Josephine protested, but he ignored her, launching into a tirade about loose women. Anna let him run on for a minute or so before holding up her hand.

'Monsieur Bernier, I appreciate your position, but I need to progress my investigation and find out who attacked Louise. I cannot do that without asking hard questions. May I continue?'

Bernier scowled and turned away. Anna took this as permission. She looked at Armand.

'What about this morning? What did you see?'

Armand flushed an even deeper shade of red. 'I was not there this morning either,' he said, shamefaced. 'I thought it would be advisable to meet in the very early hours of the morning because the men on patrol would be tired and less likely to notice us if we kept far away from them. But I fell asleep.' He looked to Louise. 'I am so sorry. When François arrived earlier, I knew at once that something must have happened. I feel terrible.'

Bernier snorted. 'Please, Monsieur,' Anna chided. 'Now Armand, this is important. Was anyone else aware of your plans? A servant, perhaps? Your brother?'

Armand shook his head. 'No one.'

'How do you communicate?'

Louise's sobs subsided and she cried quietly, hiding her face in the handkerchief. Armand looked at her, his own face contorted with pain and sorrow. 'We signal to each other from a window. Sometimes we exchange letters after church while everyone is talking.'

Bernier made a strangled sound and Josephine tutted, although she said nothing. Her lips were a thin, straight line, but they were trembling, and her bosom heaved now and then with the effort of holding her emotions in check. The de Vauxs sat mute, frozen in disbelief.

'So, it is impossible for anyone to have known you would be in the cemetery at that hour?' Anna pressed. Armand nodded.

'We confided in no one, Mademoiselle. There is no way anyone could have known. Unless they saw Louise heading in that direction, of course.'

'This brings me to another question. What did you see while you were in the cemetery?'

Louise shook her head, struggling to catch her breath so she could speak. 'I swear to you, Mademoiselle...I was hiding and saw almost nothing. It was as I told you before. I only left out the part about meeting Armand.' She took a deep breath. 'I wish I had seen more. Then this might all be over.'

Anna nodded. 'That is why I need you to tell me everything. The smallest detail may be the one which leads to the answer.'

Louise sighed. 'I went to the cemetery and found myself a little hiding place not far from the entrance...'

'The entrance near your farm?'

'Yes. I was waiting just inside, standing between two of the larger tombs in the shadows, like last time. But then I heard footsteps and realised the men were patrolling. I tried to squeeze between the back of the tomb and the cemetery wall, but there was too little space. There was nowhere for me to hide... the men would see me easily when they passed. I peeked out. No one was in sight, so I ran across the path, where the tombs are closer together and easier to hide amongst. I wove my way between them, trying to find a place where I could see the path without being seen myself. I found a spot, but just as I reached it, I was grabbed from behind.' She stopped, closing her eyes, and took a deep breath. Josephine squeezed her hand. 'It was like before. His hands on my neck, his mouth on my skin. Then he whispered, 'Leave this place,' and pushed me. I staggered forward and fell flat, and when I had got to my feet and looked around, there was no one there.'

Anna leaned forward. 'And the feel of his hands?'

Louise looked at her. 'Warm, Mademoiselle...yet the voice was old Monsieur de Vaux! I screamed when I fell. Monsieur René was not far away... it must have been his footsteps I had heard on the path. He ran to me, and I screamed again, not realising at first that I was safe. He brought me home.'

'What of the other men?' Escoffier was making notes in a small, neat script.

'They arrived not long afterwards.'

'Who was there?

Louise shook her head, biting her lip. 'I am afraid I did not take in much after that, Inspector. I could not say who was there.'

'We have had a description of the scene from François Archambeau,' Anna said. 'René should be able to corroborate that information.'

Escoffier nodded and made a note. 'Where do you think your attacker went after he pushed you?'

'I could not see. He must have made his way through the tombs as I did. I suppose if the patrol men were walking along the paths, he could have stayed in the middle of the tombs. It would have been easy to conceal himself among them.'

'Can you think of anything else? Any smell? Did you touch him?' Anna asked.

Louise thought for a moment, then shook her head. 'There was no particular smell, Mademoiselle, but it happened so quickly that I didn't have time to think. I am not sure if I did touch him. I froze. I can't remember.' The tears came again, and she dabbed at them with the handkerchief.

'Do not worry,' Anna said in a gentle voice. 'Something may come back to you once you have slept.'

Louise gave a miserable nod and sank even further into the cushions, as though trying to become invisible. Josephine brushed some hair away from her daughter's forehead and indicated the forgotten cup of coffee on the table next to her. 'Try to drink something, ma chère.'

The girl automatically reached for the cup and raised it to her lips, but I doubted she tasted it. She looked exhausted and her eyes were unfocused. Escoffier was watching her, eyes narrowed.

'If I may, I would like to see Mademoiselle Bernier's injuries,' he said, addressing Bernier. 'After that, I think we can let her retire and get some rest.'

'Indeed. There is nothing further I need to ask of her at present,' Anna said.

Bernier gave a dour nod but said nothing. Josephine took Louise's cup and the girl fumbled with her collar again, opening it so Escoffier could examine the marks on her neck. Satisfied, he thanked her and returned to his seat, where he made a few more notes. Josephine rose and helped Louise to her feet, slipping an arm round her waist.

'Do you wish to speak with René now, Inspector?' she asked. 'He is waiting in the kitchen.' Escoffier nodded.

'Yes, please, Madame. Thank you.'

'And thank you, Inspector, for attending us personally,' Josephine said. 'We greatly appreciate it. It is a comfort indeed, to know you are dealing with this horrible situation.'

Escoffier rose and bowed to her as she left the room. It was only after she had led Louise out and the door had closed, that I realised I should probably have acknowledged her, too. However, de Vaux had also remained seated, staring into space with a devastated expression on his face. Armand, just beyond him, looked like he might start crying at any moment.

Footsteps creaked along the hallway, and I heard Josephine calling for Julie. Escoffier turned a page in his notebook and paused for a moment, then said, 'And you say you were asleep during all this, Armand?'

Armand started as all eyes in the room fixed on him, and he flushed scarlet, looking as though he wished he could sink through the floor. 'I sat up in my room with a book. I have slept very badly these past few weeks, so I thought it would be easy enough to read until I was due to leave the house. The next thing I knew, someone was knocking at my door, telling me to dress quickly and attend you, Mademoiselle Stenberg.'

Anna gave him a small, sympathetic smile. 'It must have been hard for you,' she said.

'It was. I should have been there.'

De Vaux rounded on him. 'You should have been there? Well, I thank God you were not!'

'Louise could have been badly injured!' Armand retorted. 'I should have been with her.'

'We will discuss this at home, young man,' snapped de Vaux.

'You keep your son away from my daughter,' Bernier growled between gritted teeth. 'He is nothing but trouble. Enticing my daughter out of the house in the middle of the night and damaging her reputation!'

268

'How dare you!' De Vaux shot to his feet, fists clenching. 'If you want to protect your daughter's reputation, I suggest you teach her how to behave correctly around young men. Sneaking about in cemeteries is hardly fitting behaviour for any young woman!'

Bernier began blustering, his accent thickening so much in his rage that I could barely understand a word, which was probably just as well. Armand blanched and de Vaux turned puce, taking a step forward. Escoffier got to his feet, an imposing, commanding presence in the room.

'Gentlemen, please,' he said with quiet, but unmistakeable authority. 'If you are going to discuss appropriate behaviour, I suggest you begin by demonstrating it. I do not wish to have to make any arrests in this case apart from the person who has been attacking Louise.'

Bernier paused mid-sentence and for a terrible moment, I thought he was going to ignore Escoffier and launch himself at de Vaux. My heart pounded in my chest and panic rose in my throat. Would they expect me, as a young man, to do something to intervene? Would I betray myself if I remained where I was, sitting stiff and uncomfortable in my seat, watching the scene play out on front of me? Anna was bolt upright in her seat, eyes flicking from Bernier to de Vaux, so there was no opportunity for me to pick up a hint as to what I should be doing. I set my cup down and tugged at my collar, which felt suddenly restrictive. Escoffier caught my eye and read my fear.

'Sit.' It was incredible how he conveyed so much authority in a single word. Both de Vaux and Bernier froze and stared at him, then each found a seat and dropped into it, Bernier clearly furious, de Vaux almost rigid with disbelief, anger, and despair. Armand had sunk down into his chair, cheeks scarlet with embarrassment. Seeing him so miserable, a wave of pity surged in me. He had made an error of judgment and was only now starting to realise the scale of the consequences.

At that moment, Julie knocked and ushered in René, who was clutching his hat, looking uncomfortable in Escoffier's presence. He ran through his side of the story very quickly, confirming what Anna and I had already learned from François. Escoffier listed the names of all the patrol members, and he and Anna both questioned René, but learned nothing new.

'All I would be doing is giving you my opinion,' he said with a shrug, 'and given everything that has happened, I do not think it would be helpful.'

'You are quite right,' Escoffier agreed. 'Well, if Mademoiselle Stenberg has no further questions for you, you may go.'

'There is nothing else I need to ask,' Anna said. 'Thank you, Monsieur René.'

'I will show you out,' said Bernier. René gave the room a quick, awkward bow, then followed Bernier.

'How could she have heard my father's voice?' de Vaux whispered.

Anna was frowning, as though she herself was musing over that very point. 'I should go and examine the grave again,' she said. 'If there has been further disturbance, it will change my current thinking.'

'What is your current thinking?' de Vaux asked, a note of desperation in his voice. Anna took a deep breath before she spoke, clasping her hands in her lap.

'I am almost entirely convinced there is no vampire.'

De Vaux began to express his relief, but she held up a hand and he stopped mid-sentence. 'The difficulty here is situations like this one, with Louise and Armand. It has distracted us all. We have been focused on who has been sneaking around in the cemetery, who has been there when they should be at home. Yet it seems all we have done is unmask a man having an affair, and a pair of young lovers who simply wished to be together.'

Armand hung his head, but Anna did not indulge him with an acknowledgement. She continued, her voice rising passionately. 'My work is not easy. Most of the time, I can be confident in which type of creature I am dealing with. Here, however, I am still not certain what is going on. It could be the work of a human, but there remains the possibility that this is a creature which I have not encountered before.' She looked at Escoffier. 'Is there any way we can secure the cemetery? I do not want to find myself chasing yet more of Frossard's little spies. I am tired of my time being wasted.'

'Frossard's spies?' Escoffier narrowed his eyes.

'Viktor and I joined last night's patrol. It was a busy night. We discovered Monsieur Joubert hiding in the bushes watching us, and it turns out he works for Frossard.'

'Does he, indeed,' murmured Escoffier, making another note.

'He swore he did not damage the grave and was not involved in the attack on Louise,' I added. 'It seems he was asked to watch what happened while Anna and I were there, and report back to Frossard.'

'You said something about a man having an affair?' Escoffier said. 'What has been happening? This was all last night?'

I gave him a brief explanation of all that had occurred during the patrol, and he shook his head. 'Quite the drama,' he said. 'I agree that something needs to be done to tighten security around the cemetery. We need to look into the odd noise you heard, and I suggest someone be found to replace Christophe if he cannot take it seriously. When is he due to patrol again?'

'Probably not until Saturday,' I said. 'They work in strict rotation, do they not? One day on, two days off?'

'Yes,' said de Vaux. 'That is my understanding.' He glanced at Escoffier. 'Frossard seems determined to proceed tomorrow. Is there anything which can be done to delay him? Anything at all? I can pay – '

Escoffier held up his hands. 'Guy, please! Think what you are saying, and where you are!' He lowered his voice. 'The last thing you need now is to be accused of trying to bribe a police officer.'

De Vaux shook his head and turned away. 'I am sorry, Jean, I was not thinking. Forgive me. Of course, I would never do that. My thoughts are all over the place. Forget I said anything.' He took a deep breath. 'Is there any hope that we can delay him? Any hope at all?'

Anna and Escoffier both remained silent, and de Vaux leaned his elbows on his knees, head in his hands. Armand was grey. Tiredness suddenly surged over me, and I had to quickly raise a hand to my mouth to stifle a yawn. Anna, too, was pale. When she spoke, her voice was strained.

'There is always hope, Monsieur, but I cannot say how much. Viktor and I will return to Madame Archambeau's through the cemetery and check

Monsieur de Vaux's grave as we pass. Perhaps you should come with us,' she added, looking at the three men. Escoffier frowned.

'I will come, of course,' he said. 'Tell me, how much sleep have you had?'

'About an hour, perhaps a little less,' Anna replied.

Escoffier shook his head in disbelief, taking in her pallor and the dark shadows I knew were beneath my eyes. I wished the subject had not come up, because now, I wanted nothing more than to collapse into my bed and sleep. Yet there was still so much to resolve. As my exhausted brain saw it, we had made very little progress, although clearing away the distractions would hopefully bring the crux of the issue into focus. We had one day left before Frossard took matters into his own hands, but I knew if I did not sleep soon, I would be good for nothing for the rest of the day and no help to Anna whatsoever.

'In that case,' Escoffier said, all businesslike efficiency, 'I suggest we escort you to Madame Archambeau's, stopping at the grave on the way past. I will see what can be done to secure the cemetery again, although I cannot promise anything. Is there anyone else I should be speaking with this morning?'

'I have not spoken to Matthieu and Jean about this latest attack,' Anna said. 'My suspicion is that they will simply corroborate René's story and have nothing fresh to add. You should also speak with François Archambeau, as he has been of great assistance to us thus far and is an observant young man. That may need to wait until later in the day, though, as he was also on patrol the night before and I am not sure how much rest he has had.'

Escoffier made a brief note and slid the pad and pencil into his pocket. 'What is keeping Bernier?'

'Speaking with René, perhaps.' Another yawn threatened and I struggled to hide it. Anna reached out and took my hand.

'We should go. If Monsieur Bernier is outside in the yard talking to René, we can say our farewells then.'

We all made our way along the hall to the front door. Julie met us just as we reached it, apologising profusely for being unaware that we intended to leave. Anna reassured her and asked if she knew where Monsieur Bernier had gone, but the woman shook her head.

'Forgive me, Mademoiselle, but I have no idea. I was waiting for Monsieur to ring for me.'

She fussed round us for a moment, ensuring we had our hats and coats, then opened the door for us, curtseying. I thanked her and she gave me a sweet smile, her eyes crinkling with warmth. 'It's my pleasure, young Sir.'

René and Bernier were in deep discussion at the yard entrance and Bernier turned at the sound of our footsteps, looking apologetic. 'Please forgive me,' he exclaimed. 'I did not realise how long we had been talking. Is there anything else you need from me?'

Escoffier said that he and Louise would need to attend the police station later that afternoon to sign a witness statement, and asked René to do likewise. We bade them farewell and heard them fall back into conversation as soon as we were out on the street.

'What must we accomplish by tonight?' I asked as Anna slipped her hand into the crook of my arm. We started walking up the hill, turning left into the little road which led to the cemetery, de Vaux, Armand and Escoffier following.

Anna gave a heavy sigh. 'Last night was not as bad as it could have been, but I still need to sleep before I can organise my thoughts.'

'How could it have been worse? It was chaos!'

'It was, yes, but think of what has been resolved.' She lowered her voice, and I leaned down to hear her. 'If we go out again tonight, which I expect we will have to, we should have no interference from Christophe's amorous adventures, and Joubert should also keep his distance after being so clumsy. I cannot imagine we would see Louise or our young friend back there, either.'

'Without all of those things, whatever remains must surely be connected somehow to the case,' I said, considering.

'Exactly. And do not feel obliged to join me tonight. I appreciate your help and enjoy your company, but I do not expect anything. If you are tired, which I imagine you are, then stay at Christine's tonight.'

'What? And miss all the excitement?' I exclaimed. 'I am sure I will be fine after a few hours' sleep. In any case, I have to go to the telegraph office and see if Uncle Geoffrey has sent anything.'

She smiled. 'I can imagine. Why don't you ask Christine if Céline might run an errand for you while you rest? It will either save you a wasted journey, or a telegram will be waiting for you when you awaken.'

'Good idea.' I yawned, unable to help myself, and Anna squeezed my arm. 'François might even be willing, if he's awake before us, particularly if he needs to go into town to speak with the Inspector.'

We entered the cemetery, pausing to detour to the de Vaux grave. It was just as we had left it, and the relief from all of us was evident, although no one spoke. The de Vauxs left us at that point, Armand dragging his heels in his father's wake as they went back along the path and turned left out of sight. I did not envy Armand the discussion I was sure would follow.

Escoffier, Anna and I continued along the paths towards the main gate. The Inspector was looking around interestedly, occasionally scribbling in his notebook. We had almost reached the gate when, all at once, he gave a sharp cry and darted off the path into the marble jungle to our right. There were mainly plots like the de Vauxs' in this part of the cemetery, some topped with marble slabs, others with statues. Most had a headstone and either a low fence or a chain surrounding them. We stopped and turned to watch Escoffier as he wove his way between them.

'What has he seen?' I asked, just as Escoffier gave a shout. Anna started running towards him, ducking between the headstones with sure-footed grace. I followed more carefully, heart thumping as I saw the two of them staring down at something on the ground. The grass between the tombs was long here, the dew soaking into the hems of my trousers and making them flap wetly around my ankles.

Anna and Escoffier were standing with their backs to me, looking down at a grave. It was a plot like de Vaux's, with an ornately carved headstone of white marble. As I drew level with them and followed their gaze, I saw what Escoffier had spotted.

The grave had been roughly dug into. Chunks of turf lay scattered round about, and there was a ragged hole in the earth. As I peered down into it, I was relieved to see it was still not deep enough for the coffin to be visible.

'Almost the same as the de Vaux grave,' Escoffier muttered, his face dark, brows pulled together in a frown. 'And not a new grave, either.'

'This one is a little deeper, I think,' Anna said, kneeling down and looking more closely. 'I would say it has been dug by hand.'

'How can you tell?' Escoffier squatted next to her, and I leaned over her shoulder, peering at the clumps of grass, the scattered soil, trying to see through Anna's eyes. To me, though, it was simply soil.

Anna pointed. 'Look here,' she said, indicating the edge of one of the chunks of grass. 'See this indentation here? I think someone dug this out with the toe of a boot, perhaps. And here, too,' she added, pointing to another. 'See what I mean?'

Escoffier and I leaned in, and as I craned my neck, tilting my head from side to side to see it from different angles, I realised what she meant. 'I see!' I exclaimed. 'So, they would have used their toe to loosen the turf, and then…dug the earth by hand?'

'Wait a moment,' Escoffier said. 'How do you know this isn't the work of an animal? A dog, maybe?'

Anna reached for the nearest chunk of turf and lifted it carefully, turning it over to show us the underside. 'If it is a dog, where are the claw marks?' she asked. 'There are no paw prints anywhere, either.'

Escoffier muttered an expletive under his breath as Anna set the clump of turf down where she had found it. He peered at the details on the headstone. 'Jeanne LaMarque,' he murmured, more to himself than to us. 'I need to find Arnal. I must speak with this family as soon as possible.'

'Are they connected to de Vaux or Frossard in any way?' Anna asked.

Escoffier shook his head. 'I am not familiar with the name at all. I cannot think of anyone at Frossard's office, and I have never heard Guy mention it either. I will make enquiries, though. Any connection between them may well be of significance.'

Anna made to stand and I shifted backwards out of her way, but the sudden movement made me dizzy. I staggered backwards off-balance, caught my arm on the edge of a gravestone and landed hard on my right hip, hands flailing as I tried to break my fall. Anna cried out and leaped up, Escoffier alongside her, and both leaned down to pull me to my feet. I retrieved my hat and brushed my overcoat down, cheeks flaming with embarrassment, my head swimming. Fortunately, my hair had not escaped from beneath my collar, but I ran a self-conscious hand over it anyway as I jammed the hat back onto my head. My hand was stained green from the grass, and I felt in my pocket for a handkerchief to wipe the worst of it away.

'I'm fine,' I mumbled, batting away their concerns.

'You need to sleep,' Anna said.

'You both need to sleep,' Escoffier corrected. 'Leave this with me, Mademoiselle. I will have someone send you an update as soon as there is anything to report.'

Anna nodded and quickly scouted around the area. I was not sure what she was looking for, but whatever it was, she clearly did not find it. She took my arm, assured Escoffier that we had his card and would be in touch later, and then we set off for Christine's. My arm throbbed painfully where it had hit the headstone, my grass-stained palm stung, and I still felt light-headed.

'It's not a vampire,' Anna said as we made our way onto the street.

'But that horrible noise we heard,' I protested. 'If it wasn't a vampire, what was it?'

'Remember what I told you about investigations?' she asked. 'How I often find myself helping people with illnesses which make them think they are vampires?'

A chill rippled its way down my spine. For some reason, I found that thought more alarming than the idea of a vampire. 'I remember,' I said slowly.

'I don't believe the cry we heard was a vampire,' Anna said. 'I think it was the sound of a desperate man.'

Chapter 27

For the rest of the short walk to Christine's, my exhausted brain played with the concept. The faces of Frossard, Joubert, de Vaux and Armand crowded my thoughts, shoving away all thought of sleep. Trying to focus on Frossard, I followed Anna into the house like a sleepwalker, barely managing to acknowledge Céline as she opened the door for us. She looked alarmed and ushered us into the parlour to sit before the fire as we had earlier.

'I will bring you something warm to drink,' she said. 'Also, Madame and I are going out into town later this morning. Can I do anything for either of you while I am there?'

'Oh Céline, that would be so kind of you!' I exclaimed. 'Please could you go to the telegraph office for me?'

'It would be my pleasure, Monsieur.'

Handing her some coins, I explained what I needed, and she nodded, flashing me a reassuring smile as she left the room.

Anna was curled up in her armchair, a blanket tucked round her, looking at us both from beneath heavy eyelids. I stifled another yawn, settling myself more comfortably. The soothing crackle of the logs in the hearth set my eyelids drooping. I could hear Anna's voice, but her words were no longer registering. As they faded into a quiet murmur, sleep wrapped its arms around me, and I fell into blissful oblivion.

Something awakened me and my eyes snapped open. The house was silent, and Anna still slept in the chair opposite. The dark hearth indicated we had slept for some time, and I squinted at the clock on the mantelpiece, which told me it was almost noon. Bright daylight glowed around the edges of the heavy drapes, which were still drawn across the window. There was plenty of daytime left for the investigation, but would it be enough to stop Frossard?

The chair was comfortable, and it was difficult to stir myself to move, so I mused over the case instead. How desperate was Frossard? If he was taking bribes, the criminal elements in Amiens must have some sort of hold over him. If de Vaux's popularity was threatening the status quo, how far would those people go in order to maintain it?

Yet there were a couple of niggling thoughts which persisted, one of which was the attacks on Louise Bernier. The whole scenario felt too random. No one knew about her assignation with Armand, so it was pure chance that she had been there at the very moment the perpetrator was damaging de Vaux's grave. Yet Louise had been scared more than harmed, on both occasions. Was the damage to the grave supposed to distract from a failed or half-hearted attack, or vice versa? And what of the new disturbance? My heart went out to the family who had been thrust into the midst of this drama. Would they get a visit from Frossard too?

As my thoughts wandered, I let my eyes do the same, travelling over the knick-knacks and furniture in the darkened room. My gaze passed over the writing desk and paused there as the other niggling thought pushed its way to the front of my consciousness. I tried to ignore it, but it persisted, clinging like a limpet to a rock. After several unsuccessful attempts to dismiss it, I gave in and stared at the desk. Remembered images of François hunched over the papers, and snippets of his argument with Christine flitted through my mind. I pushed the blanket to one side and went to listen at the parlour door for any sign of life in the house.

Opening the door a fraction, I looked out into the empty, silent hall, straining my ears. A horse clopped by outside, and the sounds of women's voices drifted in from somewhere further along the street, but the house was quiet. I decided to go to the kitchen to check on Céline. If she was there, I would ask for a glass of water.

The kitchen was large and spotless, everything neatly arranged on shelves and a huge oak dresser. I checked all the doors, discovering the larder and the cold room, and peeked out into the yard, but the kitchen table was clear except for a book of recipes and a pencil. There was nothing on the range and nothing baking in the oven, although I could detect the faint, lingering aroma of bread. It seemed Christine and Céline had not yet returned from town. This was my chance.

Hating myself for my inquisitiveness, I made my way back to the parlour, treading as quietly as I could. I did not want to wake Anna, and François, too, must still be sleeping. Closing the parlour door softly behind me, I went to the desk and eased open the drawer. Anna slept on.

It was simple enough to identify the papers I needed. They were bundled together in an untidy pile, a ribbon wrapped round them and secured with a loose knot. Holding my breath, I slid them towards me, one eye on the door, my ears straining, my heart skipping a beat at every tiny sound. This was wrong of me. I was prying. Why could I not leave it alone?

As I tried to rationalise my appalling curiosity, I leafed through the pages, my hands shaking, and found that I was looking at Christine's private correspondence from a woman named Anne Marie, who lived in Paris. A quick glance here and there told me the two women were friends, so I skipped over the letters, searching for the newspaper cutting I had seen François scowling at. It was about a third of the way down the pile. I drew it out and held it up, just able to make out the words. One corner was crimped, as though something had been folded into it. A quick search showed that it had been sent attached to a letter.

'Ma chère Christine,' I read.

'Life here is much the same except for a great and terrible excitement concerning the dreadful business in the cemetery in Montparnasse which I told you about in my last letter. I have enclosed a newspaper cutting for you, as the details are too terrible for me to write. The good news is that they have caught someone! Papa told me a trap of some kind was left in the cemetery, and it caught a piece of the man's uniform. He was a soldier, of all things! Can you imagine? You will see from the news report. But Christine, that is not all. Look at his name. Is that not the name of the soldier we met in Amiens that day, when we were returning to your house after the final fitting of your wedding gown?'

I stared at the loopy, girlish writing in shock and fumbled for the newspaper article. There was no date, but Anne Marie's letter was dated March 1849. I would have been three months old.

As soon as I started reading, I felt something shift in my thinking, but I was so dumbfounded that the thoughts were loose and unformed. I could see why Anne Marie had been too uncomfortable to write the details out herself. They were horrific.

A soldier named Bertrand had been arrested by the Parisian police for scaling the wall into the cemetery in Montparnasse and desecrating graves. He had not simply dug into them though, as I had seen here in Amiens. This man had actually dug up the bodies. When he was finished with them, he left them where they lay, to be found by whatever unfortunate person was the next to pass by. After he had evaded capture on several occasions, a trap had been set for the criminal by members of Bertrand's regiment, and when he had turned up at a hospital with injuries, the doctor realised he was dealing with the man who had been dubbed the Montparnasse Vampire.

Nausea swept over me, and I looked away from the report, biting my lip and swallowing hard, trying not to think about the details. Bertrand had, it seemed, been popular and well-liked by his colleagues, yet he was concealing terrible urges. I had never before heard even a suggestion of anyone doing what this man had apparently done. My stomach lurched and I choked involuntarily, making Anna jerk awake in the armchair.

'What?' she exclaimed, half-asleep. 'What time is it? How long have I been asleep? Why on earth didn't you wake me?'

She squirmed round in the chair to face me properly and saw the papers, the news cutting. 'Viktor,' she breathed. 'What are you doing?'

'This is important,' I whispered. 'You need to see this. I think this must be what everyone has been referring to. Look at this letter, here.' I held out the letter and pointed to Anne Marie's reference to Amiens. 'Something happened in Amiens sixteen years ago, something which involved vampires. Surely it must be this?'

She hopped up out of the chair and came to stand next to me, taking the letter. Her eyes widened as she read, then she turned her attention to the cutting, catching her breath now and then. When she finished, she hurried to the door and stood by it.

'Put them back exactly as you found them,' she said in a low, urgent voice. 'We need to wash, change our clothes, and go and see Escoffier. This sheds a whole new light on things.' She peered out into the hall as I had done a few minutes earlier, waving an urgent hand at me to be quick. I slid the pages into the pile. I had not undone the ribbon, so all I needed to do was ensure the bundle still looked messy, and that the cutting was not protruding anywhere. That done, I stood, closed the drawer, and went across the room to pull back the drapes, letting the midday sun dazzle us, then folded the blankets neatly and left them over the arm of one of the chairs before joining Anna at the door.

Together, conscious that François was likely to be sleeping, we climbed the stairs as quietly as we could, hurrying into our rooms. The water in our washstands was cold, but we both stripped off our clothing and scrubbed ourselves, gasping as goosebumps rose on our skin. I laced Anna into her corset, and she helped me hide my hair, smoothing the macassar oil into it with gentle hands. She brought her clothes into my room, and we talked in low voices as we dressed, keeping an ear open for the sound of footsteps on the landing outside.

'What are you thinking?' I asked as I fiddled with my cravat.

'That case was sixteen years ago.' Anna sat on my bed and worked her button hook along her boot. 'If we assume this soldier Bertrand was in his twenties at the time, then he would be in his thirties now, or maybe early forties. But he could be older.'

'So, we cannot discount any of the people we have met here.' I turned wide eyes to her. 'What if one of them is this Bertrand, Anna? Jean used to be a soldier...'

'This is what we need to see Escoffier about,' she said, her voice grim. 'I no longer know whether we can trust anyone involved in this case. Let's think about Jean. Yes, he was a soldier. He was on patrol last night. If he attacked Louise and ran off, as she describes, it would make sense for him to let one of the others find her, wouldn't it?'

I thought back to what François had told us. 'He took a huge risk,' I said. 'François and Matthieu were not far away. One of them could easily have seen him.'

'Perhaps there was something in his military training which helped,' Anna suggested. She went over to my mirror and studied her reflection, smoothing her jacket and adjusting the pins in her hair.

Visions of my father in his uniform flashed up before me and I closed my eyes to shut them out. My fingers fumbled the cravat, and I muttered something unladylike under my breath as I started again. Anna came over and gently brushed my hands out of the way, tying the cravat with deft fingers. She gave me an appraising look, a little half-smile on her lips.

'You do make a good boy,' she said. 'And I am impressed that you listened to your instincts about what was in the desk.'

'It would not rest,' I said, with a little shrug. 'I thought if I satisfied my curiosity, I could put it out of my mind and focus properly on the case. I never for a moment imagined that the key to the case might be in Christine's desk.'

A thought struck me, and I froze. 'What?' asked Anna. 'What is it?'

I looked at her, my eyes wide as something fell into place in my head. 'Anna,' I whispered, 'what if we are wrong about Jean?'

She frowned. 'What do you mean?'

'What if the person Christophe was going to meet was … was Christine?'

Anna gaped at me, her mouth falling open. All at once, I made another connection and gripped her arm in excitement.

'I remember now!' I exclaimed, forgetting to lower my voice, and Anna flapped her free hand at me, grimacing. 'Christine said something the night we arrived which sounded odd for some reason, do you remember? I have been trying to think of it ever since.'

'I remember.' Anna was looking up at me with sparkling eyes full of anticipation.

'She said something about not believing in vampires.'

'On more than one occasion, as I recall,' Anna said after a moment's thought.

'Well, that being the case, why would she need to worry about François being out on patrol?' I asked triumphantly. 'Of course, it could simply be concern about a violent man being out there and François putting himself at risk, but what if her main concern was that she herself has been going to the cemetery and doesn't want her son to see her?'

Anna blinked. 'This is Christine you are talking about, Viktor,' she said, frowning. 'I just cannot see her doing something like that.'

'Think about it,' I urged, almost hopping up and down in my excitement. 'She and Christophe are similar in age. In that letter, her friend said they were on their way back from a fitting for Christine's wedding dress. It should have been the highlight of the day, surely? Yet they both met a soldier that day, and remembered him. He must have been significant to them in some way. What if he was this Bertrand? What if he is back?'

'Why would she want to see him again after all these years, though, especially after what he did?' Anna countered, the frown deepening between her brows as she turned the possibility over in her mind. I stopped, my shoulders slumping a little, thinking furiously.

'Blackmail?' I suggested.

This time it was Anna's turn to freeze, her eyes widening. After a moment or two, she relaxed again. 'Let's not jump to conclusions,' she said. 'Although, if the meeting was not a formal one, then you may be on to something. I just cannot see it, somehow, and I am not sure how we might go about finding out, unless we ask Christine outright. I would like to keep her out of the investigation if it proves irrelevant. There are already far too many reputations at stake here.'

'But if she knew Bertrand, she is involved anyway, now his name has come up,' I said.

'And how did his name come up? By you snooping in her private papers,' Anna reminded me. 'I am hoping to hear from my employers today. Whether they mention his name or not, we can at least use it as a cover when we speak to her.'

'All right,' I said, taking a deep breath to try to calm my racing heart. 'Is there anything else we need to do?'

Anna ticked the items off on her fingers. 'See Escoffier to ask about the old vampire case and find out how his enquiries are proceeding. I hope there is a message waiting for me downstairs. We must speak to Jean. Arnal, too. I want as much information as possible before I speak with Christine. Are you ready?'

I said I was, and we went out of my room and down the stairs to the hallway. Escoffier had indeed left word for Anna, asking her to attend him in his office to maintain the confidentiality of the case. As I pulled on my overcoat and carefully set my hat on my head, arranging my hair, I thought I heard a slight click from upstairs, as though a door had just been carefully closed. Was that François? I paused, cocking my head to listen, but the house was silent, and I guessed he must still be sleeping, which was understandable. Making as little noise as possible, we let ourselves out of the house and headed for town.

We did not see Christine and Céline on the way, so we made the telegraph office our first port of call. Town was busier than I had expected, people bustling to and fro, horses, carts and carriages turning the roads into interesting adventures whenever we needed to cross. Gangs of filthy children scampered past us now and then, and at one point, a washerwoman, even taller than myself and with arms like tree trunks, almost knocked Anna into the road as she strode along with a huge bundle of laundry balanced on her hip. I caught Anna's arm to steady her, and she muttered something uncharitable about the woman's manners which made me raise my eyebrows. She glanced up at me, saw my expression and chuckled.

'I am corrupting you terribly, am I not?' she said. 'I forget myself sometimes. Pay no attention.'

Laughing, I offered her my arm and we continued on our way. It was a beautiful day, bright and sunny, with a cold enough breeze that we were glad of our coats. Thoughts of Christine tumbled against each other in my mind, and something suddenly struck me.

'Anna,' I said. 'You thought all along, did you not, that the attacks on Louise were clumsy?'

'Yes,' she said. 'Why?'

'Well, think about the news cutting,' I said, my brain shifting the puzzle pieces of my thoughts around at break-neck speed. 'There was nothing to suggest that Bertrand ever attacked anyone.' I gulped, feeling nauseous. 'No one alive, anyway.'

'He was a soldier, though,' Anna reminded me. 'He would know any number of ways to truly disable or injure someone. I am still not sure what to make of Louise's involvement.'

'I am thinking of everyone we have met and whether any of them really are who they say they are,' I sighed.

'We need to keep an open mind,' Anna said. 'Listen to everything, trust nothing. And,' she added, slowing down, 'read your letters, with a bit of luck.'

I looked around and saw we had reached the telegraph office. Our mail was still there, waiting for us: a thick packet of papers for Anna, two telegrams and a letter for myself. I posted my letter, then, thanking the clerk, we stepped out into the sun again and went to find a café where we could sit and read. One of my telegrams was from Uncle Geoffrey and as we walked, I tore it open with trembling fingers, desperate to hear his news.

'All well. Father found. Letter following. Come home.'

The sense of relief which flooded through me was so overwhelming that I staggered, and Anna had to put out a hand to steady me. 'What?' she demanded, turning an anxious face up towards mine. 'Is something wrong? Is it your uncle?'

'No…no, everything is well,' I said, breathless, my head swimming. 'My father has been found. Uncle Geoffrey wants me to go home.'

Anna blanched a little. 'Will you?' she asked, a note of uncertainty in her voice.

I waved the letter at her. 'This is from him also. Let me see first what he has to say.'

She nodded and busied herself with looking around for a tea-room while I read and re-read the telegram, stumbling along beside her, my emotions in turmoil. I was safe again! My father was back in St Bernadette's, and I was free to return to my old life.

The more I considered this, the more my spirits sank, and by the time Anna pulled me into a pretty café, I was despondent. This adventure in which I found myself was nothing more than a dream. How could I possibly go to Paris with Anna, much less meet with her employers? The money I had taken from my father's desk would not last forever, and if I was ordered home, and chose to disobey, at least one of my aunts would immediately petition my grandfather to have my allowance stopped.

Anna said something to the waiter who came to take our order, but I did not catch the words. The blood was rushing in my ears, and I was only vaguely aware of what was around me. Anna caught my arm and gave me a little shake.

'Viktor!' she hissed. 'What is it?'

Blinking, I forced myself to focus. 'Nothing...'

Anna raised an eyebrow. 'Ridiculous. You looked devastated.'

I sighed. 'I was thinking about my future.'

'Ah.' She lowered her gaze to her gloved hands, neatly clasped in her lap. 'You can go home now and pick up your life again.'

'So, it seems,' I said. 'Part of me does not want to.'

Anna smiled. 'I remember that feeling well.'

'How did you reconcile it?' I asked, curious. 'Do you ever go home to visit your family?'

Anna gave an offhand shrug. 'Not often. I did at first, but it does not take long to become tired of people telling you what a disappointment you are.' She eyed me, looking thoughtful. 'I suspect you might have the same issue.'

'Very much so,' I said with a humourless chuckle. 'Lots of reminders about expectations and my duty to the family, too, knowing my aunts.'

'Sometimes women puzzle me,' Anna remarked. 'The way they do their part in keeping the rest of us in line.'

'They cannot help it,' I said, feeling a sudden rush of defensiveness. 'Their upbringing taught them what was expected, and they cannot see beyond it. People like you and I, though, can see broader horizons.'

'A blessing and a curse,' Anna remarked. 'Yes, we have options, but whichever one we pick will cause difficulties. For me, as I suspect it is with you, it was either a lifetime of dullness and conformity, or the ever-present likelihood of being disowned and cast out by my family. So far, at least, they have chosen to ignore my work. I believe they have told some of their friends that I am at a Swiss finishing school.' She chuckled. 'I would have needed a significant amount of polish if that was actually the case. I have been doing this work for some years now. They will need a new lie soon enough.'

'I have an extra complication,' I said, choosing the words with care. 'My family has a certain amount of prominence and there are expectations of me which most people would not have.'

'A life under the microscope?' she asked.

I nodded. 'This is my one rebellion in an otherwise unblemished record.'

'You had a genuine and frightening reason to do what you have done. It is not like you grew tired of attending balls and parties and ran away.'

'True,' I said, with a little shudder. 'However, my uncle advises me that my father has been found, so they will all expect me to return home.'

She smiled. 'Read your letter. You have all the time in the world for decision-making.' She opened her own packet, revealing a bundle of papers, which she began scouring.

I picked up Arthur's telegram first. It was brief and to the point. 'Message delivered. All well.' A rush of gratitude shot through me. I would ensure that Arthur was well-compensated for the assistance he had given me.

The waiter brought our drinks, and I tucked the telegrams into my pocket while he set out cups and offered hot milk. Anna thanked him and he bowed, melting into the background. I tore open the envelope and withdrew a couple of pages covered with Uncle Geoffrey's spiky scrawl.

'You cannot know the relief I felt when Mr Phillips called on me to advise me that you were safe. I confess I was surprised when I heard you had left for France without a word, although Mr Phillips's explanation does go some way towards addressing the issue. I trust that now your father is safely back here at St Bernadette's, you will make arrangements to return home immediately. Everyone has been beside themselves with worry. I cannot understand how you ended up in contact with this Miss Stenberg, but she sounds like a sensible and capable young woman. Who is she? Who are her people? I hope you are being careful of your reputation. The season starts in a few days' time, and I understand from Mrs Armitage that you have an appointment at the dressmaker's next week.

'Your father was discovered down at the docks, not far from the Lord Warden Hotel. He evaded us for far longer than I expected, and as a result, I have been forced to increase his security level. I am uncertain whether you are aware that he attacked my driver Robert while I was waiting for you. It was fortunate that Soames appeared when he did. He is a capable man. Sadly, your father is also a capable man, and managed to give us the slip before I could summon the secure wagon to transport him. Please be assured that he did not attempt to enter the house, and everyone is safe and unharmed. Robert has a nasty cut to the head, but he will recover soon enough.

'I am uncertain whether you have money with you, or how much, so I have taken the liberty of contacting your grandfather's man in Paris to have money made available to you at the main bank in Amiens. He will also assist you in arranging your journey home. His name is Sébastien. I have provided an address for you to contact him. You will arrange to meet him in Paris, and he will make the Montmartre apartment available for your use while he deals with your tickets and luggage. He will also engage a chaperone in order that you might divert yourself with some sightseeing and shopping while you are there.'

There was another paragraph of expectations and instructions for my journey home, and I set the letter aside, feeling nauseous. Anna regarded me as she sipped her coffee. 'Problems?'

Shrugging, I turned my attention to my own cup, adding a little hot milk to the steaming coffee. 'Nothing I was not expecting,' I said. 'Seeing it written down, though, brings my choices into sharp focus.'

'You are expected to return home, I take it?'

I gave her a brief summary, omitting the part about Sébastien and the apartment and saying only that an agent had been engaged to assist me. Anna picked up her spoon and stirred her coffee, deep in thought. When she spoke, her voice was soft, and she glanced around the café to ensure she was not overheard.

'You have a choice to make, Viktor. A difficult one, too. It is not the kind of decision which should – or even can – be made overnight. You need the luxury of time to consider your options and at the moment, time is the one thing we do not have.'

'I want to stay and see the case through to its conclusion,' I said. 'I am not about to board a train for Paris simply because my uncle says I must. It will be easy enough to delay both my uncle and his agent. After we have seen Escoffier, I will send some telegrams.'

Anna nodded, the tiniest sparkle in her eye and a little twitch of a smile at the corner of her mouth. 'Let us finish our drinks and get on with our work!' she said. 'Time truly is of the essence today.'

'Is that often the case with your investigations?' I asked, sipping my coffee and wishing I had been less liberal with the hot milk.

'There is always an element of urgency. Delay puts lives at risk.'

I blinked, turning the thought over and over in the chaos of my mind. Now I had confirmation I was safe, that my father was once more in St Bernadette's and no one had been injured, something seemed to give way inside me. Thoughts of my choices, and the consequences of each, swam around, jostling for prominence. It was with some effort that I shoved them into the background and turned my full attention to the case. That was my priority. Once it was resolved, I would have all the time in the world to attend to my own issues.

'What have you there?' I asked, indicating the papers.

'This is the full file on the Montparnasse Vampire,' said Anna. She pushed them towards me, and I started leafing through them. There were news cuttings very similar to the one in Christine's correspondence, and a number of reports in different hands, some easy on the eye and others almost impossible to decipher. I squinted at them, fascinated, as we finished our drinks.

We went to find Escoffier. The police station was busy. A harassed-looking sergeant stood behind the desk, half a dozen people waiting to speak with him. Anna and I joined them, and I gazed around with interest. I had never been inside a police station before, and the activity was intriguing. An elderly woman in a black shawl was talking to a man who was sketching. She pointed to the drawing and gesticulated, and the man made some changes before holding the sketch up for her inspection. A young lad ran past them with a large pile of files in his arms, disappearing through a door in the far wall. Two men in uniform were looking through a bundle of papers, another was searching through a cabinet and yet another was putting pins into a large map of Amiens on a board in a corner. The sergeant crossed the room to speak quietly to a man in a neat black suit who was working at a small, cramped desk. He looked up and nodded, and the sergeant beckoned to the man at the front of the queue, who went to join them. The man in the suit pulled up a chair for him, and once they were in conversation, the sergeant returned to his post.

It took a while for him to reach Anna and myself and when we asked for Escoffier, he frowned, the corners of his mouth turning down and making him look disagreeable. 'What is your business with him?' he asked. 'He is a busy man.'

Irritation surged through me, and I drew myself up to my full height, looking down at him. 'We are in communication with the Inspector regarding the recent incidents in the cemetery, Sergeant,' I said before Anna could even open her mouth. 'We, too, have pressures on our time, as I am sure you can imagine, given the circumstances.'

The sergeant looked at me and seemed to decide that arguing would be unwise. He nodded, asked us to wait and vanished through one of the doors at the far end of the room. A few minutes later, he returned with the Inspector, who raised a hand in greeting and beckoned to us. We made our way between the desks and greeted Escoffier, who showed us into his office, closing the door.

Anna launched into a description of the Bertrand case and Escoffier nodded. 'Yes, I recall it well,' he said. 'That was partly what inspired me to join the police. Terrible, terrible case.'

'What do you know about Frossard, Christophe and Jean, Inspector?' asked Anna, drawing her notebook and pencil from her bag.

'In what context?' asked Escoffier.

'Were they born here? Have you known them a long time?'

Escoffier eyed her curiously. 'Christophe, yes, I have known for some time, as it happens. His family lived nearby when I was growing up. Frossard, to the best of my knowledge, has lived here his entire life. All I know of Jean is what I have seen during this investigation. He was a soldier, I believe. Why?'

'What if Bertrand is back in Amiens?' I said quietly.

Escoffier gaped at me and sat back in his chair. 'You think that is possible?'

'The attacks on Louise were not made by a vampire, Inspector,' Anna said. 'They were clumsy and ineffective. She was frightened more than harmed, and not a single member of the alleged vampire's own family has either encountered a vampire or been hurt by one.'

'No one knew Armand was due to be meeting Louise,' I added, 'so it seems unlikely that he would be the target.'

'Louise was in the wrong place at the wrong time,' Escoffier mused, nodding. 'What made you focus in on those three men in particular?'

'Christophe was sneaking around the cemetery with a woman,' I said. 'Although we do not know who she was. We found a torn piece of petticoat at the place where he said she climbed over the wall.'

'You did not see her?'

I shook my head. 'No, Inspector, and Christophe refused to give her name.'

'Christophe is who he claims to be,' Escoffier said, 'but I will have him brought in so I can speak with him. Jean, too.' He sighed. 'Christophe cannot be Bertrand. I know him.'

'And Frossard?' Anna asked.

Escoffier got up, went to the door, and looked out into the main office. He called to someone and a moment later, a uniformed man with a white beard appeared. Escoffier ushered him in and closed the door. 'Mademoiselle Stenberg, Monsieur Stenberg, this is Albert Pelletier.' We exchanged greetings. 'Albert, you know the Frossard family, do you not?'

The man nodded, a frown adding creases to an already heavily lined face. 'I do, Inspector, yes. My parents worked for his parents. How can I help you?'

'Was Mayor Frossard ever in the army?' asked Escoffier.

Albert gave a sharp bark of a laugh. 'Ha! Him? A soldier? That would have been a sight to see, Inspector. No, he was a lazy student who grew into a lazy young man who did only what he could not avoid.'

Escoffier nodded, keeping his expression blank. 'Useful to know, Albert, thank you,' he said. 'That was all I needed. Dismissed.'

The policeman nodded and let himself out of the room, a puzzled expression on his face. Once the door had closed behind him, I looked at Anna and Escoffier. 'It cannot be Frossard after all, then,' I said.

'If we are on the right track with this, then no,' Anna said. She was scanning one of the pages from the case file. 'I am no longer sure about Jean, either. Look here.' She laid the page on Escoffier's desk, and we leaned over it. It was a physical description of Bertrand. I read through it, puzzled, then realised what she was getting at. Escoffier sat back in his chair and whistled through his teeth.

'It says here that Bertrand was twenty-two,' I said. 'Making him thirty-eight now.'

'Which discounts Jean and Frossard. De Vaux, too.' Anna tucked the page back into her packet of papers, frowning.

'You didn't seriously think that de Vaux...' Escoffier began. Anna shook her head.

'No,' she said. 'One only has to look at the poor man to see how badly he has been affected by all this.'

'It does not discount Christophe,' I said quietly. 'Or Matthieu. Or René.'

'It's not Christophe,' Escoffier said, a note of impatience in his voice. I subsided into silence, my cheeks warm, and pretended to study the page again.

Anna looked at me, frown deepening. 'Matthieu and René... what do we know about them?'

Escoffier started to rummage through a sheaf of papers on his desk. 'I know nothing of Matthieu, myself,' he said, 'and know only what I saw of René at the Berniers'. Let me see where we are with the interviews.'

He pushed back from the desk, excused himself and left the room again, closing the door behind him. Anna watched him go. 'We have been extremely lucky with the Inspector,' she said, her voice low, beckoning me close. 'The police are, more usually, suspicious of me and tend to obstruct rather than help. Escoffier is a blessing indeed.'

'How do you manage in such circumstances?'

'It is a challenge, and incredibly frustrating. Most of them ignore me altogether. Some try to make life harder, which requires intervention from my employers to smooth the way. Others are sarcastic and spend most of the time sneering, only to be rapped across the knuckles when the creature, whatever it happens to be, makes an appearance.' She smiled. 'You might not have quite as many difficulties if you work as Viktor, though. I am convinced that most of my problems arise simply because I am female.'

We both rolled our eyes and smiled at each other, but her words brought back all my concerns about my future. I struggled to quell them as Anna launched into an amusing anecdote about a London policeman who had gone from swaggering bravado to cowering behind her skirts as she discussed a territorial dispute with a three-hundred-year-old vampire. I half-listened, smiling and nodding, forcing the unpleasant thoughts back into a corner. It was a relief when Escoffier reappeared.

'I have sent one of the men to speak with Matthieu and René,' he said, efficient and business-like. 'He will report back as soon as he can, and I have instructed him to send word to you at Madame Archambeau's, regardless of whether anything pertinent has arisen.

'Thank you, Inspector,' Anna said, getting to her feet and holding out her hand. Escoffier took it and raised it to his lips, eyes twinkling. All at once, I envied Anna. No one had ever looked at me that way, and I suspected no one ever would. The pit of my stomach gave an uncomfortable lurch and I busied myself with my shirt cuffs. Escoffier shook my hand and escorted us back to the reception area, where a different sergeant, younger, ruddy-faced and built like a pipe-cleaner, was listening to a middle-aged woman talking about a pickpocket.

We said our farewells and went back into the street. 'Where next?' I asked.

Anna considered. 'In light of what we have just learned, I am not sure that speaking with Jean would achieve much,' she said. 'Let us go and see if we can find Arnal.'

'What exactly are you hoping to learn from him?' I asked, curious.

'Gossip,' Anna replied.

I looked at her, puzzled. 'Gossip? How will that help?'

'I am looking for ways to direct any conversation we might need to have with Christine.'

'Oh!' I gaped at her. 'And you think Arnal will be able to provide them?'

'In his role as sexton, he will most definitely be able to tell us something about the Archambeaus,' Anna said. 'He probably prepared Monsieur Archambeau's grave.'

I had not considered that and lapsed into silence as we turned our steps towards the cemetery. My calves were aching from all the walking, which did not surprise me, given the speed at which Anna tended to walk, and my own new and unfamiliar masculine gait. We reached the cemetery, using the side entrance by the Bernier farm for convenience. Anna paused and wandered back and forth in front of the tombs next to the wall where Louise claimed to have been waiting for Armand, then hid between two of them and instructed me to walk along the path to see how easy it was to spot her. I did so and found that once I was opposite her, there was no way she could have avoided detection.

'It would have been getting light when Louise was here,' she murmured. 'Even if the patrol man did not have a lantern, he would still have seen clearly that someone was hiding here, would he not?'

I agreed. The tombs in this area had been built right up against the cemetery wall, so there was a gap of perhaps six inches behind them. Louise had chosen a cul-de-sac as a hiding place.

Anna went across the path, and I trailed after her as she wandered around. Although the tombs and graves were fairly close together, and the grass here was overgrown, there was sufficient space around each for a man to move undetected. We spent a little while walking between them and quickly came to understand why Louise's attacker had escaped so easily. Even with one line of tombs between us, we lost sight of each other almost immediately, and the long grass muffled our footsteps, so it was difficult to work out where we were in relation to each other. At one point, I started to panic, for I had lost Anna and she was not responding to my calls. I stopped, heart starting to race, staring at the marble all around me, looking for the path. A minute or two later, I heard

Anna calling my name. I hurried towards her, emerging onto the path to see her standing a little way away, looking around.

'I thought something had happened!' I exclaimed, unable to keep the note of panic from my voice.

'I was testing a theory,' she said, looking contrite. 'I left you and ran through the tombs to the path over there.' She gestured off to my right. 'If you had not known where I was originally, where would you have imagined I came from?'

I looked where she was pointing and thought of the layout of the cemetery. 'It's the path which eventually takes you to the de Vaux grave,' I said. 'And if you were a patrol man, I would have imagined that that is where you had been.'

Anna nodded, satisfied. 'Thank you for indulging me, Viktor, and I am sorry if I scared you by disappearing like that.'

'I'm all right,' I said, although my heart was still beating much more quickly than usual. 'It was a useful exercise to shed light on Louise's version of events.'

'And hopefully Arnal will be able to shed light on past events,' Anna said, approaching me and taking my arm. 'Come, let us see if we can find him.'

We walked in silence for a while, looking at the names on the graves as we passed. The cemetery was peaceful and still. The only sounds were our footsteps, the merry chirping of sparrows in the trees, and the occasional clatter of a cart from the road. Even the Berniers' cows were quiet, and I could picture them chewing the cud in benevolent contemplation.

We approached a corner, passing a gnarled old rhododendron whose boughs obscured much of the view ahead. I heard the sound of footsteps tapping along the path and as we got to the corner, Christine appeared, almost colliding with us. She clutched Anna as Anna reached out to her, and I had to sidestep quickly to avoid them both.

'Please forgive me!' Christine exclaimed, straightening her bonnet. 'I was not looking where I was going.'

Anna assured her all was well, and Christine nodded, the tiniest flicker of a smile lifting the corners of her mouth. 'I was just on my way to my husband's grave,' she said. 'Will you walk with me, or are you engaged?'

'We will be delighted to accompany you,' Anna said, and we fell into step alongside her. Christine moved with great dignity, her steady, measured pace giving our little procession a suitably grave air as we made our way along the paths. The breeze lifted some strands of hair, tickling them against my cheek, and I raised my hand to brush them away. It was only when I caught the tip of my finger on the brim of my hat that I realised what I was doing and hastily shoved my hand into my pocket. Anna and Christine were walking slightly ahead of me and could not have noticed, but I cast a surreptitious glance around, just in case. Everything was still and quiet, and there was no sign of Arnal. A cow lowed and faint male voices shouted to each other, but it seemed the cemetery was cocooned, the world beyond its walls muffled and indistinct.

Franck Archambeau's grave was a large and elaborate mausoleum towards the northern wall of the cemetery. The tombs were very close together here, almost touching, leaving room for only the most slender of people to squeeze between them if they were minded to do so. Anna might have been able to manage it, perhaps, but it would still be a struggle.

This appeared to be an older area, judging by the dates on the tombs nearby. Christine stepped off the path onto the grass next to the tomb, and Anna and I paused at a respectful distance as she reached out her gloved hand to touch the marble scroll with her husband's name engraved on it, along with his date of birth and his date of death. I saw with a start that he had been fifty-eight when he died.

'Franck was a great deal older than I,' Christine murmured, running her hand over his name. 'I was eighteen, he was fifty. At first, I resisted the suggestion of marrying a man so many years my senior. I clung to my girlish hopes of marrying someone dashing, someone who enjoyed dancing as much as myself. Someone with whom I could grow old, rather than watching time trap him in its net and ravage him while I was still so young.' She gave a deep, heartfelt sigh. 'That, however, was not my destiny.'

'It still could be,' Anna murmured. 'Have you given any thought to remarrying?'

Christine turned to look at us and the sadness in her eyes sent a physical jolt of empathy through me. 'Franck worked hard his entire life to ensure we could live well, and I would not wish to either jeopardise François's future or disrespect the memory of the man who did so much to secure that future for him.'

'I understand.' Anna's eyes were misty, and her voice filled with emotion. 'There are unscrupulous people out there.'

'Indeed.' Christine began to trace the letters of Franck's name with one finger, slowly following the incisions in the stone. 'I cannot think of myself until François is settled in his own home. After that, who knows what the future may hold? Until then, I have my charity work and I have my boy, and they take up all my time and much of my thought.' She sighed. 'They grow up so fast,' she said in a wistful voice. 'One moment, they are sitting in your lap while you read to them, and then one day, you awaken and realise you cannot recall the last time you felt their arms about your neck.'

Sudden tears threatened as my parents' faces loomed large in my mind and I caught my breath. Christine glanced at me, then blinked and gave herself a little shake, trying to smile.

'Goodness, that was unusually serious of me,' she said, her voice full of forced levity. 'Come, let us return home and I will ask Céline to serve us something delicious in the parlour.'

We nodded, and after making a show of removing a cobweb and some dead leaves from various nooks and crannies in the carvings around the tomb, Christine stepped back onto the path, carefully lifting her skirts. I remembered to offer her my arm, which I probably ought to have done before, instead of trailing around behind the two of them. She accepted with a smile, slipping her hand into the crook of my arm with the lightest pressure, and the three of us began to make our way along the path. There was no sign of Arnal. Anna was looking around her with interest, but Christine's words had cast a shadow over my mood, and I lapsed into silence as she and Anna chatted, my thoughts consumed by memories of my parents when we had been together, and happy.

Walking along the seafront at Dover, watching the fishermen with their boats and the women on shore, skirts tucked into their waist bands as they hung the fish on frames or packed them into baskets for the market. Mother reading to us in the parlour as I snuggled on my father's lap on the couch, she leaning against him, his arm around her waist. Parties at my grandfather's estate, long ago, in the days before talk of marriage and duty, when all was laughter, dancing and hide and seek with cousins.

I was jolted back to myself when Christine paused near the main gate and let go of my arm. Blinking as I collected my thoughts, I watched as she went over to admire a cluster of daffodils growing next to the path. She stooped elegantly, raising one of the drooping golden trumpets to her nose, then straightened with a rueful laugh. 'Such a pity their scent is not as beautiful as they are!'

Anna chuckled. 'Personally, I think few flowers can beat the perfume of a hyacinth or a rose.'

Christine agreed with enthusiasm and as we left the cemetery and strolled along the road, the two of them chatted about various gardens they had visited, comparing the scents of different flowers. I trailed after them again, feeling strangely disconnected from everything around me, as memories of my mother in her rose garden crowded my thoughts.

All at once a chill shot through me and I froze, mind racing back to something Christine had said. As I turned it over and over, examining it from all sides, puzzle pieces began falling into place, making my heart pound and a thin sheen of sweat break out across my back and forehead. Yes, it had to be… there was no other explanation.

I reached the house in a light-headed blur, blood rushing in my ears. Amidst a lively cacophony of chatter, I removed my overcoat mechanically and handed Céline my hat, then Anna took my arm and whisked me upstairs. She pulled me into my room, closing the door behind us, then took me into her room and sat me down at the chair before her dresser, turning my face gently towards her so our eyes met.

'All right, what is the matter?' she whispered. 'You have been behaving oddly since we met Christine. What is going on in that head of yours?'

Who is Anna Stenberg?

For a moment, I simply stared at her wide-eyed, mouth hanging open, mind frantically trying to order my thoughts even as it struggled with them.

'I know who the vampire is,' I breathed.

Chapter 28

Anna stared at me, a soft flush of colour rushing to her cheeks. Eye glittering with curiosity, she backed up and sat heavily on the end of the bed. 'Tell me.'

I took a deep breath, rearranging my thoughts, then began. I talked through all my observations, testing them, trying them for size to see if they fitted together. Anna listened intently, nodding now and then. At one point, she went to her bag, retrieved her notebook, and scribbled a couple of lines. When I finished, she stood and walked to the window, looking out onto the street below.

She stayed there for some minutes, unmoving, tapping one fingernail in a soft staccato rhythm against the window frame. There was a distant look in her eyes, the little crease of a frown settling between her brows and her lips pressing together into a thin line. When she turned to me, there was something different in her demeanour that I could not place.

'It fits, does it not?' she said. 'Yet it is all still circumstantial. It is just as likely a scenario as Frossard setting de Vaux up, so he loses the mayoral election, or Armand and Louise working together to make the police look ineffective so de Vaux wins.'

My heart sank a little. I had been so sure, but now I had aired my thoughts, I could see what she meant. Yes, everything looked suspicious enough, but there was no actual proof. I felt a sudden shift inside me, as though some undiscovered part of my being had fallen into place. So, this is what it feels like to have a purpose, I thought. In that moment, I knew I would not return to Dover. Not yet at least.

'What do we do now?' I asked.

Anna bit her lip and looked at me for a long moment, fingertips steepled in front of her as her expression flitted between concerned and resolved. Resolution won. 'We need to have a conversation,' she said. 'But first, we need to gather together every scrap of information we have. Run and fetch your journal, will you? I heard your pen scratching away the other day, and you're very observant.'

'What was Henri doing for you? Was he investigating too?'

'He was liaising with some of his contacts here, trying to find out more about Frossard. Everything he has sent me so far tallies with what we learned at Escoffier's office today. Frossard is a venal, self-serving man who does as little as possible himself in order to achieve his goals. Henri managed to speak with one of his clerks and learned that they tend to view Frossard as a man lacking in vision and imagination, which is why his popularity as mayor has fallen away in recent times.'

'That suggests he might not have dreamed up this scheme himself, but one of his lackeys might be more creative,' I observed, and Anna nodded.

'Investigating Frossard will take time I do not have, and I don't have it because of his insistence on proceeding with the exhumation order tomorrow,' she said, a touch of frustration in her voice. 'That alone makes him worthy of suspicion, but Henri has never heard even a whisper of underhanded tricks at election time before.'

I got up and went to my room to fetch my journal. 'Has Frossard ever believed himself likely to lose the election before, though?'

'Good point.' Anna's tone was grim. 'Here is what I think we need to do. Firstly, we share all our information and look at each of the suspects in turn. Once we have done so, we will need to follow up your suspicions, and I'd like to do so as soon as possible. After that, we will either have our vampire, or one line of investigation can be closed off. We must move fast, though. We are running out of time.'

For the next hour, we sat at the table in Anna's room, heads bent over our notebooks. Anna retrieved a couple of leather-bound books from her trunk and flipped through them now and then when a thought occurred to her, then set them aside with a frustrated tut and continued writing. After the third time, I asked, 'What are they not telling you?'

She turned a puzzled expression to me, and I indicated the books.

'Oh!' She poked one with an ink-stained forefinger and shook her head. 'Similar cases keep popping into my head, but there were vampires involved in two of them, and we are dealing with a human.'

I nodded and turned my attention back to my journal, where I was sketching out the skeleton of my argument, with Anna adding in her information. When we had finished, my argument had by far the greatest amount of detail, but Anna went through each item and put dots next to some of them. 'These are all circumstantial, and that one there is just opinion,' she explained. 'We cannot rely on them as evidence, but we can use them as prompts to try to obtain evidence.'

Taking a deep breath, I stared down at the page, each of Anna's dots sending spikes of doubt through me. She was right. My gut feelings were not evidence. Whilst there was a compelling argument in favour of each of the points I had made, there were also alternative explanations for all of them.

Anna sat at her dresser and began methodically tidying her hair. I watched idly as she drew it back into a neat, tight bun, tucking in every loose strand, surprised at how it threw the angle of her jaw into sharp focus, how her cheekbones suddenly stood out more, how severe the style was on her. As she worked, her eyes were fixed on her reflection, and when she removed the pretty lace jabot she had been wearing and replaced it with a sombre cameo brooch, I realised this was Anna preparing to go into battle. Gone were the soft lines and the curves and in their place appeared someone self-assured, business-like and detached. I thought briefly about perhaps changing my own appearance, but this was Anna's moment, not mine. She knew how to present the information we had gathered. My role was to watch and learn.

Pushing back from the dresser, Anna stood and smoothed down her skirt, then turned to me. 'Are you ready?'

'Yes,' I said, picking up my journal and pocketing it. 'Do I need to...' I gestured vaguely to my hair and general appearance, and Anna flicked her gaze over me critically.

'No, you look perfectly presentable,' she said. 'Turn around so I can check your hair.'

I did so, and a moment later felt her hands on the back of my neck. 'There,' she said. 'Perfect.'

She moved around so she was standing in front of me and reached out to take my hand. 'Don't get your hopes up,' she said quietly. 'I think your argument is an excellent and well-considered one, but that does not mean it is the answer. I don't want you to feel disappointed, or that you have somehow failed if it proves incorrect. Eliminating lines of enquiry is a valuable part of the investigative process, not a failure.'

'All right,' I said. 'I understand why. It makes it easier to focus on the more likely aspects of a case.'

'Yes.' She nodded, looking pleased for a moment, then her expression darkened. She drew herself up to her full height and took a deep breath. 'Let us go.'

We were greeted by the aroma of baking bread as we stepped out onto the landing, and I paused for a moment to enjoy it. Anna descended the stairs in front of me, and as we reached the hall below, I was struck by details I had never spotted before; the faint trace of beeswax lingering in the air from the polished woodwork, a neatly rolled umbrella next to the coat stand, the gleam of the brass doorhandles. My stomach lurched uncomfortably at the alien familiarity of this homely place which was not my home, and I gulped audibly, making Anna turn around.

'Are you all right?'

'Yes... yes, I am.'

I took a breath and composed myself. Anna gave me a searching look, then flashed a quick smile and turned back to the parlour door, raising her hand to knock discreetly. From within, Christine's voice called, 'Come in!'

Anna opened the door, and I followed her inside. The room was bathed in bright sunlight, glinting off the knick knacks on the shelves and surfaces.

Christine was sitting at the writing desk, pen in hand, and half-turned as we entered. Her welcoming smile faltered as she looked at Anna. Her gaze did not reach me at all.

'Christine, I think we need to discuss something,' Anna said quietly.

The colour drained from Christine's face and the pen fell from her fingers, splattering ink drops on the letter she was writing. She got up and hurried to the door, almost bowling me out of the way, and for a moment, I thought she intended to leave the room. However, she shut the door firmly and leaned her head against the wood, eyes closed, before turning to us.

I will never forget the haunted, desperate look in her eyes as her gaze met mine, nor the sudden pallor of her skin. She raised a trembling hand to her throat and whispered, 'You know, don't you? You know who the vampire is.'

'I think we do, yes,' Anna said.

Christine blanched again, her skin whitening so abruptly that I thought she was going to faint. She swayed, and put a hand out to steady herself against the doorframe, then turned helpless eyes to us.

'I have done something terrible,' she whispered. 'And now I don't know what to do.'

Chapter 29

For a moment, none of us moved or spoke, then Anna reached out, took Christine's arm and led her to the chairs by the fire, settling her comfortably. She took the chair opposite, then indicated that I should sit next to her. Hitching my trousers legs as I had seen my father do, I leaned back against the cushion, heart pounding, trying to make myself seem small and unthreatening. Christine was still sheet white and I hoped Anna had smelling salts. It looked like we might need them.

'We are here to help, Christine,' Anna said in a soft, gentle voice. 'Not to judge.'

The woman nodded and turned away from us to look into the hearth. She was fighting with some strong emotion, hands tightly clasped in her lap, the knuckles taut and white. From time to time, she gulped as though choking back tears.

Anna let her sit in silence for a while to compose herself, then asked quietly, 'Would you like me to ring for tea, Christine?'

'No!'

I started at the sudden, desperate cry. Christine edged forward in her chair; hands outstretched beseechingly. 'No, please… I do not want Céline to know anything and if she sees me upset, she will plague me with questions.' She let her hands fall into her lap again, limp and lifeless now. 'I would not be able to cope with her questions.'

305

'I understand.' Anna thought for a moment, then asked, 'Would you find it easier if I explain what we have discovered, and you correct me if I go wrong?'

Christine took a deep breath, sat up and squared her shoulders, facing us. Her expression was a mixture of desolation and resolve. My heart lurched, and in that moment, there was nothing I wanted more than to throw my arms around her neck and hug her. A horrible sick feeling wormed its way into my stomach, and I shifted in my seat, biting my lip.

'That will not be necessary,' Christine said in a low voice, glancing towards the door. 'I need to talk about this. It has been eating away at me and...' She sighed. 'I have no idea what to do.'

'Talk to me,' Anna said gently. 'We can deal with this together.'

Christine nodded and took a deep breath, collecting her thoughts, then began to speak.

'I was introduced to Franck Archambeau when I was just sixteen,' she began. 'He was a business associate of my father's, many years older than I was, already well past forty. At first, I did not particularly notice him, because he was just another dinner party guest. He started appearing at our table more and more frequently over the following months, but it was not until I was approaching my seventeenth birthday that my parents started speaking of marriage. I was horrified. I had never seen him as anything other than a friend of Father's. I had no idea he was coming there to see me. I was polite to him, as I was to all our guests, but he held no special significance for me. As far as I was concerned, at the tender age of sixteen, he was an old man. Certainly not someone I would be interested in romantically.'

It was all I could do to stop myself going to hug her. I knew those thoughts so well.

'I protested, of course; who would not? I was a young girl with my entire life ahead of me. Selfish as it sounds, I did not want to find myself nursing an elderly husband while all my friends spent their time socialising and dancing with their young, vibrant, healthy husbands.'

'I think it sounds perfectly reasonable and not selfish at all,' I commented, then added, as Anna caught my eye, 'I would not want that for my sister. It is no life for a young woman.'

Christine gave a mirthless smile and shrugged. 'But what can we do, we women?' she asked. 'What choice have we but to do as we are instructed? That is why you fascinate me so much, Anna. You have managed to escape the confines of society to pursue your own individuality, and I admire you for it.'

Anna shook her head. 'It is not as glamorous as it seems, I can assure you. It has its own penalties and consequences.'

Christine's dark eyes roamed over Anna's face searchingly and she nodded, looking thoughtful. 'Yes,' she said, almost to herself, 'yes, there are always consequences.'

As I puzzled over that, she continued with her story, her voice low and trembling with emotion. Despite her protests, a marriage had been arranged between herself and Archambeau and she had found herself in a whirlwind of preparations in which she had no interest whatsoever. Her well-meaning but overbearing relatives sounded exactly like my own and I cringed inside as I listened. She described her mother dragging her to the dressmaker's, florists calling at the house, an endless search for a veil which her mother would deem good enough.

'We received word that my veil was finished,' Christine said. 'Usually, Mother would have dealt with the note when it arrived, but it happened that she was unwell that day, and unable to leave her bed. She suffered terribly with headaches. I did look in on her, but she was asleep, so I sent a note back myself, to say I would attend the shop in person that afternoon. Then I arranged to meet one of my dearest friends, Anne Marie, who was to be one of my bridesmaids. We went for afternoon tea, and as we were leaving, Anne Marie felt faint and almost fell down the steps in front of the building. A young soldier was passing by and caught her just in time. He was polite and amusing and insisted on escorting us back inside so Anne Marie could sit down, even though she assured him she was perfectly well. The poor girl was horribly embarrassed, but I could see she was very pale, and her hands were clammy, so I summoned a waiter, explained what had happened, and he found the three of us a table.'

The soldier introduced himself as Sergeant François Bertrand. He was a voltigeur, part of an elite skirmish unit in the French army, skilled in marksmanship. Voltigeurs tended to be extremely athletic, and Bertrand was no exception. He was charming, good-looking, and intelligent, with impeccable manners, and both Christine and Anne Marie found him to be excellent company. His regiment was stationed in Amiens to carry out some military exercises, he told them, and he was greatly enjoying his time in their beautiful town. They chatted over a pot of tea, then Anne Marie asked the waiter to call her a cab, as she still felt unwell.

'Sergeant Bertrand escorted her to the cab when it arrived, then came back to finish his tea,' Christine went on. 'There was something about him that I liked. He was easy to talk to and seemed to really listen. He asked intelligent questions. I found myself opening up to him about my wedding, and how much I was dreading it. We talked for so long that I almost missed my opportunity to collect my veil. If I had been any later, the shop would have closed for the day.

'The Sergeant insisted on paying for the tea, then escorted me to the shop and waited outside discreetly whilst I pretended to be delighted with the veil. When I had concluded my business in the shop, he walked me to the corner of the road I lived on, and by the time we got there, I realised I wanted to keep talking to him. Foolishly, I said this. He smiled and suggested I might like to meet him that night.'

Christine had been affronted, as I expected from a girl of her breeding, and Bertrand graciously accepted that he had overstepped a mark.

'Just as I was turning to leave, he said something which changed everything,' Christine said, her voice shaky and thin. 'He said, 'Such a beautiful rose to be placed in a vase next to a withered bouquet.' It stopped me in my tracks. I had been about to march off in indignation, but something happened within me at his words, something I couldn't quite explain. I did not turn to him, just paused, long enough for him to give me a time and place. I hurried home, not daring to look back.'

Christine went on to describe the quandary she had found herself in. Her mother, who was awake and sitting in bed sipping broth, had been delighted by the veil, to Christine's relief. She expressed concern about Anne Marie and insisted Christine send a note to check how she was, fearing she might be unwell for the wedding and upset the seating arrangements. Christine, gritting her teeth, had begrudgingly done so, choosing her words carefully in an attempt to disguise her mother's selfishness.

The evening had passed in a blur for her. Christine found herself staring at the clock on the parlour mantelpiece after dinner, watching the interminable drag of the minute hand as her mother twittered about weddings and whether the final pieces of the trousseau would be finished on time, and how lovely the veil had proven to be. Christine responded almost mechanically and excused herself as soon as she could, escaping to her room and sending her maid away.

'I lay on my bed, fully clothed, thinking about what the Sergeant had said.' Christine's voice dropped even further, and Anna and I both leaned in so we could catch her words. My heart thumped so hard against my ribs that I felt sure both Anna and Christine must be able to hear it. 'All I could think of was myself as a freshly-picked rosebud next to a bunch of withered flowers and it broke my heart. There were plenty of eligible young men in Amiens. My friends' parents did not seem to struggle to find suitors of a similar age to the daughters they wanted to marry off. I alone was to be saddled with a man older than my own father.'

She paused and looked ashamed. 'I contemplated many alternatives to marriage, all of which would have been devastating to my family. But I had to do something for myself, just once, just to experience it...' Her tone turned almost pleading. 'I was about to be married to a man more than twice my age and... I wanted to know...'

Her face crumpled and Anna and I both leaped from our seats, Anna tugging a handkerchief from her sleeve and pressing it into Christine's hand. I knelt by Christine's chair as she mopped delicately at her eyes, keeping her face turned away from both of us. Her shoulders shook with repressed sobs, and it was several minutes before she had recovered herself sufficiently to speak again. Anna and I waited patiently in silence, Anna gently reaching out to clasp her hand over Christine's as it lay trembling in her lap. At one point, I thought I heard someone in the hall, so I got up and went to see who it was. When I opened the door, however, the hall was empty, so I went back to my chair.

'Please do not think badly of me,' Christine whispered. 'Please. I was a fool. I know that. Of course, I know that. And yet, there was something inside me crying out for …' She paused and shrugged helplessly. 'I can't put it into words, even after all these years.'

'You wanted a taste of independence,' Anna said quietly. 'To be able to make your own decisions about your body. I understand completely, and I can assure you neither of us would ever think less of you for that.'

I shot a glance at Anna even as I acknowledged the truth of her words, yet inside I was conflicted. Christine's revelation had shocked me. One of the Dover set had done something similar a year or so previously and she had been removed from the social circle immediately in the midst of a flurry of gossip. The last I had heard, her family had moved to the other end of the country and we had heard nothing from her since. I wondered what implications there had been for Christine. Her actions had not prevented her marriage and she had spoken of her late husband with great affection, so she must have remained undiscovered.

The feeling of nausea gripped my stomach and twisted, and I pressed my lips together. swallowing. Christine's actions went against everything I had been raised to believe, yet now, having chosen a different path myself, a new understanding rose in me, along with guilty thoughts about those towards whom I had been uncharitable in the past. I realised I might return to Dover to find a similar fate awaiting me. I could think of two aunts in particular who would advocate for a much older husband to keep my unseemly, adventurous spirit in check. The thought made me shudder, and I was thankful when Christine continued her story.

'I slipped out of the house,' she said, her voice wavering. 'I met him. He was amusing and charming, yet somehow, it was not what my foolish romantic notions had expected.' She took a deep breath. 'Then it was over, and he was gone. I managed to get back into the house undetected and stood at my washstand for over an hour in the darkness, scrubbing my skin, terrified someone would know. Yet no one did.

'The wedding went ahead as planned and still no one suspected anything. Then I found out I was pregnant.'

The implication of her words was clear, and I stared at her in shock. She caught my eye and a bright spot of colour flared in her cheeks, making her look even more unwell. I reached out a hand to her, stroking her arm soothingly.

'I did not know who François's father was,' Christine whispered. 'Fortunately, he favours me in looks, so there was never any question of people suspecting that Franck might not be his father. Of course, Franck was delighted to have a son so soon after our wedding. It was he who chose François's name, and I am sure I don't need to tell you what an awful feeling it gave me at first. I thought he knew, or at least suspected. For the first few months, I lived in an agony of anticipation, waiting for the axe to fall, but it did not. Franck bought me anything I wanted. I had the best of everything all through my pregnancy and he was so kind and solicitous. I soon realised I had misjudged him terribly and that he was an exceptionally good man. Unlike many husbands, he encouraged my love of books and learning, and we would often spend afternoons reading to each other or discussing something in the newspaper. I lived on a knife-edge in spite of that, though, always afraid I would be found out.'

She sighed and dabbed at her eyes again. 'The years went by and gradually, I realised my secret was safe. I had a beautiful healthy son and a loving husband…what more could I ask? Then we lost Franck. I chose not to re-marry, although I had offers. I had been well provided for, and there was a part of me which believed I owed it to Franck to respect his memory in this way, to make up for the lack of respect I had shown him at the beginning of our life together.

'I first noticed something strange in François's behaviour about a year ago,' Christine continued. 'Consciously, at least. I thought it was nothing more than the surly disposition of a growing young man, so I paid little heed at the time. Oh, how I wish I had been more observant.'

She lapsed into silence, biting her lip. Anna caught my eye, the familiar little frown between her brows. She looked tense and drawn, as though the burden of our looming deadline was weighing heavily on her.

'What did you notice first?' I whispered.

She turned her beautiful eyes to me, moist with tears. 'I realised I could not recall the last time I had felt his arms about my neck.'

Anna stiffened beside me and sat back on her heels as I caught my breath, anticipating Christine's next words. Christine gave a deep sigh. 'You may think, of course, that it is entirely natural for a son to abandon childish demonstrations of sentiment. It was the first time he gave me one of those strange little stiff bows of his, one evening as he was going to bed. I held out my arms to him when he came to bid me goodnight, and he simply bowed. It took me by surprise, and I made a little harmless comment about growing up, but he barely reacted, so I let the subject drop. After that, he was somehow detached when he and I were alone together, although in company, as you have seen, he is bright and pleasant. I began to watch him, but saw nothing of concern, so I pushed my worries aside, dismissing his behaviour as typical of a young man on the brink of adulthood. Then he began to ask questions about his father. Innocent-sounding questions. What did he think of a particular subject, how did he behave in these circumstances, and so on. I answered as best I could and thought little of it. He was young when Franck passed, and it seemed natural for a son to be curious about his father. Then the questions took a darker turn.'

She stopped again and this time, she got up and went to ring the bell. Remembering her words, I took my seat again and Anna did likewise, lending an air of normality to the room. Céline appeared a couple of minutes later, took Christine's order for tea, then left, her eyes darting between the three of us, alight with curiosity. Christine maintained a soft smile until the moment the door closed, then she sank into her chair and took a deep breath.

'Would it help if I took over from here?' Anna asked, 'Let me tell you what our investigations have uncovered.'

Christine twisted the handkerchief between her fingers and gave a brief nod. Anna settled herself more comfortably and began to explain how the case had come to the attention of her employers. She covered a lot of detail we had spoken about before and I was about to point it out to her when there was a tap on the door. I got up to admit Céline, laden with the tea tray, and helped her to pass round the cups while Anna spoke about the patrols and her own observations. I realised she was creating an illusion for Céline, and added in a couple of observations of my own, which Anna acknowledged with the tiniest of nods and the ghost of a smile. Christine murmured a soft response here and there and managed to smile at Céline as she accepted her tea. Céline gave her mistress a searching look, but said nothing. As she left the room, I noticed she was frowning, so after the door closed softly behind her, I hopped up and went to listen to the sound of her feet retreating along the corridor. Pressing my ear to the cool wood, I heard the door closing at the far end of the hallway and returned to my chair. I had half-expected her to remain there, listening.

As soon as I sat, Anna leaned forward and set her cup to one side. 'Christine, we know about Sergeant Bertrand,' she said. 'His name came up in the course of the investigation, from different sources.'

The cup rattled on the saucer in Christine's hands, and she froze, closing her eyes. A tear slid down one cheek and it was two or three minutes before she spoke.

'So, you know everything.' Her voice was as brittle as autumn leaves, barely a whisper. 'Imagine how it felt. I did not know whether he was François's father, or if Franck was. Anne Marie was living in Paris with her own husband by then. She wrote to me after Bertrand was discovered and sent a news clipping.'

Her voice cracked and she raised the cup to her lips, taking a tiny sip. 'The newspaper quoted some of his words,' she went on. 'He was describing what he had done to…to one of the…bodies.' Her face twisted in pain. 'I knew straight away. The soldier I had met here in Amiens was the man they were calling the Ghoul of Paris. One phrase stood out for me. He had told me that were I his bride-to-be, he would cover me in kisses and press me wildly to his heart. That was exactly what he said he had done to…to…'

She crumpled and it took several minutes for her to compose herself. I was horrified. I could feel the nausea clawing its way up my throat, and it was only by taking the tiniest sips of tea that I was able to control it.

'I was ill for weeks,' Christine continued. François was so young at the time that he would not remember, but poor Franck was terribly worried. He cancelled all his business commitments and spent the entire time sitting by my bed, reading to me, or holding my hand. He sent for the best doctors. We spent three months in Italy, which was a delight and lifted my spirits greatly, but the horror never left me. I learned to hide it from him and how to manage it, and over the years, as François grew, it did ease, although it is always in the background. Sometimes I manage to forget it entirely for a while. Recently, though, it has been ever in my mind.'

Anna nodded and murmured something soothing and reassuring, reaching out to take the cup from Christine and set it aside so she could hold her hands. I found myself staring unseeingly into my cup, mind racing as I thought of the pain Christine's risky choice had caused her. An image rose in my mind of my reflection in Anna's looking glass as I tidied my cravat, and she arranged my hair. Christine's indiscretion had been fleeting. I had been living and breathing mine for days. Gone was the tall, awkward young girl, and in her place was a young man, fully inhabiting his height for the first time, but what implications did my choices hold? Dover was calling, and the call would only become more insistent as time passed.

I snapped back to attention at the mention of my name and found Anna looking at me, an earnest expression on her face. 'Viktor? Will you explain to Christine what you observed?'

Fighting the urge to leave the room, and feeling horribly awkward and self-conscious all of a sudden, I finished my tea and returned my cup to the tray to buy myself a few precious moments to arrange my thoughts. As I sat, tucking the cushion behind me more comfortably, I was suddenly strongly aware of its smooth texture, the plush fabric soft against my fingertips. I settled myself as comfortably as I could, and was about to start speaking when the parlour door was flung open and François stood there, his face white, hair in disarray, staring at us. Christine caught her breath and went to stand, but François crossed the room in a moment and flung himself at her feet.

'Help me, Maman, please help me,' he begged, clutching at her skirts. 'I don't know what to do. I don't know how to stop it.'

Christine's face crumpled and a strangled sob escaped her throat as she laid a trembling hand on her son's head. Her mouth opened, but the words would not come, and all she could do was gaze at him helplessly. He turned to Anna, and I could see tears glinting in his eyes.

'Can you help me?' he whispered. 'Please. I don't want to be like this.'

'Like what, François?' Anna said gently. 'Talk to me. I am here to help if I can.'

He laid his head on Christine's knee and turned beseeching eyes to Anna.

'I don't want to be like my father,' he whispered. 'I don't want to be like the Vampire of Montparnasse.'

Chapter 30

A hush descended on the room. For several long moments we sat there unmoving, the only sound the ticking of the clock. Christine's fingers trembled in François's hair while he clutched at her skirts, crumpling the fabric. Anna was breathing slowly and steadily, hands clasped loosely in her lap, as calm as ever. I was a tangle of jarred sensibilities, turning Christine's words over and over in my mind, trying to suppress the ingrained disapproval which caught in my throat. At the same time, a flare of triumph was blazing in my gut.

'Will you share with us, François?' Anna asked in a soft, low voice. He started and turned his head slowly so he could meet her eye. She shifted forward in her chair, leaning down to him, the rustle of silk unnaturally loud, emphasising our stillness.

'I can't.'

His voice was barely above a whisper. Anna and I both leaned in at the same time, then Anna slipped from the chair and seated herself on the floor opposite François, tucking her skirts around her modestly. She reached out and laid a hand on his. He started to move back, but she tightened her fingers around his, holding him there.

'I can help you, François,' she said, and the assurance and confidence in her voice gave him pause. He had half-risen, but now lowered himself back to the floor, leaving his hand in hers. 'Please talk to me. I think I already know how I can help you, but I would like to be certain. Will you share with me?'

'You can?' He looked so lost as he spoke that my heart went out to him. What was he going through? What anguish and confusion were sending his thoughts into a spiral of turmoil? I kept my expression neutral until his fearful eyes met mine. The bewilderment and pain sent a stab of empathy straight into my heart and I almost reached out to him. Catching myself just in time, I gripped my knees instead.

'Yes, and I will.' Anna tilted her head to one side, appraising him. 'Will you permit me to do so?'

Silence fell once more. Christine, it seemed, was holding her breath, and it was a moment or two before I realised I was doing the same. Then François started talking. He was hesitant at first, but all at once, he understood he was safe, that there were people who could help him. More importantly, people who wanted to help him. The words flooded the room in a deluge of panic and self-loathing.

'I found a dead cat,' François began. 'A while ago, in the lane beyond the cemetery. It had been attacked by something, a dog or a fox, I expect. There was a wound in its belly, and I could see...'

He paused, trying to compose himself. 'The entrails. I saw the entrails. They fascinated me. I tried to continue on my way, to walk past, but something struck me forcefully and I had to stop. It was a strange feeling I did not understand...that I still do not understand.'

Meeting Anna's eyes with a beseeching look which almost broke my heart, he whispered, 'Please believe me, Mademoiselle, I do not know what came over me. I knelt down and peered at it. Everything seemed to be in sharp focus: the individual hairs in the skin, the deep red of the blood, the textures and the light shining on the –'

He caught himself, flushing a deep red. Christine had closed her eyes and turned her face towards the hearth, but now she looked down at him, her face streaked with tears. 'Oh, François,' she whispered.

The room suddenly felt oppressive, and I had to fight the urge to get up and bolt. The intensity was overwhelming, and as Anna started speaking soothingly to François, encouraging him to share more, I tried to unpick the various conflicting emotions within me. The anguish on both Christine's and

François's faces was terrible to witness and I was still torn between shock, disapproval and understanding at Christine's indiscretion and the implications it had for her family. Was François indeed the son of the Vampire of Montparnasse? Or was he simply a young man struggling over hurdles towards adulthood and attempting to do so without a father's guiding hand? Had he found Christine's correspondence and recognised himself, or had he tried to adopt Bertrand's tendencies for some reason? A thin sheen of perspiration broke out on my forehead, and I raised a hand to my collar, which suddenly felt constricting, and tugged at it.

'Tell me about the cemetery, François,' Anna said, her voice low and soothing. 'What happened? Things had moved on from the dead cat, hadn't they?'

He nodded, miserable, and fumbled in his pocket for a handkerchief, scrubbing his face hard as if he wanted to remove a layer of skin. 'Seeing the cat awakened something in me which I do not understand. I kept thinking back to it, even going out of my way to look for other dead creatures, hanging around the farm gate to see if there were animals to be slaughtered. Louise noticed me one day…we talked. I pretended I was merely watching the cows as I passed along the lane. Louise is pleasant to talk to but speaks far too often of Armand de Vaux.'

I caught my breath as a realisation hit me and flicked my gaze towards Anna, who was focused entirely on François, leaning forward in her seat. Her eyes glinted and her lips were slightly parted, watching every flicker of expression as it travelled over his face. Curiosity piqued, I found myself leaning forward, too, hardly daring to breathe.

The floodgates had opened. Words began to tumble from François unbidden, a stream of consciousness. He spoke of fascination with Louise, disdain for Armand and revulsion towards himself. Anna let him, glancing now and then at Christine, who sat rigid, her face drawn and marble white. Eventually, François began to talk of Louis de Vaux's death.

'The night I learned of it, I lay in bed, thinking about how he had been in life. I wondered what he looked like in death, and the moment the thought entered my head, I knew I had to find out. We went to pay our respects, and seeing him lying in the coffin so small and frail and shrunken, well, something shifted within me. Part of me wanted to reach out and touch him, to press my fingertips into his flesh to see what it felt like. I kept my hands clasped behind my back, so tightly that after we left the house, my joints ached when I tried to straighten them.' He paused, gaze fixed somewhere in the middle distance, and flexed his fingers. 'The funeral came and went, and after the burial, I found myself thinking terrible things. What it would be like to dig down into the freshly-turned earth.' His face crumpled. 'I didn't think beyond that. I let myself quietly out of the house and went to the grave. I knelt there and put my hands on the soil, feeling the texture of it. I started digging, but it was a lot harder than I expected, especially without any tools.'

Realising he needed a shovel, yet still without any real thought in his head other than to dig into the grave, François had gone in search of the sexton's hut. As he made his way between the memorials and graves towards the cemetery wall, he had spotted movement. Creeping over to see who was there, he recognised Louise.

'I knew exactly what she was doing,' he said, his voice bitter. 'She was waiting for him. I couldn't have that. The thought of it made me feel ill, and I panicked. I couldn't have her see me, but equally, I had to do the right thing and frighten her away, so she did not make a terrible mistake.'

He looked up at his mother then. Christine stared back, her face a mask of horror and disbelief. She slumped back in her chair and immediately Anna was on her feet, grasping Christine's hand and reaching out to gently touch her cheek with her fingertips to make sure she was still conscious. Anna reached into a pocket and withdrew a little bottle, removed the stopper and wafted it under Christine's nose, making her start and splutter. She waved Anna away.

'This is what you meant,' Christine said, her voice flat and lifeless. 'All those questions about your father. You weren't asking about Franck. You meant something quite different.'

'If you mean your shocking little secret, Maman, then yes, I know all about it. You should lock your personal papers away.'

Christine looked defeated. 'You read my correspondence?'

François did not answer, just met her gaze. I could not see his expression, but whatever Christine saw there made her pause. I saw the realisation on her face, chased away by a helpless bitterness.

'Of course, you did,' she said. 'I did not recall leaving the pages in such disarray.'

A rush of heat and discomfort shot through me, the memory of searching through Christine's writing desk rising to the forefront of my mind. I bit my lip, noticing that Anna was pointedly not looking in my direction. Guilt gripped me and my stomach gave an uncomfortable lurch. I should have followed Anna's advice and stayed away from Christine's papers. In my eagerness to be useful, I had violated someone's privacy in the worst way. Nausea rose in my throat, and I swallowed hard. What had I become in this handful of chaotic, bewildering days? Everything around me was already so alien to me: the place, the people, the situation, discovering that the world had far more secrets than I could ever have guessed at. I had to remain true to myself.

Even as the thought crossed my mind, I knew deep down that, in fact, I was being true to myself. Not the self which lived in Dover and tried to live up to her family's and society's expectations, but a self I was just beginning to realise existed. A bolder, capable self, someone with the potential to be of use to society rather than a mere adornment. A self who could give her life purpose and meaning.

'I read those letters and the newspaper article,' François said. He shifted suddenly, sitting up on his heels, two bright red spots appearing on his cheeks. 'And I knew. Suddenly, things seemed to fit into place and make sense. But I did not want to do the terrible things he did. I just wanted to look. And I had to get Louise out of the way. I had to. I could not let anyone see me. I could not let them see my shame. But I had to look at him. I had to. I could not stop myself. It was overwhelming, as though something was controlling me and I was simply being carried along, an unwilling passenger.'

'What happened with Louise?' Anna asked. François turned to her, and his face twisted suddenly into an ugly sneer. Her eyes widened a little, but she did not flinch or otherwise react. She waited, her face alight with interest.

'You already know,' François said. 'Why do you have to hear it from me? I crept up behind her. It was easy. She was hiding and it was simplicity itself for me to dodge between the tombs. I do not know why I tried to bite her, though. On reflection, that was unwise.'

'Unwise?' Anna repeated, raising an eyebrow.

'Things took a rather unexpected turn.'

'Unexpected in what way?'

He gave a short, mirthless chuckle. 'I expected to scare her away and then continue what I was doing. She was clearly somewhere she should not have been. I thought she would run home and stay there.' He paused, as though he was thinking back to that night. 'I became flustered. Finding Louise there made me nervous so after I frightened her, I wove my way back between the tombs, only to reach de Vaux's and realise I had forgotten to look for a shovel. My heart was pounding. I knew I should return home immediately, but couldn't bring myself to abandon the opportunity. I began digging with my hands again, but not long afterwards, I heard voices and saw lamps, and I ran. I did not think to fill in the hole I had dug, and doubt there would have been time to do so even if it had occurred to me.' He paused. 'I wish now that I had thought of it.'

Anna nodded. 'I can understand that,' she said. 'Tell me what went through your mind the following morning.'

François launched into a long explanation of the confusion and panic which had gripped him when he realised the implications of his actions. Horrified, he had immediately volunteered to take part in the patrols, in part to keep abreast of what was happening, but also to deflect suspicion away from himself and to see if there was any opportunity to right the wrong. On encountering Louise a second time, however, he had once again been gripped by jealousy at the thought of her with Armand de Vaux. 'It made me furious, too,' he added. 'Despite everything, she was still running around the cemetery. It was clear what had to be done. I had to stop her making a terrible mistake. I had to do something to make sure she never went there at night again.'

'François, that was not your responsibility,' Christine said quietly, her voice thin and brittle. 'Noble as your intentions are, Louise's morals are for her to manage herself.' She sighed. 'I know I have disappointed you. I know I made a foolish and stupid mistake, and that my life – your life – could have been very different. Fortune smiled on me. It does not smile on the unfortunate women I try to help. I know some of them will move on to better things. They may find work and be able to afford a room. Others will not, and will come back to us time and again, having made the same mistakes over and over. All we can do is pick up the pieces and attempt to educate them. It is for them to decide whether they accept that learning. Just as it is with Louise. Her parents have taught her morality. They are good people. What she chooses to do with those lessons is her responsibility, François, no one else's. Why are you so concerned with Louise's morality all of a sudden? Is it because you read my correspondence?'

'It is because I do not wish my future wife to shame me in the way that you shamed Father!'

Silence fell. Christine's jaw dropped. Anna blinked and locked her gaze on François. I froze. My heart rattled against my ribs. What was he saying?

Christine recovered first. 'Your future wife?' she whispered. 'What are you saying, François? You are intending to marry Louise Bernier?'

François threw up his hands in exasperation and leaped to his feet. All three of us started at the sudden violent movement and a sharp gasp escaped Christine's lips. 'How can I marry Louise Bernier?' he demanded. 'She thinks only of that wretched Armand. I would make a far more suitable husband for her, yet she sees no one but him.'

'François!'

Christine rose to her feet, drawing herself to her full height. She clasped her trembling hands in front of her, knuckles showing white through the skin. François froze as her voice sounded in the room like the crack of a whip.

'There is to be no more of this talk,' Christine said. 'I will not tolerate it. Louise Bernier is not for you. She is a pretty girl, I admit, but that is of no importance in marriage. Looks fade. The most important matter to consider is whether your personalities are a good match, whether she would be a good wife to you, and you a good husband to her.'

I shot a glance at Anna. Her lips parted, as though she was about to speak, but she remained quiet, listening intently.

'That was one of the mistakes I made with your father,' Christine went on. 'I chose to focus on the superficial and ignored what was truly important. He and I, despite the age difference, were an excellent match. I learned over time, and after much needless heartache.'

'I can make my own decisions,' François retorted.

Christine rolled her eyes. 'You are not of age! We have discussed this.'

'You control everything! No wonder the men in the patrols ignore and belittle me!' He threw up his hands in exasperation.

'Was this your way of seizing control?'

Anna's voice rang out clear and firm and both Christine and François started. Christine blinked and recovered herself, sinking back into her chair. François hovered, shifting from foot to foot, colour flooding his cheeks. He gave a petulant, inelegant shrug.

'This was something you could control, direct,' Anna went on. 'Something you could use to punish and frighten people. The problem was that it escaped you almost at once, did it not? You lost control and it was removed from your grasp. You tried to claw it back, with the second attack on Louise.'

'She should not have been there!' he burst out. Christine hushed him, to no avail. Only when Anna snapped out, 'Enough!' did he freeze mid-sentence.

'This helps no one,' said Anna, emphasising each word. 'You have created havoc in this town, François. You have cast a slur on the good reputation of the de Vaux family, and on Louis de Vaux in particular. Louise Bernier has suffered because of you.'

François opened his mouth to retort and at that, Anna stood, pointing to a chair. 'Enough of this! Sit!' she instructed.

For a moment, I thought he would leave the room. His gaze swept over Anna and Christine, then he locked eyes with me. I gazed steadily back.

'I suggest you do as she says,' I told him, indicating the chair.

He shifted uncomfortably, his expression flitting from scared to furious to irritated. It settled on condescending, and he slumped into the chair with ill grace. He looked like a petulant schoolboy for a moment, but his fingers plucked at the hem of his coat in a restless staccato rhythm. I stared at him, at the line of his jaw, the well-shaped lips. Had he asked me to dance at a ball, I would have accepted in a heartbeat. Looking at him, there was nothing to indicate that he was the doorway to a lifetime of agony and heartache.

'May I use some of your notepaper, Christine?' Anna asked, indicating the writing desk. Christine looked puzzled but nodded.

'Yes. Yes, of course. Please use whatever you need.' She paused as Anna got up and moved to the writing desk, seating herself comfortably. 'Is this something to do with helping François?'

'It is entirely to do with helping François,' Anna said, opening the ink pot. She smoothed a sheet of notepaper on the blotter and selected a pen. 'In order to end this business to the satisfaction of all, several things must happen. First and foremost, I must convince this town that there is no vampire, and thus restore the reputations of the de Vaux family in general, and Louis de Vaux in particular.' She dipped the pen into the ink and began to write. 'I must also provide an explanation for the attacks on Louise which both resolves the difficulties François created and deflects attention away from him.'

'How?' Christine shook her head in despair. 'How can that be achieved? Surely it is impossible.'

'I have at my disposal all the resources of a large and wealthy organisation,' Anna said. 'In cases such as these, where the identity of the person responsible has to be kept secret, I may need to call on some assistance.'

Interested, I listened to the scratching of her pen on the paper, waiting for her to outline her plan. Christine, however, looked aghast.

'Assistance?' she exclaimed. 'No, you cannot! I cannot have people learning about this! I would never have breathed a word if I had known you would tell others.'

'Please,' Anna said, looking up from her writing. A frown creased her brow. 'Let us not jump to conclusions.' There was an edge to her voice which made all of us pause, a harshness I had not heard before. She took a deep breath, lips pressed together, then began to speak with renewed authority.

'Christine, I need you to arrange to see Catherine de Vaux. Call on her, invite her here for tea, whatever you need to do. In your conversation with her, casually mention that you are thinking of spending a few days in Paris. Viktor and I have been talking about it with you and it has awakened a longing in you to see some of the sights we have mentioned. Perhaps you have a letter from an old governess or a distant cousin – someone far enough removed that your deception could not easily be uncovered – inviting you to visit. Can you do that?'

Christine blinked and nodded. 'Yes, I will call on her. I have not done so for a day or two, so it will not seem unusual.'

Anna nodded, satisfied. 'Thank you,' she said, turning her attention to her writing once again. 'It will be incredibly helpful. It will also provide a reason for you to travel to Paris with us. Do not, at this point, make any mention of when you might go, other than perhaps vague references to a time after the vampire issue is resolved.'

Christine gave another nod. 'I understand,' she said. 'And what of you, Anna? You have to convince Frossard that he should not go ahead with the exhumation order. However will you do that? From all I have heard, he seems absolutely determined to go ahead with it.'

'I hope you will understand when I decline to tell you,' Anna said, a small smile flickering across her lips. Christine bristled a little, but before she could retort, Anna continued. 'The fewer people who know my plan, the more convincing everyone else can be when it plays out.' She leaned forward, her expression earnest. 'Trust me, Christine,' she said. 'I have done this before. All will be well. For everyone.'

She glanced at the clock. 'Christine, how do you feel? Do you think you are well enough to visit Catherine de Vaux today?'

Christine's eyes widened and her mouth opened and closed once or twice before she collected herself and straightened her back. 'Yes,' she said, her voice surprisingly firm. 'I will go and ready myself now, if you will excuse me.'

'Of course,' Anna said with a soft smile, and I nodded. Christine left the room in a rustle of skirts, leaving behind the faintest aroma of rose water. My stomach lurched as I recalled smelling it on François that night at dinner, and a wave of nausea roiled uncomfortably within me. Swallowing hard, I picked up my cold tea and took a tiny sip.

'What do you need me to do, Mademoiselle?' François asked. He had paled again, looking as drawn and tired as his mother. Anna gave him a kind smile.

'Strange as it may seem, François, all I need to ask of you is that you behave as normal. Maintain any routine you have or go to places you would usually visit. Do nothing out of the ordinary.' Her smile widened. 'After all, today is just another ordinary day, is it not?' She gave him an encouraging nod, prompting a weak smile to flicker briefly at the corners of his mouth.

'I understand the image you are trying to create,' François said. 'I know all of this is to help me, so you may be assured, Mademoiselle Anna, I will do my part.'

'Thank you, François.' Anna held his gaze for a moment, then turned her attention back to her writing. Dipping the pen in the ink, she scratched out another line, mused for a moment, then took another sheet of notepaper and wrote what appeared to be a brief letter. She folded and sealed it, then asked me to ring for Céline. I rose, went to the bell, and tugged the rope. François scrambled to his feet and hovered for a moment, uncertain, before abruptly turning on his heel and leaving the room, closing the door behind him with a sharp click. I let out a long breath and Anna gave me a reassuring smile.

'All will be well,' she whispered, then turned to the door as we heard Céline's light tread approaching. I turned to the fireplace and pretended to study one of the knickknacks in what I hoped was a nonchalant manner.

Céline tapped on the door and Anna bade her enter. She handed Céline the letter and fished a coin from her pocket. She gave the maid instructions and Céline bobbed a curtsey before hurrying off. Her footsteps receded along the corridor, and I heard the door swing shut. A few minutes later, she passed the window in her hat and coat.

'An urgent letter, then?' I commented.

'Yes.' Anna was scribbling something else by this time. 'We need to see Inspector Escoffier, because if he will not help me, I shall need to send word to Paris for help.'

I went to sit down, curious. 'What are we going to do?'

Anna finished writing, tidied the pen and blotter away and folded the page of neat writing, tucking it into her pocket. She stood and closed the writing desk, then went to the door and beckoned to me.

'Come,' she said. 'There is a lot to do, and I will need your help.'

'I will do anything I can,' I said. 'What must we do first?'

Anna went out into the hall, and I followed her, closing the parlour door behind me. There was no sign of François. Anna paused at the foot of the stairs, tilting her head, and I listened too, but the house was quiet and peaceful, a far cry from the strife we had witnessed between Christine and François. Satisfied, Anna turned to me with a broad smile.

'First,' she said, 'we need to get rid of our vampire!'

327

Chapter 31

Anna refused to tell me anything. As I leaned against the doorframe between our rooms, trying not to scowl, she took her case to the table and opened it. I forgot to be annoyed as I had my first proper look at what it held. Like a magnet, it drew me to her.

It was lined with rich, deep blue velvet and had several compartments housing tiny glass bottles. Anna took a couple out and held them up to the light. They contained a clear liquid. She replaced them with care, then produced a small pistol, checked it was loaded and set it down on the table.

There was a rosary in a soft leather pouch, three crucifixes of varying sizes, a wooden mallet and about half a dozen wooden stakes with wickedly sharp, fire-hardened points. Peering into the case, I spotted a pocket-sized Bible, a couple of small folding knives, and an entire section filled with little paper twists, presumably containing mustard seeds like those she had given to François and myself.

Anna glanced up and gave a soft chuckle, but continued in her work, methodically taking each item out, testing it and then returning it. Only after she had finished, and the lid was firmly snapped shut did she indicate one of the chairs. I sat expectantly, hoping to find out what role I was to play in the final act of the drama.

'What are all of those things for?' I asked. 'Will we be using them later?'

'This is a collection of useful items I have gathered, which help me to create an illusion,' she said. 'You may be surprised to know that if a grave ever does need to be opened, and if a vampire is discovered and needs to be given peace, it is the sexton's shovel, most often, which is the method of choice. It's quick and relatively easy as long as your aim is good.'

An involuntary shudder rippled down my spine and Anna immediately changed the subject. 'We need Escoffier's help to conclude this, Viktor. If he will not co-operate, and there's no real reason why he should, I need something which looks suitably impressive and final in order to convince people that the threat to them is over. I do need to be careful here, however, which is why I need Escoffier more than he will realise.'

'Why?' I leaned forward, interested.

'Think of what Christine said, and your own interpretation of what you have seen around you,' she said. 'What are we dealing with in this case?'

I thought for a moment. 'We are dealing with a human, not a vampire,' I said, slowly feeling my way through my thoughts. 'But all of those things look like they are for getting rid of a vampire.'

'Precisely!' She nodded, looking grim. 'I need to have these things ready, in case of need, but if I bring them out straight away, what will people instantly think?'

Frowning, I stared at her, not following what she meant. Suddenly, it hit me. 'Oh! Of course! If you march into the cemetery armed with an arsenal of weapons, everyone will instantly believe Monsieur de Vaux is a vampire after all. And this is as much about protecting people's reputations as it is about dispelling the vampire hysteria, is it not?'

'It is.' She pressed her lips into a thin line. 'Inspector Escoffier needs to assist us in creating a different kind of illusion.'

I smiled. 'He seems rather enamoured of you. I am sure you will be able to persuade him to help you.'

Anna gave a mirthless laugh. 'The difficulty I have is that my suggestion will take him somewhat beyond the law, and police officers, particularly senior ones, do not usually take kindly to such suggestions.'

'Ah, I understand.' I considered this thoughtfully. 'So, what is the alternative, if he does not?'

'A mixture of science and the occult,' Anna said. 'With a little more emphasis on the occult. Except it's tricky and may well result in collateral damage for Louis de Vaux's reputation, so I am very much hoping Escoffier will help.'

The next half hour was taken up with dealing with a number of callers. Escoffier's officers had completed their enquiries and either sent messages or were nearby and decided to attend Anna in person to update her. No one had anything to report. René and Matthieu were exactly who they claimed to be, thus closing another line of investigation. Céline had returned from her errand and kept us well-supplied with refreshment. Anna read her letters between callers, sipping coffee, her expression terse, and I wondered how badly affected she was by the potential repercussions of what lay ahead. While she was occupied, I re-read Uncle Geoffrey's letter, which was still in my pocket. My stomach churned uncomfortably all the while as I considered the choices with which I was faced, which were nowhere near as serious as those facing Anna. Once again, my thoughts flitted around like restless butterflies, and it was a relief when the doorbell sounded, making both of us start. Anna folded her letters as Céline's light tread passed the parlour. A moment later, we heard the low murmur of voices and the sound of footsteps in the hall. I slid the letter into my pocket.

The parlour door opened, and Céline ushered Escoffier into the room. We stood, and he and I bowed to each other.

'Inspector Escoffier, Mademoiselle,' Céline said quietly. 'Will you be requiring more coffee?'

'Yes please, Céline,' Anna replied, as Escoffier took her hand and raised it to his lips. Céline curtseyed and left the room, closing the door behind her. Escoffier held out his hand and I shook it firmly.

'Thank you for coming, Inspector,' I said, trying to pretend I knew what was going on. 'Please do sit and make yourself comfortable.'

'It's my pleasure, if it means we can bring this matter to a close,' Escoffier said earnestly, settling himself into a chair. 'Thank you.'

Anna smiled. 'I truly hope we can. We need to reach a certain level of agreement before that can be achieved, however. There are a limited number of options open to us, which is why we need your help and co-operation.'

Escoffier regarded her appraisingly, much as he had in de Vaux's study. Anna met his gaze steadily, and his lips parted as the two of them gazed at each other. It looked as though time had stopped for them.

'I will help you in any way I can,' Escoffier said softly, a tiny, ragged note in his voice. He cleared his throat and shifted in the chair, fiddling with his shirt cuffs. Anna kept her eyes locked on his, her expression serene as she thanked him. He was clearly enamoured of her. I could well understand that, for I myself found her intriguing, albeit in a different way. Did she often have to resort to feminine wiles to bring cases to satisfactory conclusions? I did not possess such skills. Could I, as Anna suggested, work as Viktor? He was certainly a more comfortable body to inhabit than my own.

'Is Madame Archambeau joining us?' Escoffier asked.

Anna shook her head. 'No, not for this conversation. It needs to remain between us. She has, I believe, gone to call upon Madame de Vaux. It seems that Viktor and I created a longing in her to see the sights of Paris, with all our talk at dinner of our favourite places. I believe she is planning to visit a childhood friend there and thought it would be an excellent distraction for Madame de Vaux if she joined them.'

Escoffier smiled, his eyes twinkling. 'What an excellent idea. I recall you mentioning that Madame Archambeau was uncomfortable with François taking part in the patrols, so perhaps there is a mother's protective instinct involved also.'

Anna gave a soft chuckle and nodded, her eyes lighting up. 'I think you are absolutely right, Inspector. She gave me the impression that she was proud of his maturity and desire to assist his community, whilst at the same time fearful for his safety. However,' she added, reaching out a hand to touch the letters almost unconsciously, 'I am firmly of the opinion that there is absolutely nothing to fear in the Cimitière de la Madeleine.'

Escoffier leaned forward, keen. 'There is no vampire?'

331

Anna shook her head. 'No, Inspector. This case has all the hallmarks of a prank, frankly. I have seen many. I have also seen many vampires, but there is nothing here which leads me to believe that Monsieur de Vaux is anything other than a pleasant old gentleman who has sadly passed away.'

'What is the case missing in terms of the vampire angle?' asked Escoffier, sounding genuinely curious. 'And have my officers sent word to you yet regarding their enquiries? Nothing had arrived before I left my office to attend you.'

'They have indeed.' Anna tapped the letters with a slender forefinger, and I saw Escoffier's gaze flick to her hand before returning to her face. 'The lines of enquiry regarding the patrol members are closed. All of the men are exactly who they say they are.'

'And this leads you to believe it was a prank?'

Anna nodded. 'It would not surprise me to learn that a vagrant had been sleeping in the cemetery.'

Escoffier narrowed his eyes. 'Oh, yes?'

Just then, Céline tapped at the door, and I went to assist her with the coffee. Escoffier sat back in his chair with an amused smile playing at the corners of his mouth as Anna continued to sit calmly, her expression enigmatic. Watching them, I was overcome with a sudden desire to laugh, so I busied myself offering milk and passing around the plate of biscuits Céline had brought, biting the inside of my mouth to stop myself giggling. Part of it was nerves, I knew, but it was amusing to see Escoffier falling head over heels for Anna. I hoped that whatever her plan was, he would support it.

Céline retreated, closing the door behind her, and the three of us drank in silence for a couple of minutes. Escoffier tilted his head, listening, as we were, for signs that Céline had returned to the kitchen. We caught each other's eyes and chuckled.

'Well,' Escoffier said, 'now we are certain we will be undisturbed, perhaps you would be so kind as to explain how I can assist you, Mademoiselle.'

Anna smiled, a genuine, warm smile which made Escoffier catch his breath audibly. She placed her coffee carefully on the table next to her, folded her hands in her lap and began to speak.

'There are a number of issues at play here, Inspector, not least of which is the need to prevent an unnecessary exhumation. Have you heard from Mayor Frossard?'

He nodded. 'You will be glad to hear I was able to delay him. I received your message as he was leaving my office, as it happens. He was not particularly happy, as you can imagine, but I pointed out that he is campaigning for re-election and any indication of impropriety would be unwise at the moment. That gave him pause and he went rather quiet and took his leave. With any luck, it should give you the space you need.'

'Excellent,' Anna said, unable to hide the relief in her voice. 'This is my main concern. We have so many reputations at stake, Inspector, and the plain truth is that none of them need to be blemished. Certainly not in the case of a non-existent vampire.'

'What can be done to protect them?' Escoffier asked.

'It is very simple.' Anna beamed at him. 'We need to prove there is no vampire and hand them an alternative culprit.'

Escoffier gaped at her, as did I. 'An alternative culprit?' he repeated, looking blank.

Anna nodded. 'Yes. At the moment, the hysteria is centred around the possibility that Louis de Vaux is a vampire and is responsible for the attacks on Louise. We simply need to provide a convincing alternative explanation for everything which has happened. Because, not to put too fine a point on it, there is one.'

Escoffier considered this for a moment, raising his cup to his lips. When he spoke, it was clear he was feeling his way along.

'You know something,' he said. 'You probably know everything. What do you need from me? Who is this alternative culprit you mentioned?'

Anna smiled. 'He does not exist.'

Escoffier paused and did a double-take. 'I beg your pardon?'

'He does not exist,' Anna repeated. 'Our role is to ensure that everyone believes he does.'

Escoffier set his cup down with a smart click and gave Anna a sceptical look. 'I think you need to explain in detail, Mademoiselle.'

'Of course, Inspector. Please forgive me.' Anna plucked delicately at one of her cuffs. 'There are a number of issues we have to address within our solution. The exhumation is unnecessary and must be stopped at all costs. Thankfully, it appears that you have been able to delay Mayor Frossard, for which I thank you most sincerely. It is one fewer worry for me. Tied in with the exhumation is the damage to Monsieur de Vaux's reputation, which I should, with luck, be able to restore. It will be straightforward enough to disprove the existence of a vampire, but that is where I require your assistance the most, Inspector.'

Escoffier nodded, listening carefully, and drew his notebook and pencil from a pocket. Anna paused for a moment before continuing.

'One of the other reputations which has suffered is that of Louise Bernier. There is little which can be done about it, I fear, because she was somewhere she should not have been. The attacks on her have to have an explanation which will satisfy everyone. Her family, yourself, the de Vaux family, the people of Amiens.' She threw Escoffier a frank look. 'I considered a number of options. There were few available to me, however. Here in Amiens, it would be impractical to import colleagues from Paris to act out certain roles. It is sometimes possible in more remote rural communities, where the law and its application is somewhat...' she tailed off, searching for a word. '...less structured, shall we say.' She smiled at Escoffier, who had raised an eyebrow. 'I will not compromise you, Inspector, by saying anything else on that particular subject. I am quite sure you would be horrified by the vagaries of the law in certain parts of France. Let us focus on the case.'

She picked up her cup and finished the last of her coffee. I indicated the pot, she nodded, and I stood to refresh her cup. The Inspector declined with murmured thanks, and I returned to my seat, topping up my own cup and setting the pot back on the table.

'The attacks on Louise were quite clearly the work of a human, not a vampire,' Anna continued. 'We need to establish that someone, a vagrant, was sleeping in the cemetery and that Louise disturbed him. She was not physically harmed beyond some bruising. He was not aiming to harm her. He simply wished to be left in peace. I suspect the activity in the graveyard scared him off, which is why nothing else happened. Perhaps he left something in the cemetery and needed to return to look for it. However, he was disturbed once again by Louise and was forced to scare her a second time.'

'This is too far-fetched,' Escoffier said. 'No one will believe it. You know who is responsible, don't you?'

'You have to trust me, Inspector,' Anna said smoothly, sidestepping the question. 'Please. I know it is a lot to ask of you.'

'I am not even certain what it is that you are asking,' Escoffier said. He looked harassed, and his eyes darted from Anna to myself and back again. I attempted to keep my expression neutral.

'I'm asking you to support my theory that the culprit is someone from outside of Amiens, who tried to pass a night in the cemetery, but was disturbed,' Anna said. 'If we could find a bundle of belongings, perhaps hidden in a gap between a mausoleum and the cemetery wall, for example, it would add weight to the story.'

'Why?' asked Escoffier. 'Why go to such elaborate lengths? Why the deception? What you are asking, Mademoiselle, goes against my instincts. If Louise Bernier's attacker is at large and known to you, you will be in serious trouble if you do not reveal his identity. He must be made to face his crime.'

Anna gave a thoughtful nod, her expression grave. My heart rattled in my chest, and I held my breath, waiting to see what would happen and half-expecting Escoffier to arrest us both for harbouring a criminal.

'In this type of work, I see many things, Inspector,' she said quietly. 'I see families ravaged by grief and loss, much like the de Vauxs, and worse. I see families dealing with these terrible things whilst having to come to terms with the fact that their beloved relative has become one of the undead. I also see families where there is a kind of sickness, a very specific sickness.'

Escoffier turned this over in his mind and nodded briefly.

'The law, in some cases, is not always the most appropriate tool for resolving issues like the one facing us,' Anna went on. 'It is an unwieldy tool and can often be applied in too heavy-handed a manner. Very occasionally, circumstances require me to take a softer, more gentle approach. This requires me to create an illusion, and that is where I need your help, Inspector. I need you to help me make Amiens believe a vagrant passed through the town, was disturbed, frightened a young girl, and has since moved on, leaving behind some of his possessions. Are you able to do that?'

Escoffier stared at her for a long moment and flicked his notebook shut with a sharp motion which made me start. Getting up, he began to pace the room, his hands clasped behind his back. I cast a worried look at Anna, but she gave me a small smile and an even tinier shake of her head. Uncertain what she meant, other than to hold my tongue, I followed Escoffier's movements. He looked like a tiger pacing an enclosure at London Zoo. He reminded me more than ever of Arthur and, like Arthur, there was a presence about him which I found deeply comforting. At that particular moment, however, it seemed he was about to upset all of Anna's plans. Sitting in the elegant parlour, surrounded by Christine's photographs and ornaments, seemed somehow incongruous given the nature of the discussion. As the silence stretched between us, my discomfort increased, yet Anna sat calmly, hands folded in her lap.

Pausing at the window, Escoffier turned his back to the room, his large frame blocking much of the light. He remained there, unmoving, for some time before turning to regard Anna thoughtfully. A frown creased his brow, but his expression was unreadable, and I found myself holding my breath. It seemed that the success of Anna's plan rested almost entirely on Escoffier's co-operation, and I could understand his hesitation. Anna was probably breaking a law, and the thought of the consequences of that, particularly for myself, was enough to make me shudder. The empty cup rattled on its saucer and Escoffier and Anna both looked at me. I dropped my gaze to the cup as I rose to place it back on the tray, then returned to my seat and pulled out my notebook and pencil, pretending to jot something down.

'Anything I do to assist you absolutely must be off the record and in the strictest confidence,' Escoffier said finally, his rich voice dropping low. 'Can I trust you both to make no mention of this anywhere?'

Anna's face softened and her eyes sparkled. 'You can, Inspector. Have you ever heard of my organisation before?'

Escoffier shook his head. 'I cannot say I have, no.'

She let the statement hang in the air for the Inspector to digest. He looked even more thoughtful, frown deepening, then gave a deep sigh. A little smile flared briefly at the corners of Anna's mouth.

'I do not like this at all.' Escoffier sounded resigned. 'Yet there is something about you, Mademoiselle, which speaks of integrity and capability. You are right; I have never once heard of your organisation. Nor, indeed, have I ever heard of other agents such as yourself.' He flashed her a lopsided and rather endearing grin. 'I am willing to discuss the matter with you to see if we can reach an agreement which will not lose me my job.'

'My organisation has absolute respect for the law, Inspector, but unfortunately, we must acknowledge the fact that creatures exist within the world which do not fall under any jurisdiction but their own.' Anna smiled up at him. 'And, sometimes, mine.'

Escoffier returned to his seat, perching on the edge as though he was trying to reduce the distance between himself and Anna as far as possible whilst maintaining respectability. 'Very well,' he said. 'Let us devise a plan.'

Chapter 32

The next few hours passed in a frenzy of discussion, organisation and preparation as Escoffier and Anna put together their plan. I kept to the periphery, volunteering a comment or opinion when asked, but otherwise sitting quietly to listen and absorb. A series of ragged neighbourhood children with matted hair and filthy faces were engaged to carry messages all across Amiens, and Céline kept us well supplied with refreshment, appearing at the parlour door so frequently that Anna was eventually obliged to ask her to remain in the kitchen until called. Christine returned part-way through, her mood much improved, enthusing about the trip to Paris. Catherine de Vaux had been grateful for the opportunity to spend some time away from home and had accepted Christine's invitation immediately. Christine gave us some highlights from their conversation, thanking us for putting the idea in her head. The four of us chatted for a while about places in Paris which we particularly enjoyed, then she excused herself and went off to the kitchen to speak to Céline. The house buzzed with activity, and eventually François volunteered to wait by the front door, so Céline did not have to keep leaving the kitchen to deal with the stream of callers either collecting or passing on messages.

At one point, I excused myself and went to my room, leaving Christine to act as Anna's chaperone. During the course of the day, Escoffier seemed to become increasingly besotted with Anna, and showed no sign of leaving. Amusing though it was at first, I soon began to feel awkward and was relieved when Christine returned and could take my place.

I laid my father's journals on the table, chose one at random and began flipping slowly and methodically through the pages. Afterwards, I took up another, and then another. I was not looking for anything in particular, nor did I read every single line; rather, I let my gaze bounce around the pages randomly. It was unlikely that my father, in the depths of his mania, had knowledge Anna did not, with the wealth of experience available to her through her mysterious organisation, but what if there was a tiny snippet of information she had not considered, and which would help her resolve the case more easily? Her plan was full of pitfalls, and I had a persistent feeling of nausea crawling around in the depths of my belly.

I reached for another journal and as I did so, a soft tendril of mist swirled before my face. I started and recoiled, a cry escaping my lips. The chair rocked and caught on the carpet, and I had to catch hold of the table to prevent it from tipping me backwards. Righting myself, I stared at the table, waving my hands around over the journals. The mist was gone.

Leaping to my feet, I looked around frantically, but there was nothing. The room was innocuous, ordinary. As I hurried around it, peering into corners, behind furniture and under the bed, seeing nothing, I wondered what had prompted the mist's appearance. Had it been trying to guide me to one of the journals in particular?

Returning to the table, I stood staring down at the journals for a moment, then began rearranging them into neat lines. They had become jumbled when I grabbed the table to keep my balance. I worked slowly and methodically, eyes peeled for any sign of the strange mist, but nothing happened, not even when I picked up the journal I had been reaching towards.

All at once, a wave of frustration descended. The mist, the strange creature it concealed, Anna's plan, Escoffier, François... everything crowded into my brain, making me dizzy. The room swirled around me, and I caught my breath, gripping the table as strange dark dots danced at the edges of my vision. The collar and cravat felt tight suddenly, and I sank to the floor, leaning my head against the table leg as nausea rose within me.

I sat there for a long while, I think. Noises floated up from the hall, but I did not really register them. My ears buzzed and I squeezed my eyes shut, breathing deeply and hoping the feeling would soon pass. A shudder ran through my body, leaving behind a strange chill which raised the hairs on my arms and the back of my neck. Suddenly, the sheets and blankets looked welcoming and inviting, and I crawled across the room, heaved myself on the bed and curled up, pulling the bedclothes tightly around myself.

'Viktor? What is wrong? Are you unwell?'

I cracked open one eye, trying to focus. Anna was hovering next to me, concern etched on her face. She reached out a hand and touched my forehead gently, then bit her lip.

'You feel hot,' she murmured. 'Let me ring for some water.'

She moved to the bell and rang for Céline, returning to me immediately. I struggled to sit up, taking in the darkened room in some confusion. Anna saw me looking around and smiled softly.

'You have been asleep for a while,' she said. 'Escoffier has gone, and everything seems to be in place for tonight. Will you be up to it, do you think?'

I blinked at her for a moment. 'Will it work?' I asked. 'There seem to be so many things which could go wrong.'

'It's always the same,' she said with a little shrug. 'All I can do is hope. Escoffier is trustworthy, at least. I have had to place my faith in so many people – police included – who were far less approachable and open-minded.'

'What do you need from me?'

'I need you to stay with François and watch him. He is scared and could be unpredictable.'

I stared at her. 'What on earth am I supposed to do if he becomes unpredictable? I wish you would remember that I am not a boy.'

'No, you are an extremely capable young woman, who needs to realise she has a good brain and quick wits,' Anna said in clipped tones which revealed her irritation. I was about to retort when we heard Céline coming up the stairs. A moment later, she tapped at the door. Anna bade her enter and asked her to bring some water, explaining I was overtired and feeling unwell.

Céline expressed dismay and disappeared immediately, returning a few minutes later with water and a small bowl of broth. Anna had cleared the journals from the table, and we sat there together while I ate. The broth was thin but full of flavour and by the time I had finished, I felt a great deal better. We had moved on to chatting about everyday subjects while Céline was coming and going, and once she had cleared the bowl away, Anna returned to her plan.

'It is unlikely that François will do anything, I think. He is scared and knows what is at stake. However, I need you to be aware and ready, should anything happen.'

I stared at her helplessly. 'Ready?'

'I know it is a lot to ask, but there are so many people involved that having you as an extra pair of eyes and ears will be invaluable. Please watch François for me.'

I threw my hands up in defeat. 'Very well, I will do my best. I know how important this is, and I cannot help but think I am the weak link in the chain.'

Anna flashed me a quick, rather mirthless smile. 'Do not be so quick to diminish your abilities,' she said. 'Now, I need to prepare. Please excuse me for a moment.'

She went through the connecting door into her own room, closing it softly behind her. I heard faint sounds of rummaging, of drawers and cupboards opening and closing. Walking to the window, I unlatched it and pushed it open, drinking in the cool evening air. Someone was laughing in the distance, joined by a number of other voices, and the aroma of something meaty and delicious greeted me as the breeze shifted in my direction. I hoped it was Céline's cooking, although I had little appetite. A chill settled over my heart gripping it tightly. For a moment, my vision clouded, and I dug my fingers into the windowsill, staggering a little. A few deep breaths settled my ragged breathing and calmed my racing heart somewhat, but as I sank into one of the chairs, I noticed my hands were shaking.

A couple of hours later, I was standing in the hall with Anna and François. Anna carried her case and was wearing an outfit in a rich dark blue, jacket buttoned to the neck and a heavy woollen shawl wrapped around her shoulders. Her eyes glittered and her expression was serious. When she spoke, it was in short, clipped sentences. There was an air of barely contained energy about her, as though the moment she left the house, she would be running.

François, too, was clearly full of nervous anticipation, fingers plucking unconsciously at his lapel, at his cravat, at his shirt collar, his cuffs. He shifted from foot to foot, avoiding eye contact with both of us. Out of sympathy, I turned slightly away from him, focusing my own attention on Anna, and waiting for her instructions.

Christine appeared at the parlour door, her face white and drawn. She, too, had a shawl pinned over her dress in spite of the fire crackling in the hearth. Looking past her into the room, I saw she had been reading. A book lay open on the table next to her armchair.

'Everything will be all right, will it not?' she asked, unable to disguise the quaver in her voice. She reached out a hand to François, but he moved away, and I found myself between the two of them. Awkwardly, Christine withdrew her hand, two bright spots of pink flaring briefly in her cheeks.

Instinctively, I reached out and took Christine's hand. She looked up at me, a weak smile flickering across her lips. 'Please try not to worry,' I said, with far more conviction than I felt. 'I know that is easy for me to say, but Anna's plan is sound, and we have Escoffier assisting us.'

Anna nodded and lowered her voice, glancing along the corridor in case Céline appeared. 'I have done everything within my power to divert attention away from François. Not even Escoffier knows about him. That is how it shall remain. You have my word.'

Christine pressed her lips into a tight, thin line and gave a barely perceptible nod. I squeezed her hand, then she pulled away and tugged her shawl more closely around her. The three of us exchanged glances and Anna opened the front door.

'Let us go and resolve this situation once and for all,' she said, determination in her voice.

François straightened and gripped his cudgel. 'Yes,' he said. 'Please. I want it to be over.'

We left the house and walked along the road towards the cemetery gates. There were few clouds in the sky, but the moonlight was dim, deepening the shadows around us. Anna's step was quick and light, François striding along beside her. I hung back, my mind racing. The task ahead was daunting, especially with so many lives and reputations at stake, and once again, fear rose in my throat. No matter what Anna said, or how reassuring she might sound, there was no avoiding the uncomfortable truth that I was the weak link in her plan.

Escoffier was waiting at the main entrance. As we approached, he bowed to Anna and held out his hand to François and myself. Even in the watery moonlight, I could see his grim expression.

'We are all prepared?' he asked, his voice soft.

'Yes,' Anna whispered back.

'Good.' He turned abruptly and led the way into the cemetery, moving swiftly, his step surprisingly soft for such a large man. We hurried after him, looking all around us as we made our way to the de Vaux plot. The cemetery was still and shrouded in deep shadow, the moonlight picking out here and there the tip of a wing, the corner of a mausoleum, the top of a gravestone. We did not light the lanterns we carried. Anna wanted to attract as little attention as possible.

As I followed along behind François, glancing over my shoulder every few feet, I suddenly became aware of a familiar scent, the strange, musky, cloying aroma which clung to the creature in the fog. It filled my nostrils, and I caught my breath, peering into the darkness. Was there fog? It was too dark to tell, and I could not feel its damp chill on my face or hands. Perhaps I had imagined it. Yet why would that, of all things, have invaded my thoughts at that moment?

I puzzled as we continued walking. The odour faded, leaving me more convinced than ever that I was imagining things. Taking a few deep breaths, I fought to calm my racing heart, but as we neared the de Vaux plot and I saw the faint glow of a candle, and the silhouettes of a group of people, all my efforts were in vain. My heart hammered against my ribs, and I fell back a pace or two, convinced that someone must be able to hear it.

Anna murmured a greeting as we reached the group. De Vaux was there, Armand at his shoulder. Jean and René stood near them. Arnal was leaning on a shovel and smoking a cigarette. There was another man beyond Arnal, shifting from foot to foot, but it was not until he stepped forward to mumble a greeting that I realised it was Maurice Bernier.

Seeing everyone, François tensed and took a step back, bumping against me. I put a hand on his arm and leaned in to whisper in his ear. 'Stand firm,' I murmured. 'Remember they know nothing.'

He turned his head towards me, his expression contorted by the feeble glow into an almost lupine leer. I blinked, my heart jolting, but he turned away again almost immediately. Unnerved, I focused instead on Anna as she greeted everyone.

All at once, something happened.

As Anna spoke, that scent once again filled my nostrils for a brief moment. I glanced around, but there was nothing to be seen. Shaking my head a little, I dragged my attention back to Anna. She was speaking but seemed distracted.

'Our first task is to ensure that we have the area covered,' she was saying. 'Wherever you position yourself, please make certain you can see at least two other people, and –' She broke off and tilted her head suddenly, and I could just make out her frown. I wondered what she was doing.

Then I heard it.

From somewhere off to my left, a voice rose in an ethereal ululation, rising and falling as if carried by the wind. It seemed there were words, although none I could understand, and the melody was like nothing I had ever heard before. It was nowhere near us, yet it seemed to surround me, filling my senses, lulling and soothing. A warmth bloomed around me, and I was suddenly filled with the urge to find the singer. I turned in the direction of the voice, staggering a little. The world seemed different somehow, warmer, less frightening. I took a couple of uncertain steps towards the voice.

'Viktor!'

I blinked and the voice quietened, making me catch my breath, afraid that the singer was moving away from me, that I would never find them. I took another step, then someone caught my arm and shook me, none too gently.

'Viktor!'

I dragged my arm out of their grasp, almost snarling, then stopped dead as I realised Anna was standing in front of me, her face tilted up to mine. 'You heard it, didn't you?' she gasped. 'You heard it!'

'I have to hear it again,' I said, slowly. 'I have to.'

'No!'

Her voice, loud and harsh, cut through the fog which had settled on my mind, and I fell back a pace or two. One of the men murmured something unintelligible and the air around us suddenly became tense and strained. A match flared and a warm glow enveloped us all. Escoffier had lit one of the lanterns and was holding it up so he could see me.

'What's going on?' he demanded.

Anna was peering intently into my face, but as he spoke, she turned to him. 'Unexpected development,' she said. 'Arm yourselves, please, gentlemen. Did any of you hear singing?'

'Singing?' René repeated. 'When?'

The other men shook their heads in confusion. No one had heard anything except Anna and me. It was bewildering. The voice had been some way off, but clear and haunting. How could they have missed it, in the silence?

Anna was giving instructions in a clipped, business-like voice as she knelt and set her case in front of her. 'We form two groups. Remain on the paths. That is vital. No matter what you see or hear, do not leave the path. We move together. I will follow the first group, so I am in the middle and able to reach any of you quickly.' She opened the case and handed Bernier, François and myself twists of mustard seeds. 'You three, Monsieur Jean and Monsieur de Vaux will be in the second group, and your task is to sprinkle these seeds periodically along the path as we go. If the vampire decides to ambush us from behind, it will be distracted by the need to count the seeds, which will give me time to reach it.'

Bernier took the vial almost automatically, then said, 'I thought you said there was no vampire. Yet now you are saying there is. How can we trust you? You do not know what you are talking about!'

'Bernier!' snapped Escoffier.

The farmer shot Escoffier an unfriendly look. 'It's a reasonable question,' he said in a surly tone. 'How can we trust her?'

'Because she is the expert in these matters,' Escoffier shot back. 'Hold your tongue, Maurice. Mademoiselle Anna, what will an attack look like?'

'The creature will be fast. Faster than anything you have seen before. Depending on what type of vampire it is, it may have the form of a handsome man, a beautiful woman, or a wraith in a shroud. You need to be on high alert, looking all around, and do not immediately trust what you see before you. René, you are wearing your crucifix?'

'Yes, Mademoiselle.' René, startled, fumbled beneath his collar, and brought out the silver cross on its chain. Anna nodded.

'Good. Please leave it visible and join Inspector Escoffier at the front of the first group. Armand, Monsieur Arnal, you are in the first group. We move along the path with no more than six to eight feet between the groups. We sprinkle mustard seeds behind us and to the sides as we walk. I am ready to take action. Armand, will you please carry my case for me? It is sturdy and can be used effectively as a weapon. Delivers quite a nasty blow,' she added, removing several long, pointed wooden stakes and a mallet from the case and closing it, the snapping locks unnaturally loud and threatening in the silence which had fallen. 'Report anything you see. A cat. A fox. A bat. A figure in the corner of your eye. Report everything. Until the creature shows itself, I have only suspicions as to what we are dealing with, but I can categorically confirm that we are not dealing with Monsieur Louis de Vaux. This is something else.'

Several of the men raised their voices in protestation at this, but Anna hissed them into silence, her voice sharp and her eyes flashing darkly in the lamplight. 'Quiet!' she snapped. 'Do you not think my work is difficult enough already? From here on, please remember this, gentlemen. I am the expert. I alone have the knowledge and skill to deal with whatever we are about to find. I alone have the knowledge and skill to keep the rest of you alive. I alone have the knowledge and skill to despatch a vampire. So, from now on, your job is to do exactly as I say and let me proceed with the work I have been trained to undertake. Is that clear?'

There was a shocked silence, broken by a few mumbled yeses. Maurice Bernier and Jean both cast appraising looks in my direction and it was a relief to know that they could not see the colour I could feel flooding into my face.

'Please listen to my sister,' I said, speaking rapidly, thinking that I needed to add my voice to Anna's. 'She speaks the truth. I have not had the training she has had, and her depth of knowledge in this field far outstrips mine. If you wish to stay safe and stay alive, you will follow my lead and listen to her, trust her expertise, and do as she asks.'

Some of the men shifted their grip on their weapons and shuffled their feet, exchanging glances. De Vaux made an impatient noise.

'Let us stop delaying!' he exclaimed. 'If there is some terrible creature roaming around, we need to deal with it!'

'De Vaux is right,' Escoffier said, his voice grim. 'Is everyone armed and ready?'

This time, the responses were firmer, and Escoffier nodded to Anna. 'Mademoiselle, we are in your hands.'

He was watching her closely, I noticed, perhaps waiting to see if this was part of the plan she had not disclosed to him. The lamplight glinted off something and I saw he was holding a pistol. I gave an involuntary shudder, my mind racing through dozens of scenarios, none of which ended well.

'Stay together, stay alert,' Anna said. 'Let us proceed.'

Everyone fell silent, and together, we started moving along the path, peering in all directions, expecting to see some foul creature from beyond the grave bearing down on us. A thin mist hung sullen and heavy between the tombs and gravestones, stretching its cold, damp fingers across the path about knee height. I eyed it suspiciously as I walked near Anna, casting a few mustard seeds to my left every few steps. Behind me, de Vaux's breath was a series of staccato gasps, and up ahead, René was whispering the Lord's Prayer over and over.

Anna was walking slightly apart from everyone else, her head tilted to one side. Every so often, she would slow her steps a little, then continue on. She had produced what I initially thought was a belt, but when she clipped it around her waist and slotted the wooden stakes into it, I saw it was a custom-made holster of sorts. For a moment, following slightly behind her in the dim light, I was mesmerised by the soft sheen catching the edges of the polished wood, glinting on her hip. She swung the wooden mallet as she walked and there was a lightness to her step, like a cat prowling through the night. François's breathing was hard and heavy to my right. Behind me, I could hear the air whistling in Bernier's nostrils. We moved slowly along, keeping our tread as soft and quiet as we could.

All at once, I heard something and stopped dead, cocking my head to listen more carefully. It was a strange sound, which I could not immediately place. There was something dull about it, a slow rhythmic kind of wetness. It was coming from somewhere off to my left.

'What is it, Viktor?' Anna whispered. At the sound of her voice, everyone stopped and turned to me. One or two of the men caught their breath, and I noticed Monsieur Arnal had his shovel raised to shoulder height, the light glinting off the metal.

'Listen,' I whispered. 'Do you hear that?'

There was a silence as everyone focused their attention, but after a few moments, de Vaux whispered, 'I hear nothing.'

'Nor I,' murmured Jean. Arnal and Escoffier started to speak, but Anna hushed them.

'Viktor, tell me what you hear,' she instructed.

I described the sound as best I could and she took several steps away from us, leaving the path and moving between the memorials. 'Wait there,' she ordered in a low voice. 'And make no sound.'

My heart thumped loudly and painfully in my chest as she vanished into the gloom. Instinctively, we moved a little closer to each other. The sound seemed louder and more distinct. Whatever it was, it seemed to be drawing nearer, and panic rose within me. 'Anna!' I whispered. 'Come back!'

There was the sound of footsteps hurrying through the grass and a moment later, Anna appeared. 'This way!' she hissed, darting past us all and running along the path ahead of us. It took a moment or two for us all to gather our thoughts and start running after her. Up ahead, I could hear Escoffier demanding to know what was happening. The frustration in his voice was plain, and I hoped he would not try to take over. This was clearly not part of the plan, and only Anna had any idea what was happening.

'What is it? What are we dealing with?' Escoffier hissed. Anna wheeled to a halt, spinning around on the path, forcing us all to an abrupt stop.

'It's a revenant,' she said, speaking quickly. 'A reanimated corpse.'

'Reanimated? Reanimated how?' Escoffier asked, but Anna ignored him.

'Viktor, what can you hear now?'

I started, then closed my eyes and listened. The strange sound seemed to float around before settling in a particular direction. 'Over there,' I said, pointing further along the path. 'I think it is moving. A strange, wet sound. There's a loose rhythm of sorts to it.'

There was a silence, then Bernier muttered, 'Can't hear a thing.'

Anna hushed him sharply. 'There is a reason why only certain people can undertake the work I do,' she chided. 'There are things I can see and hear that you cannot. Monsieur Arnal,' she said, looking towards him. 'I may be in need of your shovel. Are you prepared?'

Arnal huffed out a long breath, then grunted a rough Yes. 'Didn't think I would have to do this, though,' he added in an undertone.

'Do what?' demanded de Vaux. There was a quaver in his voice.

'Decapitate it,' Arnal said shortly. 'Let's move, shall we, Mademoiselle?'

In stunned silence, everyone followed Anna as she led the way along the path. I glanced at François, who had been silent throughout, and wondered how he and the equally silent Armand were faring. All of a sudden, François spoke, making me start a little as he raised his voice.

'What is this noise you are hearing?'

Anna slowed very slightly. 'It's the revenant chewing on its shroud,' she said quietly. 'We need to corner it so I can stake it and Monsieur Arnal can take off its head. That's the only course of action with this type of vampire, sadly. They do not speak, or think, or reason. They are, quite literally, hollow shells. But they are sometimes quick, so be wary. Above all, do not let it come close enough to bite or even graze you with its teeth. Just corner it. I will do the rest.'

There was some dark muttering, a low whistle and the sound of René slapping his cudgel into his palm. 'Let us go,' he said. 'We must deal with this evil.'

All at once, the horrible sound grew louder and I gave a cry as something lurched out of the shadows to my left, bearing down on me. A foul stench overwhelmed my senses and I staggered away, colliding with François and Bernier, who both instinctively clutched at me. François dropped his seeds and let out a ragged curse, falling to his knees and scrabbling frantically in the grass at the edge of the path. The lamp fell from Escoffier's hand, plunging us back into the gloom of night. The creature raised skeletal arms from the folds of the decaying woollen cloth wrapped loosely around its body, reaching towards François. Bernier yelled and swung the stick he was carrying, knocking the creature's arms violently away. It staggered to one side, regained its balance, and lunged for Bernier, whose scream of terror etched itself into my brain. He fell backwards, landing next to me, and I found myself staring directly into the creature's face, the skin taut and paper-thin, eyes sunken and vacant, yet somehow inherently malicious. It hissed at me, lips pulling back to reveal long, pointed, razor-sharp canine teeth, its foul breath hitting me full force, as though I had run straight into a wall. François had scrabbled desperately out of the way and was frozen on Bernier's other side, arrested part-way through getting up, his eyes fixed on the horrible spectacle before him.

The creature turned its attention back to Bernier, gripping him tightly by the collar as it sat astride him. The stench was overpowering, the sweet, cloying stench of decay mingling with the earthy mould of the grave. I retched, rolling away, and as I did, Anna's boots flashed past my face.

Time stood still.

As if in slow motion, I saw Anna raise the sharp wooden stake and bring it down, piercing the creature's back. It let out the most ghastly, unearthly screech I had ever heard, releasing its grip on Bernier and trying to reach behind itself to get to the stake. Anna was still holding the stake, and now brought down the mallet, driving the wooden point right through the creature. It screamed and writhed, and Bernier, frozen with terror, could only stare up at it helplessly with panic-stricken eyes as it thrashed.

'Arnal!' shouted Anna.

He was by her side in an instant, shovel raised. 'Bernier, move!'

Bernier simply stared at the creature, his mouth hanging open slackly as some of the other men added their voices to Arnal's, urging the farmer to get out of the way. Jean and de Vaux, both of whom had been standing shocked and frozen themselves, suddenly snapped into life and sprang forward. They each grabbed an arm and dragged Bernier away from the creature.

Anna put her boot in the small of the creature's back and shoved it forcefully to the ground, pinning it. 'Now, Arnal!' she cried, gritting her teeth as the creature screeched and thrashed. Arnal took a step forward, putting his own foot on the creature's ribcage next to the stake and adding his weight to Anna's. He raised the shovel high above his head, then brought it rapidly down, blade first, on the creature's neck. There was a sickening crunch as bone splintered. The head jerked violently to the right and the creature fell silent. Arnal brought the shovel down again and again, grunting with the effort. Four blows in total, each seeming to my eyes to be more savage than the last, until finally he knocked the severed head away from the shoulders.

A thick blanket of silence fell as we all stood or lay around the stinking corpse, hardly able to believe what we had just witnessed. Anna was breathing heavily, but when she spoke, the triumph in her voice was clear.

'We did it, gentlemen,' she said. 'Congratulations and thank you for your assistance. Monsieur Bernier, are you all right?'

Bernier made a strangled noise in his throat and Jean, still crouched next to him and gripping his arm, released him and stood, then leaned down and pulled the shaking farmer to his feet.

'Let me help you,' René insisted immediately, tucking his cudgel into his belt. He went to Bernier's other side, picking up the farmer's stick when his foot caught it. The three men moved a little distance away, murmuring quietly together.

Anna huffed out a little short breath and when she spoke, I could sense an edge in her voice. 'These creatures are fast, evasive and cunning, despite being little more than reanimated corpses,' she said. 'They are creatures of instinct. I suspect that such a large number of us in close proximity was sufficient to attract its attention and draw it from its place of rest.' She looked to Escoffier. 'Which we will need to locate and deal with.'

'Deal with?' he repeated.

'Armand, my case, please,' Anna said, and Armand, after a few moments' pause, moved to her as though in a trance, although he gave the creature a very wide berth. Anna took the case, knelt, and set it on the ground before her. 'Thank you. May I have some light, please?'

Escoffier cast about for the lamp and de Vaux, sidling away from the remains, handed him a tinderbox. Escoffier lit the lamp and went to Anna, holding it above her. De Vaux went to Armand, who had backed away, and put his arm around his son's shoulders in an unexpected and touching display of love. The two of them stood silent and unmoving, watching as Anna lifted a tray out of the top of the case and withdrew a sack from a compartment beneath. She replaced the tray, closed the case, and returned it to Armand. Shaking the sack open, she carefully rolled the head into it with the toe of her boot.

'Monsieur Arnal, Inspector Escoffier,' she said, straightening. 'Might I beg your assistance, please? We need to return this to its place of rest. Can you drag the body between you?'

I thought for a moment that Escoffier would baulk. He gaped at Anna, then handed the lamp to me and stared down at the stinking body. He had holstered his gun and stood there flexing his fingers. 'Gloves,' he murmured, more to himself than anyone else, and delved into his pocket.

Arnal had no gloves, so de Vaux offered his own. The sexton took them with grateful thanks and pulled them on, then gripped the tattered shroud, wrapping it around one of the corpse's bony ankles. Escoffier did likewise. Arnal held the shovel, blade down, over the corpse, ready to jab at it if needed. Escoffier, seeing this, quietly unholstered his gun.

'Where are we taking it?' François asked suddenly, his voice barely above a whisper. I shone the light on him briefly and saw the horror etched into his face. Whatever fascination the cemetery had once held, I felt certain had been firmly banished the moment the unspeakable creature had stretched its arms towards him. He looked so young and afraid.

'We have to place it back in its grave and take steps to ensure that it cannot rise again,' Anna replied. 'Monsieur Arnal, may we be guided by you? We need to systematically check the cemetery to discover where this creature came from.'

Arnal nodded. 'I have a route I take. Start over there.' He indicated back the way we had come, and, leaving the lamp with them to act as a marker, we congregated at the corner where the paths met.

Arnal and Escoffier remained on the path with their foul burden while Arnal directed the rest of us between the memorials and graves. Anna slipped one of her stakes into my hand as she passed me. 'Hold it like this,' she said wrapping my fingers around it, 'and when you strike, strike straight for the heart, like this.' She raised my arm, moving it in an arc to demonstrate, then vanished behind an angel statue before I could say anything. I hefted the smooth wood, feeling the weight and finding a comfortable grip, then turned my attention back to the row of tombs I was meant to be checking. Running my hand over the cold marble, checking for anything which seemed out of place, I had a moment of blind panic as Anna's instruction finally sank in. If anything lurched towards me out of the shadows, that sharpened stake was the only chance I had of saving my own life. It was a chilling thought.

We worked our way through the cemetery, row by row, tomb by tomb, until we heard François calling.

'Here! Over here!'

Chapter 33

We stumbled through the darkness, following the sound of François's voice as it carried on the crisp night air. Most of the group had reached him by the time I found my way there and were all gathered around one of the burial plots. Like the de Vaux plot, its outline was marked by a low, ornate iron fence, but the grave contained within was in turmoil. A huge heap of overturned earth was clearly visible, even in the dim moonlight, and its damp, loamy smell filled my nostrils. Anna dug around in a pocket and produced a candle, which de Vaux lit for her. The tiny flame leaped uncertainly, casting strange shadows all around us. I could not help but shudder as she held it close to the wrecked grave.

The coffin lid had been fully dislodged and was standing almost upright in the ragged hole. One corner could be made out, the wood rotten and deformed, distorted even further by the flickering candlelight. Matthieu crossed himself and backed away.

'I will fetch Arnal and the Inspector,' he said, and hurried away out of sight.

Anna was peering into the grave with detached professionalism. 'Could those of you with mustard seeds please come and empty the vials completely into the grave?' she asked. 'Scatter them as well as you can. We do not want them all in one place.'

François and I stepped forward. The stench of decay was, thankfully, not overwhelming; the corpse had clearly been long buried. Even so, the smell coated the insides of my nostrils, and I raised my sleeve to my face, wishing I had a scarf to cover my nose and mouth. We sprinkled the seeds into the dark, gaping maw of the grave.

'Is there a rock or stone anywhere nearby?' Anna asked. 'Not a pebble, something larger, perhaps the size of an apple.'

We all cast about in the dim light, leaning down to feel around by our feet. After a couple of minutes, Armand held out an object to Anna and asked, 'Will this do, Mademoiselle?'

'Yes, this is perfect,' Anna said, weighing it in her hand. She looked over to where Escoffier and Arnal were approaching with their gruesome burden, the lamp light bobbing eerily over the stonework as they picked their way carefully between the memorials. As they reached us, I peered at what Anna was holding. It looked like a chunk of fallen masonry.

Several minutes were spent with Anna guiding the two men as they lowered the corpse back into its resting place. Once that was done, Anna requested that she be helped down into the grave, and Escoffier and Arnal each took one of her hands and carefully lowered her down. François took up the lantern and held it aloft, and we all peered down at her as she balanced carefully amidst the rotting coffin timbers.

'Please can you pass me the head?' she asked. Shuddering a little, Arnal lifted the sack containing the head and knelt at the edge of the ragged hole, leaning in to hand it down to her. He stayed there, watching intently as she set it carefully amidst the rotting wood, down by the corpse's feet. Everyone had gathered around, watching in morbid fascination as she prised open the jaws and carefully inserted the chunk of rock.

'Viktor, in my case, there are some strips of fabric,' she said.

Armand immediately knelt and fumbled with the catches. Escoffier swung the lamp over me, and I rummaged around, producing two narrow rolls of fabric which resembled bandages. I handed them down to Anna, waiting to see what she did. Armand must have spotted the candles, because a moment later, there came the sharp sound of a tinderbox striking, a flare of light, and then a steady, warm glow. Armand lit three candles and passed them around before focusing his attention on Anna once more. Armed with light, the group moved a little closer, curiosity overcoming all of us.

Anna unrolled one of the strips of fabric and began tying it firmly around the corpse's jaw, knotting it on top of the head. De Vaux, who was holding a handkerchief to his nose, coughed a little, then asked, 'Why are you doing that, Mademoiselle?'

'This will help to keep the rock in place for as long as possible,' Anna replied, not looking up from her task. 'There is an ancient belief that the act of chewing on the shroud is what creates the vampire, although my organisation disagrees in principle with the theory. We have not yet managed to disprove it, so we have to adhere to the old precautions.'

She tested her knots, then gestured to the men to help her out of the grave. 'This should suffice,' she said, when she was once more standing next to me, brushing earth from her skirt. 'The creature should not wake again, but if it does, the seeds will distract it, and it cannot chew the shroud any longer.'

'Why is the head by its feet?' asked François. His eyes were still wide with the horror he had seen, but he had edged closer to the mouth of the grave and was peering into it. His sunken cheeks and eyes aged him significantly.

'To confuse it. It won't know how to move about. The head can be left above the neck after severing, but it is vital that you place something between the two. A sturdy piece of wood usually works. It prevents the head from reattaching and enabling the creature to rise and walk once again. However, my preference is to separate head from neck as thoroughly as I can, for the extra reassurance.'

An involuntary shudder rippled through me as my mind, despite my best efforts, played image after gruesome image of undead wraiths such as this one working out how to reattach severed heads. Anna must have felt me trembling, because she slipped a hand into mine and gave it a quick squeeze.

François made a non-committal noise and wrapped his arms tightly around his torso. As Anna spoke to Arnal about filling in the grave, and the men dragged themselves out of their shock and into action, I watched François. He stood unmoving, and I could not see whether he was watching the activity around the grave or lost in his own thoughts. At least his terrible secret was safe. With any luck, it would remain so, and he and Christine could escape to the anonymity of Paris. Were there really people there who could help him? I thought of François incarcerated in an institution like St Bernadette's and shuddered again. The image of Christine having to face some of the things I had seen whilst visiting my father or my uncle at the asylum brought unexpected tears to my eyes and I blinked them away furiously.

Anna stepped back from the grave and let Arnal take control. He instructed the men to collect shovels from his storage shed, and René, Armand and François hurried off, returning a short while later with four or five, which they handed round. Arnal had reluctantly climbed down into the grave to secure the tattered remnants of the coffin lid, the sound of the mallet on the nails loud and jarring in the thin night air.

Inevitably, a crowd soon started to gather. The light, noise and activity had woken several of the families whose houses backed onto the cemetery. De Vaux noticed them first, standing a little way away, watching. 'Inspector,' he murmured, 'we appear to have an audience.'

Escoffier, Anna, de Vaux and Bernier went to speak with them. There were about a dozen men and three or four women, all wide-eyed with curiosity and fear. I remained near the grave, trying to watch and take in everything at once, whilst simultaneously appearing as though I had seen this countless times before. The coffin secured, Arnal climbed out of the grave and he, René, Jean, and Armand began to fill it once more. The sound of earth hitting the coffin was loud and unexpected, and the little crowd of spectators fell silent for a long moment as the stark reality of the situation hit them. Feeling uncomfortable, and not a little nauseous as the loamy earth smell assailed my nostrils, I went to stand near Anna, nodding to those in the crowd who caught my eye. Most of them were carrying lamps, which cast long, eerie shadows over the graves and mausoleums as those holding them swung them around, trying to get a better view of what was happening without having to get too close.

'Whose grave is it?' one of the women asked suddenly. 'This isn't the de Vaux plot.'

'That's what I was trying to explain,' de Vaux said, exhaustion in his voice. 'My father is not and never was a vampire, as I have always maintained.'

'The family will be informed, you may rest assured,' Anna said soothingly. 'May I ask a favour of one of you? The grave needs to be blessed. Might someone be able to rouse Père Michel, please?'

'I can do that, Mademoiselle,' said a tall young man, and set off at a run. The crowd muttered, and behind me, I could hear the rhythmic sound of shovel blades cutting into loose soil, the rattle of small stones against metal and the soft thud as each shovelful of earth landed in the grave.

'I owe you an apology, Monsieur de Vaux,' said the woman quietly. 'I knew your father from church, and knew he was a good man. I am sorry for the part I played in gossiping about him.'

'I appreciate that,' de Vaux said, and one or two others added their voice to the woman's. Anna nodded in satisfaction.

'Perhaps you can all now take steps to undo the damage which has been done to the de Vaux family's reputation, and Monsieur Louis de Vaux's, in particular,' she said.

'Yes,' Bernier said. 'The bad feeling between our families is well-known, but it is an age-old argument, and I am man enough to set it aside and add my truth to theirs. Louis de Vaux was not a vampire. Whatever the creature might have been, I saw with my own eyes that it was not Louis de Vaux.'

De Vaux held out his hand to Bernier, and after the briefest of pauses, the farmer took it. As they shook hands, the crowd rippled back to life, assuring de Vaux that they, too, would do their part in defending his father's reputation and making sure the truth was known. Escoffier, who had been speaking quietly with Anna, spoke up.

'Please also spread the word that, from now on, there will be penalties for anyone found in this cemetery after dark,' he said. 'I will be posting a guard each night. Tell as many people as you can. There will, of course, be formal confirmation of this from my office in due course.'

'Are we safe?' asked an older man, whose white hair stood out in unbrushed tufts. He appeared to have a nightshirt tucked into his breeches, with a jacket thrown over it. He had a poker in one hand, and I guessed that all of these people had armed themselves with whatever was to hand as they hurried out of their houses to investigate the disturbance in the cemetery.

'Yes,' Anna said before Escoffier could reply. 'The vampire has been neutralised and will not rise again. You need not fear it.'

'Then why do we need guards?' asked another man. 'If it won't rise again, what are they guarding against?'

'Hoaxers,' said Escoffier shortly.

'Please remember,' Anna added, 'that there is much to pity in vampires. Something stirs them, and once roused, all they can think of is returning to their family. If they manage to find their way back, the blood lust overcomes them, with tragic results. A vampire's existence is one of self-loathing, no matter how they may appear outwardly.'

That silenced everyone for a while and we all stood in the chilly night air, musing over Anna's words. I had never imagined I would feel pity for an undead creature, yet the image of one trapped in its coffin, yearning for its family, struck me unexpectedly and hard, and this time, I had to turn away, so no one saw my tears. I wandered back to see how the men were getting on with the grave.

Several of the onlookers were also goaded into action and approached cautiously, asking if they could take a turn with the shovels. Arnal kept going, as did Jean, but Armand and René handed theirs over and stood back, René plucking at his crucifix with restless fingers. Armand watched the diggers for a moment or two, then turned away, wrapping his arms around his torso and staring down at the ground. Bernier left de Vaux and went to Armand, murmuring something quietly in his ear, and the young man nodded. Bernier clapped him on the back briefly and returned to de Vaux, who was deep in quiet conversation with three or four of the crowd. Armand remained unmoving, hunched over, as though trying to disappear inside himself. How would he fare, once this crisis was fully behind him? Would Anna have a way to provide some kind of help for the bereaved family? This mysterious organisation of hers seemed to have endless resources at its fingertips. And what of the relatives of the poor unfortunate whose grave we were all gathered around, a sombre tableau in the half-light? How would she break the news to them? Thinking about what had happened to the shrunken, rotting corpse made me shudder violently and I hoped I would not need to be present for that particular conversation.

The crowd lapsed into silence, and we stood in the cool air, listening to the rhythmic sound of the shovel blades cutting into the earth, each person lost in their own thoughts. Roused by the sound of running footsteps, the diggers stopped and the rest of us peered around, grips tightening on weapons, lamps swinging back and forth trying to see who was approaching.

It was the young man who had gone to wake Père Michel. The priest, breathing hard, stopped short when he saw the crowd and looked around, his jaw dropping when he saw the diggers, shovels in hand, returning to their task once they realised who the new arrival was.

'Mother of God, what has happened here?' breathed Père Michel.

Anna briefed him, quickly and concisely. He stood staring at her blankly, shaking his head now and then, his mouth occasionally trying to form words which never made it beyond the confines of his thoughts. 'Will you bless the grave, Father?' Anna asked. 'Give this poor soul rest?'

He nodded, fumbling in his coat pocket. Withdrawing a Bible, he opened it and moved cautiously to the side of the grave. The diggers were making good progress, but there was still a sizeable mound of earth to shift. Père Michel watched them for a while, then seemed to collect himself. He made the sign of the cross over the grave and began to pray. One by one, the crowd moved closer, adding their voices to his, each finding comfort in the familiar call and response of the prayers. It was unexpectedly moving.

All at once, the realisation hit me that I had not seen François since he returned from Arnal's store with the shovels. I was about to panic when he stepped forward from behind a tomb and took the shovel from Jean. Breathing a sigh of relief, I cast about for Anna, and saw her at the edge of the crowd gathered around the grave. My tired mind started losing focus as the prayers continued around me, and parts of the eventful night replayed in my head. Christine's pale, drawn face. François. The horror of the creature as it lurched towards us, stinking of death and decay. The eerie, otherworldly singing.

As my mind strained to recapture the melody I had heard, a question bubbled to the surface. Anna had not explained the singing, and it was clear that only she and I had heard it. That being the case, did it mean it really was otherworldly, and I, too, was able to hear such things?

And if it was otherworldly, I thought, heart racing, why had I heard it *then*?

Chapter 34

The rest of the night passed in a flurry of activity which left us all exhausted.

Père Michel, under Anna's instructions, blessed a number of graves, tombs and memorials next to the vampire's. She explained that this was a precautionary measure only, as there was no sign of disturbance in any of them. Some of the crowd followed the priest from grave to grave, solemnly responding to the prayers, faces serious and thoughtful. One or two of them cast glances over their shoulders every so often, as though expecting some terrible entity to leap at them. Others drifted away, hoping to sleep for a couple of hours before the day's rigours began once more.

The grave had been restored and blessed, and the shovels were returned to Arnal's store by the tired diggers, who trailed back to the grave site slowly, one or two massaging weary muscles. The cold fingers of dawn were prising the clouds apart to peer through, revealing a ragged gathering of subdued, shocked people in the half light. Several others had swelled the crowd as dawn arrived, having heard the commotion during the night, but not brave enough to investigate it at the time. Necks craned and hands plucked anxiously at collars and aprons as Escoffier and Anna sought to reassure and offer explanations, and de Vaux reiterated his father's innocence.

François had slunk to the periphery of the untidy knot of people and was watching everything with an expression of horrified fascination. At any other time, this might have attracted unwelcome scrutiny, but one glance at the

362

crowd and I could see the same expression reflected in several of the onlookers. Out of all of us, Armand looked the worst, his cheeks sunken and dark shadows beneath his eyes gaunt and ill. Jean, who had been silent for most of the night, was standing with him, grim-faced, one hand toying with the hilt of the sword at his waist. I made my way around the edge of the crowd until I was next to François. He started as I drew near.

'Oh, it's you, Viktor,' he said in a low voice tinged with relief.

'Are you all right?' I asked. He gave a soft, mirthless chuckle and leaned towards me to whisper.

'It seems I am, in spite of everything. I never imagined anything like this.'

'It's shocking, isn't it?' I replied, without thinking. François shot me a look.

'Even for you, who has seen it all before?'

'I have not seen everything,' I said hastily, trying to recover. 'My sister has seen so much more than I. Even so, regardless of one's exposure to them, such events are always going to cause distress and be extremely hard to deal with, are they not?'

He took the chide well and ducked his head in acknowledgement. 'Forgive me, I did not mean to imply that you were unfeeling. I can clearly see you are not.'

I nodded and turned my attention to Anna, who was still deep in discussion with several of the onlookers. I thought of going to stand with her but decided against it. This was, after all, her work, and my place was beside François.

Even as I thought it, my mind started firing questions around. What exactly had happened? No one had seen any sign of this vampire until tonight. François had admitted his part in Louise's unpleasant experiences, and it had seemed that the entire thing was simply a prank which had spiralled out of control. Yet here we all were, numb and wide-eyed in the aftermath of an actual vampire attack.

Before I could delve too deeply, a commotion distracted me, and I saw the little knot of people scatter as they were joined by a familiar figure. Frossard, with Joubert on his heels, strode to Escoffier and demanded to know what was going on. His voice cut through the tense early morning atmosphere, and everyone stopped what they were doing to turn and stare at him. If he noticed, he did not show it, and in the end, Anna and Escoffier were obliged to take him some distance away to talk to him. Even from a distance, I could still hear his voice carrying through the thin, cool air, although the words were indistinct.

'The man's a fool,' muttered François. 'When I think about what he wanted to do to poor Monsieur de Vaux…and now I have seen it for myself with the poor wretch in the grave.' He shook his head. 'Had I but known…'

'Hush, François,' I cautioned softly. 'Let us focus on the future now. Think of Paris.'

He grunted and lapsed into silence, turning slightly away from me. Frossard's voice rose beyond us, quivering with indignation. 'An actual vampire?' A few moments later, he strode back into our midst, looking around until his gaze fell on the freshly turned earth. 'This one?' he asked loudly, of no one in particular. No one responded, so he edged towards the grave, peering at it suspiciously, his cane held out in front of him. Escoffier and Anna hurried up to him.

'This is the one?' Frossard asking, not taking his eyes from the grave. 'This is where it was?'

'Yes,' Anna replied shortly. 'The grave has been blessed and the poor soul within will now have peace and rest.'

'Yet you are inciting a panic,' Frossard whipped back. 'Why are you telling people there may be others here? What evidence have you? You told us there was no evidence of any vampire. Why should we believe you?'

Anna paused before responding and when she did begin to speak, it was in the clipped, brisk tones I had come to recognise as her thoroughly annoyed voice. 'If a panic ensues from the advice I give, Monsieur le Mayor, at least my advice is given after having dispatched the vampiric creature which attacked members of the patrol. You, too, incited a panic with your talk of exhumations and your refusal to provide proper assistance to the police, and you did that with no evidence whatsoever.'

Frossard's mouth opened and closed a few times and there was a muffled snort of laughter from the back of the crowd, followed by a low ripple of comments. The mayor started to bluster once more, hurling accusations left and right. Anna was a charlatan, he said, and if anyone thought they had seen a vampire, they were either deluded or drunk and should not be out on the streets. This roused the ire of the patrolmen and things looked to be taking an ugly turn. Joubert stepped forward to stand at Frossard's shoulder, cudgel in hand, and Jean half unsheathed his sword as the patrolmen loudly denounced Frossard. It took the combined efforts of Escoffier and, to my surprise, Père Michel, to subdue the situation and calm the men. Anna stepped away from the confrontation and came to stand with me.

'Not the ending I might have hoped for, but we have fulfilled our part,' she murmured. 'It is always difficult to leave a case behind, but the manner in which people readjust their lives is not our business. Our role is to rid them of the threat and educate them in preventative measures.'

'Is it always like this?' I asked.

'Like what?'

I gestured towards Frossard, who, having failed to win any sympathy from the onlookers, was striding off towards the main gates, Joubert trailing after him. 'Do you always have this much trouble?'

Anna gave a soft chuckle and reached out to squeeze my hand. 'Oh Viktor,' she said. 'Compared to some, this one has been remarkably easy and straightforward. Escoffier truly is a gem. Normally everyone I encounter is a Frossard, or worse.'

I shook my head in disbelief, wondering yet again at Anna's fortitude, all the more convinced I would flounder were I in her shoes. Yet something was tugging at my thoughts. Lapsing into silence, I let my mind tumble where it would as I watched Escoffier start to disperse the crowd and send runners to the police station. He looked tired and drawn, yet there was a fire about him, a gleam in his eye. Perhaps this incident would mean the end of Frossard as mayor and Escoffier was looking forward to having someone more reasonable on the opposite side of the bargaining table. I hoped it would be de Vaux.

Bernier came over and took Anna's hand, clasping it between his own. 'My sincere thanks, Mademoiselle,' he said. 'I confess that, at first, I was doubtful of your ability, and I am ashamed. We all owe you a great debt, and you will always be most welcome in my house.'

Hearing this, de Vaux joined us, Armand trailing after him. 'Monsieur Bernier is right,' he said. 'We owe you so much. The de Vaux house will always be open to you should you be passing this way and need accommodation. Thank you, Mademoiselle, from the bottom of my heart, for restoring my father's reputation. I am forever in your debt.'

Anna smiled. 'Please, do not speak of debt,' she said. 'My skills are a gift, which I give freely. Should you wish, you may consider making a donation to my organisation.'

She was interrupted by the sound of running footsteps and we all turned to see who was approaching. It was Louise, wearing a simple day dress of soft grey fabric, a heavy shawl pinned around her shoulders. Seeing us, she faltered and slowed to a halt, a little flush appearing on her cheeks. Anna gestured to her. 'Come and join us, Mademoiselle Louise, everything has been resolved, and you are quite safe.'

Bernier held out a hand to his daughter and she approached slowly, placing her hand in her father's and staring around her. 'It's safe?' she repeated. 'So there really was a vampire?'

'There was,' Bernier, said. 'Saw it with my own eyes. Terrible creature. Unspeakable.'

Louise gaped, then realised and raised a hand to cover her mouth. 'And I thought it was a man,' she whispered.

From where I was standing, I could see Anna's profile, and caught the slight narrowing of her eyes. Louise's story about the warm hands on her skin rumbled through my mind, and from the way François's head snapped up at her words, it was clear we were all thinking the same thing. Was Louise going to push the point? And if she did, would Anna have a plausible response?

'But the hands…' Louise began. 'The hands I felt. They were warm.'

Bernier and de Vaux both looked at her. Anna paused for a fraction of a moment, then said, 'Sometimes with these creatures, their hands are so cold that when they touch you, they burn slightly and thus feel warm.'

Louise stared at her for a long while, turning this over in her mind. A heavy silence descended on us, which stretched on and on until Bernier muttered, 'Well, I have seen it for myself and would not like to feel those terrible hands on my skin. Come, Louise, we should return home. The danger is over, thanks to Mademoiselle Anna.'

'Thank you, Mademoiselle,' Louise said almost automatically. There was a little frown wrinkling her forehead and my heart pounded in my chest as I realised she was trying to make everything fit her experiences and discovering that not everything did. Yet there was nothing in particular which would lead her to François even if she did keep questioning what she knew. To the best of my knowledge, he had never declared himself to her, which was fortunate.

Bernier shook de Vaux's hand again and then turned to Armand. 'I do not approve of the manner in which you have been meeting my daughter,' he said gravely. 'Yet I am not an unreasonable man. Perhaps the feud between our two families has run its course at last. We should look to the future, and pick our own fights rather than inheriting them from others. Once all this has been concluded and the dust has settled, come and see me, young man. We will talk.'

Armand could only stare as Bernier shook his hand firmly, then put an arm around Louise's shoulders and led her away. De Vaux watched them as they vanished behind the jungle of marble, then looked at his son. 'We should return home also, my boy. Your mother will be worried, although I doubt the commotion would have carried as far as the house.'

'Yes, Father,' Armand replied. He still seemed stunned, barely focused on what was happening around him. He had not so much as glanced at Louise. Would they be able to salvage their fondness for each other, or would they forever be reminded of these terrible few weeks? What indelible marks had been left on all of these people?

De Vaux once again shook our hands, bending over Anna's and kissing it. 'You have saved my father from suffering a terrible indignity, Mademoiselle. I say it again, my family will always be in your debt. You are returning now to Madame Archambeau's?'

'Yes, we need to sleep before making any preparations to return to Paris.'

He nodded. 'Understandable. We, too, should rest. I shall attend you at Madame Archambeau's later, with your permission.'

'Of course.' Anna smiled up at him. 'It would be my pleasure.'

De Vaux straightened and bowed to her. 'Then I bid you good day for now and thank you again for all you have done.' He put an arm around Armand, and together, the two of them started making their way between the tombs, quickly disappearing from view.

Escoffier watched them go, then turned to Anna. 'I need to remain here to instruct my men when they arrive,' he said. 'Go and rest, and I, too, will attend you later, if I may.'

'You may,' Anna replied, giving him her hand, and once again I saw a look exchanged between them. Pretending to find a nearby inscription suddenly fascinating, I moved discreetly away, aware all at once of how heavy my limbs felt, how blurred my thoughts. The idea of sleep was intoxicating.

A few minutes later, there was a gentle touch on my arm and I looked down into Anna's tired face. 'Let us go and sleep, Viktor,' she said. 'There are still some things to be finalised before we can think of leaving for Paris, but they are mostly formalities. There is the family of the poor unfortunate vampire to speak with, and a visit to Frossard's office, too. We should be able to leave the day after tomorrow if that will suit you?'

'It suits me well,' I said, 'but then, I have nothing pressing upon my time.'

She chuckled. 'Maybe you will before much longer,' she said lightly, slipping her hand through my arm and leading me back towards the path to the main gate. François followed at a distance, and Anna occasionally turned her head to check he was still there.

We walked in silence, too exhausted for conversation. My mind was slowly turning over the events of the night, picking over them one by one. Something kept bringing me back to one thing, and try as I might, there was no way to explain it.

'Anna,' I said hesitantly, glancing behind me to see where François was. He was trailing us by some distance, well out of earshot, as we walked along the road towards the house. 'The strange singing. What was it?'

She was silent for a few moments. 'I'm not sure,' she said softly. 'It was something I had not encountered before.'

'Really?' I exclaimed. 'Yet you seemed so confident, as though you knew exactly what was happening.'

'Oh, I knew what was happening,' she replied. 'Or, to be more accurate, I suspected what was happening. I am just not sure what was singing.'

'It was a 'what', rather than a 'who', then?' I asked, chills creeping up my spine as I recalled the ethereal, crystal clarity of the voice.

'I fear so,' she said. 'I think it may have been some kind of siren call, which would usually suggest that the creature's sire was in the area, watching us and ready to wake it from its sleep. Yet it makes no sense. There is only one scenario I can envisage which does make sense, but that sheds a completely fresh light onto the situation.'

'What is it?' I asked, curious.

'It was as though something knew we needed help, needed a distraction to deflect attention away from François,' Anna murmured, lowering her voice even more. 'It was just too convenient, don't you think? A vampire turns up at just the right moment, where, a day earlier, there had been no indication of one.'

'That puzzled me,' I admitted. 'The grave had no connection to the de Vauxs, so if you had seen traces of activity, you had no need to hide them. They were, as you say, exactly what we needed, in the circumstances.' I paused, mulling this over. 'What are you suggesting?'

Anna turned to glance over her shoulder once again.

'I think,' she said slowly, 'perhaps someone has a guardian looking out for him. Someone from the other side.'

'The other side?' I repeated. 'You mean... someone deceased? De Montfort?'

'Possibly,' she said, 'but I think it more likely that François has attracted the attention of something from the fae world with his nightly activities in the cemetery. That's why we need to get him away from here and into safe hands in Paris as soon as we possibly can.'

Chapter 35

As we reached the house, the front door opened and a worried-looking Céline ushered us all into the parlour, where Christine, her face drawn with concern, was standing by the hearth, a crumpled handkerchief twisted around her fingers. She tucked it hastily into her sleeve and reached out to Anna and I, squeezing our hands, before going to François, taking him by the shoulders and looking into his eyes. Anna and I sank gratefully into the armchairs, wrapping ourselves in the blankets laid out for us. Christine murmured something into François's ear, and he nodded, then excused himself and left the room. Christine sighed, then turned to us, composing herself.

'It is done?' she asked.

'It is,' Anna replied. 'You need fear no longer. Inspector Escoffier is taking charge of patrolling the cemetery from now on.'

A look of intense relief flooded Christine's face, then she paused and frowned. 'Escoffier? Then… there is still a need for vigilance? There is still some danger?'

'It is mainly to keep people out,' Anna explained. 'Quite often, incidents like this occur when human activity disturbs or catches the attention of the undead or the fae. We were able to prove beyond doubt, however, that Monsieur Louis de Vaux is definitely not a vampire. The vampire was someone else entirely, someone with no connection whatsoever to the de Vaux family.'

Christine's eyes widened. 'There was a vampire, then?' she exclaimed.

'There was.' Anna stretched her hands towards the fire, rubbing her palms together. 'It has been dealt with and will now rest peacefully and cause no further problems.'

'That poor family,' Christine murmured. 'Will someone have to tell them?'

Anna nodded. 'It is in hand. Escoffier and I will attend to it.'

Christine nodded. 'If I can assist in any way before we leave for Paris, please do not hesitate to ask,' she said. 'I am intending to finish packing today so I can have the trunks sent on ahead.'

Anna smiled. 'Viktor and I are intending to leave the day after tomorrow, which should be plenty of time to bring this matter to a conclusion. I suspect there will be a number of visitors before then, for which I apologise in advance.'

'There is no need!' exclaimed Christine. 'You have performed a great service for this city. I will advise Céline and ensure there is plenty of refreshment available. Speaking of which...'

She broke off as a light tap sounded at the door. I got up and opened it, admitting Céline and a large tray of cocoa and toast. She set the tray down and bustled about, ensuring we were comfortable, setting side tables within our reach and prodding the fire. The flames leaped higher, sending a burst of warmth and a bright glow throughout the room, and all at once, I felt soothed. The crisis was over. All I needed to think about for the moment was eating, drinking, warming up and then sleeping, which I hoped would not be too far in my future. My eyelids were heavy and although I was following Anna and Christine as they spoke, my own words would not form into sentences, so I simply listened, sipping the cocoa, and nibbling the toast as the chill in my bones gradually eased.

'Viktor?'

I blinked. Anna was leaning over me, a little smile on her face in spite of how exhausted she looked. I had fallen asleep in the chair. Struggling into a more upright position, I babbled an apology, but Anna hushed me.

'We need to sleep, and you will be more comfortable upstairs, I assure you. Come.'

I set the blanket aside and stood, letting Anna take my hand and guide me from the room. Christine was coming down the stairs as we emerged into the hallway and gave me an indulgent smile. 'You poor boy, you look exhausted. Go and sleep. I will make sure you are not disturbed.'

'Thank you,' I mumbled, and followed Anna up the stairs and into our rooms, where I lay fully clothed on my bed and fell immediately into a deep, dreamless sleep.

I awoke with a start, and a vague feeling of unease, completely disoriented and with no sense of the time. I lay there for a moment, staring up at the ceiling and trying to order my unruly, sleep-jumbled thoughts, but they would not behave, so I gave up and closed my eyes again. The house was silent. No one would object if I had another five minutes of rest before getting ready to deal with the aftermath of the vampire.

'Viktor? Are you all right?'

My eyes flew open at the sound of Anna's voice, and I started as her face loomed over me. I blinked and struggled to focus on her concerned expression, the last, wraith-like threads of a disturbing dream slipping from my mind like sand through fingers.

'You were crying out in your sleep,' Anna said softly. She rose from where she had been kneeling by the bed and sat next to me, reaching down to brush a strand of hair from my face. 'What is wrong?'

I shrugged and whispered, 'Bad dreams, nothing more. I don't even recall what they were.'

She smiled and squeezed my hand. 'You were incredibly courageous last night, you know,' she said. 'You should be proud of yourself.'

I scoffed a little. 'I did almost nothing, Anna.'

'You remained with me. You did not cry, or scream, or run away, as virtually any other girl your age would have when faced with such things. No, you remained.'

'I was frightened, Anna. I have never seen anything so terrible before in my life.'

Her fingers tightened reassuringly around mine and her smile widened. 'No. Few have. And yet, despite the horror, you were there beside me, doing your part to help that pour soul finally find rest.'

We fell silent for a moment, and I knew that she, like myself, was replaying the awful scenes in her head. The stink of the grave came flooding back into my nostrils, along with the sight of the rotting flesh and yellowing bones, and the ethereal, other-worldly singing.

'Anna,' I said suddenly, 'are we truly finished here? Don't we need to investigate the strange singing we heard?'

Her face clouded and the little frown settled into place between her brows. 'Did you look at the grave, Viktor? The one the vampire emerged from?'

'Not really. I was too focused on the creature itself.'

A little smile played on her lips. 'Understandable.'

'What did I miss?' I asked, curious.

'When we first explored the cemetery, there were no signs of disturbance around the grave at all,' she said. 'We were thorough. It was as innocuous as Louis de Vaux's own.'

I frowned up at her, not understanding. 'What do you mean?'

Anna bit her lip and glanced towards the door, then leaned closer. A lock of her hair fell over her shoulder and tickled my cheek, and her subtle perfume wafted gently towards me. 'Don't you think it was all a little too convenient?' she whispered. 'I know I said François has some kind of guardian watching over him, but somehow, it just doesn't fit in with the rest of the facts as we know them. It has been bothering me.'

'What can we do?'

She huffed out a breath and looked off into the middle distance for a moment. 'I can request that another operative examines the site, one with different skills to my own. We often do so, as a precautionary measure. I can't sense everything. I would like to return to the cemetery later, after dark. It may be that an answer presents itself.' She turned to me again, tilting her head to one side and regarded me appraisingly. 'You appear to have some ability, too. My mentor will be intrigued.'

I felt heat flood my cheeks and looked away, my gaze settling on the stack of journals on the table. 'Would your mentor be able to look at my father's books?' I asked. 'I've seen the expression that crosses your face sometimes when you are looking at them, and I know you recognise things. Maybe you even know what they are. They are not simply the ramblings of a madman, are they?'

Anna took a deep breath and paused for a moment, twisting round a little to glance behind her. When she spoke, her voice was low and firm. 'No. They are not.'

My heart leapt at her words. The shame of my father's enforced incarceration had run rife through the family, and there had been a number of unpleasant visits from disapproving aunts and inquisitive cousins in the early days. If there was a chance to prove he was not insane, then surely, I had to take it.

Yet even as I thought it, my mind was filled with a jumble of overlapping, chaotic questions. If my father was not insane, and the scribbles and sketches and words and diagrams were familiar to Anna, did that mean my father was also sensitive to these otherworldly creatures? If so, how had it come about? Was that how the fog creature had latched on to me as it roamed the docks back in Dover? I had always assumed his condition was as a result of the trauma he had experienced in the army, and the guilt I knew he carried as one of the few survivors of the Light Brigade. What if that was not the full story? If I had inherited a strange ability from my father, perhaps there were others in the family who shared it. Why was I only experiencing it now if it had always been part of me?

Anna rose from the bed, making the springs creak, and crossed the room to the bell cord. She gave it a couple of tugs, then went to the table, gathered up the journals and tucked them out of sight beneath the bed. 'I am expecting Inspector Escoffier and Monsieur de Vaux,' she said. 'We both need to attend to our toilette and make ourselves presentable. Frossard may also call, but if he does not, I will go to his office.' She regarded me thoughtfully for a moment. 'You should send word to your uncle that you will be in Paris.'

I sighed deeply, not wishing to consider that particular crossroads. 'You are right, I should.'

She leaned down and tilted my chin towards her, forcing me to meet her eyes. 'I know they will demand that you return to England,' she said. 'You have a lot to lose, Viktor. If you feel you have no choice but to obey, then you must go. We can correspond. It should not be difficult to arrange for my mentor to accompany me to Dover to meet with you there instead.'

My mind raced at the thought of convincing Mrs Armitage to permit me to attend such a meeting without a chaperone. Slumping back onto the pillows, I shrugged helplessly. 'I doubt I would be able to, Anna. I am not allowed anywhere without a chaperone.'

She smiled. 'Young men do not need chaperones.'

I stared up at her open-mouthed. Just then, there was a light tap at the door and Anna called out, 'Come in.'

Céline entered the room and curtseyed. 'What can I do for you, Mademoiselle?'

'Please could you bring us some water, Céline? We desperately need to wash.'

'Of course!' Céline smiled. 'Would you both like to have a bath this evening?'

'That would be most welcome,' I said. 'Thank you, Céline.'

'After I have brought your water, would you like coffee in the parlour?' Céline asked.

Anna said it would be delightful, thanked her and sent her off for the hot water. I got up from the bed, suddenly aware that I ought to have done so when Céline entered the room. I took off my suit coat and went to hang it up, shivering a little. Anna retreated to her own room, and as I loosened my cravat and collar, and went to stare out of the window, I could hear her bustling around, opening drawers and humming softly under her breath.

Céline returned with the water, and I washed thoroughly, keen to scrub the stench of the cemetery from my skin. The scent of the soap, mingled with the aroma of coffee wafting up the stairs from the parlour, made me suddenly and inexplicably homesick.

After I had dressed again, I went downstairs without waiting for Anna, suddenly desperate for a cup of coffee. François was standing by the parlour window, looking out into the street. He turned as I walked in.

'Viktor!' he exclaimed, his face lighting up in genuine pleasure. 'Are you rested? I have come in here to hide from my mother. She and Céline are fussing over packing and travel arrangements, so this is probably the safest place for me at the moment.'

He glanced beyond me to the door as I settled myself in one of the armchairs, then lowered his voice conspiratorially. 'How did she accomplish it?'

I blinked at him. 'How did who accomplish what?'

'Mademoiselle Anna. How did she get the creature to appear?'

'François,' I began, but the door opened just then, and Céline bustled in with a tray of coffee and cake. Both François and I moved to assist as she set the tray down and began to arrange the cups and plates, and a moment later, Anna came into the room. François went to her and bent over her hand in an unexpected and rather endearingly gallant way.

'Mademoiselle Anna, you are a marvel!' he exclaimed, his voice full of admiration. Anna smiled at him, withdrew her hand gently and seated herself. Céline caught my eye, and a little smile brightened her face, too. She handed each of us a steaming cup of coffee, then curtseyed and left the room.

Immediately she was gone, François set aside his cup and went to Anna, kneeling beside her chair, his eyes earnest. 'I owe you a great deal,' he said solemnly. 'Perhaps even my life. Something happened to me last night, seeing that creature. What I did, the... the urges I had...' He broke off, his cheeks flooding with colour as he struggled to voice his thoughts. 'I was appalled at myself before, but something drove me to seek answers to the questions I had. Now I have seen with my own eyes, and I never wish to look upon such a creature again.' His expression changed to one of pleading and his voice sank to a whisper. 'Can I be cured? Can your doctor in Paris truly be of assistance to me?'

There was empathy in Anna's eyes as she looked at him, and when she replied, her voice was soft and gentle. 'I do not know, François. I can only offer you my assurance that he is a learned man and one of the most open-minded people I have met.'

François nodded, biting his lip, then rose and picked up his coffee and returned to the window, sipping thoughtfully as he watched the bustle in the street outside. A baby was crying nearby, and the loud, staccato clopping of hooves echoed off the house fronts as carts and carriages rumbled along. The carters called out to each other in deep, coarse voices. A man walked past the window, looking down at the folded newspaper he held. No doubt the local presses would soon be turning out stories of the Amiens vampire.

My question was soon answered. François lapsed into silence, finished his coffee, then excused himself, bowed and left the room. Anna was looking at the calling cards which had been left for her and making notes in her little book. I refilled my cup and was just reaching for the milk jug when the doorbell was rung loudly. A few minutes later, Céline announced Monsieur de Vaux and Inspector Escoffier.

I remembered to rise as they entered and shook hands. Christine appeared and greeted them and the five of us slipped into easy conversation as Céline brought more cups and another pot of coffee. After she left, Escoffier leaned forward to Anna.

'I have spoken to the family,' he said. 'As you might expect, they are bewildered and upset. I offered them your card, but although the wife was keen to speak with you, the husband forbade it. The victim was his father.'

Anna nodded. 'It is too much for many people,' she said. 'At least they are aware that, should they wish to speak with someone, there are people to whom they can turn.'

De Vaux nodded solemnly. He looked like a new man. He was no longer an ashen grey, and the lines in his face had smoothed out. Reaching into his pocket, he withdrew two small boxes and handed one to Anna and the other to me. 'A small token of my family's deep and unending gratitude,' he said quietly. There was a soft catch in his voice, and when I looked into his eyes, they were bright with emotion. 'I cannot begin to describe how much you have done for us, or the extent of the debt we owe you. Please accept these, and our sincere thanks.'

Anna opened the box to reveal a stunning diamond brooch with three pearl drops. My gift was a diamond tie pin, a solitaire, whose exquisite, perfect facets glittered as I turned it to the light, admiring it. 'Monsieur,' I exclaimed, 'you are too generous.'

'No,' said de Vaux firmly. 'These are mere trinkets. There is nothing on this earth which could possibly represent our gratitude. I hope that when you wear them, you will be reminded of the immeasurable good you do.'

Emotion overcame me and I could only nod, fixing my attention firmly on the diamond, trying to will away the tears which were threatening. Murmuring her thanks, Anna took the brooch from its box and started to pin it to her collar over the lace ruffle she was wearing at her neck. Escoffier smiled as he watched, then set his cup down and moved forward in his seat.

'May I?' he asked, indicating the brooch. 'It is a little lopsided.'

Anna blushed and nodded, and Escoffier knelt by her, their eyes fixed on each other, his large hands carefully sliding the pin into the fabric. I smiled softly. When Escoffier had finished, and returned to his seat, the brooch was even more lopsided than before.

'You are returning to Paris, I believe?' he said, suddenly awkward as he realised we had all been watching. Anna, blushing, confirmed that we were, and Escoffier nodded. 'I may have business in Paris in a few days,' he said nonchalantly.

The bloom in Anna's cheeks deepened and she dropped her gaze to her hands. Escoffier huffed a half-cough and busied himself with his coffee cup, and I tried to hide a smile. Anna and the Inspector would make a handsome couple, I thought.

'May I ask if there are any further instructions for myself or my family?' de Vaux asked, breaking the awkward silence which ensued as the pair pointedly stirred coffee and avoided each other's gaze. With relief in her voice, Anna, cheeks still attractively pink, explained she would be sending a colleague with a different skillset to oversee the cemetery for a period of time, to ensure that the activity had definitely been curtailed. Escoffier immediately shifted into his official persona. He set his coffee aside, took a small notebook from his pocket and wrote a few lines, asking a question here and there about what signs to look for, and any items his men should carry to protect themselves. At this, Anna looked thoughtful.

'A police force armed with anti-vampire tools will serve only to cause alarm. You are trying to reduce panic, not sustain it. However, that said, I understand some of the men will be loathe to patrol the cemetery without something of reassurance about their person. I would be inclined to equip them with seeds. Knotted string also works, but it takes time to prepare. You could also ensure that they have access to stakes and mallets and shovels in the cemetery itself. Perhaps Monsieur Arnal will be able to assist you with the arrangements.'

'Indeed.' Escoffier nodded and made a note, and de Vaux spoke up. 'Should equipment be required,' he said, 'I am fully prepared to pay for its provision. Privately. I will not politicise this unfortunate incident. I will leave that to Frossard. Inspector, please advise me of any requirements you may have, and I will attend to it.'

Escoffier gave de Vaux a sincere, grateful nod and I thought again what a lovely sight it would be to see Anna walking along on his arm. The two men clasped hands, and I could see the understanding passing between them. Anna watched, lips curved in a smile, nodding with satisfaction. 'Thank you, Monsieur,' she said quietly. 'You have no idea how much it means to me to leave the matter in your capable hands. So often, I meet with nothing but resistance from officials, so it truly has been a pleasure to find so many people in Amiens who were willing to work alongside me.'

Both men smiled warmly, declaring their admiration for her abilities and fearlessness. Listening to them, I found my mind wandering, picturing myself in Anna's place. Whatever skillset I possessed; it did not feel other-worldly.

De Vaux and Escoffier rose to take their leave and Anna and I stood also. The men bent over Anna's hand and shook mine, then Escoffier passed Anna what looked like a calling card. She took it, glanced down at it, blushed and slipped it into her sleeve without a word. When she looked up at him, her eyes were sparkling.

Once the door had closed behind the two men, Anna and I were caught in a flurry of activity to prepare for Paris. Christine and Céline were bustling around with dustsheets, so we decided to call on Frossard, which would also give me the opportunity to send word to Sébastien about my arrival. I had to uncover the secrets of my father's journals, and I firmly believed there was someone within Anna's organisation who would be able to assist me in my quest. The walk to Frossard's office passed in a blur, taken up almost entirely in imagined scenarios where I attempted to defend my decisions, with varying degrees of success, to a gathering of disapproving relatives.

We were greeted in the lobby of Frossard's office by a tall, thin clerk who stared disapprovingly down his nose at us as we approached, a feat made all the more impressive by the fact that he was sitting at his desk. I drew myself up to my full height, looked down at him and gave him a pleasant nod, and Anna requested a moment with Mayor Frossard. The man stared at us both for a moment, then, with great reluctance and a tremendous show of effort, reached for a large book and opened it, flipping slowly through the pages, as if turning them was an extreme form of manual labour. Irritation rose in my throat.

'Have you an appointment?' he asked in a pinched, nasal voice. 'Mayor Frossard is a very busy man.'

'I do not,' Anna began, at which the man gave a loud, melodramatic sigh and snapped the book shut.

'In that case, you will need to arrange one,' he interrupted. 'You cannot simply walk in and expect time with the mayor.' He leaned forward, a supercilious sneer twisting his lips into a parody of a smile. 'I don't expect you to appreciate fully the nature of the important work the mayor does...'

My eyes widened in disbelief at the sneering condescension, but before I could say a word, Anna, her voice dripping with intense dislike and carrying clearly across the entire foyer, said, 'And I do not expect you, sir, to understand what it is to be summoned to assist with a vampire which is causing problems in your city, and to spend night after night amongst graves, searching for the creature. I do not expect you, sir, to understand what it is like to drive a stake into the heart of such a creature, or to separate its head from its body to protect the population from its predation. I do not expect Mayor Frossard to understand the nature of the important work I do, either, but I return to Paris imminently and I *will* see him. If it is too much trouble for you to escort us, I am more than happy to escort myself.'

The man's eyes widened, and his mouth fell open at the mention of the vampire. Immediately, he began to bluster as Anna stepped back from the desk, looked around, then marched to a door in the far wall. 'Wait!' he exclaimed, pushing his chair back. 'You cannot simply- '

Anna paused, hand stretched out towards the doorknob, and turned to regard him coolly. 'I believe I can, but I will give you an opportunity to exercise your office before I exercise mine. I am Mademoiselle Anna Stenberg and wish to speak with Mayor Frossard regarding the conclusion of my investigation into your vampire. Please advise him that I would speak with him immediately. What I say may well have bearing on his mayoral campaign.'

At this, the man started visibly, got up and went to Anna, opening the door to allow her to pass through. I followed, giving him another pleasant nod, struggling to maintain my composure whilst seething inside. Without a word, he led us along a plush panelled corridor, our feet whispering over the rich, deep carpet. Dark paintings of former mayors glared down at us from the walls, the sombre lighting from the few lamps casting strange shadows over them. Our guide stopped at an ornately-carved door about half-way along the corridor, sighed deeply, then knocked. A voice within bade him enter and he opened the door a fraction, just enough to permit himself to slip inside, leaving Anna and I standing awkwardly in the corridor. I saw Anna's eyes narrow, and as I started to wonder what she was thinking, she pushed the door open and strode past him. I hurried to follow her, finding myself in a spacious, panelled room. There were windows along the opposite wall and Frossard, sitting behind a large desk, was silhouetted against the afternoon light. He looked up as we entered, then pushed his chair back and got to his feet, his protestation dying on his lips as he realised who we were. He came around the desk and made a graceless bow to Anna, then shook my hand. His grip was limp and brief, and he was clearly flustered. Whether that was over our sudden appearance, or due to the nature of our visit, it was impossible to tell. He took a large white handkerchief from a pocket and mopped his forehead with it as he gestured to the two chairs in front of the desk. I glanced at the clerk as I settled in the chair, taking more delight than was strictly appropriate at his discomfiture. He murmured something and left the room, closing the door behind him sharply, the snap of the latch loud and crisp in the otherwise silent room.

Frossard dropped heavily into his chair, the leather creaking beneath him, and leaned forward, resting his elbows on the open ledgers in front of him. 'What can I do for you, Mademoiselle Stenberg?'

In a clipped, efficient manner, Anna gave him a precise description of the events of the preceding night. Frossard paled as she spoke, and I guessed he was picturing what she described, as I was. He reached out and picked up an ornate silver letter opener, turning it over and over in hands which trembled slightly. I watched the chunky fingers dispassionately as he set it down again, and when I lifted my gaze to his face, I was startled to realise he was looking at me. He clasped his hands together in front of him, the knuckles showing whitely through the skin.

'Well,' he said slowly when Anna reached the conclusion of the night's events, 'it certainly sounds like our city owes you a debt of thanks.'

In truth, spoken as it was between gritted teeth, it sounded quite the opposite, but Anna, gracious as always, merely smiled a little and inclined her head. 'I am delighted,' she said, 'to have been able to bring the matter to a satisfactory conclusion. It is a great pity that another family is now faced with the heartbreak, shock, and trauma of discovering that a relative has been turned.' She gave Frossard a frank, direct look under which he shifted uncomfortably. 'I trust your office will be offering them support?'

Frossard flushed and his fingers tightened around each other until it seemed his knuckles would break through his skin. He harrumphed and huffed a little. 'Are you quite certain that the threat has been dealt with?' he asked.

Something snapped inside me. 'Perhaps you did not fully appreciate the fact that the creature was decapitated, Monsieur le Mayor,' I said crisply. 'My sister has taken appropriate measures to ensure it remains in its grave from now on, and at peace. Amiens needs have no fears for the future.'

Anna glanced at me, an inscrutable expression on her face which gave me pause, and my heart thumped. I hoped I had not spoken out of turn. Frossard spluttered for a moment, then controlled himself with what appeared to be a supreme effort, and turned slightly in his seat, away from me and towards

Anna. I bristled, pressing my lips together, but said nothing. Anna stared steadily at Frossard, also saying nothing, until he visibly wilted.

'Of course,' he murmured. 'The family will have anything they need.'

Anna nodded in satisfaction. 'Thank you, Monsieur,' she said.

'However,' Frossard continued, raising one of his meaty hands, 'I would appreciate your assurances that this unfortunate incident is now finally at an end, and will not have unfortunate repercussions.'

Anna narrowed her eyes. 'The incident is indeed concluded to my satisfaction,' she said. 'As for possible repercussions, I cannot say. I think much will depend on the manner in which those involved in the case have been seen conducting themselves.'

At this, Frossard inhaled sharply, and choked on his own spittle. Coughing hard, he shoved himself away from the desk and staggered across the room to a small table, on which was set a jug of water and several glasses on a silver tray. He slopped water into a glass and drank deeply, replacing the jug rather more heavily than was necessary, then moved to the window, breathing hard and looking out over the view of the surrounding buildings. Anna and I waited, watching his outline against the daylight outside. Eventually, he turned.

'As I said, Mademoiselle,' he said in a taut voice, 'the city owes you a debt of gratitude. I appreciate this visit, but I regret that, unfortunately, I have a great deal of work to do. Allow me to escort you back to the foyer.'

I blinked, my eyes widening at the blatant dismissal, but Anna was already rising smoothly from her chair and thanking him. I followed suit, straightening my coat and setting my hat carefully on my head. Frossard went to the door, clearing his throat noisily. We followed as he led us back along the corridor and into the foyer, Anna slipping her hand through my arm and giving me the tiniest of smiles. The clerk looked up as we entered, disapproval etched into every line on his face.

Frossard shook my hand and bent over Anna's, then bade us good day and turned towards the clerk's desk. We responded politely, I tipped my hat and together, we walked with quiet dignity across the foyer. I opened the door for Anna and followed her out. As I did so, I heard Frossard hissing angrily at the clerk and glanced over my shoulder as I turned to close the door. The mayor was leaning over the desk, both hands planted on it, and the clerk was sitting rigid and upright, an outraged and hurt expression on his face. I chuckled softly and let the door close behind me, taking a long, deep breath of fresh air.

'How do you tolerate people like him?' I murmured as Anna took my arm again. She sighed.

'Most of the people I have to deal with are like Frossard,' she said. 'De Vaux and Escoffier are delightful exceptions.' She looked down at the ground for a moment as we made our way back towards the main part of town. 'I will be interested to hear what my colleague has to say on the subject. It is not sitting comfortably with me. Something about it was unusual.'

'François is unusual,' I pointed out.

'He is not the first person I have encountered with such interests,' Anna murmured. 'Perhaps it is connected to his father, and I am simply reading too much into it. Yet...'

She broke off and lapsed into silence, tucking her hand into my arm. A thousand questions burned inside me, but I reined them in, leaving her to her thoughts. Instead, I began composing telegrams to my uncle and his contact Sébastien in Paris. We turned our steps towards the post office, walking in companionable, if distracted, silence.

When we reached the post office, Anna smiled up at me and vanished inside straight away. I remained outside, mind running frantically over different phrases, trying to find a combination which made my intentions clear without causing too much offence to Uncle Geoffrey. He was only acting in my best interests, after all. If he could see me now, standing in the centre of Amiens as a young man, he would be appalled and embarrassed. The moment anyone found out, I would be labelled a disgrace.

Something occurred to me suddenly, almost out of nowhere. Would I end up in St Bernadette's alongside my father, under Uncle Geoffrey's professional care? Would they see me as suffering some sort of insanity for choosing to protect myself with this disguise? For a moment, fear gripped my heart and crushed it in fingers of steel, leaving me gasping and breathless. Glad that I was standing right next to the building, I put an unsteady hand against the bricks to support myself as the world trembled around me. I gritted my teeth, determined not to faint, and leaned against the wall, forcing myself to breathe steadily, even as my heart leaped around in my chest. I had not considered the asylum as a possible consequence of my actions. Yet the more I thought about it, the greater a threat it seemed, and the world went foggy around me, the edge of my vision closing in.

'Viktor?'

Anna's voice snapped me out of my panic, and I looked round for her, startled to see that the fog had not been part of my imagination, but was, even now dissipating slowly, soft tendrils curling around me and rolling up the brickwork before fading into nothingness. I blinked at Anna, who was staring at me. 'What?'

She came to me, clutching at my hands, finding them clammy. 'Did something happen? Are you all right?'

I mumbled something about the asylum, and she paled, the colour draining from her cheeks. For a moment, she simply stared at me. Then she took a breath and when she spoke, her voice was soft, calm, and steady, exactly the reassurance I needed.

'Let us be practical,' she said. 'Have you told your uncle that you maintained your disguise?'

I racked my brain, trying to remember the contents of the letter I had sent. 'No, I said only that I was exercising discretion.'

Anna smiled gently up at me, squeezing my hands. 'Then all we need to do is ensure that you are attired as a girl when you meet anyone connected to your family. They never need to know about Viktor. You can explain everything you did without once needing to explain how you were dressed.' She chuckled. 'Besides, who is ever likely to even consider that you were dressed as anything other than a girl?'

I blinked. 'You're right. It would never occur to anyone, would it?'

'Put it from your mind. Go inside and send your telegrams. Reassure your uncle. Agree to meet his man when we reach Paris. I would suggest, though, that you maintain your disguise until we reach headquarters. It will be far more discreet than, say, taking a room at a hotel as a young man and leaving as a young woman. You do not want to leave any clues.'

I nodded, seeing the sense in this. Anna smiled again, and stepped back, releasing my hands and looking around me thoughtfully. 'Did you see the creature?' she whispered. I started.

'The creature?' I repeated. 'When? Where?'

Anna frowned. 'When I came outside, you were wrapped in a thin veil of fog, Viktor. Didn't you see it?'

My reply died in my throat as she suddenly gave a soft cry and clutched my arm. 'Viktor! You were thinking about the asylum, weren't you?'

'Yes,' I whispered. 'Why?'

Anna tightened her grip on my arm. 'You were frightened, yes?'

'Yes, very, but - '

'Think about all the other times you've seen the fog. What did they all have in common?'

I gaped at her, trying to understand. 'Well, the first time was in Dover, then the time when we heard the wolves, but they have nothing in common.'

'Fear.'

'What?'

She sighed in frustration. 'Fear, Viktor. The common factor every single time has been your fear. Think about it. You feared for your life with the attacker in Dover, and again with the wolves. I am guessing it was the same when we arrived in Amiens.'

My mouth dropped open. 'Yes, it was. I was terrified. Yet there are a couple of instances which don't fit. I saw the fog in my room at Christine's when all I was doing was looking at my father's journals, and the fog didn't appear when the vampire did.'

'No,' Anna said slowly. The little frown appeared between her brows as she mused. 'No, the fog didn't appear, did it? Something else happened, though. The singing.'

Now I was truly dumbfounded. 'You think the fog creature was the one singing?'

'Think about it. It makes perfect sense. The creature attached itself to you in Dover and has acted as a kind of protector ever since. It even came when you pleaded for help. What if it senses your fear and comes to your aid when you are most in need?'

I turned the matter over in my mind. Anna was certainly right about the creature appearing just when it was most needed, but that did not explain the appearance of the fog in my room, and I pointed this out to her. She bit her lip thoughtfully.

'Was there something in the journal which could have triggered its appearance?' she asked.

I shook my head. 'Nothing which frightened me. In truth, I am not even sure if I was fully concentrating on them. I think I was musing about what it might be like to be part of your organisation.'

An inscrutable expression crossed Anna's face and she let go of my arm. A faint smile played at the corners of her mouth, but it looked forced to me, as though I had upset her somehow. 'Let us keep this in mind, and discuss it later,' she said. 'I am keen to return to Christine's, so hurry inside and send your telegrams.'

I did as she bade me, once again using only my initials and reassuring my uncle of my safety. I agreed to meet Sébastien in Paris, but added that afterwards, I wished to travel. I knew this would cause a degree of consternation in some quarters at home, given that the social season was due to begin in a few days' time, after Easter. There would, no doubt, be some form of compromise required to keep the peace and I thought about what I could offer. Agreeing to return home for my presentation at Court would be most likely to appease, even though the very thought of it made my blood run cold in my veins. I would keep the suggestion in reserve until after I had had the opportunity to gauge Uncle Geoffrey's reaction. Surely, though, if there was a chance of discovering what had happened to my mother, he would support my decisions?

The second telegram, to Sébastien, was far more straightforward. I said simply that I would contact him upon my arrival in Paris and arrange to meet him. I did not anticipate the meeting being a long one, so even if we did not arrive until the evening, I would still have sufficient opportunity to get it over and done with as soon as possible. I asked him to leave word for me at the telegraph office.

We visited a few shops and made some small purchases for the journey, although it would not be a long one. I was careful with my expenditure. The spectre of an enforced return to Dover loomed over me, as did the other unpleasant alternative – being left without funds. Still, as Anna had said, all I needed to do was ensure I was wearing my usual attire when I met my uncle's contact. No one need ever know about Viktor. Even if word reached one of my relatives that my companion had been seen with a young man in Amiens, it would never occur to them that the young man was myself. I clung to the thought. It was one of the only comforts I currently had.

By the time we arrived back at Christine's I was exhausted. The stresses and terrors of the previous night were weighing heavily on me, and it was with a foggy mind that I dragged my case out from beneath the bed and packed my few belongings into it. I seated myself at the table and reached for one of my father's journals, listening with half an ear to the sound of cupboard doors opening and closing in Anna's room. Turning the pages idly, I scanned the scrawling script, not taking anything in.

The doorbell startled me, and my eyes snapped open. I was slumped in the chair, the journal on the floor at my feet. I blinked, trying to orient myself, and reached down for the journal. It had landed open and face-down, crumpling the corners of a couple of pages. Setting it on the table, I began to methodically smooth them back out.

Céline's light tread sounded on the stair, and a moment later the sound of quiet, muffled voices drifted in from Anna's room. The two of them descended the stairs together, then there was silence. I leaned back in the chair again, closing my eyes and drifting into the comforting arms of sleep.

When I opened my eyes again, it was to find Anna leaning over me, smiling. The lamps were lit, and she had dressed for dinner. She was wearing a scarlet gown which rustled softly as she stepped back.

'I am sorry to have to wake you,' she said, apologetically. 'You looked so very peaceful. However, it is time for you to dress for dinner. You need to eat. We both do.'

Squinting around the room, my eyes growing accustomed to the light, I struggled into a more upright position and watched as Anna laid out clothing for me. There was a lightness in her step, a little flush of rose pink in her cheeks, and now and then, a small smile twitched at the corner of her mouth. She moved to the window and drew the curtains, humming a sweet tune I did not recognise, then crossed to the lamps and increased the flame, sending a bright, warm glow dancing over the room.

Sighing, I pulled myself to my feet, stifling a yawn, and slipped out of my jacket, shirt, and cravat. I went to the washstand and splashed water on my face, hoping it might make me more alert. As I dressed, I watched Anna. She was toying with the edging on her lace shawl, the enigmatic smile still curving her lips. I wondered what – or, more likely, whom – she was thinking about, and suspected I could guess. 'You look happy,' I said, my tone a little more mischievous and teasing than I had intended.

Anna started, blushed deeply, and ducked her head. 'You miss nothing.'

I laughed. 'It would be rather difficult to miss this, Anna. You are positively glowing.'

She smiled. 'I had a visitor earlier, after we returned.'

'Escoffier.'

She raised an eyebrow. 'You were awake?'

'The bell woke me, and I heard you go downstairs.' I eyed her, smiling. 'Did you arrange to meet with him in Paris?'

'I did.' She turned a broad smile to me, light dancing in her eyes. 'Oh, Viktor, he is so ardent, yet such a gentleman about it. I am not one for men's romantic chit chat, usually. It annoys me more than I can say. But there is something about Jean which intrigues me. I would be happy to know him better.'

'Well, you make a delightful couple,' I told her. 'I have thought so on a number of occasions.'

She crossed to me and reached up on tiptoe to kiss my cheek. 'You are very sweet,' she said. 'However, we must not run before we can walk. Let us see what happens.' She picked up my cravat and began to tie it for me, her fingers working busily. 'Let us go and eat. I am only just starting to appreciate how hungry I am.'

I dealt with my hair, smoothing macassar oil into it, then rinsed my hands and put on my jacket. The reflection in the looking glass reminded me forcefully of photographs of my father as a young man, and a little shudder rippled inexplicably down my spine. Pulling myself together, I accompanied Anna to the dining room, where Christine and François were chatting about their travel arrangements and the sights they wished to see.

'Your investigation is truly complete?' Christine asked, nodding to Céline to pour the wine. Anna smiled and replied that it was, at which Christine gave a sigh of relief and threw her a look of gratitude. Céline filled our glasses, beaming happily, then served the meal as we chatted about the various delights of Paris. François, who was pale and rather quieter than usual, offered a toast to Anna before lapsing into almost complete silence. He listened attentively but did not volunteer anything unless directly addressed. His hands were shaking, I noticed. The forthcoming journey, and what lay at its end, must be weighing heavily on his mind.

At the end of the meal, we retired to the parlour, where Céline served coffee. As we sipped, Christine asked Anna about the headquarters from which she operated.

'It is on the outskirts,' Anna replied, sipping her coffee. 'A large, sprawling, private estate with significant grounds. I hope I will be able to entertain you there whilst you are in the city. I need to confirm with my employers first, however, and seek permission.'

'Of course,' Christine said. 'I completely understand, given the unusual nature of what you do.'

François excused himself and slipped from the room, closing the door quietly behind him. Christine watched him go, then let out a long breath and turned tired eyes to us.

'He is struggling,' she murmured. 'I do not know how to help him. I pray that your expert will be able to provide the answers I do not have.'

'I hope so, too,' Anna said softly. 'Time will tell.'

We chatted for a little while longer and Anna outlined our travel plans for the following day. Henri was coming to collect us in time for the lunchtime train, which meant we would be in Paris by evening. My heart skipped around in my chest, rattling against my ribs, making me uncertain whether François or I was more uneasy about the impending journey.

'We will be taking the evening train,' Christine said, finishing the last of her coffee. She set the cup down, then went to sit at the desk. 'This is our address,' she said, reaching for a sheet of notepaper and writing quickly. 'Please feel free to call on me at any time. I am anxious about François and will ensure that I am available to meet with your expert at his convenience.' She rose, closed the desk, and handed Anna the address. Anna thanked her, folded the page, and slipped it into her sleeve.

Christine took her seat once more, but the conversation faltered, and it was a relief when Anna stood, excusing herself for the night. Christine and I got to our feet and exchanged our own goodnights. Christine was clearly as exhausted as we were, and I wondered if the shadows beneath my eyes were as pronounced as Anna's, or my cheeks as sunken as Christine's. I suspected all of us looked the worse for wear, and was glad to retreat to my room, change into my nightshirt and collapse into the bed. Rolling myself up in the blankets, I snuggled into the pillows and closed my eyes, knowing sleep was waiting for me.

Chapter 36

I opened my eyes to a bright, sunny morning. The curtains had been drawn and the connecting door to Anna's room stood wide open. The sound of humming drifted softly through to me, and I could hear the sound of fabric rustling. Anna must be packing the last of her belongings.

I sat up, yawned and stretched, my back stiff and my legs aching. At first, I couldn't understand it, then remembered the walk to and from town the previous day and sighed at myself. From now on, I would take a brisk walk every single day, whether I was in Dover or Paris. Perhaps it would still be necessary to play the role of the dutiful daughter when I returned home, but no one was going to prevent me from going for a walk. If walking was good enough for the Royal Family, it was certainly good enough for a baronet's granddaughter.

A smile teased the corners of my mouth, and I spent a moment imagining myself using that line in conversation with Mrs Armitage. It would only work once, so if the situation arose, I would need to make it count. Mrs Armitage did not tolerate impudence.

A shiver rippled down my spine as I thought of the day ahead. Part of me was excited beyond measure at the thought of seeing Paris again, and of visiting Anna's mysterious headquarters. Although she had been somewhat close-lipped about it, resisting my various attempts to prise information out of her, a picture had formed in my mind of a sprawling castle full of secret rooms, mystery, and dark, panelled corridors. Rolling my eyes at myself for such ridiculously romantic notions, I dragged my body reluctantly from the comfortable embrace of the warm blankets and went to the washstand, my joints and muscles protesting the whole time. I washed and dressed quickly, fingers fumbling with collar buttons and cuffs, then went around the room, making certain I had packed all my belongings. That done, I locked my new travelling case and heaved it over to the door. It was somewhat heavier than the previous one, and I hoped I would be able to get it down the stairs without falling, dropping it, or otherwise making a spectacle of myself.

Anna peeked around the door and smiled. 'Ready? Good. Leave your things there, Viktor. Henri will bring them down when he arrives.'

Relieved, I abandoned the case just inside the door. 'Do you need help with packing?' I asked. 'I warn you, though, I am not very good at it.'

'Lack of practice, that is all,' she said, with a little chuckle. 'Thank you, but everything is packed. Let us go down to breakfast, shall we?'

'Céline has not been up yet,' I said, suddenly realising.

'I expect Christine told her to let us sleep,' Anna said. 'We have plenty of time before the train, and I appreciated the opportunity to rest.'

'As did I,' I agreed fervently. 'Although I am not sure I have much appetite for breakfast this morning. My stomach is a little unsettled.'

Anna regarded me for a moment. 'Are you excited, or nervous?'

'Both.'

A smile softened her lips and her eyes twinkled. 'I understand. You should eat a little, though, if you can. We will take luncheon at headquarters, but that will be a few hours from now.'

I smiled and took a deep breath. 'I should have something. Shall we?'

Anna nodded and I opened the door, allowing her to walk past me into the hall. She paused as she drew level with me, adjusted my cravat, smiled mischievously at me, then went out into the hall and started down the stairs, humming softly. I chuckled, touching the cravat a little self-consciously, then followed her.

Christine was already at breakfast as we entered the dining room. She threw us a broad smile and invited us to sit. We settled ourselves comfortably, and a moment later, François walked in. He paused briefly on seeing us, then gave one of his stiff bows and joined us at the table, sitting to my left. Christine was on my right at the head of the table, and I had deliberately left the seat next to her free for François. Anna, sitting opposite me on Christine's right, caught my eye. Her eyebrow twitched almost imperceptibly.

A pained expression flickered over Christine's face, and she paled. She turned her attention to her coffee cup, murmuring a greeting to her son as she raised it to her lips. Her hand shook slightly. François responded politely but blandly, and the conversation faltered. I toyed with my cuffs, looking around the room, admiring the paintings and the elegant decanters on the sideboard. The silence was just starting to become intolerable, and I was on the verge of saying something, when Céline arrived with a tray of steaming croissants and a selection of cheeses which made my mouth water. All of a sudden, my appetite returned with a vengeance, and I found I was able to enjoy a hearty meal. Anna winked at me from across the table and I smiled into my croissant. The food was a welcome distraction, especially as Céline was as bright and cheerful as the morning, and lifted all our spirits with her sweet, enthusiastic comments as she served us all. Christine threw her a grateful look and relaxed a little, and even François made a joke or two. By the end of the meal, the atmosphere was greatly improved.

We were just finishing our coffee when there was a knock at the door. We heard Céline answer, the sound of soft voices, then a moment later, she tapped on the door and peeked in.

'Mademoiselle Anna, the gentleman is here with the carriage,' she said. 'He is asking about your luggage. Is there anything you wish me to do for you?'

Anna smiled at her. 'The cases are all packed and ready, Céline, thank you,' she said. 'Please ask Henri to bring them down.'

'Afterwards, Céline, please take him to the kitchen and give him a good breakfast,' Christine added.

Céline nodded and vanished, and a moment later, we heard Henri's firm tread on the stairs. Christine sighed.

'It's truly been a delight to have you both here,' she said. 'Not just for François and myself personally, although you have helped us more than I can possibly express. You have also helped the community in a time of great need, and I would like to show my gratitude somehow. Please tell your employers that if any of your colleagues require lodgings at any time, they are most welcome here, and always will be.'

Anna gave her a warm smile and reached across the table to squeeze Christine's hand. 'That is an incredibly generous offer, and I am very grateful. Thank you. I will convey it to my employers when I return to headquarters today.'

I thrilled at those words, the reality of the situation sinking in a little further. Today! After days of imagining, today I, too, would see these things. Of course, I also had to navigate a meeting with Uncle Geoffrey's agent, which was far less appealing, and would need careful handling. My stomach gave a little lurch at the thought, and I paused, the final bite of croissant part-way to my lips. Christine noticed and turned a concerned expression to me.

'Is everything all right, Viktor?' she asked gently.

Blinking, I forced myself to smile. 'I distracted myself with thoughts of arrangements for our journey,' I blurted. Christine smiled and nodded, I choked down the last piece of croissant and the conversation moved on. François sat silently listening for the rest of the meal, his presence casting a pall over the room, and I was glad when breakfast was over, and we could start preparing to take our leave. The house became alive with chatter and activity. Céline bustled about with packages of food for our journey. Henri appeared from the kitchen smiling broadly and waited at the foot of the stairs while Anna and I checked our rooms one final time for anything we had overlooked. Anna and I hugged Christine, accepted one of François's bows, and I held out my hand to him. He looked at it for a moment before taking it and we shook hands.

'All will be well, François,' I said quietly. 'Place your trust in my sister and her knowledge. And, François, try to enjoy Paris. It is a diversion. Take advantage of it.'

He frowned at me a little and I wondered for an awful moment whether I had overstepped and said the wrong thing. Then his expression relaxed, and a smile appeared. 'You have both helped me far more than you will ever realise,' he said, his voice soft so as not to be overheard. 'Thank you.' He looked over to the carriage, where Henri was just offering his hand to assist Anna up the step, and said, more loudly, 'Have a safe journey, both of you. I look forward to seeing you in Paris.'

Anna turned and smiled at him. 'We will find a beautiful little café somewhere to sit and watch the world go by,' she said. 'I hope you both enjoy a pleasant journey later.'

Christine and François thanked her, and she took Henri's hand, stepping lightly into the carriage and settling herself on the seat. I nodded to Henri and climbed in after her, patting my jacket pocket to ensure my uncle's correspondence was tucked safely inside. The rustle of paper reassured me, and I leaned back against the seat as Henri swung himself up on to the box, the carriage bouncing on its suspension.

Anna opened the glass and gave Christine her hand, pressing her fingers. 'All will be well,' she said. 'Trust me.'

Christine nodded wordlessly. Anna released her hand and called out, 'All right Henri!' I heard the snap of the reins, and the horses began to move off. We waved, watching Christine and François doing likewise until they vanished from view.

Anna leaned back in her seat and let out a long breath. 'Well,' she said, 'I shall be glad to return to headquarters. I enjoy travelling. I see and learn so many fascinating things, but at the same time, one needs home.'

I blanched at this, and immediately her expression became contrite. A deep flush bloomed in her cheeks, and she bit her lip. 'Oh Viktor, I am so sorry. That was thoughtless of me, given what you need to deal with today. Forgive me?'

'Of course.' I managed a small smile, although my heart was thumping, and I felt suddenly nauseous. 'You live out of a travelling case so much that it is easy to understand why you feel that way.'

'How do you think your meeting will go?'

Shrugging, I shifted in the seat, my discomfort rising. 'I cannot say. I expect to be spoken down to, as always. I am a mere girl, after all, who knows nothing of the world, or even of her own mind.' Anna snorted at this. 'Yet I may have hope. My uncle felt my mother's disappearance most strongly, and I suspect he has many unanswered questions. This is where I need to direct my appeal. To the search for the answers he lacks.'

Anna nodded. 'I truly hope one of my colleagues will be able to help you,' she said earnestly. 'The things you've shown me in your father's journals leads me to suspect that he has already been in contact with someone from the organisation. Also,' she added, in a thoughtful tone, 'we need to work out what the fog creature is and where it came from. Whether there are more of them somewhere, and if anyone else has ever encountered one. I cannot recall a single mention of such a thing in all I have read in our library.'

We chatted about the fog creature as the carriage bore us to the railway station. Anna asked me for my thoughts and how it made me feel, and wrote notes. It felt good to be able to share such a strange set of experiences. Dealing with them alone would have been unthinkable. There was not a single person at home with whom I would have been comfortable sharing the story. Not even Elizabeth, despite her being my best friend.

It was not long before we arrived at the station. Henri found a porter and dealt with our luggage, while Anna looked over the travel arrangements. The train was waiting at the platform, the smell of coal hanging sharp in the air, penetrating our clothing and hair. We found our compartment, and between them, Henri and the porter loaded the cases. Anna pressed a note into the porter's palm with thanks, and the man bowed over her hand before vanishing into the crowd.

'Is there anything else you require of me?' Henri asked.

'No, Henri, thank you,' Anna replied. 'You have been wonderful, as always, and a true credit to the organisation. Thank you for making the journey so easy. I appreciated it greatly.'

He flushed with pride and smiled. 'It is my pleasure to do whatever I can for the organisation, Mademoiselle,' he said. 'Thank you.'

'Do you have another assignment lined up?' Anna asked.

He shook his head. 'No,' he said. 'I shall return home until I am required.'

Anna took his hand in both of hers and squeezed. He raised her hands to his lips and kissed both. 'Thank you for everything, Henri,' Anna said sincerely. 'I look forward to seeing you again soon.'

'And I you, Mademoiselle. It is always a great pleasure.' Henri released Anna and turned to me. 'I am delighted to have met you, Monsieur, and hope to see you working with Mademoiselle again at some point.'

I shook hands with him, telling him how fortunate we were to have had him with us during the journey. It was difficult to say all I wanted to, though, because I was thinking as an uncertain girl who had been terrified more than once during that journey, and I needed to speak as a self-assured young man. I added my thanks and appreciation to Anna's and was rewarded with a broad, attractive smile. He bowed deeply to both of us, closed the compartment door behind him, and was gone.

We sat looking at each other for a few moments, listening to the activity outside on the platform. People shouting, the buzz of lively chatter, the clatter of doors, the hiss of steam. A family passed by in the corridor, father leading the way, mother bringing up the rear after three small girls with pretty russet-coloured curls. I took out my letters and glanced over them, then stuffed them back in my pocket and turned my attention to the scenery beyond the windows, while Anna withdrew a book from the small bag she had with her and began to read.

With much shouting and loud whistles from the guard, the train slowly pulled away from the platform. As it gained speed, I was lulled by the gentle rocking and the rhythmic clack of the rails. Buildings, then countryside, blurred as we sped past, until my tired eyes could no longer keep up. Letting my eyelids droop, I settled more comfortably in the seat, the sounds washing over me into a soothing lullaby. It was with some surprise that I started as Anna gently shook my arm.

'Viktor, wake up,' she said. 'You have slept all the way here!'

'Hm?' I mumbled, blinking up at her. She chuckled and nodded towards the window. Following her gaze, I realised the train had stopped, and we were in Paris. People were hurrying about like ants on the platform. Porters struggled along between them with trunks and cases, weaving precariously in and out of the chaos. For a moment or two, I watched, leaning forward, enjoying the scene. Anna touched my arm again, smiling down at me.

'Come, Viktor, we need to meet our driver and see to the luggage.'

Nodding, I got to my feet and straightened my hat, coat, and cravat, self-consciously checking my hair was still under control. I followed Anna out into the corridor, past two empty compartments and down the steps to the platform. We moved to a quieter area away from the train, and Anna looked around. Spotting someone, she caught my hand and tugged me along the platform to a tall, wiry man with a weatherworn, lined face, who smiled broadly on catching sight of her and bowed as we reached him.

'Mademoiselle!' he exclaimed. 'What a delight to have you home safely once more! I hope you enjoyed success on your travels?'

Anna smiled and gave him her hand. 'Thank you, Guillaume, how good to see you again! Viktor, this is Guillaume, one of our coachmen. Guillaume, my brother Viktor.'

We shook hands, Guillaume appraising me with a slightly puzzled look on his face. I noticed him glancing between Anna and myself, searching for a family resemblance he would never find. Anna informed him that we needed to stop at the telegraph office before embarking on our journey, then sent him off to deal with the cases while she went to a nearby news stand and purchased a newspaper. He returned a short while later, with a porter pushing our luggage on a trolley. Anna and I followed slowly. Anna was scanning the paper, and I glanced over her shoulder a few times, wondering if there was something in particular she was looking for, or if she was simply catching up on what was going on in Paris. I thought back to the Dover newspaper. Perhaps she was looking for another of those strange, coded messages in the Personal section.

Guillaume led us to a beautiful, luxurious carriage, supervised the loading and securing of the cases, then assisted Anna inside. He thanked the porter, I heard the clink of coins, and the man touched his cap before hurrying off. Guillaume swung himself into the driver's seat and soon we were rattling along the Parisian streets. I pressed my nose to the glass, drinking in the beautiful view. It did not take long to reach the telegraph office, and I jumped down from the carriage, hurried inside and collected a message from Sébastien, which essentially said that he was at my disposal and would meet with me at a time of my choosing. I settled on late afternoon at my grandfather's apartment, thinking there would be sufficient time to settle at Anna's headquarters and change my clothing beforehand. That done, I returned to the carriage and updated Anna on my plans, while Guillaume urged the horses into a trot.

We passed close to the stunning Sacré Coeur, sunlight gleaming on its towering basilica, then headed into a series of narrow streets. I looked left and right, enjoying the familiar and unfamiliar, my heart feeling lighter suddenly.

'How far is your headquarters?' I asked. 'We seem to be heading towards the outskirts of the city.'

Anna gave a very Gallic shrug. 'Perhaps half an hour's drive,' she said vaguely, then turned her attention back to the notebook she was writing in. Curious, I shifted a little in my seat, tilting my head to see if I could read upside-down. It looked like she was writing notes on the case, and I realised she would have to submit a report, something which would probably end up in the library and which would be used by future generations of agents to help them in their work.

My heart rattled in my chest, echoing the rattle of the wheels over the uneven streets. I sat forward, watching the buildings pass by as the horses trotted briskly along. The sound of their hooves rang around us, mingling with the sound of children playing. Several women were scrubbing windows or doorsteps, calling to each other in cheerful voices as they worked. Something about the scene brought a smile to my lips and a great sense of calm settled on me all at once. Leaning back into the cushions, I let the world pass by, happy to catch glimpses of the lives of others, little moments in time. A mother smiling down at her baby as she leaned against the wall next to her open front door, two other children sitting on the step. Three boys playing with a ball. A man on a bicycle, whistling a lively tune. A group of girls holding hands and dancing around in a circle, singing. I was struck by their ragged clothes, and once again, a vigour surged through me. Everywhere, there were people who needed help. Was this where my path lay? Was this how I would find my purpose in life? If, as Anna claimed, I possessed some kind of unusual skill, it would be wrong to let it lie dormant and not put it to use for the good of others.

Even as the words formed in my thoughts, I found myself racking my brain for anything in my life which had marked me out as unusual. The one thing which kept cropping up was my height. Maybe I had been so fixated on being tall that I had been oblivious to anything else.

Those thoughts were uncomfortable, so I dismissed them and took to staring blankly out of the window, letting the scenery blur before my eyes. After a while, the houses started thinning out, and just beyond the very edge of the city, the coach stopped at a pair of large, ornate gates. Guillaume jumped down to open them, led the horses through, then closed the gates with a clang which sounded unnaturally loud amongst the surrounding trees and shrubs. The carriage swayed as Guillaume climbed back up to his seat, and we set off up a long, sweeping driveway, bordered on each side by a thick hedge of rhododendrons, their dark leaves glossy in the early afternoon sun. I leaned out of the window a little way, but the drive curved around to the left, disappearing beyond the foliage, frustrating my attempts to see our destination. Anna put away her notebook and pencil and watched me in amusement.

'We will be there soon enough,' she soothed. 'You have waited this long, after all.'

I sank back into my seat and laughed. 'All right,' I said. 'You win. I will be patient.'

The drive wound on, first one way, then the other, twisting and turning its way through trees and shrubs. An occasional statue or stone bench appeared now and then, but on both sides, the dense foliage was impenetrable, and I had no sense of what might lie beyond it. Were there open fields? Wooded areas? Gardens? A lake?

All of a sudden, Guillaume slowed the horses and I realised we were pulling up outside a vast castle. Catching my breath, I craned my neck, staring up at the austere brickwork and statuary, the elegant Gothic windows. A graceful fountain, topped with winged angels, sat in the centre of a large, circular driveway in front of the castle, and Guillaume steered the horses around it, halting directly opposite the enormous main door. He jumped down and gave his hand to Anna. She descended the steps with her usual grace, and I followed more slowly, looking all around, trying to drink in every detail.

The castle was even more Gothic than in my imaginings. It really did have the soaring turrets I had pictured. It was surrounded by trees of all types and sizes, some so tall and broad that they must have been hundreds of years old. The garden beds and grass around the fountain were neat and well-kept, bursting with pretty spring flowers. But it was the castle itself which drew my gaze. As I stood staring up at it, I was only half-aware of Guillaume unstrapping the cases from the carriage. The air around us was silent of birds, which lent an eery, other-worldly atmosphere to the place. I took in the long front edifice, which stretched away from us on either side of the heavily studded main door under its ornately carved stone canopy. The place was vast, more so than I had expected, and I found myself dizzy with excitement at the thought of what lay within.

Anna touched my arm, and I started a little, torn from my reverie. I looked down to see her smiling up at me, a twinkle in her eyes.

'Welcome, Viktor,' she said warmly. 'Welcome to Castle Rochenoire, home of the Sabbatarians, and headquarters of the Order of Guardians.'

Chapter 37

As I stood gaping, the huge main door swung open and two liveried footmen appeared. Their jackets were a deep, rich burgundy, with a tasteful, discreet amount of gold frogging at the epaulettes and lapels. They bowed, and the taller of the two, a stocky man with a large moustache and sharp eyes, bade us welcome.

'Thank you. It is good to be home,' Anna smiled. 'Philippe, Michel, this is my brother Viktor. Has a room been prepared for him, do you know?'

Michel, the shorter man, nodded as he stepped forward to take our bags. 'Yes, Mademoiselle.' He turned to me and bowed. 'A pleasure to meet you, sir. Your room is next to your sister's. Madame LeFévre, our housekeeper, thought you would appreciate being close to her.'

I bowed in response. 'Thank you,' I said. 'That was very considerate, and I am grateful.'

He gave me a searching glance, a little frown furrowing his brow, then turned his attention to our luggage. Colour flared in my cheeks, the heat searing my skin, and I pretended to adjust my cufflinks. For once, I was too distracted to worry about being discovered. Anyway, Anna spent so much time in disguise that my own would probably not even raise so much as an eyebrow.

Anna gently touched my arm and indicated that we should proceed inside, so I followed her, the two footmen bringing up the rear with our luggage.

I found myself in a large hallway which stretched out to my left and right. Occasional tables stood at intervals along its length, with vases or knickknacks. Small lamps glowed dimly on the first two tables, so most of the corridor was in darkness, with only a random shaft of light from an open door further along indicating its length. Heavy-looking framed paintings lined the walls above dark wood panelling, disappearing off into the murk.

In front of us was an imposing central staircase leading to an upper gallery. An archway on either side led deeper into the house, and as I stepped forward to peer upwards, I saw there were three floors above us. The centrepiece was a vast chandelier full of candles, its crystals glittering with rainbows wherever the light struck them.

As we walked past the ornate carved balustrades towards one of the archways, a butler stepped out of a side room, his eyes lighting up as he saw Anna.

'Mademoiselle Stenberg, what a delight!' he exclaimed. 'May I take your coats and hats?'

'It is good to see you, Sylvestre!' Anna exclaimed, beaming as he took our hats and coats. She introduced me and Sylvestre bowed, his blue eyes giving me a frank, appraising look. Inwardly, I squirmed beneath his scrutiny.

Sylvestre excused himself and went back into the room he had just vacated. Anna raised an eyebrow at me. 'Is it as spooky and mysterious and deliciously Gothic as you imagined?'

I chuckled. 'Even more so!' I admitted. 'And a good deal larger than I expected.'

'Agents from all over the world use Castle Rochenoire as their base,' Anna explained. 'All our records are here, as are a significant number of unusual artefacts which agents have collected during their work. Also, there is the library, of course, which is probably our most valuable asset.'

'More valuable than our brave agents, who face untold dangers with every case?'

I whirled around, startled, to see a woman in her fifties, wearing an immaculate black dress, her dark hair pulled into a neat coiffure at the nape of her neck. Her eyes, almost as dark as her hair, sparkled with delight and she opened her arms to Anna, who went to her. They embraced tenderly, the woman smiling into Anna's hair. 'How are you, dear one? Are you well? It is lovely to have you home once again.'

Anna smiled up at her. 'I am very well, Madame, thank you. It's good to be back. I missed you!'

The woman chuckled. 'You missed me bringing you coffee in bed and pressing your clothes for you, I am sure,' she said teasingly, turning her gaze to me. 'And who have you brought to us, Anna?'

Anna introduced the woman as Madame LeFèvre, the housekeeper. I bowed, and as I straightened, Madame LeFèvre released Anna, stepped forward and tilted my chin so I was looking down at her. She was only an inch or two shorter than I. Her eyes softened as she took in every detail of my face, and she nodded to herself. Lowering her voice, she leaned close to me and murmured, 'You make an excellent young man, my dear. Quite splendid! Your height is an advantage for such a disguise.'

'Madame!' Anna protested in a whisper, smiling. 'Viktor's disguise has convinced everyone so far. She has travelled from England in this manner and assisted me with my investigation. Not only that,' Anna added, lowering her voice still further, 'she has some talents of her own.'

I blushed and Madame LeFèvre regarded me with renewed interest. 'Indeed? Well, I am very pleased to make your acquaintance, and look forward to getting to know you,' she said. 'Let me show you your room.'

I nodded wordlessly as she headed for the stairs, taking in coats of arms on the walls, more heavily-framed portraits of scholarly-looking elderly gentlemen, and the scent of wood oil rising from the balustrade as I started to climb. Madame LeFèvre took us to the third floor and turned to the left. We followed the corridor along until it turned to the right, and I was amazed to see how much further it continued along before appearing to turn to the left beyond our sight. We stopped outside a door on our left, which I noticed had a small, discreet number 27 just above the lock. Madame LeFèvre produced a key, unlocked the door, and opened it. A stream of bright light flooded the hall and I blinked, squinting a little, my eyes having become accustomed to the subtle light in the castle. I went into the room and looked around.

To my right, an ornately carved four poster bed dominated the room with its rich scarlet drapery and plush, inviting pillows in crisp, white cases. A wardrobe, washstand, and dresser, in the same dark wood as the bed, stood to one side. Light bathed the room from three tall arched windows opposite the door, and to my left, half the room was taken up with bookcases, a large desk, armchairs and occasional tables arranged in front of the marble fireplace, in which a cheerful blaze was merrily dancing.

'I hope this will suit,' Madame LeFèvre said. 'The bellpull is next to the fireplace there, and if you wish to bathe, simply ring and one of the servants will attend to your requirements. Dinner is usually served at eight, and luncheon at noon. I have arranged for some food to be brought up for you, however, and your luggage is on its way. Michel or Philippe will unpack for you.'

'No need,' I said, perhaps a little too hastily. 'I can do it.'

Madame LeFèvre looked at me for a moment, then smiled kindly, her eyes softening. 'Our Anna here has arrived home in a variety of guises,' she said, 'although, admittedly she has never turned up dressed as a young man.'

Anna chuckled softly. 'I am not tall enough to carry it off with the aplomb and authority Viktor has,' she said.

Embarrassed at being caught out so easily, I bit my lip and looked down at my feet. Anna reached out and squeezed my hand, drawing a reluctant smile from me.

'Viktor does have an engagement in the city this afternoon, Madame,' she said. 'She will need the carriage, if it is available. Please could you ask someone to confirm with me? Also, she will need to be attired in female clothes, and I suspect would appreciate the assistance of a lady's maid. Is Violette able to assist her?'

Madame LeFèvre nodded. 'Of course, I will ask her to come straight up to assist and bring you both some hot water and tea. Would it be appropriate to serve your food half an hour from now? I will make enquiries about the carriage, also.'

'Thank you, yes.' Anna smiled broadly at her. I nodded in agreement. If everyone here was like Madame LeFèvre, I had certainly been extremely fortunate in finding myself amongst them.

Madame LeFèvre handed me the room key, and excused herself with a small bow, closing the door quietly after her. I stared down at the key for a moment, then curled my fingers around it, feeling its weight and solidity as it nestled in my palm, cool against my skin. The comfort it brought me was a surprise, and I caught my breath as tears pricked my eyes. Whatever I had expected, it was not this warmth, this sense of home and family. It was something I had not experienced in so long, not since my mother's disappearance, and all at once, her loss struck me painfully, and I sank to my knees, sobs rising in my chest. Anna dropped to the floor beside me, gathering me into her arms, her face full of concern.

'Viktor, what is it? What's wrong?'

The words would not come. All I could do was shake my head at her and cling to her as she gently rocked me, rubbing my back and murmuring words of comfort in a soft, soothing voice. After a few minutes, aware that Violette was likely to appear at any moment with our hot water, I took a few deep breaths and fumbled in my pocket for a handkerchief. Anna took it and carefully dabbed at my eyes.

'Everything will be all right,' she said. 'You have carried so much during these last two weeks. You have stood strong, whether you believed you could or not, and never faltered.'

I looked at her, blinking back fresh tears. 'What was that word you used earlier? Sab...something. What was it?'

'Sabbatarians,' she said. 'We all have one thing in common, we agents. All of us were born on a Saturday, and, as a result, all of us possess the ability to see, hear and communicate with otherworldly creatures.'

'I was born on a Saturday,' I whispered. 'And...the fog creature...'

She nodded. 'Yes. Exactly. This is why I think you need to spend some time here, exploring your abilities with one of my experienced colleagues, who will be able to guide you far more skilfully than I ever could.'

'I have never experienced anything even remotely unusual in my life, though,' I protested. 'Why am I only seeing strange things now?'

Anna considered for a moment, dabbing at my face with the handkerchief and smoothing back my hair. 'Trauma,' she said simply, her voice soft. 'You feared for your very life, and at that moment, the creature came to you. Whatever traumas you have suffered in the past, none were as intense as that particular occasion, and it was then that your power was triggered.'

I nodded thoughtfully, accepting the logic of her words. 'I didn't fear for my life when my mother vanished. It was a different kind of agony. And although my life was in danger from my father back in Dover, the danger was never immediate, not like it was in the alleyway with that horrible man.'

'No, you were removed from it in both cases,' Anna agreed. 'I truly hope that somewhere in our library will lie an answer to your difficulties. Perhaps later, we should spend some time with your father's journals.'

'For what purpose?' I asked, curious.

'You should show them to one of my colleagues. I would recommend one of the older agents, if any are here at the moment. They have seen much and know more. I recognise some things in those pages, but only a fraction of what is there.' She smiled and squeezed my hand. 'We should try to work out if there is some kind of progression of thought contained within them, if they have an order or are truly random.'

I sighed. 'Don't forget that I could not bring all of them,' I reminded her. 'I simply grabbed a few from the top of the pile.'

She nodded. 'Even so, there may still be something which gives us a clue.'

'Which gives *you* a clue,' I retorted. 'I am completely in the dark.'

Anna conceded. 'Maybe for now,' she said lightly, 'but I assure you, it will not always be so.' She stood and pulled me to my feet, then took my hand and tugged me towards one of the tall windows. Drawing aside the drapes and lace curtains, she opened the sash. 'Get some fresh air for a moment,' she suggested. 'Violette or one of the other maids will be here soon enough, and you are a little blotchy.'

I nodded and leaned out into the cool air. All around me were trees, as far as I could see in every direction. There was still no birdsong, which I vaguely registered but did not focus on, and a fresh, light breeze danced past, carrying with it a tang of loamy soil. A few deep breaths later, I felt more settled. I closed my eyes and let everything wash over me for a moment, trying to keep my focus on the solidity of the window frame beneath my hands, the wall pressing against my legs and belly as the cool air soothed my hot face. A few minutes passed, then I felt a light pressure on my arm and turned to see Anna looking up at me, her face full of concern.

'Better?' she asked in a soft voice. 'You've been so still and silent.'

I nodded. 'It's calm here. There is space for thinking.'

She smiled. 'Yes, there certainly is. You will be happy here.'

Before I could answer, there was a tap at the door. Anna went to open it and admitted a maid. She was tall and slender, with very blonde hair pulled back into a neat bun at the nape of her neck. I estimated her age at mid-thirties and liked her immediately. She had kind, twinkling eyes and an air of efficient capability which I found reassuring.

Anna greeted her and introduced her as Violette. She curtseyed to me and set about her work, taking the jug of hot water to the washstand and filling the basin for me, then turning her attention to my luggage while I went to wash. Anna excused herself and went to her own room, leaving me alone with Violette. I removed the jacket and shirt, feeling horribly self-conscious at my disguise being so exposed, but Violette did not react at all. I splashed the hot water on my arms, thinking how good it felt, and reached for the soap.

'If I may say, Mademoiselle,' Violette said as she took my skirt from the case and shook it out, tutting a little at the creases, 'I have so much admiration for you, doing what you do, and the disguises and so on.'

I turned to smile at her as I lathered. 'Thank you, Violette,' I said. 'All this is new to me, though.'

She raised an eyebrow for a moment, then returned the smile. 'I understand, Mademoiselle. The descriptions I hear from other agents always make their lives sound so glamorous, but I know it is not really like that.'

'No, it isn't, is it?' I agreed. 'You must have heard some fascinating stories. I hope I will hear some, too.'

'You will be with us for a while?' she asked.

I rinsed my face and reached for the towel. 'I am not certain. I shall know more by this evening. I hope to be able to remain here for a time, but unfortunately, there are certain pressures upon me which need to be addressed. If my family were to discover that I have been travelling around France dressed as a young man, there would be consequences.'

Her face softened and she gave a sympathetic nod. 'I understand, Mademoiselle. We will have you looking pretty and elegant and feminine in no time, I promise!'

Violette was as good as her word. She finished unpacking my case, confirmed that I had no other female clothes with me, then disappeared with my garments. When she returned, it was evident she had pressed them. There were still some creases, but they were nowhere near as pronounced. Violette helped me to dress, checking how I liked things to be done, then settled me in front of the mirror and dressed my hair, coaxing it into a simple but beautiful style which let it ripple down my back. I was amazed as I watched the reflection of her deft fingers, and delighted with the result, which was far less severe than my usual coiffure. Violette added a tiny dot of colour to my cheeks, then stood back to consider her work. I beamed at her in the mirror, and she returned the smile.

'You are pleased?'

'I am, Violette. Thank you!'

There was a knock at the door and Violette went to open it. A maid and a footman carried in a bottle of wine, a glass and a tray on which was a silver salver. They set everything on the small table near the fire and invited me to sit. I did so, pushing the stool carefully out of the way beneath the dresser before settling myself in the comfortable chair next to the hearth and turning my attention to what was being set before me.

The light meal was delicious, beautifully cooked and well-flavoured, and the wine complemented it perfectly. I sipped slowly, feeling some of the stress easing. Violette and the two other servants hovered unobtrusively whilst I ate, the footman, Laurent, occasionally stepping forward to offer to refill my glass, which I declined. I needed to be fully focused during my meeting with Sébastien.

After I had finished, Laurent and Ernestine, the maid, cleared everything away and left the room. Violette, having finished unpacking my case, excused herself and followed them. I got up and wandered to the full-length mirror in one corner of the room, admiring Violette's handiwork. I looked every inch the respectable young lady. There was nothing in my appearance which would give Sébastien any cause for alarm.

Anna reappeared a couple of minutes later, tapping quickly on the door and letting herself in almost before I had had an opportunity to respond. She looked me over critically, nodding her approval with a little smile. 'Violette does good work. You look lovely.'

'Thank you,' I replied, reddening. To distract myself, I crossed to the wardrobe, realising something all of a sudden. 'Oh! I have no coat,' I exclaimed. 'I have only my father's overcoat.'

'There should be a cloak in there,' Anna told me. 'I took the liberty of advising that you would be in need of some clothing, so Madame LeFèvre will have left you something suitable.'

Opening the wardrobe, I saw a number of unfamiliar items hanging alongside my own meagre supply. There was a thick tweed cloak, just as Anna had said, and I took it out, the rough fabric contrasting with the gentle caress of the silk lining. There was also a small, slightly nondescript hat, which would have to suffice. Returning to the mirror, I quickly pinned it into place, then wrapped the cloak around myself. 'There. Will I pass inspection, do you think?'

Anna chuckled. 'Most certainly. No one would ever suspect the adventures you have had.' Her expression grew serious. 'Viktor, would you like me to accompany you? Not to the meeting itself, of course,' she added hastily. 'I can wait in the carriage for you.'

'Much as I would truly appreciate you being there,' I said, after a moment's thought, 'it would be better if I went by myself. I need to give the impression that I am able to cope alone. It will add weight to my argument.'

She nodded. 'I understand. Don't forget to take some money with you. Oh, and here, keep this in your glove, perhaps,' she said, taking a small card from her pocket. I looked at it, puzzled. 'It is one of my safe houses in the city,'

Anna explained. 'If you have difficulties, you can go there, show the housekeeper this card, and be given sanctuary on my authority.'

I blinked and slipped the card into the waistband of my skirt, realising I did not have gloves. 'I hope that will not become necessary,' I murmured.

Anna flashed me a reassuring smile. 'You will be strong and confidant,' she said. 'While you are out, I shall find my mentor and see if we can speak with him tonight after we have eaten.'

I nodded. 'I would like that. Anything which can shed light on what happened to my parents will be so very helpful.' I paused. 'Even if the answer proves to be something unpleasant.'

'At least you would know.' Anna nodded in understanding. 'And Viktor… you *can* cope alone. You do not need to give an impression. You can simply be yourself.'

I smiled and pulled the cloak more closely around myself, then checked the mirror. 'I should take some money with me.'

Anna hurried out of the room, telling me to wait for a moment, and returned with a small black reticule studded with jet beads, which she handed to me. 'Here, take this.'

Thanking her, I stuffed some money, Anna's card, Uncle Geoffrey's correspondence and a handkerchief into the purse, then added a pencil and tore a few sheets from the back of my journal, folding them and tucking them in carefully. I wasn't sure exactly what had prompted me to do so, but I would need to get word to Anna if anything happened to prevent me returning to the castle. I sincerely hoped they would not become necessary, and that Sébastien proved to be reasonable.

Anna walked me down the stairs and out of the main door, where the carriage was waiting, and introduced me to Pierre, the driver, who bowed solemnly, his intense blue eyes looking up and down appreciatively. He was taller than I, heavily built, and had a reassuring air of capability. Anna hugged me tightly, then watched as Pierre helped me into the carriage and closed the door. I opened the glass and leaned out to her. 'If there are any problems, I will send you word,' I said. 'I am not certain how, but I will.'

'Arrange with Pierre to be out of the meeting by a certain time. If you are not, he will know what to do.'

I nodded, my stomach knotting and turning somersaults as Pierre shook the reins and the horses began to walk down the drive. Anna waved until the carriage turned a corner and I could no longer see her. Leaning back against the plush upholstered seat, I tried not to panic, but my attention was soon diverted by how uncomfortable I was in my corset, and how my skirt and petticoats kept tangling around my legs every time I shifted in the seat. After a few minutes, I was thoroughly frustrated, wondering how on earth I had ever managed to do anything in such constricting garments.

The journey to my grandfather's apartment in Montmartre was pleasant enough. I spent most of it re-reading the letters and telegrams Uncle Geoffrey had sent, thinking about how the conversation with Sébastien might develop. When Pierre reined in the horses, I was startled out of a reverie and blinked at the familiar surroundings. It was a few years since I had last been here, but very little had changed.

Pierre jumped down from the box and opened the door for me but leaned in as I was moving forward to get up. 'Mademoiselle,' he said in a low, discreet voice, 'do you know how long you are likely to be?'

'I am afraid not,' I said. 'However, I cannot see the need for the conversation to be any longer than an hour. Hopefully, it will be far shorter than that, but I have no idea what to expect. What do you need me to do to raise an alarm?'

'Nothing which puts you in danger,' Pierre said firmly.

'Pierre, the man I am meeting is a family agent. He is not looking to harm me.'

'Perhaps not,' Pierre said, his piercing blue eyes raking mine. 'He might lock you in a room, however, or prevent you from leaving in some other way. You know this man?'

I blinked at him. 'No, I have not met him before.'

Pierre nodded. 'In that case, you would be wise to exercise the same kind of care as you and Mademoiselle Anna exercise on your field work.'

His words made sense and I nodded. 'Please give me an hour, Pierre. If I am not back by then, I take it you will do whatever is necessary to raise the alarm.'

He stepped back and gave me a little bow. 'Indeed, Mademoiselle. You need have no fear.'

I gave him a smile that I knew did not reach my eyes and allowed him to help me step out of the carriage. He swung himself back up onto the box, took out a book and started reading. I noticed it was one of Byron's poetry collections.

Taking a deep breath, I turned to the building behind me and walked up the steps to the front door, tugging on the bell with a little more force than was strictly necessary. A maid opened the door, curtseyed, took my cloak, and accompanied me to the apartment, opening doors for me and chatting pleasantly about the weather. I responded in kind, making sure to keep my tone bright and my comments suitably bland, as befitted a young lady.

Sébastien was waiting for me in my grandfather's reception room. He was a tall, broad man, no more than thirty years old, with dark hair and, to my surprise, a large beard, above which brown eyes regarded me kindly as he bowed over my hand and invited me to sit. Wishing my stomach would stop turning somersaults, I settled into an armchair and looked up at him with the pleasant, demure, expectant expression my aunts preferred in their nieces. I was offering him nothing until I had some idea of what was going to be asked of me. Sébastien ordered coffee and pastries and the maid curtseyed and left the room. He seated himself opposite me, carefully and deliberately straightening his coat tails with precise, elegant fingers.

'It is a relief to see you, Mademoiselle,' he said, with a warm smile. 'And looking so well, too. Your uncle tells me there has been a great deal of consternation in the family regarding your absence.'

I maintained my own smile even as indignation flared in my breast, and it was a moment before I had framed a suitable response. 'Indeed, and for that, I am regretful. However, I made sure to keep my uncle informed at every possible opportunity, as I am sure he has told you.' I regarded him evenly, making sure I was not betraying any emotion. 'It was extremely unsettling to be obliged to leave my home with almost nothing, but I was fortunate indeed to have fallen into the company I did.'

Yes,' Sébastien said, his tone thoughtful. 'This young woman you mention in your correspondence. Tell me about her. Who is she? Who are her people?'

'She is an extremely capable and intelligent person, with a background similar to my own,' I said, choosing my words carefully. 'She is refined, elegant, resourceful and witty.'

Sébastien nodded slowly, turning my words over in his mind. I could almost see the cogs spinning behind his eyes. 'You were a little vague when explaining how you met her,' he commented. Irritation surged in my belly and my smile started to feel false, plastered on.

'Not vague,' I said, letting a little edge creep into my voice. 'I daresay that you have never had to go into hiding because your father had escaped an asylum and was bent on harming you. Believe me, it does little to encourage social niceties and a great deal to encourage innovation and one's survival instinct.'

Sébastien had the grace to redden slightly and inclined his head. 'Forgive me,' he said, his voice softening unexpectedly. 'If I may say so, Mademoiselle, I admire you. So many young women your age would have crumbled and had no idea what to do. Yet here you are, alive, well, and in safe company. You are impressive.'

This was not what I had expected, and I blinked at him, uncertain how to respond. The maid returned at that moment, sparing me the need to reply immediately, and as she set out the cups and plates, I ran through a few potential responses in my head, hoping the arrival of coffee meant the moment had passed. Luckily, it had. Sébastien took a sip of coffee, dismissed the maid, and then set his cup down and went to the writing desk in the corner of the room. He took out an envelope and returned to his seat, tapping it thoughtfully on the arm of the chair.

'As you may expect,' he said, sounding almost apologetic, 'now the danger has passed, your family wishes you to return home immediately. I have made the necessary arrangements, and will either accompany you myself, or ask the housekeeper if she will act as chaperone.'

There it was. Just as I had expected. As my heart sank, Sébastien outlined my travel plans. I would immediately move my belongings into the apartment and remain there for the rest of my time in Paris. I would take a train to Calais, and then the ferry to Dover, where the carriage would be waiting to take me home. Two of my aunts were already travelling to Dover to take care of me when I returned.

Sipping my coffee almost unconsciously, I let his words wash over me as my mind scrambled around for a response. I could feel panic rising at the thought of returning to my dull, contained life without first having the chance to learn whatever I could about my mother's disappearance. The more I thought of it, the more I realised I needed to know.

Sébastien lapsed into silence and took up his coffee again, and I frantically considered responses, finally settling on the one which I thought would best demonstrate my willingness to comply, whilst simultaneously providing me with the chance to have my own way.

'If you are my family's trusted agent,' I said, 'I imagine you are aware of my situation.' He inclined his head and I nodded. 'I will return to Dover, of course. However, it may not be for a few days.'

He smiled. 'You require time for sightseeing?'

'No.' I set my cup down on the table, in case my hands began to tremble. A rattling coffee cup would not help me in my cause. 'During my travels, I came across some information which suggests that I may be able to discover more about my mother's disappearance.'

Whatever Sébastien had been expecting me to say, it was not this. The smile which had curved his lips started to fade, and by the time I paused, he looked decidedly uncomfortable. 'Information? What information?'

I thought of the notebooks in my father's desk and wished I had thought to lock them away and take the key, so no other prying eyes could see them, or use the information to beat me at my own game. How to describe the information? I should probably keep that part to myself. The last thing I needed was for the family to believe I was chasing my father's mania.

Lowering my voice, I leaned towards him. He did likewise, shifting to the edge of his seat. 'I shouldn't reveal that just yet,' I said. 'Uncle Geoffrey was as devastated as I when my mother disappeared. I would hate to give him false hope that we might finally discover what happened to her. He has been so good to me, and this is an opportunity for me to repay him for all his kindnesses.'

'Maybe so, maybe so,' Sébastien said, 'but what exactly are you talking about? What information, and who possesses it?'

'This is what I need time to determine,' I said. 'The nature of the information is vague, but there was enough detail to make me question the source of my father's mania.'

'Oh?' Sébastien's eyes were glittering and alert. I had his attention and would need to tread carefully.

'We have always assumed it was related to his experiences in the army, have we not?' I asked, waiting with interest for Sébastien's response so I could determine just how much he knew about my family.

'We have,' he replied. 'Are you saying those experiences were not the root of his affliction after all? It was more than reasonable to think they were. Being one of the few survivors cannot be an easy burden to bear.'

'It is not.' I paused and took a breath before continuing. 'Those experiences damaged him, Sébastien, there is no denying that. My mother's disappearance made everything worse. I have been given an opportunity to determine whether there is anything more to learn about what happened to her, to give the family some peace of mind, some answers.'

'And how will you do that? This is no task for a young girl.'

I regarded him coolly. 'If you know as much about the family as I imagine you do, then you will be aware there is talk of marriage awaiting me when I return home. If I am considered old enough to marry, then I am certainly old enough to meet and speak with someone about my mother.'

'Meet with whom?'

'All I know is that he is a scholar of some kind, incredibly knowledgeable, and has dealt with unexplained disappearances before in some capacity. More than that, I cannot say.'

'This should not be a task for you,' Sébastien began, but I interrupted.

'Who knows my parents better than I? Who is more likely to spot a fraudster, or catch him out in some inconsistency? Who was with my parents when my mother disappeared?' I leaned forward. 'That day is etched into my mind, every detail crystal clear. If this is some kind of deception, I will know. I will recognise it in a way no one else can.'

He sat back and regarded me, but his expression was not one of horror, or annoyance, or frustration. He looked full of admiration.

'When would this conversation take place?' he asked.

'The scholar is travelling at the moment, and due to return to Paris in a few days, I understand,' I lied. 'I was intending to engage a chaperone for my new friend and myself and do a little sightseeing and shopping whilst I am here. Paris is such a beautiful city, and I have not been here in some time.'

'And you speak the language as though born to it.'

I smiled. 'My parents wished me to be able to communicate as well here as I do at home. It is good to have a chance to make their wishes reality, even in these circumstances, which have been less than ideal. Especially if, in doing so, I can help the family as a whole.'

Sébastien regarded me and sighed. 'You realise the ripples this will cause?'

Straightening my back, I regarded him evenly, although my heart was racing. What did he mean by that? It wasn't an instant no. He was not scoffing at me, or laughing, or patting me on the head. I held my breath and waited. Sébastien shifted in his seat and picked an invisible thread from his trouser leg, then drummed his fingers on the arm of the chair for a few moments. I continued to sit calmly, watching, my comfort increasing even as his reduced. It seemed as though I had the upper hand, but I could not allow myself a moment of complacency.

'How much time will you need, do you think?' he said quietly. 'I should not be doing this. I should be marching you to your lodgings to collect your possessions and then accompanying you everywhere.'

Curious, I edged forward in my seat. 'You are willing to help me?' I asked, incredulous. 'I am grateful, but confess I am also surprised. Why are you doing this for me?'

He shook his head. 'I have done many things for your family,' he said. 'I have worked for you all for a number of years, although my path has never crossed yours before. Your mother's disappearance always struck me as odd. If there is a way to shed some light on it, or even to finally close the door, I think it will be time well spent. I can see you are best placed to uncover any underhanded intentions on the part of this scholar. I am uncomfortable at the thought, however. Would they speak to you if I accompanied you?'

I sighed delicately. 'I fear not. They would be happy if my friend acted as chaperone, however. I was quick to establish that.' The lies tripped off my tongue with an ease which startled me. 'In addition, I insisted that the scholar should meet me in a public place.'

Sébastien nodded, lapsing into silence again. I picked up my coffee, pleased to see my hand was steady. Could I have found an unexpected ally in Sébastien? It would certainly be useful to have someone bridging the gap between myself and Uncle Geoffrey. What would I have to promise, though, in order to be able to remain at the castle? Would there be consequences for Sébastien if he was flouting Uncle Geoffrey's instructions?

'If I help you, Mademoiselle, I will need some assurances in return.' Sébastien's voice was firmer than before and startled me as it cut crisply through the air. 'I am willing to delay our travel arrangements for a few days. It would be reasonable, I think, that after the upheaval of the last two weeks, you would need some space and time to relax and gather your thoughts, which I can certainly provide. In addition, I have instructions from your uncle to provide you with any money you require. He advised me that you might need to add significantly to your wardrobe.'

'He is correct,' I said. 'My departure was so sudden that there was no time to pack properly. I have managed perfectly well, however. I was able to make a few purchases whilst travelling here.'

He nodded. 'And your lodgings? Will you move to the apartment, as the family wishes?'

'In time,' I said. 'I just arrived, and arrangements have been put in place for me. It would be ill-mannered and ungrateful to simply turn my back on them, and I wish to give a good impression of myself and our family.'

Again, he nodded, and I hoped I was not putting too much emphasis on the family. However, when he spoke, he surprised me once more. 'You are capable and fearless, it seems,' he said. 'I have great admiration for those qualities in a young woman and will be happy to serve you in any capacity you wish whilst you are in Paris. I understand you want to provide answers so everyone can come to terms with what happened to your mother, but I also understand this is something you need to do for yourself more than anything. It is not unreasonable for you to ask to have a conversation with someone, and I am happy to facilitate. All I ask is that you move to the apartment at the earliest opportunity that etiquette and manners permit.'

I thought of the small but elegant room I usually used in the apartment, and how it contrasted sharply with the old-world grandeur of the vast room which had been allocated to me at Castle Rochenoire. I had not stayed in the apartment for some years, but it had that tang of the homely, the familiar, which part of me so desperately craved. Yet even as I looked around at the ornaments, the drapes, even the andirons in their rack by the hearth, memories crowded my thoughts. My father, using the poker as a sword in a mock battle with one of my uncles. My mother playing the piano and singing softly. Myself, small and beloved, standing between them, looking out of the window to the street below, waiting for my grandfather's arrival. It was overwhelming, sweeping through me and leaving me breathless. The coffee cup rattled in its saucer, and I hastily set it down, clasping my hands tightly, knuckles showing white through my skin.

'What is it?' Sébastien asked. His voice was surprisingly gentle, but then, a lot of things about Sébastien had surprised me so far. I looked across at him, swallowing hard and trying to hold tears at bay.

'Everywhere I look in this apartment, I see my parents,' I began, and he immediately held up a hand. I caught my breath. It had not occurred to me that my memories would make the apartment unbearable. If Sébastien insisted I stayed there, I was not certain how I would cope with it. Perhaps that was his intention, I thought, my lip curling, so I would be keen to go home, where the family wanted me.

'Say no more,' Sébastien told me. 'I understand completely. Please forgive me for my thoughtlessness. Perhaps you would permit me to select a good hotel as an alternative?'

Again, I stared at him for a moment, taken aback. This was very strange indeed. It was as though he actually saw me as a person, rather than the family's latest commodity to be parcelled up and sent off to some dull, aged husband. He met my gaze steadily, his eyes full of compassion, and I realised, with a jolt, that this man truly cared. This man, who I had never met, despite his apparent years of service to the family, cared more about me in this moment than my relatives.

Taking a deep breath, I forced a quavering smile. 'It is a kind offer, Sébastien, but the expense is completely unnecessary. I have exceptionally comfortable lodgings with my companion, far more so than even the best hotel in Paris. Plus, it has the added bonus of being completely new to me. I can rest and recover there, far more easily than I would be able to here.'

'Of course.' He nodded. 'I will explain your reasoning to your uncle. He will understand.'

'Why are you helping me?'

The question left my lips even before it had truly registered, and I looked down at my hands, feeling heat searing my cheeks. I began to stammer an apology, knowing I had lost any semblance of control over the conversation.

'Please, there is no need to apologise,' Sébastien said. 'I am helping you because you have made a good argument to explain your requests and decisions, and I respect that. I confess I expected you to rail against your uncle's requirements. Of course,' he added, his eyes twinkling at me, 'in a way, that is exactly what you are doing, but you are doing it in a sensible, mature manner. Plus, I feel everyone has the right to an adventure at least once in their life. Perhaps this can be yours.'

Returning the smile, I blinked back tears and glanced over at the clock on the mantelpiece. There was plenty of time before Pierre would become concerned and raise the alarm, which pleased me. I found I liked Sébastien, which I had not expected. Without exception, the family's agents were older gentlemen, dour and unsmiling, who executed their instructions to the letter. Sébastien was as refreshing as a cool breeze on a warm day.

'Of course,' he said, his voice thoughtful, 'there will naturally be conditions.'

I blinked at him, my heart sinking. Here was the sting in the tail.

'In order to ensure you are able to pursue your adventure, the family will need some reassurances regarding your safety.' Sébastien refilled his cup, eyeing me over the rim before taking a sip. 'Would you be willing to permit me to act as your manservant? I appreciate that it will be somewhat difficult if you are intending to reside with your friend, but I am sure that if you and she are intending to shop or take in some of the delights of Paris during your stay, you will require a chaperon.'

I thought of Anna, her calm demeanour, self-confidence and commanding voice. I thought of the creatures she dealt with, and a little smile tickled the corners of my mouth. If only Sébastien knew.

However, his suggestion was sensible. If he was acting as my de facto guardian, the family would be less likely to throw up its collective hands and demand my immediate return to Dover. I also felt somewhat indebted to him for making it possible for me to remain not only in Paris, but also at Castle Rochenoire, at least for the time being. It remained to be seen just how indebted I was making myself, but for the moment, I was more than happy with the outcome of our conversation, and sincerely hoped Sébastien would prove himself the friend and support he seemed to be.

'You knew my parents,' I said quietly. Sébastien nodded.

'They were a pleasure to serve,' he said. 'I admire your father greatly, and your mother always had a kind word and a smile.'

That jolted me. Something about it sent a flurry of butterflies skittering around my stomach. Trying not to shift uncomfortably in my seat, I set my cup down, wondering what was wrong. Tendrils of mist suddenly curled into the edges of my vision and set my heart racing in panic. I could not let Sébastien find out about the fog creature. The family could not know. Trying to quell my panic even at it rose in my throat, I sent out a silent message to the fog creature, begging it to stay hidden. Over and over, I thought the words, whilst trying to appear to be listening intently. To my relief, the fog dissipated almost as quickly as it had appeared, and Sébastien continued speaking, seemingly oblivious. I interlaced my fingers on my lap, forcing my focus onto Sébastien just in time for him to finish speaking and lean forward with a smile.

'At least you can have that reassurance,' he said, with an encouraging nod. I nodded back, shocked at how few of his words had registered in my panic to keep the fog creature away.

'I should take my leave, Sébastien,' I said. 'The sooner I can attend to my business, the sooner I can return to Dover. The carriage is outside waiting for me.'

Sébastien nodded and rose to ring for the maid. He and I chatted about the sights and beauty of Paris while the maid helped me with my cloak, then he dismissed her to wait by the front door. As soon as she had left the room, Sébastien reached into his coat and produced a bulky envelope. He looked at it for a moment, weighing it in his hand, then held it out to me. I took it, puzzled, and opened it carefully. My eyes widened when I saw it was stuffed full of francs.

'Your uncle sent it for you. He was concerned that making arrangements through the bank might not be the best method for you.'

I nodded, tucking the envelope safely out of sight, deciding to refrain from commenting on Uncle Geoffrey's concerns. Instead, I looked at Sébastien with a serious expression. 'Please be assured that I will be discreet,' I assured him, 'and I sincerely thank you for your service, Sébastien.' I paused. 'I hope you will not encounter any difficulties from the family for the help you are giving me.'

He smiled, his eyes softening. 'As long as we ensure our stories are consistent, there is no need for anyone to know anything. Of course, should you uncover new information, it will be impossible to maintain the fiction.'

'What will we do in that eventuality?' I asked.

He looked thoughtful again. 'I will need to prove to them that there was no dereliction of duty on my part, which will, in turn, help you justify your choices.'

I nodded, seeing the truth in this, and held out my hand to him. 'I will keep you informed,' I told him as he bent to kiss my fingertips. 'I have no desire to cause problems for you or the family, but this is something I simply have to do if I am to live with myself for the rest of my life.'

'I understand,' he said, his tone sincere and earnest. 'Let me escort you to the carriage.'

We descended to the street, and I noticed the relief on Pierre's face when I emerged unscathed. He leaped down from the box and opened the door so Sébastien could hand me into the carriage. As I settled against the plush upholstered seat, I heard the murmur of their voices, and slid over to the window to look out. Pierre was handing Sébastien what looked like a calling card, and I realised I had not told him precisely where I was staying. It was strange that he had not pressed the issue, but as I had turned up unharmed and on time, and in a carriage, as befitted my status, he had clearly decided there was little to be worried about.

Sébastien nodded to Pierre and bowed to me. The carriage rocked as Pierre took his seat once more, and as we moved off, I kept my eyes on Sébastien until we turned a corner, and he was gone.

Chapter 38

When I returned to the castle, there was a flurry of activity in the hall. Maids and footmen were scurrying around, some with cleaning equipment, some with vases and armfuls of flowers. Feeling awkward and uncertain of myself, I skirted around them, accepting their greetings and apologies, and made my way to the stairs, trying to remember the route to my room. What was going on? There seemed to be too much bustling for the staff to simply be preparing for dinner.

I found my room and, to my delight, discovered Anna sitting next to the fire, scribbling in her notebook. She looked up as I walked in, her eyes searching my face. 'Did it go well?' she asked. 'Come, sit, tell me all about it.'

'Everything went surprisingly well,' I told her, draping the cloak over the back of a chair. Briefly, I summarised the key points of my conversation with Sébastien, and she raised an eyebrow.

'Well, well,' she murmured. 'He sounds unusually accommodating.'

'Compared to every other agent I have ever know, he is a breed apart,' I agreed.

'At least you have the freedom to remain here and begin your investigation,' Anna said, her eyes shining. 'Something exciting is happening, too. It seems our founder has returned after an extended period away from the castle, and will be joining us for dinner tonight, which is a rare occurrence.'

'Ah, that explains the activity downstairs,' I said. 'Who is the founder?'

Anna paused, biting her lip thoughtfully. 'I think it is probably best if you discover that for yourself,' she said.

I frowned. 'That's a very vague and unhelpful statement.'

'Forgive me. I am not being deliberately obstructive. There are some things which need to be discovered rather than passed on, and this is one of them. You will understand when you meet him.'

'You won't even tell me his name?'

She smiled. 'Perhaps I can distract you instead. Would you like a tour of the castle?'

It was impossible to hold on to any frustration after such an offer, so I swallowed my retorts and smiled at her. 'Yes, please.'

'Let me just finish this,' she said, nodding at her work. 'It will only take a few minutes, then we can start at the library.'

My smiled widened. 'I am looking forward to seeing it,' I told her sincerely. 'Will your mentor be there?'

'Possibly,' she said, glancing at the clock. 'He may have retired to his room by now, especially given that dinner will be an exciting affair tonight. He prefers the company of books to that of people and needs to prepare himself for large gatherings.'

'There will be a lot of people at dinner?' I asked, suddenly thinking of my attire. I rose and went to the wardrobe, peering thoughtfully at the unfamiliar gowns hanging there.

'More than usual,' Anna said. 'A lot of us do tend to have dinner served in our rooms, especially if we are working on something. However, tonight is a special occasion.'

There was a pretty sky-blue satin gown in the wardrobe, and I stroked the soft, cool fabric, enjoying the way it slid over my skin like water. Hopefully it would fit me. It looked rather short, and there would be insufficient time for Violette to make any alterations to it. A smile passed over my face as I mused about going to dinner as Viktor.

As Anna wrote and paused to think, I moved around the room, looking at the paintings. Most were landscapes, but there were one or two portraits, almost obscured with years of grime. I peered at them, curious, thinking how immaculate the rest of the room was, but they did not strike me as being particularly significant. One was a man, the other a woman. Perhaps they were former agents. Had they both used this room at some point in the past? What had become of them?

I moved around the room to the windows, running my hands over the heavy silk brocade drapes, enjoying the luxury of them. The sun was sinking in the sky, setting the clouds on fire. A lone crow rose from one of the trees and soared off, silhouetted against the deep, incandescent orange glow beyond. I watched it as it wheeled and dipped in the evening air. A light touch on my arm brought me back to myself, and I turned to see Anna smiling up at me, her eyes alight.

'Shall we go and explore in the library?' she asked.

I agreed with enthusiasm, and she led me out of my room and back towards the staircase. We climbed to the next floor and turned right along the corridor; our footsteps muffled by the thick carpet. We turned another corner and Anna made her way to the end of the corridor, opening a door to our left. I followed her in, and my mouth dropped open.

Whatever I had been expecting, it was not the airy, spacious room which I saw before me. The ceiling soared overhead at least twice the height of my own room, and a gallery ran around the entire space, with spiral staircases in the two far corners. In front of us were rows of long, low bookshelves with a bank of desks and chairs beyond. The walls to left and right of us were an expanse of floor-to-ceiling shelves, each one crammed with ancient tomes, journals and packets of letters tied with ribbon. A fire burned merrily in a large, ornate marble fireplace in the right-hand wall, the bookshelves sitting snugly alongside. The crackle and fizz of the burning logs gave life to the room, and the soft glow of dancing flames transformed the austere space into something almost homely and comforting, despite its size.

We moved into the centre of the room. Everywhere I looked, tiny details impressed themselves on me. A small door leading out of the gallery above. A stained glass rose window in the wall opposite, between the spiral staircases. The subtle vanilla tang of old paper, mingled with wood polish. And somewhere, what sounded almost like a soft humming. I paused, tilting my head, listening, but as soon as I tried to focus on it, the sound died away, leaving only silence in its wake.

'Look at these,' Anna was saying, gesturing to the bookcase next to us. 'These are hand-drawn maps which our agents have brought back over the years. If you discover what your fog creature is, you might be able to trace its origins in some of these. They date back several hundred years and show the locations of various populations of entities and fae creatures.'

Fascinated, I moved to the bookcase and reverently touched the very tips of my fingers to one of the rolls of paper. Anna took it carefully and laid it out on a desk, unrolling it with practised hands, and together, we leaned over it, reading the tiny, neat writing and admiring the artwork. It was a map of Italy, showing the location of a vampire clan on the outskirts of Venice in the year 1523. Around the edges of the map were sketches of the vampire, a terrifying creature with sunken eyes, clawed hands and sharp fangs. These I pored over, leaning close to the page.

'This vampire looks nothing like the one we saw in Amiens,' I murmured. 'Or like de Montfort.'

'No, indeed. This is a different species entirely,' she agreed. 'Vampire enclaves and clans differ wildly. Each retained some traits from the vampire who originally founded the clan, and over time, these differences have become more pronounced, especially in the most powerful clans.'

'Why those in particular?' I asked.

'Because their original founders are still alive,' she said quietly. 'Vampires of great age and even greater power. They are able to reinforce and strengthen those traits in a form of communion with those they have created, who then reinforce it in those they have created, and so on. Come and look at this.'

She rolled the map up and set it back in its place, then led me to one side of the room and knelt next to a bookcase which held some of the largest, heaviest books I had seen in my life. One had a spine almost as thick as my thigh and was a good two feet tall. The others were a little more slender, although not by much. Many looked like vast, oversized ledgers. All were ancient.

'These are all handwritten, and incredibly valuable,' Anna said. 'They can only be moved by three people working together. Some of them were written by vampires.'

'They are so old,' I whispered, eyeing the bindings. She nodded.

'These books hold one of the greatest resources we have. Vampire lore, told by the vampires themselves.'

I stared at the shelves, trying to fathom the incredible amount of information at my fingertips. Would I ever understand it? The things Anna was talking about were so far removed from my world. It felt so odd to be discussing vampires as easily as we might discuss the contents of a picnic basket, or a poem we had enjoyed. Yet, no matter how otherworldly and strange it felt, there was also a part of me which knew I was exactly where I needed to be. Instinct told me the answers I sought lay somewhere in one of these books.

'I spoke to a colleague, albeit briefly,' Anna said, taking my arm and tugging me towards the desks. 'He suggests you write down everything you can remember about the circumstances of your mother's disappearance. Include every detail, no matter how small or insignificant you might believe it to be. The more you can recall, the better placed my mentor will be to help you.'

She settled me at a desk and bustled around finding paper, pen, and ink, laying them out before me as I watched in bemusement. 'I have to do it now?' I asked, my heart sinking a little at the thought.

Something in my expression gave her pause and she bit her lip. 'Forgive me. I did not realise how much I would enjoy having you here, and my excitement overrode my common sense. It was insensitive of me.'

Reaching out, I took her hand. Her skin was soft, warm, as I gave her fingers a gentle squeeze. 'I understand why he needs the information,' I said, 'but I cannot just sit down and dredge up those feelings on command. They are still too raw, even now. My father's unfortunate situation keeps them closer to the surface than I would like.'

She nodded and asked for forgiveness again, and I bestowed it accordingly. Her eyes began to dart around the room like hummingbirds, finally settling on a bookcase near the fireplace. 'Let me show you this,' she said, 'and then perhaps you might want to wander around and look at everything in your own time, until we need to dress for dinner.'

I got up and followed her to a shelf which was crammed with journals of all shapes and sizes. Anna selected a couple at random, marking their positions carefully, then handed them to me. 'Field journals,' she explained. 'Have a look.'

Curious, I flipped the first book open and scanned the neat, spidery script. The writer had been in Greece, investigating the case of a child which was thought to have been stolen by fairies and replaced with a sickly fae child. There were sketches, carefully drawn maps of the area around the child's home, studies of plants and insects made with a skilled hand. Settling on the carpet in front of the fire, I leafed carefully through the pages, trying to follow the progress of the case.

Anna took a stack of journals from the shelf and came to sit with me, spreading them out on the carpet around her before selecting one and opening it. As she did, the library door opened and a tall, thin man in a dark suit entered, his nose buried in the book he was carrying. Almost absently, he closed the door behind him and picked his way to one of the desks, never once lifting his eyes from the page, yet navigating the room flawlessly. Anna's face broke into a broad smile, and she leapt to her feet, tugging the journal from my hands, and pulling me up after her.

'Michael!' she exclaimed, and the tall man started, whirling around in his chair to face us. When he saw Anna, he relaxed visibly and turned back to the book. 'You're back, then.'

His voice was dry and brittle, and I was startled to realise he had spoken in English. His accent had a slight northern lilt to it.

Anna chuckled softly. 'Yes, and I brought an enigma for you.'

He did not look up from the book but drew a small notebook from his coat pocket and took a pencil from the desk drawer. 'An enigma? From Amiens?'

'Not quite. From Dover, actually.'

That caught his attention, and he looked over, seeing us for the first time. His eyes flitted over Anna, then came to rest on me, raking me uncomfortably. I looked steadily back, lifting my chin a little. 'And you are?'

'This is my new companion Viktor,' Anna said. 'We met in interesting circumstances in Dover. Viktor, this is my mentor, Michael Grant. He has been an agent for many years and taught me almost everything I know.'

'Viktor?' Michael looked at me quizzically. I blushed, feeling suddenly awkward in my feminine attire. Anna rolled her eyes.

'Oh Michael, you remember nothing,' she said mildly. 'I wrote to you about Viktor.'

Michael frowned slightly, still looking blank, so she quickly described the circumstances of our meeting. Part-way through, he slid his books to one side and sat forward in the chair, listening intently. I put his age at anywhere between forty and fifty. His shock of greying hair looked as though he had repeatedly run his fingers through it, and there was an ink stain on his right hand. His eyes, however, gleaming in the firelight, were bright and keen, and for a moment, I felt as though he was gazing into my soul. As Anna finished her explanation, he leaned his elbows on his knees, steepling his long fingers.

'Well, well,' he said quietly. 'It sounds like you and I may have some interesting conversations ahead of us. I take it you are interested in discovering the nature of this creature you have attracted.'

'I am, yes, although that is not my main reason for being here.'

He raised an eyebrow. 'Oh?'

'My mother disappeared under mysterious circumstances, and Anna believes I will find answers here.'

He nodded, looking thoughtful, and fired a few questions at me. 'It happened in Germany, you say? Interesting place, Germany. Always something new to be discovered there, more so than almost anywhere else in the world. Of course, the Grimms are partly to blame for that.'

I blinked. 'The...Grimms?'

He eyeballed me. 'You didn't think their fairy tales were figments of their imaginations, surely?'

There was no answer to that; at least, none presented itself. As I stood gaping at him, I heard Anna's soft chuckle at my elbow, and felt a reassuring squeeze of my fingertips.

'Michael don't tease her. I would suggest thinking back to your own introduction to the organisation, if it hadn't happened all the way back in the Middle Ages.'

To my surprise, he threw back his head and laughed heartily. 'I do hope, Viktor, that your manners are better than Anna's. Sometimes I am embarrassed to call her my protégé.'

I chuckled as Anna feigned offence, and Michael waved his hand vaguely in the direction of the journals on the floor. 'Please, do not let me distract you from your research. Anna has shown you where you should look for reports about German cases?'

'She has,' I confirmed, and he gave a satisfied nod, turning back to his own work. Sensing the conversation was over, I settled myself on the carpet once again, turning to watch the fire for a moment. As the flames danced, I suddenly became aware of an acrid tang to the smoke, and wondered what logs were being burned. I reached for one of the journals at random and flipped it open without paying much attention to the title or author.

All at once, I realised tendrils of hair were tickling my cheek. I raised my hand to brush them away, then froze as a breeze started to swirl around me. Anna, who was still standing next to me, looked around in consternation. 'Michael...' she murmured.

Instantly, he was on his feet, head tilted to listen, eyes darting around the room as the breeze picked up. I grabbed at the journals as their covers flapped violently open, trying to gather them up, but the breeze was so powerful that it seemed to be holding me back, pinning me in place as I reached out to them. Anna staggered backwards with a sharp cry as a whirlwind appeared between us. I tried backing away but could not move in any direction. Panicked and confused, I looked to Anna, then to Michael, my fear rising as I saw the expression on their faces. This was clearly new to both of them.

Even as the thought struck me and dread followed, the whirlwind changed to dizzying, swirling fog and from its murky depth, the fog creature launched itself into the room. Michael yelled out a warning at the same moment as Anna cried, 'Viktor!'

'No!' I shouted at the creature. 'Not here! Stop!'

It turned to stare at me with its sunken eyes, then whipped round to face Michael, who was staring at it with wide, fascinated eyes. In the midst of my panic and confusion, I recognised the same expression I had seen on Anna's face when she had first seen the fog creature, the glint, the fascination. All I felt was horror.

The creature swung its head around, taking the three of us in. Opening its jagged mouth, stretching its paper-thin skin even further, it threw back its head and screeched, an ear-splitting, blood-curdling sound. Suddenly, it lunged towards Michael, who yelled and fell backwards, tripping over his chair. He landed heavily, grunting, and scrambled backwards with an agility which surprised me, all the while keeping his eyes glued to the creature.

It took a step towards him, then stopped and turned its head towards Anna, who was standing frozen next to me. She glanced down at me, and I saw the fear in her eyes. Something was different this time. This was not protective, this was threatening, dangerous. It hissed at her, then leaned close to me and hissed even more viciously. Fear gave me strength and I broke free of the invisible force which was holding me, scrambling across the floor until my back hit a bookcase. A couple of books landed beside me as I pressed myself against the shelves, trying to make myself as small as possible.

Anna took a step towards me. I shouted, 'No!' as the creature turned its focus back to her and lunged. Anna screamed, Michael yelled something in a language I did not understand, and at that moment, time stopped.

As the creature lunged, stretching out its long fingers towards Anna, she staggered backwards, off-balance, arms flailing as she slipped on one of the journals and fell. As if in slow motion, she struck her head on the corner of the fireplace and lay still.

'Anna!' Michael shouted. 'Anna!'

There was no response. She lay unmoving. As I stared at her, frozen in horror, I saw the firelight glinting on a tiny trickle of something escaping her ear. My breathing faltered, my jaw dropped, and all the misery, anguish and despair of the past few years seemed in that moment to crystallise into a maelstrom of emotion which ripped through me. A harsh, animalistic scream rent my ears, and it was several moments before I realised it was coming from my own throat.

Staggering to my feet, half-blind with tears, I faced the creature. 'What have you done?' I cried; my voice thick with anguish. 'What…have…you…done?'

The creature paused, swinging its head between Anna and myself, and in that brief moment of calm, I felt hysteria bubbling to the surface. 'Anna!' I screamed. 'Anna!' Over and over, I shrieked her name, my throat raw, shoving the creature aside to run to her, falling to my knees at her side and seeing the glazed eyes, the frozen expression. All at once, pure fury seized me and I whirled on my knees to face the creature, glaring up at it. 'She's dead! You killed her!' I screamed. 'Why? WHY? She's dead!' Over and over, I screamed, other sounds penetrating the red fog which had settled behind my eyes as I railed at the thing before me. There were footsteps, shouts, an alarm bell, Michael muttering in that unknown language, the crackle of the fire, a scream from somewhere to my left.

'GO!!!' I screeched at the creature. 'Go! Leave me!'

With a dull roar which sent all the loose papers in the room spinning through the air, the creature stepped back into its wall of fog and vanished with an audible whoosh, leaving in its wake the rustle of settling pages and the harshness of the screams I could not stop.

Chapter 39

I came back to myself two days later.

Opening my eyes to an unfamiliar ceiling, unfamiliar bedclothes, light beyond the windows which danced in a rhythm I did not recognise, I panicked. Leaping out of bed with a cry of alarm, I staggered as a wave of dizziness gripped me and forced me to the floor in a sudden rush of nausea. All at once, there were footsteps and the rustle of skirts, and Madame LeFèvre appeared in front of me. She knelt and brushed the hair back from my face tenderly, her eyes full of anguish. Blinking, I tried to place her, knowing she was familiar but uncertain how we knew each other. It was a minute or two before things snapped into focus.

'Oh Madame,' I whispered, bursting into tears as the memories crowded my thoughts. She wrapped her arms around me, rocking me gently, and I clung to her, aware of how badly my entire body was trembling. The tears would not stop. I did not try to stop them. I gave myself to my devastation, the loss of Anna a lead weight in the pit of my stomach.

We sat like that for some time. When Madame LeFèvre released me and sat back, her eyes searching my face, I saw the traces of tears on her cheeks and dark shadows beneath her eyes. She looked grey and pinched, and guilt swamped me for a long moment as she raised me to my feet and sat me on the side of the bed.

'Her family are here,' Madame LeFèvre said quietly. 'I thought it best not to mention you, especially given your state. How do you feel, my dear?'

I stared at her helplessly. 'I am not sure I feel anything,' I choked between sobs. 'I don't understand what happened.'

'The blow to her head... when she fell...' Madame LeFèvre's voice caught in her throat and she lapsed into silence, swallowing hard. I squeezed my eyes shut as a horrible sick feeling overtook me and I lurched towards the washstand bowl, retching. All that happened was some painful muscle spasms. I stood gripping the washstand, knuckles white through my skin, panting and choked with sobs, sweat suddenly drenching me.

'The creature...' I stammered, trying to make sense of everything. 'The creature in the fog. There was something different about it, something wrong. It protects us. At least...' My voice trailed off. 'It always has before.'

'Michael told us what happened,' Madame LeFèvre said, crossing to me and draping a robe over my shoulders as I stood there shaking and whimpering. 'There was nothing even he could have done, my dear, and he has years of experience with such things. Now, come back to bed. Would it help to speak with him, do you think?'

I let her prise my fingers from the marble stand and lead me back to bed, where she settled me, plumping pillows at my back to prop me up. I sank into them, numb and worn out. 'How did Anna's parents get here so quickly? What time is it?' It was bright outside, completely disorienting me.

Madame LeFèvre sat beside me and, taking my hand, explained that I had been hysterical in the library and the organisation's doctor had sedated me. Today was apparently the first time I had awoken and not instantly started screaming. I listened in horror, thoughts jumbling, as she described how she and the doctor had had to hold me down in the bed while he administered the sedation. As she spoke, I realised that, apart from a brief period when she had assisted in moving Anna to the chapel, she had been with me constantly, delegating her own duties to the maids.

Anna was gone.

I struggled to form the words in my mind. Anna was gone. Never again would we speak, never again would I see the little crease between her brows, or the lively sparkle in her eyes.

She was gone.

The tears came again, and I let them. A hollow had opened in the pit of my stomach and all vitality, all sense of adventure had been sucked into the void it created. Leaning back against the pillows, racked with sobs, the emptiness consumed me. Madame LeFèvre squeezed my hand, struggling with her own emotions, eyes bright with tears. We sat, unmoving, for what seemed like an eternity. My thoughts darted around like fireflies, impossible to pin down. Suddenly, they all jostled to the surface at once, a confusion of Sébastien, home, Uncle Geoffrey, the family, Anna…

All at once, I started upright in the bed, making Madame LeFèvre catch her breath and stare at me in alarm. 'What is it?' she exclaimed.

'My family… the agent here in Paris… I need to contact him!' I gasped, panic crushing my chest. 'There is something I must do while I am here, and he agreed to help me. If I lose his goodwill…'

'I am sure he will understand,' Madame LeFèvre said, her voice soothing. 'No one could have foreseen…'

She broke off as I shook my head vehemently. 'No, you don't understand, Madame. He does not know where I am staying. I was supposed to contact him. I have to send him a message right away!'

Panicked, my heart battering the inside of my ribs, I tore my hand from hers and threw back the blankets, ignoring her protests. Swinging my feet to the floor, I leaped from the bed and made for the desk, only to have my legs buckle beneath me. I fell heavily, the breath forced out of me. For a moment, shocked, I lay there, my fingers digging into the thick carpet. Something crumpled inside me, and I began to sob violently.

Madame LeFèvre murmured something and hurried around the bed, scooping me up and settling me back against the pillows, drawing the blankets over me and tucking them in securely, as though afraid I would try again. Crossing to the bellpull, she tugged it vigorously, then came back and leaned over me, stroking hair away from my forehead.

'Don't worry,' she said quietly. 'We can get a note to anyone who needs to be informed of your whereabouts. Let me bring you some paper. Write your notes, and I will have them delivered.'

She bustled around, setting me up with a little portable desk, pen and paper. I slumped against the pillows, trying to construct sentences in my mind, uncertain what to tell Sébastien. The truth was out of the question.

The rustle of Madame LeFèvre's skirts was strangely soothing and as I stared at the blank page in front of me, I realised it reminded me of Mrs Armitage and Eliza as they moved around my bedroom at home. It reminded me of my mother.

Inspiration struck and I quickly scribbled a note to Sébastien which said only that there had been an accident. I reassured him of my health, apologised for the chaos having prevented me from sending him word before now. After some thought, I added a sentence to explain that the accident had naturally affected my plans and there would now be a need to reschedule my meeting with Anna's scholar.

My focus began to return as I wrote, so I also penned a short note to Uncle Geoffrey and added a postscript to Sébastien's, asking him to forward it on my behalf to maintain discretion. After that, thoughts crowded my mind thick and fast, and I wrote to Christine, hoping her address could be found somewhere in Anna's possessions.

While I wrote, someone had responded to the bell, and Madame LeFèvre had spoken to them at the door, holding it open only a crack and shielding the person's view of the room with her body. That done, she came to sit by the bed, and for a while, the only sounds were the crackle of the fire, the pen scratching over the paper and the occasional clink as I caught the side of the inkwell in my hurry.

I folded Uncle Geoffrey's note inside Sébastien's, addressed and sealed it, then babbled at Madame LeFèvre about Christine, saying only that she was in Paris to see a specialist Anna had recommended. 'I do not know his name, Madame, nor do I know where Christine is staying.' I said, hearing a frantic note in my voice. 'But it is vital that the meeting should proceed. It is desperately needed.'

She nodded. 'I understand. The name is Archambeau, you say? Let me go and see what I can find.'

Her voice cracked and she paused for a moment, letters in hand, blinking and gulping. My own tears threatened again and all I could do in response was nod.

She left the room and a blanket of silence descended. I began to think back over the events in the library, those terrible, inexplicable events which had stolen Anna from me forever. What had prompted the creature to appear? Why had it suddenly been so hostile? Was it something to do with Michael? It had appeared particularly aggressive towards him.

I turned the questions over and over, but my mind was too numb, my heart too empty, to formulate even the vaguest of theories. Setting the little desk carefully to one side of me on the blankets, I lay back against the pillows. Before long, my eyelids began to flutter closed, and I let them, realising how exhausted I was.

The sound of the door opening started me from sleep and I let out a little gasp, half-expecting to see swirls of fog surrounding the bed. Madame LeFèvre entered the room, accompanied by a maid carrying a tray on which was a covered dish and tea things. I was wrapped in blankets and assisted into one of the armchairs by the fire, where the maid presented me with a bowl of broth. Although I was not hungry, my mouth watered as the delicious aroma wafted towards me, and when I took a small mouthful, I found it to be exquisitely seasoned. My appetite rose and I was able to finish the entire bowlful and sip the tea Madame LeFèvre poured for me. As I ate, she reassured me that she had found Christine's address and my notes had been safely delivered. The maid, who had been tending to the fire while I ate, cleared away the bowl and the tray before discreetly slipping from the room.

Madame LeFèvre drew a note from her pocket and held it out to me. 'The gentleman sent this for you, my dear.'

I nodded, having expected an instant response from Sébastien, and took the note. It was brief, expressing sorrow at the accident, relief at having word from me, and assurances that my note to Uncle Geoffrey would be sent with his next despatch to the family. I tucked the note down the side of the armchair and stared into the fire. My situation here was safe for now, but was it safe for those around me? I could not help but keep glancing around the room expecting at any moment to see one of those long, spindly hands extending towards me. If it ever touched me, would its skin feel like the dry leaves it resembled? The thought sent a shudder rolling down my spine, and seeing this, Madame LeFèvre reached for the poker and coaxed more dancing flames from the logs in the grate.

'Tell me about this strange creature,' she said quietly. 'Michael described it, but it made no sense. We have certainly never seen anything like it in the castle before.'

My heart skipped a beat, and an overwhelming rush of guilt seized me, gripping me hard by the throat and strangling my words as I tried to form them. Sensing my distress, Madame LeFèvre busied herself with the tea, taking her time while I composed myself. She handed me a cup and I took it in shaking hands, gripping the saucer. In a voice which shook almost as much as my hands, I told her a little about how I had first encountered the fog creature. The story naturally led into Anna's appearance in my life, and at that point, I lapsed into silence, the words vanishing like dreams even as I tried to pin them into coherent sentences. There was just too much pain and disbelief, too much treading water in a nightmare.

There was a light tap at the door, and I started violently, the cup rattling loudly in the saucer, some of the tea slopping into it. I muttered a curse and set the cup on the table, then clenched my hands into fists, my fingernails digging into my palms. The sharp pain made me wince, but it brought focus, and I watched as Madame LeFèvre crossed to the door and opened it, admitting Michael.

He looked like he had not slept in weeks. His hair was uncombed, his cravat askew and carelessly tied. He looked over and took me in, and I shrank a little in the blankets, feeling suddenly horribly exposed and vulnerable. Madame LeFèvre, seeming to sense this, seated Michael at the desk and quickly moved the dressing screen from its corner so it offered me some privacy.

'How are you?' Michael asked.

I answered as truthfully as I could. 'Devastated. Bewildered. Afraid.'

'Afraid?'

I took a deep breath. 'Michael, what happened in the library was not normal behaviour for this creature. At all other times, it has protected us. Was it trying to protect us from you?'

That caught him off-guard, and he was silent for a long while. I peeped around the edge of the screen. He was sitting with his elbows on the desk, head in hands, slumped. My heart ached for him.

'I don't know.' His voice was subdued and flat. 'I had no weapon, so I cannot imagine it thought I was any kind of threat. However, if it was used to you being under threat from men, perhaps that would explain it.' He paused. 'It also struck out at Anna.'

'Yes.'

I sat back helplessly in the chair, watching the steam rising from the tea and dissipating into the air, half-afraid it would suddenly solidify and reveal the creature.

'What do you fear?' Michael asked suddenly.

'That it could happen again,' I answered truthfully, 'and that my presence here is putting all of you in danger.'

Michael harrumphed by way of response and fell silent again. Madame LeFèvre returned to her seat and looked across the room at him. 'Tea, Mr Grant?'

He must have signalled a silent No. Madame LeFèvre picked up her cup, nodding briefly, and took a sip. She sat ramrod straight, staring into the middle distance as she drank.

'I have had a long conversation with our founder,' Michael said suddenly, his voice sounding loud and unnatural in the silent room. I started, a sharp little gasp escaping my lips. 'He is keen to meet you. Do you feel well enough to do so today?'

I gripped the arm of the seat, panic fluttering in my stomach. 'The founder? I suppose so. I was meant to meet him at dinner that night.' My voice cracked again, and I pressed my lips together, rubbing the fabric of the armchair under my thumbs. 'I don't even know his name.'

441

Madame LeFèvre exchanged a look with Michael which I could not decipher, and there was a moment's silence before he said, 'It is probably best if he introduces himself to you.'

Anna had said the same. I frowned. 'Why?'

Another pause. I could hear Michael shifting in the chair, the creak of the wood and rustle of cloth. 'He is a singular person, who has led an extraordinary life,' he said eventually.

That made no sense either, but I could get no more from him, and Madame LeFèvre remained passive. After a few attempts to learn more, I said I would dress and go downstairs. Michael went to wait for me in the corridor outside while Madame LeFèvre assisted me with my toilette and clothes. Not even the tugging and tightening of the corset laces shocked me out of the numbness and panic which were chasing each other around in my stomach. Thoughts of consequences, of home, Sébastien and my parents jumbled together. Inspector Escoffier's face suddenly loomed large in my mind, and I hurried to the desk, heedless of Madame LeFèvre's gentle fingers teasing my hair, to scribble a reminder to write to him. I was overwhelmed for a moment by images of he and Anna at Christine's, the sweet, gentle interest they had in each other, remembering how good I thought they would look together as a couple.

No longer.

A wave of dizziness seized me, and I leaned heavily against the desk. Madame LeFèvre, who had been pulled across the room after me, her hands still in my hair and her mouth full of pins, muttered something and nudged me into the chair. I slumped and she moved behind me, quickly inserting the last few pins before peering down at me and letting her hand rest lightly on my forehead for a moment.

'No fever.' She nodded in satisfaction. 'You are sure you feel well enough for this?'

I looked up at her. 'I cannot lie, Madame, it sounds intimidating. Yet it may as well be now as any other time.'

A little rueful smile twitched briefly at the corners of her mouth and then was gone, so fleeting that it did not reach her eyes. 'Don't be intimidated, my dear. I understand from Michael that you are quite the topic of conversation among the scholars. Anna's reports speak very highly of you.'

Her lip wobbled and she bit it, blinking back tears. I took the hand she held out to me and stood, a little unsteady. To my surprise, Madame LeFèvre gathered me in her arms and hugged me. The simple, sweet gesture caught me off-guard, and I clung to her for a moment before she released me and stepped back, looking me over.

'You are still very pale, but so much better than you have been.'

I nodded. I felt nothing. My thoughts had stilled, my emotions had shut down and retreated behind a wall, and all that remained was a shell, a ghost of my former self. Like a sleepwalker, I let Madame LeFèvre guide me to the door and usher me into the corridor. Michael was waiting at the far end, staring up at one of the portraits on the wall. As I emerged, he turned and nodded, running a hand through his untidy hair. Madame LeFèvre patted my arm and gave me a reassuring smile.

'I will wait here for you to return,' she said quietly. 'You may find you need to talk.'

Frowning at her, knowing something was being left unsaid, I murmured my thanks and began to make my way along the corridor to Michael. My legs were still shaky, and I did not dare to move too quickly in case they gave way beneath me again. My skirt and petticoats irritated me, and I realised with a jolt that I had become used to my trousers and the ease of movement they gave me.

Michael led me down the grand staircase to the main hall. There was a soft hum of voices from behind one of the heavy doors and the heady scent of wood polish. We passed an open door, and I peered in, seeing a large, beautifully decorated dining room, the long oak table gleaming in the light, the chairs upholstered with elegant red and cream striped fabric which echoed the red velvet drapes at the windows. Michael walked ahead of me almost absently, lost in his own thoughts, leading me into a corridor to our right which stretched ahead of us before turning to the left. Michael paused beside a door about half-way along and glanced at me over his shoulder.

'Are you ready?' he asked quietly.

I frowned at him, trying to quell my irritation. 'Yes,' I said shortly.

An inscrutable expression passed across his face for a moment, then he knocked softly on the door, just two little raps. Immediately, there was a responding murmur from within, too muffled, and quiet for me to make out the words.

Michael opened the door and stood beside it, holding it open for me. I entered, heart pounding, finding myself in a spacious study. Four large windows in the wall opposite cast light over the masculine, elegant furniture. To my left, four armchairs were grouped around a low table before an impressive marble fireplace which stretched to the ceiling. As I stepped forward into the room, I realised that the wall behind me was lined floor to ceiling with bookshelves, and to my right was a heavy, carved desk with more bookshelves, these ones waist-high, with portraits and a landscape hanging on the wall above. All the furniture was a glossy dark wood, almost black, while the fabrics were a deep, rich red. My footsteps whispered over the thick carpet as I drank in the luxury of the room, my eyes finally fixing themselves on the figure seated behind the desk.

Whatever I had been expecting, it was not this gaunt, slender man whose piercing eyes raked my face. He raised one hand and delicately adjusted his cravat, his expression bland and unreadable. Uncertain, I glanced at Michael as silence stretched between us, and he gave a tiny nod of encouragement. I took a deep breath, stifled my discomfort, locked away all thought of Anna and, lifting my chin, met the cool, intense stare for the first time.

A strange feeling hit me, and I had a sudden desperate need to tell this man who I was and why I was in his castle. I longed to sit by the fire and explain my family history, my father's experiences in the Light Brigade, my mother's disappearance. I wanted to tell him everything, and I had no idea why. It was an uncomfortable, unfamiliar sensation and made me slightly nauseous.

I fought the feeling, stamping it down, feeling it recede until it vanished as suddenly as it had come upon me. Confused, and regretting having agreed to this interview, I inclined my head.

'I understand you wished to speak with me,' I said, keeping my voice quiet and even. 'My name is Viktor.'

There was a slight narrowing of his eyes, and he leaned forward slightly, watching me intently. Then, as though a spell had been lifted, he rose from his chair in a graceful, fluid motion and came around the desk, his hand outstretched. He was taller than I, immaculately and formally dressed in a black frock coat and dark grey trousers. His black shoes gleamed; his grey hair was perfectly coiffed. His hand was cool and dry, his grip firm as he shook my hand then raised it to his lips. To my surprise, the kiss I expected was more a whisper across the back of my hand. He took a deep breath, his eyes fixed on mine, his pupils dilating for the briefest moment before he released me. I lowered my hand to my side, fingers toying nervously with the folds of my skirt.

'Thank you, Michael,' he said, his voice soft and melodious, his eyes still locked on mine. Michael murmured something I did not catch and left the room, the door closing behind him with a soft click.

A long moment passed, and I was just starting to feel deeply uncomfortable at such intense scrutiny when he blinked, and the tiniest glimmer of a smile ghosted on his lips. 'Please sit,' he said, stepping back and indicating a chair in front of the desk. 'Make yourself comfortable.'

He returned to his seat, and I moved to the chair he had indicated, one of a pair, feeling exactly as I did every time I was summoned to attend my grandfather in his study. I busied myself with arranging my skirts, and when I looked up again, I found him still watching intently, a glint in his eye, his expression still unfathomable. His cheeks were terribly sunken, as if he was unwell.

'I have heard much about you,' he said.

'Then you have the advantage over me, sir,' I shot back. A flicker of amusement flashed across his face for a moment.

'I cannot believe I have not been mentioned even in passing,' he murmured. I narrowed my eyes, feeling heat flood my cheeks as I tried to work out whether this was some kind of test. Irritation rose in my throat, battling the agony of loss which I was already struggling to hold at bay, and when I spoke, my voice was a good deal sharper than I had intended. I sounded, to my horror, like one of my elderly aunts.

'As the founder of a secret organisation, I should think it highly unlikely that your well-trained agents would mention you at all,' I retorted. 'I certainly found that to be the case. In fact, I still have no idea who you are.'

He raised an eyebrow. 'An amusing response from a young woman who calls herself 'Viktor', don't you think?'

I bristled a little at the sting, whilst acknowledging he did have a point. 'I adopted the name of out desperate need, and it has served me well ever since,' I said, keeping my voice even. 'There are reasons for not divulging my true name, particularly to someone who has not yet shared his.'

His bland expression softened, and a thin smile hovered at the corners of his mouth before fading. 'You are familiar with the works of Byron?' he asked suddenly.

I blinked, uncertain where the topic change was leading. 'I am. What has that to do with your name?'

He nodded, and I saw him give the smallest sigh of exasperation I had ever seen in a gentleman. 'In that case, you are already acquainted with my name,' he said. 'I am Augustus Darvell.'

Chapter 40

I stared at Augustus Darvell for a long moment, frowning as I tried to calculate his age. 'You are named after the character?' I asked, realising, even as I spoke, that this man was too old for that to be the case.

He gave a brief, elegant snort. 'Sadly, no,' he said shortly. 'I am not named for the character, Mademoiselle. I had the misfortune of meeting that reprobate Byron. Circumstances led to certain revelations being made, which he swore to keep secret. Sadly, he chose to share those revelations with the world in that awful 'Fragment of a Novel'.'

I stared at him, wide-eyed. 'You met Lord Byron?' I breathed.

He rolled his eyes at me. 'Don't go all misty-eyed over him, my dear. I have enough of that out in the world. I don't need it inside my own walls.'

'What was he like?' The question left my lips before I could help myself, and suddenly I froze, a realisation hitting me. 'Wait a moment... are you saying that he wrote 'Fragment' about you?'

'Yes.' He spoke slowly and clearly, as though to a child. 'I am Augustus Darvell.'

'But... 'Fragment' was fiction...' My voice tailed off as the eye-rolling increased. 'And Byron died over forty years ago. You would surely have been a young man, not the man Byron described.'

'He described what he saw.'

I blinked.

'He saw the man you are seeing now.'

447

I thought of the description of the gaunt grey-haired gentleman in the story, a description which perfectly fitted the man sitting opposite. Yet how could that be? He looked to be in his mid-sixties. 'Are you saying you had grey hair when you were in your twenties?'

Darvell leaned across the desk and I found myself shrinking backwards. 'He saw the man you are seeing now,' he repeated.

I shook my head, struggling with the impossibility of it, not understanding. All at once, Darvell's expression changed. For a moment, I saw beyond the suave, cultured exterior to the monster within, the beast which hungered for blood. His eyes flashed red, his teeth, for a fleeting moment, were fangs. Blinking, I caught my breath, tensing to run, but the image vanished as suddenly as it had appeared, leaving me slightly breathless, my heart pounding. I found I had half-risen from the chair and was gripping it hard, my knuckles white.

'Sit, sit,' he said, waving me back. 'I will not harm you. It is important for the purposes of our conversation that you understand who – and *what* – you are dealing with.' He waited for me to settle again, and the silence lengthened as I stared at him, frozen.

'I have read 'Fragment' and know what happened to Augustus Darvell,' I said pointedly, not certain whether I believed any of this. 'If that part of the story was real, how are you here now?'

'An unfortunate periodic requirement of the blood which created me,' he said, folding his hands in front of him on the desk. 'We do not need to discuss that now, however. We need to talk about the incident in the library.'

I slumped and nodded. 'I'll try,' I said, my voice shaky.

To my surprise, when he next spoke, his voice was kindly. 'I would not dream of putting you through the horror of reliving such an awful experience,' he said quietly. 'Believe me, I understand how you are feeling. Anna was a very special young woman, who will be sadly missed.'

He paused and I glanced at him from beneath lowered lashes, still unable to determine his mood. My thoughts were a jumble and all I could do was nod mutely, tears prickling in my eyes. I fumbled fruitlessly for a handkerchief, and

Darvell, realising, plucked one from his pocket and handed it to me. I took it and pressed it to my eyes. It was strangely cold and smelled faintly of juniper.

Darvell watched me closely as I tidied myself, waving the handkerchief away when I offered it back. 'Please, keep it,' he said. 'Your need is greater than mine.'

I nodded and tucked the handkerchief into my sleeve, taking a deep breath. 'What do you want to know about what happened?' I asked, startled at the unexpected level of confrontation in my voice.

He rose and went to the window, looked out briefly, then started pacing to the fireplace and back. I slid around in my chair, watching the loping gait, the long, slender fingers, the tilting of his head as his eyes roved around the room. In the silence, his words, 'the blood which created me' rolled around inside my mind. There was a niggling sensation in my temple which foretold the arrival of a headache, and I regretted having agreed to go ahead with the conversation. What I should have done was excuse myself and return to my room, but instead, I was talking to a man who believed he had a longer than usual lifespan. For the first time, I felt the cold caress of unease across my shoulders and down my spine, chilling me to the bone and making my heart pound.

It was ridiculous. The man was clearly in his sixties, perhaps more.

Yet my subconscious was chiding me. I had seen so many otherworldly things during these last two weeks, why on earth had I chosen to have issues with someone living longer than usual? Taking a deep breath, I closed my eyes for a moment, and when I opened them, Darvell was right in front of me.

There was no way he could have crossed the room so quickly, so silently. I cried out and flung myself backwards in the chair, tilting it alarmingly. Darvell reached out with one long, thin hand and caught the back of the chair, holding it firm and unmoving. I sat there, clutching the seat, tilted backwards, looking up at him. There was no indication on his face of the slightest effort. He was holding me up as easily as he would lift a pen from his desk.

Time slowed. The moment stretched out before me, every detail of Darvell's face suddenly crystal clear as the room around us slipped into the background. The eyes, dark, sharp and intense above the deeply sunken cheeks. The lips, mobile, well-shaped. He would have been handsome in his youth, but now, his face mere inches from mine, there was a predatory, lupine air about him.

His nostrils flared briefly as though he was inhaling me, sending a shiver down my spine. Yet in spite of this, there was something in his refinement which reassured me. With a jolt, I realised I felt far more comfortable with Darvell than I had when confronted with the Amiens men. Something told me he meant me no harm.

Gently, he righted the chair, then stepped back. I realised I was panting, my heart thumping loudly in my chest. 'How did you do that?' I whispered.

'It was one of the gifts I received when I was made in this form,' he said frankly. 'There are always two aspects of the blood of creation, Mademoiselle. There are conditions, yes, but also remarkable benefits, besides longevity. Speed, for example. Strength.'

He crossed the room to a sideboard on which stood a tray with decanter, jug and glasses. He poured a glass of water and brought it to me. I murmured thanks and sipped, grateful both for the refreshment and for the distraction. The sensation in my temple deepened into a slow, steady throb and my stomach churned uncomfortably.

'Please tell me about the being in the fog,' Darvell said. He returned to his chair and settled himself, flicking out his coat tails and reaching for pen and paper. 'With your permission, I would like to make some notes.'

I nodded absently, my focus on gathering my thoughts to answer him. A thousand questions bubbled in my mind about Darvell, about vampires, but I forced them away, needing all my concentration to revisit the horrors of the library. I had to do right by Anna. The mystery of Darvell could wait.

Slowly and hesitantly, I explained what had happened in Dover, how I had met Anna, and the various times at which either the creature or the fog had appeared. Darvell listened intently and wrote copious notes, the pen scratching over the paper, punctuated by sharp little clinks as he dipped it into the inkwell. At one point, he drew a sheaf of papers towards him, casting an eye over them, then wrote another note. As he lifted one page to check something on the one below, I was startled to recognise Anna's writing, and my heart and stomach lurched.

Darvell looked up sharply at precisely that moment. 'Forgive me,' he said. 'Yes, these are her reports. Thorough, witty, insightful.' He set the pen down and leaned forward, steepling his fingers, elbows resting on the blotter. 'She made a request in her last report.'

He fell silent once more, and I sat impatiently, waiting for him to continue. Uncomfortable beneath his intense gaze, I cradled the glass of water in my hands and looked past him to the portraits on the wall, not really seeing them. I presumed Anna's request involved the investigation of my mother's disappearance. I was not prepared for Darvell's next words.

'She wanted to train you to be her replacement.'

I blinked at him, my jaw falling open. 'She – what?' I exclaimed.

'She was a shrewd judge of character,' Darvell remarked. 'She saw something in you. Of course, the being in the fog was quite sufficient to mark you out as special, but when she came to know you, she saw qualities which impressed her. She has described those qualities in some detail, and I must say, Mademoiselle, you are remarkable.'

I shifted uncomfortably. 'I am not, Mr Darvell. I am simply caught up in circumstances beyond my understanding and doing the best I can.'

'Precisely. You are seeing things most people do not see. You are learning that the world is very, very different to how you believed it to be. Despite everything, however, you have proven time and again that you are resilient, innovative, courageous, and adaptable. I am most impressed with her description of your disguise. Most impressed.'

A flush crept into my cheeks and I murmured something inane and dismissive. Darvell's mouth twitched slightly. Was that a smile? He was impossible to read.

'Let me tell you about my organisation,' he said. 'We are the Order of Guardians. Our role is to preserve the balance between the realms, to maintain as much harmony between humankind and the otherworldly as we can. It is not easy. Humans cannot even maintain harmony amongst themselves.

Therefore, we try to ensure our work is as discreet as possible, which is challenging. People are frightened of the unknown and quick to retaliate.'

I thought of our arrival in Amiens and nodded. 'Yes, they are,' I murmured.

A stab of pain shot through my temple, and I winced. Darvell frowned, looking momentarily puzzled, then his face smoothed and became bland and unreadable. 'Are you unwell, Mademoiselle?'

'A headache,' I said, sounding a lot more dismissive than I felt. All I wanted to do was return to my room and curl up in bed, but something stopped me. Anna's words still rang in my ear, keeping me firmly in my seat.

'We can continue tomorrow, if you prefer.'

'No!' The exclamation was louder and more forceful than I had intended, and I blushed deeply, biting my lip. Darvell leaned back in his chair, and when he spoke, the pace was faster, more businesslike.

'You may not be aware, Mademoiselle, but the Guardians are few in number, considering that we work throughout the world. Not many people possess our skills, and even fewer wish to spend their life using those skills. Most, when approached, deny all knowledge.'

'People fear the asylum,' I whispered.

He nodded. 'Yes. That is part of it, certainly. No one wishes to be the odd one out, the black sheep of the family, the embarrassment.'

I cringed, and a flicker of an expression flitted briefly across his features, too quick to interpret.

'There are thirty people acting as agents at any one time,' Darvell continued, his tone a little softer. 'That is all. We are not a sprawling organisation by any means. Nor are we ancient. As I explained earlier, that rogue Byron angered me greatly by writing what he did. When I had recovered from my time in the ground, I vowed I would not be caught out in such a manner a second time. There needed to be an impartial mediator between humans and the otherworldly, and that is what I created. An organisation of intelligent, resourceful people with unique skills. Problem solvers. Ambassadors. The courageous.'

He looked at me frankly. 'You appear to have all the qualities I would desire in an agent.'

I shook my head and started to protest, but he raised his hand, stopping me mid-sentence. 'No, Mademoiselle,' he said. 'I beg to differ. You cannot deny that the being in the fog responds to you. You cannot deny you heard singing in the Amiens cemetery, or that you were able to track the movement of the vampire de Montfort. You may not understand these talents yet, you may have no control over them, but you possess them. You were born on a Saturday, I believe?'

'Yes, I was.'

He nodded. 'You are a Sabbatarian.'

'Anna mentioned that word once.'

'A Sabbatarian possesses certain powers, such as the ability to see certain types of ghosts. They can see and communicate with vampires, and often have a spirit animal to assist them.'

He paused and I caught my breath. 'The fog creature?'

'That is my belief, yes.'

'Why has it only appeared to me recently?' I asked. 'If I do possess such powers, and I remain unconvinced, then why have I not seen this creature before?'

'You were in fear of your life,' Darvell said simply. 'There was a need in you which arose from a primal place, and which called the being to you. Had you ever felt that way before?'

'No,' I said, after a long pause. 'No. Not with the kind of upbringing I enjoyed.'

Darvell nodded. 'Yes. The being has remained in the background, probably throughout your entire life, waiting for you to need it. It knows you, in its way, but not well. It reads your emotions, I think, and responds to a particular kind of primal fear. Does this fit with what you have experienced?'

I thought back. 'Only sometimes. I did not fear for my life in the cemetery, yet tendrils of fog appeared.' I paused, feeling tears threatening, and swallowed, trying to steady my voice. 'I was not afraid for my life in the library.'

'Michael explained everything. I am inclined to agree. Which tells me that this being, whatever it is, does not fully know how to read your emotions. It has succeeded on occasion, when your feelings were deep and intense, but the subtler emotions – perhaps confusion or uncertainty – those are beyond its capability to comprehend.'

'How do I prevent this happening again?' I asked, a note of desperation in my voice, throat tightening. 'Please. Help me prevent it. There must be a way.'

'You need to work with the being,' he said. 'Learn its nature. Let it learn yours. In time, you could become a potent partnership. At this moment, however, you are, at best, chaotic because you are unschooled.'

As I bristled, despite acknowledging the truth of his words, the tiniest glimmer of a smile flitted across his lips and he raised his hand, the soft daylight shining on his manicured nails. 'I meant no disrespect,' he said, 'but despite your talents and courage, you are still young, even by human standards. Therefore, I would like to make you an offer.'

He paused, and I found myself holding my breath.

'Anna spoke highly of you,' he said. 'She saw something in you which she believed would make you an asset to myself and to the Guardians. She asked that, if anything happened to her, you would become her replacement. All of these things carry weight with me. Anna was exceptional and I respect her opinion.'

Darvell lapsed into silence again, and let the silence lengthen between us, for which I was glad. My eyes were filling with tears once again, and it was a battle to keep them under control. Darvell rose suddenly and started to pace the room again, and I shifted a little in the chair to watch him, dabbing at my eyes and swallowing hard.

'How do you feel about that?' Darvell asked.

I started and tried to find some words. 'Part of me would enjoy it greatly, Mr Darvell. Yet at the same time, I feel unsuited and unqualified.'

'What did you enjoy?'

I considered, and all at once, it was as though a floodgate had opened. 'I had a sense of purpose,' I said. 'Even amidst all the fear, all the confusion, I felt alive, as though my life could actually count for something important. There is always charity work at home once I am married, of course, which is a noble cause; yet in all the times I have given consideration to the type of charity work I should like to undertake, I never once felt as inspired as I did with... with Anna. I felt a vitality I never knew I could possess. I felt a freedom unlike anything I have ever known.' I paused and regarded his outfit. 'Trousers really are a wonderful invention, are they not?'

He did smile then, albeit briefly. 'You are intelligent and speak with passion,' he said. 'The description I have read of your escape from Dover, and your ability to pass as a young man, are impressive. You may feel out of your depth, which is entirely understandable, yet you have adapted quickly and easily into the mindset of an agent.'

I blushed deeply and fixed my gaze on the treetops beyond the window, waiting for the heat to fade from my cheeks. My mind was racing, replaying Darvell's words. Surely this was too good to be true.

'Therefore,' Darvell continued, his voice soft and tinged with regret, 'I would be grateful if you would take some time to consider becoming the next Anna Stenberg.'

I stared at him, trying not to gape.

'You are already using a pseudonym,' he continued, 'and your ability to operate as both male and female is a distinct advantage. You have no female pseudonym, I take it, as everyone is addressing you as Viktor?'

I shook my head. 'No, there was no need for one until I arrived here, and I have given it no thought whatsoever.'

'And now, you do not have to.'

I stared at him. 'I don't?'

He was standing by the fireplace, running his long fingers over the carvings at one end. He turned to face me, resting an elbow on the mantlepiece. 'Anna did not explain how the system works?'

I shook my head blankly.

'As I said, there are only thirty agents at any one time,' Darvell said. 'Normally, when an agent falls, I need to spend some time seeking out a suitable candidate for replacement, yet here you are, making my life a great deal more straightforward.'

I listened, trying to make sense of the tangles.

'Sabbatarians such as yourself can come from any walk of life, Mademoiselle. The lower classes.' He paused. 'The upper classes.'

I said nothing, and hoped he was too far away to see the heat I could feel burning on my cheeks.

'Undertaking the role of an agent is not easy and can have repercussions for the family one leaves behind,' Darvell said softly. His voice was kind, gentle, persuasive, yet it rang in my head like a church bell, and it was with difficulty that I resisted pressing my fingertips to my temples. 'Early on, there was an unfortunate incident, which you may read about in the library archives when you are strong enough to do so. It became evident that agents needed to adopt a professional persona, if you will, in order to carry out their investigations. The persona becomes a wall behind which they can conceal their true identity. Something I think you would greatly appreciate, Mademoiselle Viktor.'

'I can certainly choose a name,' I said, pausing when he shook his head.

'No, Mademoiselle, there is no need. When I asked if you would consider becoming the next Anna Stenberg, I meant precisely that. In order to increase the mystery around the organisation, not only are there no more than thirty agents at any one time, there are also only thirty names.'

I frowned, now completely lost. 'Please, Mr Darvell, speak more plainly if you will. I do not understand what you are telling me.'

His eyes narrowed for a fraction of a moment, and I met his gaze steadily and with a hint of defiance, frustration rising in my throat. 'Very well. To protect my agents, I created thirty personas. Each agent adopts one of those personas during their time with the organisation.'

I caught my breath as realisation and understanding hit me, and Darvell continued. 'I am offering to teach you, Mademoiselle, to help you explore and understand your abilities, to equip you for your own personal quests. I am offering you a home here at the Castle. You have already experienced the care my servants provide. They, too, are carefully selected.'

I nodded, dazed.

'I confess that part of the offer is made for selfish reasons,' Darvell said. 'This strange being fascinates me. I have never come across anything like it and am curious to learn more about both it and yourself, as well as the connection you have. However, it is you who is the prize, Mademoiselle. Someone such as yourself does not cross my path very often.' He returned to the desk and sat again, leaning forward, his eyes keen and intense. 'Will you give it consideration, Mademoiselle? Will you become the new Anna Stenberg?'

Chapter 41

For the rest of the week, I was treated like a queen.

Dr Dupuis, the Guardians' doctor, prescribed rest, and gentle walking, so I spent my mornings wandering the corridors of the castle, one floor at a time, discovering room after sumptuous room. Madame LeFèvre put a string of maids at my disposal every afternoon as I sat before the fire in my room. Some brought refreshment, while others fetched documents and books from the library. Violette continued to help me dress, and each evening, I sat down to dinner with Darvell and the castle's other occupants. Almost everyone had returned, both due to Darvell's presence and for Anna's funeral, which was to be held the following Wednesday. Madame LeFèvre told me that Anna's parents would be in attendance, and a knot of anxiety had started twisting in my stomach, increasing day by day, along with a constant ripple of nausea. The books distracted me for a while, but every so often, everything became overwhelming. More than once, Madame LeFèvre found me sitting staring into the fire, forgotten book in hands.

During those few days, Sébastien proved himself a godsend. With Darvell's permission, I invited him to attend me at the castle, and when he arrived, I could see he was both impressed and reassured. We had tea in my room, with the maids slipping discreetly in and out with pastries, books, and papers. Sébastien smiled as his eyes followed them around the room.

'This is a beautiful place,' he said. 'I can see they are taking great care of you. How are you?'

I considered, then answered truthfully. 'My heart hurts, Sébastien. I miss Anna terribly.'

He nodded. 'She helped you a great deal, did she not?'

'More than I can say.'

'It was a terrible accident,' he murmured. 'Especially for one so young.'

Under Darvell's careful guidance, I had given Sébastien the 'public' version of Anna's death, which was that she had tripped, fallen, and hit her head, which had resulted in her death. Writing the words was difficult; speaking them was almost impossible. I stumbled my way through the conversation. Not all of my hesitations were due to grief, but thankfully, Sébastien did not press for any detail beyond what I gave him. He attended me every day after that, arriving mid-morning and staying for afternoon tea before returning to his normal duties. At first, I was concerned that someone would let something slip about either Anna or the fog creature, but I need not have worried. We were given space and privacy, and every day after Sébastien's departure, Michael came to sit with me for half an hour. We chatted gently, helping each other as best we could, both of us dreading the funeral.

Sébastien had been working miracles behind the scenes, having somehow convinced Uncle Geoffrey that the best thing for me was to remain where I was for the time being. I received several letters from Uncle Geoffrey in quick succession, at least two a day, expressing both his sympathies, and his relief at knowing I was being well cared for.

'Sébastien is a very capable and trustworthy man,' he wrote. 'He assures me that your current residence is entirely respectable and suitable for you, and that you are continuing to exercise extreme discretion with regard to your identity, for which I am very grateful. Since we recovered your father, I am pleased to report that he appears to be making more effort to work with me and to control his outbursts. He claims to have no recollection whatsoever of his escape and recapture, and, indeed, seems most remorseful. He has not mentioned you, and therefore, I have not done so, either. I shall continue to work with him and see if I can uncover the key to his illness.'

He went on to suggest that after Anna's funeral, I might wish to travel for a week or two and would arrange for Eliza to pack a trunk of my belongings. I read this in disbelief, having expected to be ordered back to Dover. It was supposed to be my debut this season, something he knew I had been dreading with every fibre of my being.

'After all,' he wrote, 'I remember how terribly worked up your mother was in the days and weeks leading up to her debut, and I cannot for a moment imagine that you are in any fit state to deal with dressmakers and deportment classes and all the rest of it. Your grandfather understands entirely and has given his blessing.'

I re-read that sentence several times, bemused. Had I been too hard on Grandfather? Or was it simply that a tall, ungainly granddaughter would be difficult enough to marry off as it was. If the granddaughter was mourning the loss of a friend, it would be even harder.

The uncharitable thought shocked me, even as a little voice in my head murmured that I was probably not far from the truth. Instead, I chose to focus on the positives, relaxing as much as my misery would let me and trying to come up with some kind of plan for my investigation. It was difficult to concentrate, however, as my mind flitted around like a hummingbird, never landing for more than a moment on a subject. Madame LeFèvre, when I complained to her about my distraction, nodded wisely.

'You are trying to take on too much,' she said, in a soft, gentle voice. 'Be kind to yourself. One thing at a time. Any more, and you will exhaust yourself.'

She was right, yet I could not put the books aside, no matter how often my attention strayed from them to the pattern in the rug, the light glinting on the andirons, the flames dancing in the grate. Although I was only taking in a fraction of their fascinating contents, there was something endlessly soothing about turning the pages, despite the subject matter being alien and puzzling. Several times, I snapped out of a reverie to find Madame LeFèvre gently sliding a book from my limp hands. My mind was scattered and, as Anna's funeral approached, my distraction increased. On the Monday beforehand, I ended up spending the entire day in bed, alternately crying, and staring at the ceiling. I refused Sébastien's visit, resulting in a hastily scribbled note which Violette brought to me, expressing concern and worry, and which I had neither the strength nor inclination to answer. Violette tiptoed out of the room, closing the door softly behind her, and a short while later, Doctor Dupuis arrived. He looked me over with professional detachment, then gave me something to help me sleep. My eyelids were starting to flutter closed as he left the room, and for a moment, before I slipped into the blessed relief of slumber, it almost seemed that there were tiny tendrils of fog swirling softly around the bed.

Darvell summoned me to his office the following afternoon. I had awoken groggy and out of sorts and had been fussing over clothes with Violette as we tried to put together an outfit for the funeral. Unsettled, and with rebellion aflame in my chest, I dressed as Viktor and went downstairs to Darvell's sanctum, where I threw myself into a chair and stared blandly across the desk at him.

He looked terrible. I recalled Byron's description of a man wasting away for no apparent reason, and once again, Darvell's phrase 'the blood which created me' flitted birdlike through my busy mind. His cheeks seemed even more sunken today, his eyes more hollow, his skin thinner somehow, almost translucent. As he steepled his fingers on the blotter and leaned forward, he looked, for a brief moment, like a wolf about to pounce.

As if sensing my mood, he omitted pleasantries. 'Anna's parents inform me that the service tomorrow will be a memorial only,' he said. 'They have decided the funeral will be family only, and we shall respect their wishes.'

My jaw dropped. 'I can't say my goodbyes?' I exclaimed.

A shadow passed over his face. 'I am sorry. The family's requirements must always be paramount. They strongly disapproved of what she did, but they want her to be buried at home.'

I nodded dumbly, certain that my family would have done the same.

'They took her last night. They will not be at the memorial.'

I stared at him, my heart skipping a beat. 'She's gone?'

He gave a barely imperceptible nod, pressing his lips together into a thin line.

I crumpled. The tears came and I let them. Darvell pushed back from the desk and went to look out of the window, hands clasped behind his back, as I sobbed and gasped. The minutes passed, and as the sobs subsided, Darvell turned to look at me.

461

'She left you something,' he said, his voice soft and soothing. I felt a twinge of a headache suddenly and raised my hand to my brow, pressing the pain.

'She did?'

He nodded. 'However, before I can give it to you, I need to know your response to my offer.'

'Mr Darvell, with respect, I am not in the best position for making life-changing decisions,' I shot back.

He let a pause hang in the air between us.

'I understand,' he said eventually, his voice the whisper of dry leaves across a frosty path. 'Believe me, I understand. May I make a suggestion?'

I nodded, trying to quell my uncharitable feelings and blinking against the dull throbbing in my temples. My collar felt tight suddenly, and, hoping I was not about to pass out, I hooked a finger into it and tugged it away from my throat.

'The memorial is tomorrow, and will take place here in the castle's chapel,' Darvell said. 'See how you feel afterwards. You may decide that none of this is for you. You may decide to avail yourself of the opportunity to learn about the being which has attached itself to you. The opportunity is offered freely, with no obligation to accept a role within the organisation. I strongly recommend that you at least spend some time with myself, so I can help you learn to manage the being.'

I nodded, then wished I had not, as my head thumped in protest.

'If, however, you decide your future lies within the organisation, as Anna did, then I can, at that point, place in your hands the items she left to you.'

I caught my breath. 'Her bequest is conditional?'

'It was an informal bequest, in the form of a comment in her report, where she clearly stated that you would make an excellent agent.' He eyed me thoughtfully, appraisingly. 'Agents often make their desires known in this way, because, as we have sadly seen, they are often denied the chance to make formal bequests.' He took a deep breath. 'Especially when they are so young.'

I closed my eyes as my heart lurched painfully. The headache was easing a little, for which I was grateful.

'You have seen the stark realities of what we do, although I am certain you are fully aware that you have merely scratched the surface.' I nodded. 'You will be making an informed decision about your future, and there is no shame in saying no. I must make that very clear. Also, if you accept my offer, you will be free to leave at any time, should you decide this life is not for you. It is not for everyone.'

'I understand,' I murmured. 'Thank you for explaining, and for giving me time to consider. I am still undecided.'

'As you should be.' He returned to the desk and sat, picking up a sheaf of papers and shuffling them into a neat pile. 'I would be reluctant to take on anyone who made a snap decision. I am responsible for every single person involved in the organisation and I need to know that they are here for the right reasons.'

Darvell lapsed into silence, and I turned his offer over and over in my mind. The images soon tangled themselves into confusion and I forced my focus back onto Darvell. He was watching me closely, the papers still in his hands. A little shiver ran down my spine as I thought of who and what he was. I supposed I should be afraid of him, especially after having witnessed his otherworldly strength and speed, but somehow, I was not. If anything, I realised with a jolt, he irritated me.

That gave me pause and I got to my feet, distracted and unsteady. 'Please excuse me, Mr Darvell.'

'Of course,' he said mildly.

I crossed the room to the door, trying not to lean on the handle as I turned it, my head spinning.

'I am here, Mademoiselle, whenever you need to discuss anything,' Darvell said as I tugged the door open and slid out into the corridor. I closed the door behind me without acknowledging his words. Even as I did so, I was uncertain why, and leaned against the wall for a moment, trying to clear my head. Why did Darvell always seem to choose the worst possible moments to summon me? Every time I entered this room, I left with a headache. Perhaps that was why he irritated me so much.

Pushing the thoughts to one side, I slowly made my way back to my room and collapsed onto the bed, where I fell asleep almost immediately. For the first time since arriving at the castle, I dreamed. They were unsettling dreams, and when I awoke to find Violette leaning over me, concern on her face, remnants of them clung to me like cobwebs. I sat up, reassuring Violette that I was quite well, but even as I spoke the words, I felt the vague disquiet which remains after forgotten, troubled dreams have dissolved into daylight.

Dinner that night was a sombre affair. I sat next to Michael, Darvell opposite. Despite being served with a delicious, aromatic roast beef, I had no appetite and picked at my plate, pushing the food around with my cutlery. No one seemed interested in eating, not even Herr Fritz, a burly German with a large moustache, whose fascinating stories had kept us entertained at table every night since my arrival at the castle. Fritz the raconteur was very much absent as we all toyed with our food and drank too much wine. Instead, he sat at the far end of the table, exchanging quiet comments with a dark-haired woman I had not yet met. Michael was mostly silent. He looked terrible, sallow, and drawn. Everyone had taken Anna's death very badly. Agents were meant to fall in the line of duty, out in the field. They were not meant to die in Rochenoire itself. The danger should be beyond the castle walls, not within.

Fritz had actually voiced this opinion during one of his stories, and I had left the table, the room falling deadly silent behind me as I pushed back from my place and stumbled blindly to the door. As I made my way along the corridor, voices were raised behind me, berating Fritz for his insensitivity. Michael's was the loudest and most vehement. Fritz had wisely refrained from repeating such sentiments, but I was wary of him, uncertain about what he truly thought of me. After all, if the danger was meant to remain outside the castle walls, I was actively working against the organisation just by being there.

I was glad when the meal was over, and I could return to my room and try to gather my thoughts in readiness for the following day. I had asked Darvell to contact Christine and Escoffier, hoping they might be able to attend. I needed to see a familiar face; even faces I did not know well. While Michael was sympathetic and attentive, his loyalties lay with his fellow agents, not some random girl whose otherworldly attendant was responsible for his protégée's death. I was particularly hoping Christine would be there. François was staying with the doctor Anna had recommended, and Christine had sounded cautiously optimistic when she responded. Escoffier's reply had been stiff and formal, and I was uncertain whether I had overstepped by asking for him to be informed.

I dreamed again that night, and when Violette awakened me the following morning, her soft voice gentle in my ears, the dream slipped away again, like sand through my fingertips, leaving behind a vague and uncomfortable feeling of dread. As I breakfasted, sitting propped up with pillows while Violette lit the fire and bustled about with hot water for the washstand, I tried to claw back some memory of the dream. Darvell had featured, and had been telling me something, but the substance was gone forever. A knot of nausea was rolling around in my stomach, and even tiny bites of hot, dry toast were not helping. Violette poured me some coffee and I sipped, burning my throat. The heat startled me into full alertness and, reluctantly, I turned my thoughts to the day ahead.

The memorial was scheduled for eleven. Having fussed over clothes, it struck me that both Christine and Escoffier would, if they attended, expect to see Viktor. It was Viktor, therefore, who descended the stairs to join the mourners assembled there. Voices were hushed, reverent. Even Fritz was quiet, and as I reached the hall and moved to stand to one side, slightly apart from them, he caught my eye and indicated that I should go and stand with him. Startled, but grateful, I went to his side and adjusted the black mourning band around my arm, keeping my eyes cast down so I did not have to see my own anguish mirrored in the eyes of those around me.

One by one, though, they moved to me, murmuring condolences and support. Hands pressed mine and there were reassuring nods in the midst of the sadness. I soon found myself in the centre of the hall, completely surrounded in a circle of kindness and empathy. It was all the more overwhelming for its unexpectedness and I was soon in tears.

The knot of people around me parted as Darvell, looking more frail and wasted than ever, began to lead the way to the chapel, which was at the back of the castle across a pretty courtyard with a fountain in the centre. Stepping out into the cool morning air, I spotted two familiar figures standing near the fountain, deep in conversation. Christine and Escoffier. I broke away from the group and hurried to them. Christine held her hands out to me and I took them, the tears flowing freely now. Escoffier, who was grey and haggard, placed a hand on my shoulder. We stood there, the three of us, frozen in the moment.

They both murmured condolences and sorrow, and I choked out my thanks, and how grateful I was to have them with me. We joined the others, slowly making our way into the chapel, and took seats just inside the door. I breathed in the scent of candlewax and incense, polished wood and that strange, light aroma which is unique to churches and chapels. A beautiful portrait of Anna had been placed in front of the altar. She was in a gown of deep red, her dark hair and laughing eyes captured perfectly in the artist's exquisite brushstrokes. It pained me to see her, yet I drank it in, knowing this would be the final time, this was goodbye.

The service was short but beautiful. There were readings from Michael, Darvell and a female agent I had not yet met. Afterwards, Darvell gave a speech in which he succinctly summarised Anna's skills and qualities, describing some of her successes, her wit, her intelligence, and courage. I sobbed my way quietly through his words, memories of Anna rising unbidden before me. Christine was giving me sideways glances, while Escoffier, sitting bolt upright on Christine's other side, stared straight ahead, lost in his own thoughts.

Afterwards, as everyone slowly made their way out of the chapel, Christine took my arm and drew me to one side, out of earshot. Her eyes, when she turned her gaze to me, were hostile, and I caught my breath, stepping back.

'Anna was not your sister, was she?'

The confusion and guilt must have shown plainly on my face because Christine nodded, pressing her lips together. 'I suspected so when I learned you were here, yet Anna was having a family burial elsewhere.'

That had not even occurred to me. There was nothing I could say. I simply looked down at her miserably, hoping I had not jeopardised our friendship.

She leaned in and lowered her voice. 'Who are you really? You make an excellent young man, I must say. I was completely fooled.'

The steel in her voice cut me. 'Christine, please, I had no choice.'

'Who are you?'

Taking a breath, I lowered my own voice and haltingly explained, without giving her my name or any specific information. As I spoke, her expression changed from scepticism to shock to disbelief. By the time I had finished, she looked ashamed.

'Forgive me,' she murmured. 'That was unfair and unkind of me. I did not mean to make you feel trapped into uncomfortable revelations, and I apologise sincerely.'

She opened her arms to me, and I fell into her embrace, tears flowing freely once again. She stroked my back soothingly, rocking me slightly. 'You're so young,' she whispered into my hair. 'You should not be carrying such weight.'

'We each have a weight to carry,' I said softly. 'Mine just has the added complication of family duty.'

'I understand,' she said, tightening her arms around me for a moment. I nodded softly, thinking of her own story, and where her one solitary moment of youthful rebellion had brought her.

She released me and took my hand, and we went back into the castle, following the murmur of muted voices until we arrived in one of the downstairs salons. The others were milling about and there was an air of quiet restlessness in the room. I settled Christine in an armchair and signalled to one of the footmen for drinks. He served us with a delicious, aromatic coffee, which warmed me right down to my toes.

I asked how François was faring, and Christine smiled wistfully. 'The doctor is kind and sympathetic, which I was not expecting. François is staying with him at the moment, as I explained in my letter.'

'That surprised me,' I remarked. 'How did it come about?'

Christine looked uncomfortable. 'It seems,' she murmured, her voice suddenly so soft that I could scarcely catch her words, 'he was inspired to become a doctor by the original case. Bertrand's.' A spasm of pain crossed her face, and I realised just how excruciating it must be for her to re-live long-buried shame. I reached out and squeezed her hand and she gave me a watery smile. 'We are making the most of the distractions of Paris,' she said, 'and trying not to focus too much on doctors and the past.'

I nodded. 'I understand and think it's a sensible approach.'

'What are you going to do, Viktor?' Christine asked suddenly, her eyes intent. 'I can see that although you are here, this is not your place. These are not your people.'

That startled me. My thoughts scrambled, rearranging themselves frantically, and all at once, there was a moment of clarity. 'They are not my people yet,' I acknowledged slowly, 'but they might be, one day. They could be. It seems I have potential to fit in here, to be useful, to serve a purpose.'

Christine nodded, listening intently. 'A purpose beyond marriage and producing children,' she said.

'Exactly. It is risky, yes, and I would need to be trained, but childbirth is risky too, is it not?'

'It is. And you have no control. You have to give yourself over into the doctor's care and trust that he knows his business.'

I shuddered a little at the thought. Christine sipped her coffee, her eyes roaming around the room. 'You would live here, if you became involved?'

'Yes, I think so. We haven't discussed details.'

'It's a beautiful place. Luxurious and elegant.' She smiled slightly. 'I imagine this is what you are used to at home.'

'My home is not this ostentatious,' I said. 'My father is a practical man who likes comfort rather than grandeur. I am very comfortable here, though. It is impossible to be anything else!'

'I can imagine,' she said, her smile widening a little. 'Does that help your decision-making? You won't be living on goodwill or moving from hotel to hotel. You will have a safe haven, a place to call home.'

'Again, I am uncertain,' I said. 'I cannot imagine that Darvell funds everything from his own pocket. If I am required to make some kind of financial contribution towards my keep, it will complicate the issue. The family seem happy enough for me to be here as some kind of honoured guest, but beyond that, I am not certain of their reaction, especially since this season was supposed to be my debut.'

Christine's eyes softened. 'Oh, my dear,' she murmured. 'As if you did not already have more than enough to manage.'

'I confess I was amazed when I received my uncle's letter and found I was being urged to recover, rather than immediately rush home to a whirlwind of deportment classes and gown fittings.'

'They love you,' she said simply. 'Do not lose sight of that. Write to them often. Tell them how much you are enjoying the culture and the sights of Paris. Thank them for this opportunity and show them you are benefitting.' Her expression changed and she looked almost mischievous for a moment. 'Perhaps, as you speak French so fluently, you might discover a worthy charity to which you could devote part of your time. It would give you a deeper connection to the city and, I am sure, is the kind of activity which your family would approve. You should also hire a chaperone.'

'Ah, I already have an ally.' I told her about Sébastien, and she listened with interest, nodding now and then, coffee cup forgotten in her slim hands.

'I would advise caution,' she advised. 'It is unusual for a retainer such as Sébastien to actively go against the wishes of the family he serves.'

I nodded. 'That does bother me. He seems sincere, but he's unlike any family agent I have ever known. He's also younger than all the others, past and present, by about thirty years.'

She raised an eyebrow. 'Indeed?'

'You think I should be suspicious of his motives?'

Christine chuckled and took a sip of coffee. 'I think you probably already know the answer to that question. In all seriousness, though, my dear, I would urge caution. You know you can call upon me, whether I am here or at home. My door will always be open to you, and I sincerely hope that one day, you will feel comfortable enough with me to tell me your real name.'

I almost told her there and then, but something held me back. A knot in my stomach told me she was right to urge caution around Sébastien, and yet at the same time, I was torn. I needed the support he was giving me, and the buffer he created between myself and my family. If I was to pursue the mystery of what happened to my mother, that buffer could be invaluable.

We arranged to meet for lunch at the beginning of the following week, when Christine hoped to have more information about François and his needs. The conversation turned to general topics, away from the darkness and tragedy surrounding us. Christine glanced at the clock, exclaimed, and set her cup down on the table.

'I must take my leave, I am afraid,' she said, delving into her reticule and producing her calling card. 'Please don't hesitate to call on me at any time should you need a refuge.'

Thanking her profusely, I rang the bell and requested that the carriage be brought round. Christine and I went down to the main hall slowly, pausing on each landing to look at the portraits. I was drawn to the women far more than the men; they had a delightful individuality about them which a line of besuited gentlemen simply did not possess in the same way. One in particular caught my eye. It depicted a beautiful young girl sitting at a desk, half-turned towards the viewer. I peered at the name plate at the bottom of the frame and was startled to read, 'Anna Stenberg, 1831.'

My heart skipped a beat or two as I took in the detail of the pages scattered across the desk, the pen in her hand, the pile of books on the floor at her feet. A previous Anna, I thought, glancing over my shoulder to see where Christine was. She had been gracious in understanding why I had deceived her as I had, and I did not want to have to tell her that Anna, too, had been using a pseudonym. Not today, at least.

Fortunately, Christine was making her way down the next flight of stairs, so I hurried after her. We reached the main hall and I nodded to Philippe, who was standing near the door. He gave a small bow in return.

'The carriage is outside, Mademoiselle Viktor,' he said, opening the door for us.

We emerged into the cool air, and I handed Christine into the carriage, Pierre standing quietly by. As Christine and I said our goodbyes, Pierre checked the carriage door, then climbed nimbly to his seat and picked up the reins. As the horses began to move off, I waved to Christine until the carriage turned a corner and vanished beyond the foliage.

I went back to my room and ordered more coffee, then sat at the desk and took out my father's journals, spreading them out in front of me. Selecting one at random, I began studying the pages, hoping some connection would be triggered by the reading I had been doing. The coffee arrived and was finished, luncheon passed, and by late afternoon, I was busily writing down my questions.

'Has anyone in the organisation, past or present, ever recorded details of a fog creature, or is it something entirely unheard of?' 'If entirely unheard of, how would such a creature come into existence?' 'If entirely unheard of, are any of us safe?'

That last one gave me pause and I sat staring out of the window, turning it over in my mind. The ramifications were significant. As things stood, I was the unschooled, unknowing link to the fog creature. Darvell was right. There was a connection of sorts, but neither of us knew the other. And if not even the Guardians could tell me what it was, or where it had come from, then I had to discover those answers for myself.

Resolute all of a sudden, I pushed back from the desk and hurried downstairs to Darvell's office. He was behind his desk, his expression as inscrutable as ever, barely looking up as I entered the room.

'Mademoiselle,' he murmured. 'How are you faring?'

He waved me to the chair, and I sat, assuring him that I was as well as could be expected. He nodded.

'Mr Darvell, I have decided to accept your offer,' I told him.

'You are certain that this is what you want to do?'

I gave him a wry smile. 'How can I not, Mr Darvell? Even if I did not have my mother's disappearance to drive me, this creature in the fog...I need to understand why we are connected. I need to be able to keep those around me safe.'

'I understand.' He steepled his fingers and tapped them against his lips. 'And you are making this choice freely? No one is coercing you?'

I narrowed my eyes, puzzled. 'No, no one. It is entirely my decision.'

'Do not be suspicious, my dear Mademoiselle. Remember, once you agree to become an agent for the Guardians, I, in my turn, agree to take on responsibility for you. It is not a responsibility I can afford to take lightly, and neither should you.'

'I can assure you that I do not.'

'Very well, then.' He rose suddenly, making me start, and went to the sideboard on which stood his jug of water and glasses. Kneeling, he opened one of the doors and from within, took a familiar case. He brought it back to the desk and set it down between us. 'You recognise this?'

There was a lump in my throat as I nodded, and my voice shook as I replied softly, 'It is Anna's toolkit.'

'And now, it is yours.' He pushed it across the desk towards me and I reached out to take it. As I did, however, the office suddenly filled with swirling, acrid-smelling tendrils of fog, all gathering around me into a dizzying whirlwind, pressing me back into the chair. Darvell leaped to his feet, shouting something in a language I had never heard. The whirlwind increased in intensity, scattering books and papers from the desk and sending them hurtling around the room. Darvell continued shouting the strange, guttural language, and I gasped for breath as the pressure around me rose.

Finally, I found my voice. 'Stop!' I cried shakily, and instantly, the wind calmed, the fog vanished, and all that could be heard were my ragged breaths and the rustling of settling paper.

Darvell rose and started methodically gathering up the documents. I rose to help him, but he waved me back into the chair and I slumped, trying to steady myself and regain control of my breath. Darvell seemed unperturbed as he moved around the room, shuffling the papers into a neat pile, then leaning down to pick up others. I watched him in silence for a few minutes as my breathing slowly calmed and my heart stopped pounding so heavily against my ribs.

'If I am to work alongside you, it appears that I am in need of more paperweights,' Darvell said mildly. 'Welcome to the Order of Guardians, Anna Stenberg.'

EPILOGUE

From that point on, my days became more ordered, more purposeful, and I was grateful for it.

Following Christine's advice, I sought out a charity for impoverished young women and offered them some of my time, which they accepted gratefully. Uncle Geoffrey, as I had expected, immediately sent Sébastien to investigate the charity, to ensure that it was genuine, and appropriate for me. Sébastien reported back positively, and from then on, I sensed a shift in Uncle Geoffrey, something I could not quite articulate. He asked me to update him weekly on how I was faring, and with any news regarding my mother's disappearance, reminding me that Sébastien was at my disposal. I happily agreed. In turn, he promised to update me weekly about my father's condition, and to discuss any changes to his treatment, which surprised me even more than his approval of my sojourn in Paris. I did not mention anything about the Guardians, the conversations I was having with Darvell, or the fact that I had been assigned to Michael for my apprenticeship, which had surprised me. I had thought his memories would be too painful, and he would want nothing to do with me once the memorial was over. Instead, I learned, he had petitioned Darvell relentlessly to ensure he was chosen as my mentor.

On the first official day of my apprenticeship, and every day thereafter, Michael and I went together to the library. I had not set foot there since the tragedy, and I was fairly certain Michael, too, had been avoiding it. He gripped the door handle and took a deep breath before opening the door and walking in. I followed, feeling awkward and uncomfortable, averting my gaze from the fireplace, and choosing a seat which faced away from it. Michael did the same. We began methodically scouring the library for any reference to the fog creature, and when we tired of finding nothing, Michael moved on to the agents' reports, looking for any strange activity around the time of my mother's disappearance and trying to determine what had been occurring in Germany while she was there. However, that also turned up very little beyond vague reports of a disturbance in a forest, which seemed to have ended as suddenly as it had begun, and with no intervention from the Guardians. There was nothing to suggest any agents had been in the area either before or after she vanished. It seemed that all we could do was travel there ourselves and investigate, so we set about learning all we could about the area, its past, and whether there had been historic connections to the Guardians. I found one passing reference to the place in a brief letter from an agent, who had stayed overnight in a house there in 1844 on his way to deal with an incident some two days' travel away. Michael found the report, which described a poorly-executed hoax designed to frighten a relative into changing their will. In frustration, I took up the report, intending to file it away, but Michael stopped me.

'Let us keep this one to hand,' he said.

'What for? There is nothing of use in it.'

He gave me a little twisted smile. 'Perhaps there is not, at this precise moment. However, we do not yet know what we will learn. It may be that this case is central to your mother's disappearance. We simply do not yet have that confirmation.'

I sighed and put the report back on the desk, slumping in my chair and stretching, listening to my joints creak as I did so. Michael winced. 'Perhaps I should have arranged some exercise for your body as well as for your mind.'

'Exercise?' I frowned at him.

'Tomorrow, you will meet Jürgen, who has been an agent for a number of years now. He has offered to sit with you for an hour or two each morning and assist you with the German language.'

I was pleasantly surprised. 'That is extremely generous of him, Michael. Thank you for arranging it.'

'If we are to travel to Germany and melt into the background there, I need you to speak German as well as you speak French.'

'You speak German,' I pointed out. 'I could practice with you.'

'No.' His voice was suddenly firm. 'Viktor, you need to understand that when you are out in the field, any tiny slip you make could kill you. People could kill you. The fae, the vampires, the werewolves... all of them could kill you. Every detail counts. If you learn German from me, you will pick up my inaccuracies and habits. Jürgen is a native speaker. You will be learning from the best.'

His logic was flawless, if somewhat intimidating, but I need not have worried. Jürgen Schmidt was a jovial mountain of a man with piercing green eyes and blond hair shot through with threads of white. He greeted me in impeccable French, then switched to German, and we passed a couple of very pleasant hours that first morning, discussing the case Jürgen had just concluded in Hungary. When the gong rang for lunch, he rose, shook my hand, and said, 'This has been a pleasure, Mademoiselle Viktor. I do not yet understand everything about your story or background, but you are a natural linguist, and it will be my pleasure to help you. Perhaps tomorrow, you will explain what you are working on. I may be able to assist.'

Assist he certainly did. The following afternoon, Jürgen accompanied Michael and myself to the library. While I wrote notes with Jürgen's translations of the more esoteric aspects of my story, and Michael worked his way methodically through a stack of agents' journals, Jürgen pored over a huge hand-drawn map of Germany, occasionally firing questions at me about my parents' travels and stopovers. He then took up a pile of reports, translating them into English at lightning speed and scribbling notes. This became a comfortable, companionable routine for the three of us, and together, we slowly compiled a case file on my mother's disappearance.

I tried to remain positive, and I did very much enjoy the work, in spite of the complex feelings it aroused within me. I was grateful to Jürgen for his willing assistance, and to Michael for taking me under his wing, but I chafed at the lack of progress and began to doubt whether the castle held any answers for me. In the turmoil of everything I'd experienced, I realised I had been clinging tightly to the castle as a beacon of hope, as the answer to the conundrum. Now I was here, sitting with my back to the fireplace, turning page after page and finding nothing, I was forced to face the very real possibility that there was nothing otherworldly about my mother's disappearance. I said nothing to Michael, though. He seemed unperturbed, pointing out on one occasion that the vast majority of an agent's work is done out in the field, not in the library. I clung to that little piece of hope.

Something else was bothering me, too. When alone in my room, I had, on a handful of occasions, spent time trying to summon the fog creature. I stood in the middle of the room, whispering to it, asking it to show itself. I laid a pile of blank paper on the end of my desk and asked the creature to send the pages flying into the air. I begged, demanded, acted disinterested. All to no avail. In truth, I had no idea how to summon it, or even what I would do with it should it appear. Darvell was yet to speak with me on the subject, so I knew I should not have any expectations. He was making enquiries, he told me one night at dinner, and would inform me immediately if any information came to light. In the meantime, I was to keep detailed records of the creature's manifestations.

I had briefly considered discussing my attempts with Darvell, but decided against it, fearing that I would – quite rightly – be censured for irresponsibility. Chills rippled through my body when the implications of my actions suddenly registered. I had focused on the skills everyone seemed to think I possessed, rather than on the risk I was taking. I was ashamed of myself and appalled that my actions had been so disrespectful to Anna's memory. Weighted down anew by guilt, I redirected my energies to research, trying to find some new glimmer of hope.

Sébastien continued his visits, and I introduced him to Michael and Jürgen one day. Christine's warnings still rang in my head, and I hoped that if there was something in Sébastien of which I should be wary, one of them might recognise it. However, the three of them quickly settled into an easy conversation about horses, of all things. I sat, prim and resentful of my constricting corset, longing for tea to be over so I could slip once again into my suit. I had thought it wise to conceal my masculine attire from Sébastien for the time being, so whenever he visited, or I met him in the city, Violette had to endure my grumbling as she laced me into my corset.

It was after Sébastien's second meeting with Michael and Jürgen that the latter commented to me how much he enjoyed Sébastien's company. 'He seems to be a good man,' he observed. 'He knows his horses, too.'

'Do you think I am wise to be cautious, Jürgen?' I asked, setting down my pen. We were, as always, in the library, and the big man was standing next to me, staring down at a map he had spread out on his desk. He chuckled quietly.

'Mademoiselle, in our line of work, caution is paramount,' he said. 'In every way. How we present ourselves. How much information we give to people. How we approach the creatures we deal with. Without caution, everything and everyone is at risk of danger, of collapse.'

I smiled up at him. 'That is reassuring. Thank you.'

'You have to consider your own personal situation,' Jürgen continued, rubbing his chin thoughtfully. 'You may decide that the Guardians are not for you, and you miss your home. Not now, maybe, nor even in six months or a year. One day, though, you may wake up in the morning and decide you no longer wish to pursue this life. If everyone knows all your secrets, well, it makes reintegration difficult. Trust me on that one, for I speak from experience.'

'Oh?' I turned in my chair so I was facing him and he nodded.

'I changed my mind after perhaps four months,' he said, his voice deepening with emotion. 'I was engaged to be married. Foolishly, I shared rather too much information with my fiancée and sadly, she was indiscreet. It resulted in my mentor being injured. I left the Guardians and returned home, but my fiancée broke off our engagement, and my family were openly hostile, feeling that I was bringing shame on them. My skills, once they became known, were feared. I was seen as a freak. It did not help that I am considerably larger than my brother and father. In the end, they asked me to leave.'

I nodded sympathetically. 'I am so sorry, Jürgen.'

He smiled. 'Thank you, Mademoiselle, but there is no need. It was the best thing for me, although, as you can imagine, it did not seem that way at the time. I returned here and was welcomed with open arms. I am accepted here. I have work which stimulates and fascinates me, as well as serving a vital function within society.'

'A society which, for the most part, knows nothing about it.'

'That is irrelevant. We do this for the good of all, not for praise or reward. Which is how it should be.'

It was heartbreaking to think of a highly intelligent man like Jürgen being run out of his home, and I wondered for a moment whether that would also be my fate. Something of my emotion must have showed on my face, for Jürgen's expression softened.

'To answer your question, Mademoiselle, yes, I believe you are exercising the right amount of caution in respect of your servant. You only met him recently, you have no prior knowledge of him, and although he seems perfectly pleasant and is certainly most concerned for your welfare, you do not yet know his motives or what he is relaying to your family.'

That had not occurred to me, and I started. 'He has to be relaying something close to the truth,' I said, quickly turning things over in my mind. 'Otherwise, my uncle would have spotted some inconsistency. Don't forget I write to him direct.'

'Sébastien does not take the letters from you to post?'

I frowned, knots forming in my stomach. 'No, I send them from here. Violette takes them.'

He reached out and placed a large hand reassuringly on my shoulder. 'Then you may rest assured that you have taken every precaution.'

I nodded and thanked him, and we turned our attention back to our work. After we had parted to dress for dinner, the subject of precautions kept swirling around in my thoughts. I dressed quickly, then turned my attention to the case Anna had bequeathed to me. I had not opened it, or even thought about it particularly, being aware of what it contained and knowing that I currently had no need of it. I had pushed it out of sight under the bed, not wanting to remember Anna's deft fingers opening the catches, or the concentration on her face as she looked through the items.

I dragged the case out and took it over to the hearth, sinking down onto the rug in front of the fire. Violette had a good blaze going, for which I was grateful. The day had been cool, and I found myself shivering, more from discomfort than the chill. With trembling hands, I reached out and opened the catches.

The contents were as I recalled them. I took out three or four of the little bottles, holding them up to the light to determine their contents, most of which were unknown to me apart from the mustard seeds. Digging deeper, my fingers closed around one of the stakes, and as I lifted it out, I noticed a book tucked beneath it. Setting the stake to one side, I took up the book and examined it.

This was the book I'd seen Anna poring over many times, I realised, the one she had carefully guarded from my sight. To my surprise, there was nothing unusual or secret about it. It was a copy of Byron's collected works, similar to one I possessed myself. I shook my head in puzzlement about why Anna had not wanted me to see the book, especially given that we had discussed Byron's work on occasion.

I settled more comfortably on the floor, leaning back against the chair behind me, and flipped the book open to a random page. The familiar verses offered a blanket of comfort, and I found myself reading them aloud in a soft voice.

As I read, I became aware of a subtle shift in the atmosphere. Sound seemed to deaden somehow, as though it was being instantly absorbed into a giant sponge. I stopped, noticing the change in my voice, and glanced around the room. All was as it should be. The bed was neatly made; the desk, by contrast, was a chaos of journals, books, and papers. I turned my attention back to the poetry, turning the pages. Here and there, I found little slips of paper which Anna had used as bookmarks, folded papers with scribbled notes, half-sentences and phrases which made no sense to me, and strings of numbers. There were also scribbles in the margins, strings of numbers again, a random word here and there.

'What does all of this mean?' I whispered aloud. 'Oh Anna, I wish you were here to help me through this.'

All at once, the atmosphere changed markedly around me and I felt an odd constriction, as though my entire body was laced into a corset. I went to set the book aside but could not move. Panic flared in me, and I gasped, a hoarse, almost muffled sound in the thick, cloying atmosphere as it swelled around me, stealing my voice. I struggled against it, my limbs heavy, unmoving, gasping for breath as fear started to grip me.

There was a sudden loud rushing sound, almost like a whirlwind, even though the air around me was still and unmoving, simply pressing my arms to my sides and my body to the floor, holding me in place against the chair. Bewildered, I turned my head as best I could, my muscles forcing themselves against the pressure from the air, and looked frantically around the room, expecting to see tendrils of fog appearing around me. Yet there was nothing to be seen. The room was still innocuous, unchanged. What I felt and what I heard was a different story, my ragged, shallow gasps, and pants of breath all but swallowed up, the sound of them only just registering. Was I losing my hearing?

The book suddenly jerked from my grip as though tugged by an invisible hand, and I let out a cry of alarm as it landed on the rug in front of me. What was going on? I tried to struggle, but my efforts were fruitless. All I could do was stare in horror and disbelief as the cover of the book slowly opened of its own accord, the pages within starting to flutter as though caught by a breeze. The roaring of the air rose to a crescendo, almost deafening me, and I tried to scream, my voice freezing in my throat against the sickening pressure. The book suddenly flipped over, landing first facedown, then on its cover, the pages riffling wildly. There was a sudden, unbearably loud pop, and I flung my arms up to clap my hands over my ears, startled as the pressure released. My hands slammed painfully against my head, and I slumped forward, crying out, not daring to tear my gaze from the book.

For a moment, it lay still. Then gradually, it began to glow, faint at first, but within moments, sending a beam of intense white light into the room. I squeezed my eyelids shut and turned my head away, ears ringing from the effects of the pressure and heart hammering agonisingly against my ribcage. Curling into a ball against the chair at my back, I held my breath, blinking away tears, waiting to see what would happen next.

Silence fell and I cracked one eye open. The white light was gone, my surroundings innocuous once again. Except now, there was something in the room with me which had not been there before.

Lying on the floor was…something. It was shapeless; a bundle of dark, draped fabric. I stared at it, wondering where on earth it had come from, what it was.

The shape twitched and I instinctively pressed myself against the chair, pushing it backwards, away from whatever was before me. I gathered my legs beneath me slowly, preparing to flee, never once shifting my gaze from the shape as it began to convulse, rising and falling in a macabre dance.

All at once, the shape resolved itself into human form, hands, feet emerging from within the folds of cloth, almost transparent. I stared, seeing yet uncomprehending, as a head appeared, one of the ghostly hands reaching up to push back the cloth to reveal its face. It turned that face to me, slowly, its expression one of incredulity. As I stared, hardly believing what I was seeing, the figure shook itself free of the dark fabric, which fell to the floor and dissipated like mist, vanishing completely. The figure and I sat opposite each other on the floor and stared, the book lying between us.

It was Anna.

She raised her transparent hands up in front of her face, gazing at them in amazement. I could see straight through her to the hearth and bookcase behind her. She was wearing the red gown from her memorial portrait, I saw. The pattern on the rug showed clearly through her skirts as they spread out around her. Her booted feet, too, were transparent.

As I gaped at her in wordless shock, she looked around the room, down at the book, then back up at me.

'Well, this is going to be interesting,' she said, an eerie echo in her voice. 'Hello, Viktor.'

THE END

Case File

(The case of Sergeant François Bertrand was taken from the historical record – here are the full details.)

NAME: Sergeant François Bertrand

DATE OF BIRTH: October 29th, 1823

PLACE OF BIRTH: Voisey, Haute-Marne, France

KNOWN AS: The Vampire of Montparnasse / The Ghoul of Montparnasse

ACTIVE: 1847-1849

Sergeant François Bertrand was 24 years old when he committed a series of atrocities in several of Paris's cemeteries, beginning in the Père Lachaise Cemetery. Bodies were exhumed, violated and cut up. Sometimes, it was clear that parts had been consumed. There was no attempt to hide what had been done; the bodies were left in plain sight, often on the paths. The perpetrator was able to evade patrolmen and guard dogs, and hysteria quickly built around the appalling incidents.

Guards were doubled, police officers patrolled, yet the incidents continued and panic heightened. Suddenly, however, they stopped. Paris began to relax, thinking the nightmare was over, but the respite did not last long. A 7 year-old girl was discovered in a suburban graveyard, the day after her burial, exhumed, mutilated and missing her heart. Authorities increased the number of guards, but it was too late – the perpetrator had already moved to a new location.

Shortly afterwards, incidents began to occur at the Montparnasse Cemetery, with such frequency that the authorities despaired. Rumours circulated about vampires and a half-human, half-animal creature, which were not eased by the assertion of medical professionals that the teeth marks were, in fact, human. Whatever was committing these atrocities, it seemed able to scale high walls and slip away unnoticed.

One night, in the Montparnasse cemetery, a patrolman heard footsteps. On investigating, he found a section of wall which had clearly been used to gain access. He set a trap, a device which fired projectiles if triggered. In March 1849, an explosion was heard in the cemetery one night, and guards were able to give chase to a figure, which evaded them by leaping over the cemetery wall. However, it seemed that some injury had been caused, as blood was discovered in the vicinity.

The perpetrator might have continued to evade the authorities, had it not been for the report of a gravedigger, who had overheard a group of soldiers talking as he worked. They were discussing one of their sergeants, who had returned to barracks the previous night after being badly wounded. He had been taken to the military hospital, and no one knew exactly what had happened to him.

Enquiries soon revealed that the Sergeant in question was one François Bertrand, a voltigeur in the 74th Regiment. This was an elite skirmish regiment, trained in marksmanship and in using initiative and cover. 'Voltigeur' translates in French to 'tumbler', hinting at the agility for which these soldiers were known – a skill which must have served Bertrand well as he scaled the various cemetery walls.

News of Bertrand's apprehension was met with disbelief and shock. He was a well-respected soldier and was of good character, having studied in a seminary earlier in life. When he appeared in court, reports stated that he looked extremely unwell.

Bertrand openly admitted what he had done, explaining how he was overcome with terrible, uncontrollable urges which led him to dig the graves up with his bare hands. He described his acts in detail, including his treatment of the body of a 16 year-old girl he had exhumed in June 1848. "I covered it with kisses and pressed it wildly to my heart," he is reported to have stated. After each incident, he explained that he would fall into a deep sleep, or trance-like state.

Doctors who examined Bertrand were unable to agree on a diagnosis, finally settling on 'monomania'. Bertrand had been a solitary and melancholy child. Some accounts of his early years suggest he was given to dissecting animals, but it seems the impulses which led to his offences did not surface fully until a couple of years prior to his activities in Paris. At that time, Bertrand happened to pass a cemetery as some gravediggers were filling in a grave. The sight produced some extreme reactions in him, forcing him to excuse himself to the friends he was with, and seek refuge in some nearby woods, where he lay on the ground and remained there in the rain, insensible, for several hours.

Despite the horrific nature of the acts Bertrand committed, and although doctors claimed he was not criminally responsible, the court sentenced him to a year's imprisonment for desecrating graves. A corpse has no rights under the law and, at the time, the term 'necrophilia' was unknown, so the only offence for which he could be punished was damaging the graves. It was Bertrand's case which gave rise to the term 'necrophilia', after eminent Belgian doctor Joseph Guislain began to use it in 1850 to describe people experiencing the same kinds of urges as Bertrand.

After Bertrand's conviction, the historical record becomes muddy, with numerous conflicting reports of both his sentence and the time of his death. In addition to the accounts of Bertrand's one-year sentence, there are claims that he was sentenced to twenty years of hard labour.

Many descriptions of Bertrand's case give his date of death as 25th February 1878, and have him moving to Le Havre in 1856, where he lived as a model – and apparently completely reformed – citizen until his death, undertaking numerous occupations such as lighthouse keeper, postman and clerk. However, there are also accounts which claim that he committed suicide after serving his year in jail. The truth of the story is unlikely to ever be clarified.

Acknowledgements

My grateful thanks to Dr Laura McWilliam, Senior Clinical Psychologist, and to Elizabeth Medland of the CPS, for taking the time to talk to me and answer my questions about the psychology of necrophilia and the application of the law. Thanks also to Dr David Waldron, who kindly sent me some news articles which proved invaluable.

Tracey Norman is an author, historian and researcher who has a deep fascination with folklore and the supernatural. She has an unhealthy obsession with sock yarn, a large collection of unused notebooks, and can often be found clutching a mug of coffee whilst trying to avoid the feline trip hazard which shares her house.